D0961547

DAYBREAK

Frank G. Slaughter

DAYBREAK

Doubleday & Company, Inc., Garden City, New York

All of the characters in this book are fictitious,
and any resemblance to actual persons, living or dead,
is purely coincidental.

CONTENTS

Lakewood

DR. *JAMES CORWIN* faced his fourth trephine since noon as calmly as an auto mechanic awaiting a call to open another crankcase. Scrubbing with his fellow house officer in the alcove just outside the student theater that housed the operating room, he was but dimly aware of the surgical team, moving like regimented shadows against the glass wall to prep the current patient. Such detachment was vital: he had learned long since to use it at will. Today (battling the doubts that assailed him when his mind veered to the future) he had need of that invisible armor.

The day had begun with an emergency call in the early morning. It was now the fag end of the afternoon, but there was no flaw in his outer serenity. He even managed a grin for Hank Gaines when their eyes met above the scrub sink—despite the fact that Hank was part of his worried musings. Young Dr. Gaines was one of his few friends at Lakewood. They were also competing for a residency on the Neurosurgical Service—a vitally important steppingstone for an ambitious doctor on the last lap of his training for a career in brain surgery.

Two months ago—before his first encounter with Taffy Cottrell—Jim would have stood aside gladly to give Hank a clear shot at the residency: with a wife and two children, his friend's need had been far greater than his own. The situation had altered when Taffy became Mrs. James Corwin. . . . Once again he wondered why he found it so difficult to think of himself as a married man. Or why (when his conduct with Taffy had been beyond reproach) he could still imagine he was her lover —the sort of lover who might be dismissed tomorrow.

"Cheer up," said Hank Gaines. "The bride won't always be working."

Before their marriage Taffy had been employed as a physiotherapist in the Thatcher Clinic. Jim had not yet informed his friend that she had resigned—or that it was now her custom to go dancing in downtown Baltimore whenever he was detained at the hospital.

"Do the blues show?"

"Only to friends of long standing," said Hank. "Ziggy will never notice. He's blinded by his own glory."

Chuckling over a shared antipathy, Jim felt some of his tension unwind. Damning the great Anton Ziegler was his only luxury in working hours—and one he could enjoy in Hank's company. At Lakewood the renowned brain surgeon was monarch of all he surveyed—and merciless to heresy in all its forms.

"I'll grant Ziegler his glory—and his genius. I still don't like his lobotomy technique."

"Ziggy isn't the first wizard who changes men to zombies with a hatpin."

"At this moment the routine of a zombie has its inducements," Jim said soberly.

"You can't be as tired as that."

Jim turned to the door. "I'm not really. But this job has me licked today, for no good reason."

"What you need is a night off."

"That doesn't mean I'll get one. Meanwhile let's remember our surgical chief will raise hell if the burr holes aren't ready when he makes his entrance."

Jim walked out as he spoke. Hank was assisting today: the ritual of precedence, en route to the table, was a tacit admission that their rivalry was real. . . . At the scrub-room door Jim paused briefly to glance at his mirrored image in a locker (this, too, was ritual, a good-luck charm for the job that awaited him beyond). As always, the tall, gaunt figure in the rumpled operating suit frowned back with the eyes of a stranger.

Lincoln, in his darkest hour, he thought. *What could a girl like Taffy Cottrell see in such a face—or the too-intent brain behind it?*

ii

It was a genuine relief to yield to the demands of his calling, to lose all thought of self in the exactitudes of a surgical process that had become almost automatic.

To a visitor the tableau under the cone of light was a far cry from the melodrama of a brain operation. Even the patient, his shaven skull propped in sandbags, was less than human as he snored tranquilly in deep pre-operative sedation. The masked figures in white, clustered about the table like fussy phantoms, seemed frozen in time, now their preliminary tasks were ended. Jim moved into the surgeon's spot—a precise advance, which stirred the silhouettes to life. So familiar was his opening gambit, he found he had measured the operative area, and traced it with a marking solution, before he exchanged a word with the team.

Six centimeters above the zygomatic process, and three centimeters posterior to the lateral rim of the orbit. The measurements were part of his unconscious memory: at the moment they were a mere echo in his brain, unreal as the refrain of a popular song. Eight times today he had repeated the litany while he measured other shaven scalps and marked them. After this cranium had been opened for Ziegler's scalpel, he would repeat the hieroglyphs on still more patients—awaiting their turns now on a crowded schedule, and closely watched by orderlies in the hall outside.

Jim stepped back from the table to draw on fresh gloves—and Hank painted the patient's scalp with a crimson antiseptic. Under this prepping solution the markings turned a deep brown, setting themselves in the skin like a superficial tattoo. The man's skull had already been draped precisely, outlining a narrow rectangle across the frontal area: two brown crosses marked the temples. Now a windowed sheet was lifted above the rectangle; its top corners were pinned to a metal frame, isolating the operative area as completely as a curtain sets off audience and stage. This was the surgeon's domain. Until Ziegler's arrival Jim was absolute ruler here.

The anesthetist waited at the head of the table, ready with a syringe of sodium pentothal. Actually no anesthesia would be used unless the patient became restless; the incision itself would be made under the numbing protection of the novocain solution Jim was now injecting beneath those two dark crosses.

When the needle grazed the skull itself, he drew it back slightly infiltrating the tissue between skull and bone. His hands still moved automatically, almost without thought. Suddenly, beneath his iron discipline, he had the illogical need to discover this particular patient's name. It was a rebel impulse, and he resisted it for a moment: this, after all, was only another charity case, from a locked ward at Rocky Point, a state hospital for the insane. . . . Like others who had preceded him, the man would occupy a cot in the neurosurgical wing for two days. Then, with the danger of postoperative complications safely past, he would return to the hospital—another statistic in the long list of prefrontal lobotomies, the operation that was Dr. Anton Ziegler's specialty.

"Who is this fellow, anyhow?"

His voice seemed strangely loud. After he had spoken, the masked faces that surrounded him ceased to be units in a well-rehearsed assembly line. Hank Gaines looked more startled than amused. Mabel Towers, the supervisor, was staring at him intently, as though the query was somehow improper. So were Joel Peters, the orderly, and Helen Bryant, the nurse presiding at the instrument tray. So (quite frankly) was Penny Ward, the so-called "dirty" nurse, who hovered just outside the circle of light that bathed the table in its harsh incandescence.

"Am I out of order?" he asked dryly.

Bruce Gordon, the assistant resident in anesthesia, put down his syringe and bent forward to read from the chart. "Catatonic schizophrenia in the excited phase," he said.

"I know that, Bruce. What's his *name?*"

"Ignaz Lavorsky."

Penny's giggle broke the tension and drew an icy glare from Miss Towers. "Ignaz," she said. "That's a mouse in a comic strip."

"You don't know him, Jim," said Hank. "How could you?"

The surgeon put the empty novocain syringe on the sterile table and picked up a gauze sponge. "You're right, Hank," he said. "How could I?"

He hardly knew why he had asked the question—but it seemed both right and proper. *A patient should be more than a chart number and a diagnosis,* he thought—*even to a neurosurgeon performing a preliminary trephine.* True, such designations were part of the verbal shorthand of all great hospitals: Dr. Jim Corwin had fallen quite naturally into the impersonal approach. . . . Looking down at the crimson rectangle of skull, he struggled in vain to tie Ignaz Lavorsky to an everyday pattern, to change this routine case into a man with ambitions, frustrations—and hope.

What could Lavorsky have in the way of hope? Jim had seen the wards at Rocky Point, the grotesques behind the bolted doors. Most of these men were buried in their cells as irrevocably as though they were already underground. If successful, the lobotomy that Ziegler was about to perform would free Lavorsky from that terrible immolation. If the success was complete, he might even take a modest part in the affairs of humanity.

Reaching for a scalpel, Jim reminded himself that he should know more of the condition for which Ziggy was operating. A surgeon who respected his job should be more than a hand skilled at manipulating a knife, the electrode of a surgical unit, the handle of a brain spatula.

"Pressure please, Hank."

Using a square of gauze, the assistant covered the small area of skin beside the cross at the right temple and pressed hard on the contact point. Jim did the same on the opposite side.

The scalpel slashed down firmly, cutting across the scalp in a single stroke. Helen Bryant had already slapped a hemostat into his palm. With a brisk click the forceps bit deep into the fascia, controlling bleeding instantly.

A mastoid retractor exposed a square of bone within the incision. Leaving Hank to pack the opening, Jim held out his hand for a burr trephine—a formidable instrument shaped like a brace and bit, with a rounded knob of metal at its end, like an acorn with cutting edges. Setting the bit in firm contact with bone, he began to rotate the brace. A faint, grinding noise, the scrape of the cutting edge against the skull, filled the room with its familiar, nerve-jarring screech; a rim of bone dust piled up swiftly around the burr.

Only a change of pitch in that muted screech told his trained ears he had penetrated the skull. He removed the steel acorn, collecting the bone dust with a curved elevator and dropping it into a brain spoon held by Helen Bryant. Next, he enlarged the opening with the elevator, chipping out wafer-thin segments of bone which the burr had only half severed. The dura mater, the lining membrane of the skull, was now in clear view—a layer of dead-white tissue in the depths of the circular crater.

A few final twirls of the burr enlarged the aperture still further. A spot of red showed on the cut surface, and he blotted this with a pellet of wax, pressed firmly against the bone. Then, closing the opening with a strip of absorbent cotton wet with saline, he moved to the second cross and repeated the surgical maneuver. Viewed by the layman, Ignaz Lavorsky was now a formidable horror indeed. Here, it seemed, was a head drilled by a gangster's bullet (though the victim, in some strange fashion, continued to breathe). Or one of those surrealist statues, a thing of hollowed temples, through which the breeze whistled at will.

Anton Ziegler entered the theater while Jim was covering the second burr hole—a squat, china-bald Viennese with drill-sergeant eyes, whose voice was a perpetual bark. Shuttling between two operating rooms, he had planned his arrival to the minute. Drying his hands on the towel Penny Ward thrust toward him on a long ring forceps, Ziegler thrust his stumpy arms into a gown and pulled on sterile gloves. Mabel Towers (an efficient mother hen) tied the strings as he charged up to the table.

"Trephine openings ready, Jim?"

"Ready, Doctor."

Hank Gaines had already moved back. It was Jim's turn to take the assistant's post, while Ziegler half crouched above the patient, his gloved palm already open for a scalpel. Jim grinned beneath his mask. The surgeon (for all his concentration on the patient) had paused directly beneath the microphone that permitted him to address the benches in the observation chamber above. Perhaps a score of students were watching today—but Ziggy would have barked the same words to an empty gallery.

"Our purpose in the operation of the prefrontal lobotomy, according to the Ziegler technique," he said in an English that had only a guttural hint of accent, "is to cut through the white matter of each of the frontal lobes in the plane of the coronal suture, just anterior to the tip of the anterior horn of the lateral ventricles. In this way the fibers of the upper and lower parts of the *centrum ovale* are cut on both sides."

The scalpel winked in the light. Jim tented the dura mater with a forceps, in response to the chief's curt nod. "You will note," said Ziegler, "that I am making a cross-shaped incision in the dura mater to expose the field. Next—so!—a three-millimeter incision in the avascular portion of the brain itself. Next, a needle is inserted, obtaining orientation with relationship to the ventricle, the *falx cerebri*, and the sphenoidal ridge."

The surgeon's hand was lightning-swift, thrusting the blunt needle deep into the brain. The patient had not stirred. The brain, though it was the focal point of the entire nervous system, was almost insensitive to pain.

"I am now passing the dissector downward," said Ziegler. "It has reached the floor of the anterior fossa, and is moving laterally, as far as the opening allows." This time the plunge of the slender metal shaft would have seemed vicious to untrained eyes. Jim knew that it was timed as precisely as the surgeon's words.

"Next," said Ziegler, "I swing the dissector—so! *Uuuupward*, along the convexity of the brain. The operation is already completed on this side." As he spoke he drew the long skewer from the brain, lifted its point for an instant as an orchestra conductor might balance his baton, then tossed it aside. Moving to the second burr hole, he strutted a little, as he always did at this moment in the operation. The murmur from the gallery was his reward. The dissection, performed blindly, had a special dramatic impact, though most of the onlookers had witnessed it a dozen times.

Jim had already tented the dura mater in the second burr hole. The surgeon's bark continued while he made an identical approach. "The physical substratum of emotion is thought to be located in the dorso-medial nucleus of the thalamus—from which fibers run to the frontal brain lobes. Along these fibers pass the stimuli responsible for the conscious experience of emotion. By cutting them—as I am doing now—I am changing the affective response. Once the connection between the thalamus and the frontal lobes is broken, tensions have no chance to accumulate. Pathological emotional conditions are thus under permanent control. Regressive and reparative behavior—characteristic of so many psychotic states—will no longer occur."

The recital ended abruptly as Ziegler drew the second dissector from the burr hole and left the table. For an instant his fiery eyes swept the faces in the gallery.

"In the technique I have described," he said, letting his voice linger on his favorite pronoun, "the severance of the thalamo-frontal radiation—as I have just told you—reduces the emotional components of the psychosis or the neurosis. At the same time it leaves enough of the frontal lobes to allow the patient capacity for productive labor—and enough judgment to make a practical adaptation to his environment." He glanced triumphantly at the wall clock and pulled off his mask.

Five minutes on the nose, thought Jim. *No wonder that grin is first cousin to a smirk.* He took a discreet step forward to pick up his cue.

"May I close the incisions, Dr. Ziegler?"

"The patient is yours, Jim." Now that he had basked in his self-generated glory, the chief sounded almost affable. "And take a ten-minute breather before you start the next case. We have both earned it."

It was a dispensation from Olympus, made with a gesture of Ziggy's right hand. The fingers (still arched slightly, as though grasping an invisible knife) looked cruel as a falcon's claws, for all their pudginess. He walked out of the theater as he spoke. Jim, pausing a dutiful second, exchanged a nod with Hank and took the surgeon's place at the table to make the closure of both burr holes.

Jim was puffing on his pipe in the lounge and refusing to think at all when Hank Gaines entered, tugging a pack of cigarettes from the pocket of his surgical jacket.

"A slick job of boring," he said. "When is the Big I going to let you handle dissections?"

Jim shrugged. "That's Voltin's job." Dr. Boris Voltin was the current resident on Neurosurgical Service. Another Ziegler in the making, he was slated to move on to greater things in the fall.

"Wonder how it feels, pushing that hatpin through a brain," said Hank. "Like stabbing cold mush, I imagine."

"If Alex were here," said Jim, "he'd resent that comparison." Dr. Alex Goldschmidt—a favorite classmate—was now a rising psychiatrist at the Scripps Institute. At the last staff meeting he had expressed his opinion of lobotomy in no uncertain terms. . . . Hank, smoking his precious cigarette in short, angry drags, did not pursue the subject: the surgical sleight of hand they had just witnessed had dampened both their spirits. Today, as always, it was simpler to ignore the fact that they had contributed to a theft—in this case, the filching of a man's higher faculties. *Not of his reason,* thought Jim. *But who can deny that*

Ziegler's probe has just destroyed the bridge linking Ignaz Lavorsky, however remotely, to the angels?

He was still struggling with that imponderable when the buzzer recalled him to the present.

"On your feet, Gaines," he said. "It's time to prep another zombie. Are you ready?"

"As ready as I'll ever be," said Hank. "Just don't ask for this one's name. It makes me nervous." He was already moving down the corridor that led to the next O.R. on their schedule—chanting as he walked, to the music of a popular dance tune:

Ignaz Lavorsky
Is no Sikorsky
He's Ziggy's zombie now—
A ship without a prow
An ape without a tree
I'm glad he isn't me!

iii

Late that night (knowing in advance that he would be returning to an empty apartment) Jim Corwin took a certain negative pleasure in bachelor habits while he waited for his mind to slough off its restlessness.

He had eaten his usual snack in the hospital cafeteria. In the library he had sat at a study table until closing time, poring over the books he was using to footnote his final thesis in the contest for the residency. At midnight (en route to the walk-up he now called home) he had paused for a beer at the Lakewood Diner—and a regretful agreement with the short-order cook that the Orioles would not finish in the first division. These harmless routines had always returned him to Taffy's orbit again, with no sense of strain. Tonight he was strangely reluctant to take the final step.

The apartment had been hers before he left the hospital to share it: when his key turned the lock, he still felt like an intruder. Switching on the drop lights above the wide day bed and the bookshelves, he wondered what a stranger would make of the hectic, slightly disordered room. The Renoir reproductions, the albums stacked beside the hi-fi set, suggested the aggressive modern. So did the books that crammed the shelves. The scarlet cushions on the day bed, the bottles in the open bar, the carnival dolls on the mantel insisted, no less emphatically, that this was the den of a bacchante. Oddly enough, each impression was accurate.

Hard though it was to picture Taffy beneath a reading lamp, Jim knew that she had devoured each book on the shelves. If she played even harder than she read these days—and had refused to give up her playtime when she became Mrs. Jim Corwin—he could still forgive that nervous, superabundant energy. Tonight his wife had gone dancing with Tom Willoughby, a former beau who drove a brick-red Triumph and spent his father's money lavishly. She had made the date with her husband's blessing. After two months of wedded bliss (the happiness, he repeated without too much conviction, far outweighed the quarrels) he knew the warring elements in Taffy's nature better than his own.

If his love had begun to mix with pity, if it was darkened at times by rage (as he pictured her laughing in Tom Willoughby's arms), he refused to regret his bargain. Taffy's living presence could wipe out most doubting instantly. It was only when he came home to find the room empty that he saw home for what it really was—a bohemian lair that needed dusting, a bachelor girl's stronghold that had kept its aura, though a husband now shared both bed and latchkey. . . .

He had first met Taffy at the Gaineses' cocktail party just before the Alpha Kappa Kappa dance. Even before their eyes met in the crowded room, he had sensed her presence, had felt he must speak to her instantly—and guessed that the urge was shared.

She had been surrounded by a group of admiring males—so large a gathering, in fact, that the Gaineses' party was in grave danger of imbalance. After Hank had introduced him, Jim was conscious only of Taffy's eyes, grave and deep and just a little slanted. It would be days before he could say if they were gray green or hazel, but he remembered their intensity—as though she had looked into his heart with that first level glance and liked what she found there. Later, of course, he would remember that she had the face of a child and the body of an odalisque. Her full lips were innocent—and made for kisses.

She gave him her hand and let it rest in his. Her voice was part of her, a vibrant, faintly husky contralto.

"Jim Corwin?" she said. "You're not *Jim*. You're American Gothic. Abe Lincoln without the beard. That's what I'll call you from now on."

"Are we on a nickname basis, Miss Cottrell?"

Taffy waved her retinue aside. "Go back to your wives, gentlemen, before they murder me. Abe here is single—and we've things to talk over." Pausing to lift two martinis from a passing tray and give him one, she tucked an arm through Jim's, steering him to a window seat.

"Are you always this direct?" he asked.

"Always. It's made me lots of friends. You, for example."

"Are we about to become friends, Miss Cottrell?"

"We're friends already. And please call me Taffy."

"Why haven't I seen you before?"

"It's your fault, not mine. I've been nearly a month in Baltimore—in continuous circulation."

"Do you work at Lakewood?"

"I do physiotherapy at the institute. Are you a Lakewood staffer?"

"Only an assistant resident, in neurosurgery."

"Aren't you a bit mature to sink that low?"

"Blame it on Korea. I had two years there."

"That's my Abe. You wouldn't deserve the name if you hadn't put country before self."

"How do you know so much about me?"

"I have a special crystal ball," said Taffy Cottrell. "It told me straight off you weren't married. Or even engaged. Which means we're dancing every dance at AKK. You dance like a dream—don't you, Abe?"

"I'm a rotten dancer."

"You won't be—after we've practiced awhile."

She had proved her statement later, on the fraternity floor. From the first step he found it easy to match her effortless response to the music. It was easier still to recall the teasing argot of college days, the half compliments that had passed for gallantry at Washington and Lee. After the dance their ritual drive to Spring Lake (and their breathless embraces in the back seat of his car) had been an inevitable climax to the evening.

He had made no attempt to go beyond kissing. It was only when he left Taffy at her door and returned to his hospital room that he realized he was in love.

Thanks to Taffy's candor, Jim had heard most of her life story between those first kisses.

Her mother (who lived in genteel poverty in back-street Washington) was a retired government employee. Her father (more wraith than man) had lingered long enough on the borders of Mrs. Cottrell's world to provide her only child with a legal surname. He had died when the child was nine, leaving his widow with the burden of raising her. It was a task the widow had taken on avidly.

For thirteen years Miriam Cottrell had worked by day in one of the marble rabbit warrens on Constitution Avenue. She had brought home extra work each night to pay for Taffy's boarding school and Taffy's brief college career at Chapel Hill. In return she had demanded only a first mortgage on her daughter's mind and heart—and assurance that Taffy, when she reached maturity, would fulfill her mother's dream picture.

This picture, Jim gathered, had included every item unhappy women invent to console them in their loneliness. At its center, of course, was a son-in-law who was both rich and a gentleman. This paragon would give Mrs. Cottrell's daughter her rightful place in society. By a special legerdemain he would also grant the mother full partnership in the union. Mrs. Cottrell had never dreamed that Taffy would think of marriage to a house surgeon at Lakewood. . . . Yet, from their first kiss at Spring Lake, Jim knew their marriage was foreordained.

He soon discovered that Taffy's ardor matched his own—though her formula for its satisfaction was simpler.

"Calling yourself a resident doesn't mean you must *live* at the hospital," she said. "Come live with me awhile."

"Do you know what you're suggesting?"

"Our steps suit, Abe. You make me laugh, even when you're serious. You can heat up a frozen dinner. Give me time, and I'll train you to mix martinis. What more does a young couple need?"

"What would your mother say?"

"Mother and I have stopped speaking. Ever since I refused to be engaged to Tom Willoughby."

"You aren't by any chance suggesting we do this to hit back at her?"

He would always remember the sudden tightening of her lips, the way her eyes seemed to turn inward under knitted brows. While the rare mood of introspection lasted, Taffy Cottrell's face was a primitive mask of hate from which all traces of civilization had vanished. The grimace was fleeting. In a flash she was her laughing self again.

"Come off it, Abe. Is this my reward for telling my life story—and offering to share my apartment?"

Realizing he had rung an emotional bull's-eye, Jim held his peace. Obviously Taffy's whole existence so far had been based on defiance of her mother. He could hardly deny that she was reveling in her freedom, or that she had welcomed him wholeheartedly as her favorite playmate. Clearly it was no time to explain that fun for fun's sake could be a dead-end street—or that marriage was the only real balance wheel for a girl of Taffy's volatile nature. . . . For the time being, he was content to enjoy his status as a favored beau—to realize (with a lift of the heart) that she would break any date to join him on the meager outings his pocketbook permitted. Even Tom Willoughby and his Triumph were rejected instantly—when a change in Jim's plans permitted an afternoon at the ball game, or a picnic on the Chesapeake.

"Why didn't you marry Willoughby?" he asked one day while they drifted in a rowboat under the Bay Bridge, trolling for stripers.

Taffy, lolling at ease with her dungaree-clad legs across a gunwale and her head on Jim's knee, snorted by way of answer.

"I'm only a so-so surgeon," he persisted, "with a fighting chance for a Lakewood residency, if I continue to flatter Ziggy's vanity. What can you see in me?"

"That's a question you should never ask a woman. But I'll answer, if you insist. On top we couldn't be more different. If we do marry someday, we'll probably fight like bobcats. But we're alike underneath. We've escaped from homes we couldn't bear—and we're both keeping our freedom."

"Aren't you dramatizing yourself just a little?"

"Nothing's more important than freedom, Abe. I'll never surrender mine."

"Not even to become Mrs. Corwin?"

"Not even then. You must take me as I am."

"Does this mean you're accepting my proposal?"

"I'm weighing it. If I *do* accept—don't forget the condition."

That afternoon, of course, she was only teasing—but there was a hard core of truth in her pronouncement. It was true that they had both escaped from families they could hardly endure. And (until they had met at the Gaineses' party) both had been lonely in their hard-won liberty.

Like Taffy, Jim had left home at the first possible moment. His father, a small tobacco farmer in North Carolina, had remained a stranger to his son—though they had worked side by side in field and smokehouse until Jim Corwin, Senior, had sold out to one of the national combines and become a merchant in Raleigh. His death had come just before his bankruptcy.

Jim's mother (who had taught school in her youth) had insisted he complete his education, no matter what the sacrifice to herself. The burden, thanks to his father's insurance, had not been too onerous; he was certain that he had been pushed into boarding school because his mother wished to rid herself of his presence. Her own death, during his last year at college, had provided an inheritance large enough to finance his medical training: there was nothing left over for such luxuries as marriage. . . . However, thanks to Taffy's apartment (the rent was paid through June), and Taffy's lighthearted certainty that two could live as cheaply as one, he had felt the risk worth while. After all, the need to save Taffy from herself was urgent.

Since Maryland was still among the states that required no blood test on a marriage license, Jim had found the paper work simple enough. Inducing Taffy to put her name on the forms and stand with him before a justice of the peace had been a trifle harder. Looking back, he realized that she had been only half aware of the actual ceremony, that the memory of the rustic parlor and the poker-faced witnesses had been filled with meaning for him alone. . . .

It was another story when the door of their motel unit on the Chesapeake closed behind them—and they stood face to face in a darkness broken only by the lattice of moonlight at the jalousies.

"You're a good man, Abe," Taffy said. "In fact, you're better than I deserve. Why do you want to reform me?"

"It's *you* I want, Taffy. Only you."

She laughed then, deep in her throat: there was an ageless note of female rejoicing in the sound. "Say what you like about me afterwards, darling. Just remember, I warned you."

"I accepted the terms, didn't I?"

"You're a strange character, Corwin. Other men have fed me champagne in the hope of seducing me. You're taking the trouble to make the seduction legal."

"Don't forget I'm a country boy—with old-fashioned morals."

She flung away from him on that. At first he feared that he had brought on another of her rages. Then he saw that she had only gone to raise the blinds. Reflected moonlight from the bay poured over her in a silver flood while she stripped off her dress. She went through the disrobing slowly: he knew she was relishing the hunger in his eyes. Then, with a happy cry, she flung herself into his arms.

"Believe it or not, Abe," she said, "I've never done this before. Don't call me a fool for wasting time."

That midnight, Taffy stretched like a drowsy kitten in the vast double bed that was a feature of the Bayside Motel—and smiled up at her new husband impishly.

"Disappointed, darling? I *am* new at this, you know."

"Don't talk about anything that's perfect," he begged. "If you do, you'll lose it."

"I wish now you *hadn't* been the first, Abe. I wish I'd had a hundred men, so I could drive you mad with sensation. Make you remember things you've never known——"

"You mustn't talk nonsense, Margaret."

"I'm *Taffy*. Don't use that other name, ever."

"You signed it on our marriage license. It must be yours."

"I'm Taffy, not Margaret! Margaret reminds me of a time I've forgotten." She pulled his head down to her breast and clung to him fiercely. "Margaret would let you down, Abe—Taffy never will. Just put yourself in her hands: she'll make life worth while."

"She already has."

"Darling, I'll never forget tonight—no matter what happens tomorrow. I won't pretend you're the first man I've wanted: I'm not that innocent. But you *are* the first I've wanted all the way. Let's hope you'll be the last."

"This is fine talk for a wedding."

"The wedding was your idea, not mine. But I won't hold that against you, Abe. Now we're here, let's make the most of it."

He would remember her words later, and the invisible wound they had made. At the moment, he was oblivious of the threat they posed to the future. Loving her with all his being, proving his love with all the ardor he possessed, he could tell himself that their hearts were joined by bonds which would outlast time. . . . Drowned in the deepest rapture he had ever known, he was unsure if he had heard her final, sleepy whisper —or dreamt it in the limbo between sleep and waking.

"Why was I afraid so long, Abe? Why did it take you to give me courage?"

He slept without answering the phantom question. . . . Then, with no sense of transition, he was staring wide-awake in an empty bed, in the smudged light of dawn. For an instant he thought the room was empty too—until he saw his wife huddled at the window.

He was beside her at once, brushing the dank hair from her forehead.

"What is it, Taffy?"

"I'm *still* afraid," she sobbed. "I thought I'd never be afraid again."

"There's nothing to be afraid of."

"The water's so gray, now the moon is gone. And this room's like prison. I tried to get through the window—but I couldn't. *Is that what you've done to me—put me in a cage?"*

Her voice broke in a wail of hysteria. Knowing this crisis of nerves for what it was, he wasted no time. When he carried her to the bed, she fought back desperately for a while. It was only when he had torn the clammy nightgown from her body and dried her vigorously in a huge bath towel that she let her tenseness go beneath his practiced doctor's hands. . . . Later, in bed beside him, with the quilt pulled about their ears, she made no attempt to resist him when he held her close.

In the morning, with the sun like a benediction across the quilt and Taffy sleeping at his side, he could almost pretend the episode had been a dream. But he was careful to leave it unmentioned until they were in the car again, on the way to their duty call on her mother.

"That dream last night. Do you have it often?"

His wife shrugged: for a moment he thought she would let the question go unanswered. Then she drew closer and tucked her hand through his arm. Her fingers were icy-cold, and he knew she was shivering.

"Too often, darling. How did you guess?"

"I know enough psychiatry for that," he told her gently. "Do you *always* feel caged—eager to escape?"

"Always, Dr. Corwin."

"Only you can't get away?"

"That's just the trouble. I'm afraid of the cage. But I'm more afraid of what's outside."

"Last night should have freed you of those fears."

"I hope you're right."

"Just go on loving me," he said. "I'll do the rest. It's my job now."

"I want to give, too, Abe. Please believe that. It's just that I can't be owned."

"That's where you're wrong, Taffy," he said, careful to keep his eyes on his driving. "You've invented this need for independence as a protection. You think a husband will rule you as your mother once did. The real you, the one I love, knows better."

"Tell it your way, Dr. Corwin."

"This rebellion has been your shield against life—because you're convinced life wants to hurt you. Your bachelor-girl pose was part of that shield. So was your offer to live with me without marriage. Am I right?"

"I'm not saying."

Her tone was light, almost bantering—but he sensed that she was listening intently—with an eagerness for self-knowledge that might not come again. "Don't fight against being a woman, Taffy," he urged. "Let yourself be loved and wanted. Above all, don't be afraid of living——"

"I'm not afraid now, Abe."

"Deep inside you are. You must tell yourself those fears have no basis. Remember I'll always be here to keep things from hurting you."

"I'll try, Abe."

"You weren't afraid last night—after you fell asleep in my arms."

"We can't always forget things that way."

"Taffy, you must learn that love and marriage are two sides

of the same coin. It will never buy happiness unless you give yourself too. Right now that seems an attack on your independence. But it's the kind of giving that makes the world go on."

"I can believe you now, Abe—with the sun shining. It was different in the dark—when I was alone."

"No one who is truly married can be alone. It doesn't matter if the partner in marriage is beside you, or half a world away. Give yourself time—you'll learn that lesson."

"I'll do my best, Abe. Just be patient."

Jim was still wide-awake, hugging his knees in the studio day bed while he watched dawn brighten the windows. . . . In the two months that followed his wedding night, there had been need of patience.

First, he had endured the screams of Taffy's mother after she had heard their news in her dingy Washington eyrie; he had shuddered inwardly at his wife's answering fury before the small, withered woman had shown them the door. Back in Baltimore he had survived his hurt surprise when Taffy resigned promptly from her job at the institute. His bride, he discovered, had assumed that his inheritance would support them both until his residency at Lakewood ended. Apparently she had also decided that he would step overnight into a practice lucrative enough to buy the things Tom Willoughby had already offered.

The first time he had returned from the hospital and found the apartment empty had shocked him to the quick. Later he had trained himself to take his wife's absences with something like aplomb, however he might rage within. After all (he told himself bitterly), she had given him fair warning.

"It isn't that I don't love you, Abe. But I can't be alone after dark. That's when the cage *really* closes. What's the harm—if Tom asks me out and you're at the hospital?"

"I don't like coming home—and finding no one here."

"*You're* used to it, darling. But I can't stand the cage."

"I've explained there's no cage, that your fears are groundless. This restlessness is only a leftover from childhood—something you must outgrow——"

"Who wants to outgrow anything? I've never enjoyed life so much before."

Jim saw that she was not even aware of the heartache she had caused—and forced himself to speak of other matters. He was now in full competition with Hank for the residency. Daydreaming of the future (when, as a successful neurosurgeon, he could afford to relax), he found escape from his doubting. Taffy (curled in his arms, in the same day bed he was thrashing on now) had listened contentedly while he built their private dream house for tomorrow.

"See, Abe? You've an escape mechanism too."

"So I have, Madame Freud. We all need a dream or two, or we'd really go mad."

"I went to a psychoanalyst once, darling."

"What did he say?"

"Not too much—I could only afford one visit." Taffy chuckled at the memory. "He advised me to fall in love, and to cultivate the dynamics of success. I'm sure he was a quack—or he'd have seen what a failure I was."

"The advice seems sound. And you must never call yourself a failure."

"But I *have* failed, Abe. Everything I've tried has fallen apart. Maybe that's why I switched men so often—until you came along to change things."

"Have I changed things, really?"

"You made me fall in love with you—just as the doctor ordered. I'd never been in love before. Just *wanted* to be."

"Has love made you happy?"

"I'm happier than I've ever been."

He had seen she meant this, too—his wife, for all her bizarre poses, was without guile. . . . Now, closing his eyes against the brightening day, Jim could tell himself that his own love was stronger than his hate. Ten minutes ago, in that forgotten country between sleep and waking (a no man's land where the Id is king), he could have strangled Taffy without a pang. Hearing her key in the lock, her careful tiptoe in the foyer, he was prepared to forgive her one more time, to cherish her as best he could.

"Don't bother," he said. "I'm wide-awake."

His wife moved into the pearl dawn light that filled the window frame: her eyes were sparkling as she leaned out to wave. From below the curb, Jim heard the cough of a departing car—an expensive cough, that could come only from Tom Willoughby's Triumph.

"Darling," said Taffy, "I've told you not to sit up for me."

"I only just wakened," he lied. "Was your evening a success?"

"We closed the Four Aces. Tom bribed the orchestra."

"I'm glad it was fun."

"Shall I get your breakfast—or come to bed?"

"Do both," he said huskily, conscious that he was trembling. "Just reverse the order."

"Damn you, Abe," said Taffy, an hour later. "Why couldn't *you* be there to bribe the orchestra?"

"Give me time," he said. "And a break with Ziegler. It's all I need."

iv

That optimistic statement, while reassuring, was hardly true. Recalling the circumstances that had prompted it, Jim felt a shiver of dread the next afternoon while he waited in Alex Goldschmidt's office as his friend completed his rounds.

He had admitted, for several weeks now, that this visit was inevitable—and he had decided to spread his cards on the table. And yet (in the forlorn hope that Taffy might still mend her ways) he had deliberately postponed it. When Alex came into the room at last, Jim still found it impossible to reveal his reason for waiting there.

The tubby, nearsighted psychiatrist had been his closest friend from their student days. The bond had grown for the best of reasons, a complete meeting of minds, a refusal to blink the realities, medical or social, that made a doctor's career so exacting. Alex (whose devotion to his calling was ascetic) had never considered marriage. Because of his eyes, he had been refused for medical service in Korea. He had just been appointed a full-time staff member at Scripps Institute and looked forward to a rewarding future in the field.

Today, in a starched coat, with a formidable casebook under one arm, he seemed the perfect, ice-cold man of science. It was only when he settled at his desk, acknowledged Jim's presence with a grunt, and stripped off heavy-lensed glasses that one had a flash of the darting mind beneath, and its unpredictable humors.

"I was hoping you'd drop in today," he said. "I need someone to argue with."

"Another run-in with Ziggy?" The hostility that kept Dr. Ziegler and Alex at sword's point was no secret at Lakewood. "I heard he was at Scripps yesterday, hunting for human guinea pigs."

"We sent him packing fast enough. The closed wards at Rocky Point are already his preserve. What more does he need?"

"He's writing a definitive text on lobotomy. He can't have too many case histories to document his theories."

"They aren't theories with Ziggy," said Alex gloomily. "They're convictions. How many skulls did you bore yesterday?"

"Eleven—in our theater. I didn't check on the others. Somehow, I didn't want to."

Alex lighted one of the cheap cigars for which his office was infamous. "See what I'm driving at, Jim? You're doing this job against your better judgment. Why not quit?"

"Because I need a Lakewood residency too badly—if I'm to support my family. And I'm not working against my will. Ziegler may be one hundred per cent right. Certainly he's tops in the field."

"And in his own estimation," said Alex. "I still maintain lobotomy is wrong, both morally and clinically. You've no right to seal off a section of a man's brain, just because his emotions don't operate by normal rules."

"We remove diseased appendices and spleens, don't we?"

"I know that argument backwards, Jim. Mental disease is different. You simply can't probe into a certain section of the brain and insist it's causing the illness you hope to isolate. That kind of thinking went out with Charcot. Man's a *whole* person. It makes no sense whatever, turning him into a robot just to quiet him down."

"Are Ziegler's cases really that bad?"

"I was at Rocky Point last week, pinch-hitting at the clinic. It was pure nightmare."

"The director's sold on the method. So's the Welfare Board."

"The director at Rocky Point isn't a psychiatrist. He's a public administrator, running a state hospital. His idea of a solution for mental illness is to turn a psychotic into a machine that does as it's told and saves the expense of extra orderlies."

Jim grinned through the smoke screen that Alex was building in huge, angry puffs. "I don't recall that the cure rate at Scripps is too high."

"Naturally it isn't. But our mental patients are still experiencing emotion. They're alive, in every sense of the word. Your lobotomies shuffle through a routine that's planned for them in advance. Cutting off part of the brain is an evasion of the basic nature of disease, not a serious attempt to effect a cure."

Alex spoke as precisely as though he were reading a medical philippic aloud. Knowing he had touched on a tender spot, Jim held his peace. Alex's chief, Dr. Hans Decker (a student of Freud and one of the world's leading analytic psychiatrists), had always preferred to seek the cause of mental derangement within the personality of the patient—and Alex was Decker's disciple, heart and soul.

"If the spark is there," said Alex, "isn't it worse than murder to snuff it out?"

"You've worked at Rocky Point—so you know most locked-ward cases are hopeless."

"Damn it, the spark's still there."

"At least you'll admit that Ziggy's technique has taken pressure off the wards——"

Alex bounced up from his desk. "Come upstairs with me: I'll show you what I mean."

Jim stood by quietly while the psychiatrist lifted a phone and gave an order: when Alex was in a lecturer's mood, he had learned not to interrupt. Nor did he offer a comment as his friend led him into one of the treatment rooms of which Scripps was so justly proud. The white-tiled apartment contained several couches, with a squat black EST cabinet at the head of each. These were the electric-shock-therapy machines that Dr. Decker and his staff used reluctantly even now—although the technique of electric shock had been seized upon by psychiatrists everywhere.

On the first couch lay a patient in hospital pajamas. Jim noted that he was little more than a boy—twenty, perhaps, and clean-cut, despite the stamp of emptiness on his waxen features. Resting between treatments, with a nurse in attendance, he was in a state of complete collapse. As he breathed, saliva bubbled at the corners of his lips. The tight-drawn face was its own death mask.

"This is Hugh Campbell," said Alex. "Recognize the condition?"

"Catatonic schizophrenia, obviously."

"He's been in this state for two months." Alex lifted the patient's arm, which remained rigidly vertical. "If I left it, he'd hold that arm stiff for hours. It's part of the rigidity of his whole body." He pressed the arm down gently. "Before the stupor he was in a state of high excitement. Destructive and almost impossible to control."

Jim straddled a chair. "What is he in normal life—a picture star? He's handsome enough."

"Hugh was an honor student at M.I.T. A born scientist, headed for a degree in astrophysics. He broke down from overwork. They sent him here, on request of next of kin——"

Jim nodded soberly. It was a heart-twisting story—and a familiar one. Staring down at the mask-like face, he found it hard to believe that this near-cadaver had been a scientist in the making.

Alex nodded to the attending nurse, who crossed to the sterilizer in the corner and returned with a syringe and a small ampule.

"I'm about to inject sodium cyanide intravenously," the psychiatrist explained. "I think you'll find the results remarkable."

"*Cyanide?*"

"An ampule too small to be toxic. It's to stimulate respiration."

Alex had scrubbed as he talked. When the nurse applied a tourniquet to the patient's arm, he thrust the needle into a distended vein and began to inject slowly. The patient had not flinched under the jab of the syringe—nor was there a visible reaction when the injection ended.

"We must wait a few minutes." Alex had begun to time the breathing of the stuporous figure on the couch. The increase in the respiratory rate was already marked. With the expansion of the boy's lungs, his cheeks became faintly pink—but Jim was even more startled by the change in his general demeanor. Little by little the muscles relaxed; the marble-death mask became a face again. Then the eyelids fluttered. Hugh Campbell was looking up into Alex's face—not with the withdrawn stare of the deranged, but with the bright warmth of intelligence.

Jim turned to speak to Alex, but the psychiatrist shook his head warningly. The patient's eyes moved from one doctor to the other, and his lips curved in a smile.

"Good afternoon, Dr. Goldschmidt," he said quietly.

"Hello, Hugh." Alex spoke without emphasis, as though this were a routine visit. "Meet Dr. Corwin, a friend of mine."

The patient held out his hand—the same hand that, a moment before, had been frozen in mid-air. The clasp of the fingers was strong, like that of any collegian his age. "Hello, Dr. Corwin," he said. "Glad to know you."

Jim controlled his voice with an effort, while he acknowledged the introduction. He could not have been more surprised had a corpse risen from the mortuary table to offer him a greeting.

"Do you know where you are, Hugh?" Alex asked.

"Of course, Doctor. This is the Scripps Psychiatric Institute in Baltimore."

"And who am I?"

"My attending physician."

"Why are you here?"

"I—had a breakdown."

"How long ago?"

"Six months." The patient's eyes went to a calendar on the wall. "Early November, it was. This is April, isn't it?"

"Why did you break down, Hugh?"

The boy's eyes clouded and his mouth trembled. He seemed to be struggling with a thought too big for words—to admit in advance that it was a losing battle. Then, precisely as though an invisible artist (dissatisfied with his creation) had passed a sponge across his face, Hugh Campbell disintegrated before Jim's eyes, to become once again a vegetative animal that scarcely seemed to breathe. Finally, the full lips flattened and began to salivate as before.

Alex shrugged and leaned across the cot to lift the hand that had shaken Jim's so heartily. Once again the arm remained vertical, without a vestige of life.

"I hoped I could get a more prolonged effect," he said. "Still, I think I've made my point."

In the office again, Jim lit his pipe with fingers that still trembled. "I won't deny I'm shaken," he said. "Exactly what happened?"

"I wish I knew," said Alex. "But I'm sure of this much. Anything that markedly stimulates breathing—or causes hyperventilation, if you want the exact term—will bring most catatonics out of stupor. A cyanide solution will do it. So will a breathing bag and a mixture of CO_2. Unfortunately, we can't make the treatment continuous. As you saw, the patient regresses immediately when it's ended."

"Always?"

"So far, yes. We've used the method to explore the personality picture while they're in a lucid state. Hugh Campbell's performance was typical. We usually lose them again before we can discover anything significant. He might have stayed out longer—if I hadn't asked why he became sick."

"Do you believe he knows why?"

"Most of them do—but the answer is well buried. Hugh was struggling to bring it out when he went under." Alex stopped abruptly and ground out the stub of his cigar. "Now tell me why I took you upstairs."

"You're trying to prove that even your most deranged patients still have minds. And that they could be brought back to normal *permanently*—if you had ways and means."

"Exactly. Here at Scripps we go to the source—the whole personality. We uncover basic trauma. Things that get people off the rails. The technique is long, involved, and frustrating. Quite apart from training, it requires a very special type of doctor. Sometimes, all too rarely, it brings its reward. Shorter methods are bound to turn up later. A new technique of hypnosis, perhaps. Or a drug that will have the same long-term effect that hyperventilation produces for only a moment——"

Alex fixed Jim with a piercing look: the eyes behind those thick lenses were hot with rage—and certitude. "We psychiatrists are still fumbling in the dark, like the doctors who fought infections as best they could before Pasteur—and before Fleming discovered penicillin. Our present treatments—inadequate though they are—cause no permanent damage. Can you claim as much for lobotomy?"

"Of course not," said Jim. "When you cut a tract in the brain, the surgery's irrevocable. Tissue in the central nervous system doesn't regenerate."

"Doesn't that mean I've won the argument?"

"Not quite, Alex. The main problem is still unsolved. Suppose you had a hundred schizophrenics under your care? How many would you hope to cure?"

"A half dozen, with luck."

"What if you had to make room for two thousand, as they do at Rocky Point? With special detention for the really violent cases, so they can't destroy themselves or hurt others? Granted, some of those two thousand *might* recover. Isn't it worth risking permanent brain damage to those few—if the others are really helped?"

"The answer is no," said Alex. "Remember the first principle of all treatment—the one old Paddy Ryan drilled into us when we were students?"

"*Nolle nocere?*"

"*Do no harm.* You can't bypass it."

"Circumstances alter cases," Jim argued. He was not sure he believed what he was saying. Brain surgery was still his profession: he felt he should uphold its honor against Alex's attack. "You must decide what's best for the largest number. Lobotomy may be the only solution—for the older, hopeless patient. I don't deny it alters the personality—sometimes markedly. But it can also turn a homicidal maniac into a useful citizen. Isn't that worth something?"

"We've enough robots walking the streets right now."

"Every lobotomy doesn't produce a robot."

"You're still begging the question, Jim. Ignoring the fact that the operation is only a stopgap. Even Ziggy wouldn't dare to call it a cure. All he really does is separate what *he* calls the troublemaking segment of the brain from the rest——"

"That isn't much different from removing part of the stomach wall to stop an ulcer from spreading."

"Contrary to the cynics, a man doesn't think with his stomach. When you take away his intelligence, you rob him of his soul."

"If you're going into metaphysics, I'll withdraw from the debate. It's getting a bit too murky."

"Then I *do* win by default," said the psychiatrist. He took off his spectacles and rubbed his tired eyes. "Besides, you didn't come here to debate medical ethics. You want my advice on Taffy."

Jim drew a deep breath. He had prolonged the argument with Alex in order to avoid his own grievous problem—but it could be put off no longer. "This time I won't argue," he said quietly.

"It *is* Taffy, then?"

"You always were a mind reader, Alex."

"You've wanted my opinion on your marriage for a long time. Being a gentleman, you couldn't open up—until you'd done your own muttonheaded best to solve the problem."

"Who said it is a problem?"

"Would you come to me if your wife weren't driving you quietly mad?"

The question answered itself: Jim could even admit a certain relief as he faced his friend across the desk. He could also understand why Taffy had disliked Alex from the first—and why she complained that his eyes were X rays, lighting forbidden corners.

"Apparently neither of us has too much talent for marriage," he admitted.

"Who does?" barked Alex. "Marriage is like driving a car, or building a log cabin—you learn by doing. By giving rather than taking. I've always known you were a born giver. Is she?"

"She loves me. I'm sure of that."

"Enough to stay home and make sure you're happy?"

"I *am* happy, Alex. Happier than I've ever been." His eyes dropped on that thumping lie. "It's Taffy I'm worried about."

"Tell your story from the beginning," said the psychiatrist. "Don't leave out a single detail—and stop covering up."

After the first halting sentences, Jim found he could state his case accurately enough. Hearing his voice go on, he took a certain satisfaction in his detachment. In Alex's presence, he felt no disloyalty to his wife. After all, he was seeking a way out for them both.

"In a sense," said his friend, when he had finished his strange recital, "this confirms my first impression. I'd say there was a chance psychiatric treatment might help her."

"Just a chance?"

"If her symptoms are based on a neurosis."

"How else could they be based?"

"For want of a better term, it may be a constitutional psychopathic state."

Jim felt his jaw harden. "What we called Section Eight in the Army?"

"To put it bluntly."

"Damn it, we're speaking of my *wife!*"

Alex shrugged. "That's an opinion, Jim—not a diagnosis."

"Sorry—I didn't mean to bark. *My* opinion is that it's only a phase—an emotional release from her home life."

"Other girls have escaped tyrannical parents and lived them down," Alex reminded him. "Burning the candle at both ends is no substitute for maturity."

"Taffy's never had a chance. Once I'm making a decent income and we've settled down——"

"Her whole life, as you've described it, has been nothing but defiance of authority. What she's doing now seems part of the pattern."

"It's rebellion, all right. But against what?"

"You, perhaps. Let's say she loves you—enough to wish she could really become an adoring, obedient housewife. Naturally, the other part of her nature would fight such a surrender."

"How can anyone help her, then?"

"I'm not saying anyone can. If she loves you enough, perhaps I can make her admit her basic conflict. Show her that it's you she's fighting today, as a symbol of the authority she rejected when she left her mother. Until she understands that much, we're helpless."

"Why does she always come back, if she hates me?"

"She doesn't *consciously* hate you, Jim. The best part of her wants to be worthy of your love. Obviously, there's a strong current of remorse in her nature—cutting down her instinct for flight, bringing second thoughts. When that mood is dominant, she realizes that you're her only hope and strength. At such times she can't run back to you too soon. While the mood lasts, I daresay she's a model wife."

"She is, Alex. Nine days out of ten."

"I'd say *five* out of ten. Maybe less."

Jim flushed but did not deny the truth. "What comes next?"

"You—and I, if she'll let me—have got to show her that her

resentment, like her fears, is completely irrational. It's a tall order, Jim."

"Which means, of course, she must come here for treatment."

"That's the first step—and a big one." Alex got up and held out his hand. "Going to a psychiatrist is like calling for help from Alcoholics Anonymous. But the mere admission you need help takes you past Milestone Number One."

v

Five minutes after Jim had left his friend's office the whole conversation seemed as unreal as a page torn at random from a freshman's notebook in psychology. He had seen plenty of constitutional psychopaths in the Army—rebels without a cause, always neck-deep in trouble when they weren't locked in the stockade. Taffy simply did not belong in the same class with those hot-eyed, hopeless drifters. . . . It was pure fantasy to suggest (even in an off-the-cuff opinion) that the girl who greeted him at the day's end was emotionally unbalanced, let alone on the verge of a breakdown.

Or so he reasoned, after his third cocktail with Taffy, in a roadhouse they favored on his evenings off. Alex (he told himself) had been inventing psychotic bogeymen as usual. Granted, she was a bit childish at times—stubborn rather than strong, and far too romantic for her good. But it was Freudian nonsense to suggest that he had replaced her mother as a detested symbol of authority.

The next afternoon (as was his custom, whenever he could steal a daylight hour at Lakewood) Jim closeted himself in the hospital library to pick up the thread of his research. All through the winter he had worked hard on the thesis he was submitting as a part of his campaign for the residency: since his marriage, he had found but little time for his books. . . . Today he bypassed the usual shelves and took down a standard text on psychoanalysis. Puzzling his way through the jungle of terms, he still refused to believe that Taffy belonged in this blighted no man's land, even as a temporary visitor.

It was a real relief to put the book aside and take up his own familiar research again—to leave the foggy bailiwick of the brain doctors (with its phobias and its phantoms) for the geometric truths of anatomy.

The title of his paper, *The Techniques of Transorbital Lobotomy,* was impressive enough. The operation, once considered daring, was now a fairly routine affair, requiring only initiative and skill on the surgeon's part. It took advantage of the fact that the roof of the eye sockets, the deep depressions in the skull that housed the eyeballs, was also a floor beneath the frontal lobes of the brain. Here the bone was far thinner than the cranium itself and easily penetrated without trephining. Twenty years ago, surgeons in both Europe and America had conceived the idea of attacking the brain via this partition, to sever the so-called thalamofrontal nerve tract radiations, a procedure vital to lobotomy. The operation was usually performed after two electric shocks, spaced to follow each other by minutes. The surgery was carried through swiftly in the coma that ensued.

The technique was simple, and would have seemed grisly only to the layman. A single instrument was used—a slender barb of steel resembling an ice pick. Inserted beneath the upper eyelid, between the eyeball and the roof of the orbit (as the eye socket was called), it entered the skull opposite the pupil and behind the frontal sinus. Driven into the brain at this precise point, the barb penetrated the frontal lobe from below—rather than from above, as in the Ziegler technique. Moved in a carefully delimited arc, it could sever the nerve tissue of the thalamofrontal tract on either side in a single stroke. The objective was identical with that of the Ziegler method. However, because of the easier approach, the severance could be made with little additional damage to the brain itself.

This, at least, was the claim advanced by the champions of transorbital lobotomy. Jim's intensive study, and a series of carefully staged post-mortem operations, had convinced him that existing literature on the subject had not exaggerated. Like all trained surgeons he would have preferred to work with full vision (the procedure, for all its safeguards, still seemed dangerously blind.) The fact remained that the approach carried with it far less danger of hemorrhage or other postoperative complications. Besides, he was hopeful that this type of lobotomy would be less likely to reduce a patient to robot level, an ever-present threat with the Ziegler method.

So far, he'd had no opportunity to test the method on a living patient. Ziggy was satisfied with his work as an assistant demonstrator of his own technique—but it would be sheer madness to suggest an alternate approach to the famous surgeon. Indeed, now that he had used up his research time on this final paper, Jim had begun to wonder (a trifle tardily) if his choice of a subject had been a happy one. And yet, much as he disliked Ziegler the man, he could not believe that Ziegler the doctor would reject his findings.

The voice of the librarian intruded on his musings. "Phone call for you, Dr. Corwin. Booth Two."

Hank Gaines's voice, reaching him across a half mile of corridors, was hurried but contained. "I'm calling from Neurosurgical Two. Better high-tail it over here."

"What's up?"

"Your boy's in convulsion."

"What boy?"

"Lavorsky—the patient you asked about day before yesterday. Step on the gas, will you?"

Ten minutes later, hurrying through his special ward, Jim turned to the door of the critical room—a cubicle at the end of the long double file of beds where patients from Rocky Point were convalescing from Ziegler's probe. A glance at the man on the hospital cot was proof enough that Hank had been wise to summon him. Lavorsky was in a state of almost constant convulsion, his body jerking so violently that two orderlies were barely able to keep him on the bed.

"Have you notified his relatives, Hank?"

"Seems he hasn't any. Few of them do at Rocky Point. Or if there is a next of kin, he's dumped his responsibility long ago."

Jim shook his head over that cynical dismissal and turned to examine the patient. Now that he had dignified the man with a name, he found it hard to believe that Ignaz Lavorsky was only another cipher in the roll call of abandoned hope. The long, melancholy profile (beaded though it was with sweat and twisted into a devil's mask of agony) had a certain worn distinction. For no valid reason he was reminded of a bust of the Emperor Augustus, a frontispiece in his high-school edition of *Ancient History*.

"He'll die if this keeps up," said Hank. "I called Ziggy—but he was hopping a train for Philadelphia."

"So we're holding the bag between us?"

Hank's eyebrows lifted. "You're the official goat, Jim. I only assisted at this operation—remember?"

"Am I to do whatever's indicated?"

"Those were the great man's orders."

"We'll have to open the wounds and examine the trephines."

"O.R. Six is ready."

"Let's go."

In this hour between shifts, Hank had been able to gather only a small crew. While he scrubbed, Jim told himself that it would probably suffice for a case of this kind, unless their explorations uncovered a real hemorrhage. In this case, if Lavorsky's life was to be saved, he would be forced to lay down a bone flap, exposing the whole frontal area of the brain. Catching Hank's eye as his friend scrubbed beside him, he knew young Dr. Gaines was reading his thoughts accurately enough.

"Still think the risk's worth taking, Jim?"

"Are you suggesting we let him go into a terminal state? He's near it now."

"The cases we lose always die in convulsion," said Hank. "Do a craniotomy and save him—you'll get yourself a medal from everyone but Ziggy, who'll wish he'd done the job himself. If the guy still checks out, it counts as an operative death on Ziggy's own record——"

"Just the same, I'm going in. So would you, Hank."

"I'm not so sure. After a season on this treadmill, I'm beginning to suspect I'm more mouse than man."

Will Eggers, the resident anesthetist, appeared in the scrub-room door a moment after the orderlies arrived with the wildly thrashing patient. "This one's a dilly, Jim," he said. "How do I get him under? To say nothing of keeping him under—without passing the danger point?"

The dilemma had troubled Jim: it was imperative that the patient be quieted before he began the delicate job of reopening the dura. When the answer came, it was simple enough.

"What about curare? Doesn't that break the connection—the synapses—where nerve impulses pass?"

Dr. Eggers brightened visibly. "That's quite an inspiration, my friend—to say nothing of a novel approach to brain surgery."

Five minutes later, when the attendants (after a prodigious effort) had placed the sick man on the operating table, Eggers forced the intravenous needle home and began a continuous drip of glucose solution, to which he had added an ampule of purified curare. Used, for the most part, to relax the abdominal wall in severe surgery, this strange drug—derived from the South American arrow poison—acted by breaking the connection between nerves and muscle. As Eggers had suggested, it was a novel specific and a dangerous one—since it might also stop the patient's breathing (this, of course, was the way it killed in the jungle). However, an anesthetist of his skill could avoid that risk by administering oxygen through a mask—and, if necessary, by applying artificial respiration.

"We'll let him ride awhile on the curare," he said. "So far, the breathing's bearing up—providing he doesn't thrash himself to death."

Since the dose was small and the rate of injection slow, it was a full ten minutes before the effect of the drug was apparent. Little by little, the convulsions slowed. Then, as the effect increased, they disappeared entirely. Lavorsky was now utterly relaxed, breathing quietly into the oxygen-filled bag of the anesthetic machine.

"Ready as he'll ever be, Jim," said the anesthetist.

Hank had already painted fresh antiseptic on the still-scarlet temples, and draped the area. Jim spread the skin clips and lifted them from the incisions. Scissors and thumb forceps made short work of the stitches that joined the fascia. Then, with a mastoid retractor, he gingerly exposed a burr hole. There was only a slight ooze of blood from cut tissues. In another moment he had scooped the bone dust from the trephine opening, washed it in saline solution, and dried it with the surgical suction machine.

Small scissors and forceps came into his hand. With these he severed the silk thread he had used to stitch the cross-shaped incision in the dura mater. His first view of the brain surface disclosed no unusual hemorrhage. The fluid oozing from the reopened dura was only slightly tinged—not grossly red as it would have been were this a genuine danger point.

"No trouble here, that's for certain," said Hank.

"We'll try the other."

An exploration of the second burr hole brought the same result. There was, of course, another possibility—a hemorrhage deep inside the brain, which would be revealed by a show of blood within the ventricle. Jim probed carefully in that area with a blunt needle. Here, as on the surface, the fluid was only faintly tinged. There was nothing to be gained by further exploration.

When the burr holes had been closed for the second time and the last dressing strapped in place, he voiced a thought that had been shaping in his mind. "Would it be too dangerous, Will—if we kept him on curare until morning? Giving those muscles a rest should help."

"It's feasible," said Eggers, "if he's watched constantly. He can still stop breathing at any moment."

Jim glanced around the circle of faces at the table. His crew had come to this emergency from other tasks—and would go off duty with the arrival of the night shift. Besides, it was a vigil he could hardly delegate.

"If you'll stand by while I phone my wife," he said, "I'll elect myself night watchman."

In the coin-box booth outside, he hesitated before dialing the familiar number, afraid that the phone would not be answered. To his surprise, he heard Taffy's voice on the first ring.

"Are you on your way, Abe?"

"No, dear. I'm still at the hospital."

"You said you'd be home at six. I've been waiting hours."

"Hank and I just did an emergency. I must stay with the patient until morning."

"I'm *lonesome*, Abe. No one has rung this phone all day."

"I'm sorry, Taffy—but I can't leave."

"Won't Hank stay with your patient?"

"It's my responsibility—with Ziegler out of town."

"Darling, you know I can't stand the dark. Please come home right away."

Picturing her all too clearly, he felt his throat contract in anger. When he spoke again, his voice was harsher than he intended. He might have been a father, scolding a willful child.

"Haven't you heard a thing I said?"

"You'd come if you loved me."

"I've a job to do here. I can't walk out on it."

"Darling," said Taffy, "I'm not the sort of girl who sits home alone."

"What's that supposed to mean?"

"Tom Willoughby's in town. If you won't be home tonight——"

"Taffy, can't you think of my side for once—instead of your own?"

"Tom's been after me to drive to Virginia Beach," she said. Her voice was curiously remote now, as though she were thinking aloud. "If you're going to be tied down, this might be the perfect time to go."

"Taffy, d'you realize what you're saying?"

"Why should I stay alone, if you can't look after me?"

"You'll be home when I return—or I'll know the reason why!" He knew he was shouting, and forced his voice to level off. "I mean it, Taffy."

"Tom's a fool," said his wife, "but he amuses me. You *know* I'd rather be with you. But if you must stay with a patient——"

He banged up the receiver in sudden fury, then sat irresolute in the booth, fighting the urge to call her back. What frightened him most was not the certainty that she had meant every word. It was the *sang-froid* she had displayed as she demolished his universe.

She had even refused to be angry, to speak above a lazy, slightly petulant whisper. . . . From Taffy's viewpoint (he saw this clearly now) she had done no wrong—and planned none—when she spoke of a weekend with Tom Willoughby. A bargain had been struck. She had merely enforced it.

vi

Lavorsky had been placed in a recovery room. All through the night Jim sat at his bedside, holding the oxygen mask to his face to make sure there was no hindrance to the steady intake and checking the intravenous needle as the curare solution continued to drip into his veins. By early morning, the improvement in his general condition was marked—enough to indicate a discontinuance of the injection. But Jim did not abandon his watchdog role until the arrival of the morning shift—including a yawning Hank Gaines. By this time, the patient was conscious—and apparently in touch with reality. In itself, this was proof of the experiment's success.

Reviewing the case with Hank over a breakfast tray in the cafeteria, Jim felt his spirits rise a little—despite the knowledge that he must leave this sanctuary in another moment and face the problem of Taffy squarely.

"So far as I can gather from my preliminary questioning," he said, "Lavorsky came out of it with his senses intact. I know it's incredible, but he's recovered his sanity overnight."

"To hear the Big I talk," said Hank, "it happens constantly."

"Another thing: you were wrong to dismiss Lavorsky as another rootless bum. Before he was taken ill, he taught math in Washington. He recalls his career perfectly."

"Since when was teaching math a career?"

"The man was on his way up. He'd been offered an instructorship at Columbia."

"Let's hope the job's still open, then," said Hank. "And that he can hold it. They don't come away from Ziggy's table with *all* their marbles, you know."

"This case might be different. It's even possible that the convulsions caused his recovery—as much as Ziegler's probe."

"Now you're really shooting the moon."

"Maybe not, Hank. Remember how we used to send patients into convulsion with insulin shock treatment—until we realized how near the danger point we were getting? Yesterday, before the orderly called you, Lavorsky was in the same state. No therapist would have dared go so far."

"What have you proved, then?"

"That my gamble with curare paid off—I hope." Jim forced himself to rise from the table. "I'll try to get back this afternoon for a second look—before we surrender him."

He climbed the walk-up stair slowly, the key already in his hand—and paused in astonishment when he heard his wife humming behind the half-open door. Evidently she had heard his step, for she thrust out a pert head before his fingers could close on the knob.

"I expected you much sooner, Abe."

He had surprised Taffy in one of her bursts of house cleaning. The tiny kitchen had been scrubbed until it shone. On the bookshelves her carnival dolls sat resplendent in new ribbons. Taffy herself was pursuing the last dust mote with a vacuum cleaner. Her hair was covered with a gypsy bandana, tied turban-fashion: save for ballet slippers it was her only costume. This was always her garb on the rare occasions when she turned domestic. Jim wondered what Alex Goldschmidt would make of the eccentricity.

His foot snared in the vacuum cord when he entered, ending her gesture at housekeeping with a burst of sparks at the baseboard. Instantly she was in his arms, kissing him with wholehearted abandon.

"Better late than never, darling," she said. "You're *always* worth waiting for."

"Didn't you go dancing after all?"

"Tom didn't make it. That's why I've been house cleaning since dawn. I couldn't sit still another moment."

So his reprieve had come purely by chance. He forced himself to go on, knowing she would never guess the pain she had caused him.

"What about this trip to Virginia Beach? Have you canceled it?"

"Of course not. It's still an open date."

"Tell me one thing, Taffy—and I'll ask no more questions. Is Willoughby already your lover?"

"*You're* my lover, Abe. You're all I ever wanted. Just promise you'll never leave me again and I'll send Tom packing. But I *can't* be alone in the night. I've told you why."

Jim turned aside to conceal his despair. Obviously she would take off with Willoughby the next time he was detained at the hospital: this had been no idle threat. Taffy (the eager maiden) had been content, to a point, with her books and her symphonies, with dancing dates and embraces in parked cars. The girl of today (who had learned what heady raptures sex could bring) was a different problem—one that was beyond his reach. Only Alex could solve this impasse, if it could be solved at all.

"Will you do me just one favor, dear?" he asked.

"Don't I—always?"

"This time I mean something different. Go to Scripps for a course of treatment."

"To *Scripps*, Abe?"

"To Dr. Goldschmidt. Believe me, you need help desperately."

The smile had melted from her face, to be replaced by the look he knew too well—the hate mask which only the frightened eyes redeemed. "You can't make me over. No one can."

"I don't want to change you, Taffy. I only want you to be happy. Eventually, you'll *have* to admit most human beings are often left alone—"

She pressed against him warmly. "I'm not alone now."

"You will be tomorrow. And the day after. That's inevitable, now you're a doctor's wife. Letting these after-dark phantoms frighten you isn't fair to either of us. Alex will help you to send them packing."

Her face was still buried in his shoulder. "All right, Abe. I'll visit your witch doctor—just to please you."

He felt his whole being relax in the ease of his victory. It scarcely mattered that he had surprised Taffy in what Alex would have called a mood of compliance.

"Just wait and see, dear," he said. "Today's the beginning of a new life for us both."

"The *old* life still suits me, Abe. I love it."

vii

Alex was at Rocky Point when Jim stopped at his office the next morning. He set up an appointment for Taffy on Monday afternoon, then hurried to his own wing of the hospital to make his final rounds before the start of the weekend. He could still not believe that forty-eight hours of continuous liberty awaited him: it would be the first extended leave he had enjoyed since his honeymoon.

He had already promised to take Taffy to the motel where they had passed their wedding night. Now that she had promised to visit Alex, it seemed an appropriate reward. A successful analysis, he felt sure, would set her feet on the path that led to maturity; in that quiet setting beside the Chesapeake, he could convince her that she must give Alex every chance to help her. . . . Opening the door of the recovery room where Lavorsky was still resting, he knew that his mind, for the first time in weeks, was free of doubting.

The patient was clearly out of danger. Yesterday, after a brief conference with Ziegler, Jim had received the great man's approval of his emergency measures. Today, face to face with the mathematics teacher (who, three days ago, had been only a snarling animal) he savored the quiet pride that only the healer knows.

"I'm glad you stopped by, Dr. Corwin." Lavorsky spoke with a tired smile, but his somber eyes were glowing. "Yesterday, there was no opportunity to thank you properly."

"Thank the curare solution, not me."

"It's true, then, that I owe my life to a deadly poison? You must have needed courage to administer it."

"Dr. Eggers gave the injection."

"But they tell me it was you who thought of it. As you see, it has brought me out of hell—quite literally."

"Are you glad you've come back?" The question was indiscreet, but Jim had asked it deliberately. When Lavorsky's lips twitched into a chuckle, he saw that the man had grasped his intent.

"Dr. Corwin, are you under the illusion that the realm of the insane is a pleasant place?"

"Some have found it so, I'm told. Some even hide there deliberately—to avoid things they can't face."

"That was untrue in my case," said Lavorsky. "I won't call myself a happy man: I was far too lonely for that. But my work sustained me—I've always had a natural talent for mathematics. It compensated for the fact that I myself was unloved."

"Will you return to teaching?"

Lavorsky shook his head. "This morning I tried to solve a problem in elementary calculus. I might have been working in Sanskrit."

Jim covered his dismay. "Did the discovery upset you?"

"Strangely enough, no. I suppose it's one effect of the operation. When I'm fully recovered, I may find I possess but half a brain. I'd still prefer that—to a whole one that's useless."

"Your resignation does you credit."

"I'm told that resignation is also a by-product of lobotomy," said the patient. "Believe me, Dr. Corwin, I'm content with my lot. Insanity is a living death for a man of intelligence: I'm vain enough to call myself that, before I was stricken. This way, at least, I can continue to be useful to society—and therefore to myself."

"What are your plans?"

"So far they aren't definite. I can tell you this. Regardless of my present powers—or their lack—I would never have returned to teaching. Most employers distrust anyone who's been in a mental hospital. And I'm not excluding our educators."

"Can you survive that, too?"

"Why not? If I've lost my skill at math, I've also lost my capacity to worry."

"It must be a strange feeling."

"And a comforting one," said Lavorsky. "Especially if you've been where I have been."

"Can I help you in any way?"

"No, Doctor. If I wish it, a job is already waiting at Rocky Point—as a hospital attendant. At the edge of hell, it's true, but safe on the brink."

Jim shook his head in wonder. He had come into the recovery room, exulting in the life he had snatched back from darkness. Now, viewing the finished product of Anton Ziegler's scalpel, he could only stare in blank disbelief.

"Perhaps you've made a wise choice at that," he said. "It's a world I know only at second hand."

"But a large world, Dr. Corwin. In America alone, it now has nearly a million inhabitants—and it is growing steadily. Ours is not an era that encourages sanity."

Two orderlies, appearing in the doorway, paused when they found a doctor in conversation with a patient. Jim knew their errand. It was time to move Lavorsky to Rocky Point for his convalescence.

"Good-by, Doctor. And thank you again for saving my life."

"Good-by, Mr. Lavorsky—and good luck."

"My luck is already good. You saw to that."

Thanks to Jim's weekend leave, his tour of duty in the wards was soon ended. On the stroke of twelve he was in the locker room changing to street clothes. The loud-speaker in the corridor began its brazen clangor when he was in the act of reaching for his hat. Long before he could pick up the words, he realized this was no routine summons—but the voice of the director himself, issuing a general call to quarters.

"Attention all members of the staff! A wing of the Downtown Hospital is afire. It is believed that several hundred patients are trapped. Effective immediately, Lakewood is on Disaster Alert."

He turned to the coin-box phone with a sigh of pure frustration. Disaster Alert was a mobilization plan set up for only the worst emergencies. Until it was lifted, no staff member could leave the grounds. At best, it meant that he and Taffy must postpone their departure until late evening.

Dialing his number at home, he was cold with fear—the certainty that this contretemps was somehow foreordained. Taffy's warm chuckle of welcome, when she heard his voice on the wire, sent his spirits plummeting. He forced himself to state the facts as calmly as he could.

"*Abe!* You're making this up to tease me."

"Turn on the radio—you'll get the details."

"You're off duty at noon. Can't you just leave?"

"You know better than that, dear. They'd call me back, even if we were at the Chesapeake."

"But it isn't fair. I want you *now.*" He knew that she was already sobbing, and sought for words to comfort her—but her voice went on rapidly before he could speak. "Remember that dream I had—about the cage? If I could be with you tonight, in that same motel room, we might drive it away for keeps."

"We'll go tomorrow. Won't that do?"

There was a pause—and there were no tears in her voice when she spoke again. "Abe, I'm not the kind of girl who waits for tomorrow. And I won't share you. It's got to be everything or nothing——"

He heard the click of the receiver. As he had expected, there was only a busy signal when he rang back. Either she had lifted the phone from the hook or was making another call. There was no time to try again. A glance through the phone-booth door told him the corridor was filling with the white-clad figures of the hospital staff enroute to their stations. From a distance he could hear Hank Gaines calling his name.

When Jim stepped into the corridor he was swept into the vast assembly line that had already changed the normal tempo of Lakewood to the complex rhythm of Disaster Alert. On the way to join his surgical team he saw the first ambulance roar in at Emergency. From that moment, cases arrived in a steady stream, to funnel smoothly to each operating theater.

Even to a war veteran who had operated under fire, the hours that followed were a blur of terror and backbreaking toil. Case after case crossed the table where Jim worked—all of them burns, since this was one of the main *débridement* teams. Today there was little time for such niceties as the excision of hopelessly damaged tissue, the clearing away of dirt fragments and burnt clothing, the elaborate light cradles that were used in cases of shock. In most instances, all he could do was apply a pressure bandage and cut down to cannulate veins collapsed too completely for the plasma needle. . . . Concentrating on the task of the moment, he found that his own racking problems had slipped from his mind. As usual, it was a jolt to straighten at last, step back from the table, and realize that the backlog of stretcher cases outside the operating room had been cleared.

"Is it over, Hank?" he asked dazedly.

Young Dr. Gaines, his forehead beaded with sweat, shook his head. "No such luck, I'm afraid. But the worst is behind us."

Jim's eye sought the wall clock. Incredulously, he noted that it was long past midnight: at least that discovery explained his throbbing weariness. He was reeling a little when he stepped out of the hard white cone of the operating lights in response to a scrub nurse's signal.

"Your wife's on the phone, Dr. Corwin. She's called several times. If you can spare a moment——"

"I think I can," he said, with a glance at the line of empty litters. "Be with you directly, Hank."

Taffy's voice, when it reached him, was both gay and strident. He realized that she was quite drunk—and guessed why before he grasped the import of her first incoherent words.

"Mos' done, Abe? I got a party goin'—just for you."

There were voices behind her, and the throb of a dance tune on the hi-fi. The sounds of revelry, in his present mood, angered him even more than the certainty that Tom Willoughby was among the guests.

"Sorry, Taffy," he said. "I'll be lucky if I get home by dawn."

"'S all right. We'll keep things roarin'."

"Why did you call?"

"T' say I love you."

"Prove it. Send your guests home and try to get some sleep."

"I can always *sleep,* Abe."

A nurse was tapping on the phone-booth door; he saw that a new case had just emerged from the shock room. "I'll join you when I can," he said, fighting hard to keep his voice casual. "Try to slow down, won't you?"

"Never goin' t' slow down again. Never goin' t' sleep alone, either. Jus' remember *that,* Abe——"

"For God's sake, Taffy!"

"Get home, darlin'. Get home quick—you *hear?*"

Again, he heard the click of a broken connection. This time he was sure her challenge had ended in a sob.

viii

The alert was lifted just before dawn. Once again Jim changed his clothes hurriedly in the locker room—and tried in vain to keep his hands from trembling. Hank Gaines, still in a work-stained operating suit, looked in at the door as Jim was donning his coat—and, seeing that they were alone, came forward to put a hand on his shoulder.

"Don't take it too hard, fellow."

Jim turned on him savagely: it was a relief to let his tension explode into speech. "Can't you mind your own damn business?"

"This is my business, Jim. I'm talking about Ziggy."

"Sorry, Hank. I didn't mean to bellow—"

"I won't pretend I wish you'd won. I need the damned residency too much."

Jim turned to face the other doctor. Hank's tired smile, the regret in his voice, seemed to reach him through an invisible wall. Even now he had only half grasped his friend's meaning.

"The *residency*, you said?"

"Didn't they tell you?"

"So far, I've been told nothing."

"Ziggy himself gave me the news just before the alert. Maybe they couldn't find you afterwards. It'll be official tomorrow."

Jim took the blow in silence, accepting Hank's handclasp along with Hank's concern. This latest buffet of fate had left him untouched. All that mattered now was his need to track down Taffy and Willoughby.

"Easy does it, fellow," said Hank. "You could never have worked for Ziegler."

"Is that a quotation from the source?"

"Now you mention it," said Hank gently, "he *was* muttering in his beard about that paper on transorbital lobotomy. Apparently you couldn't have chosen a worse subject. I wondered why you picked it."

Why indeed? Letting his mind turn dully to his career (or what had passed for a career only yesterday), Jim had no valid answer. He forced himself to meet Hank's worried eyes.

"Congratulations—the best man won."

"The best bootlicker, maybe."

"Don't feel sorry for me. I'll get along."

Hank hesitated, then spoke with an embarrassed shrug. "I know about you and Taffy too. If I can help—"

"I started that job on my own, Hank. I'll finish it."

Jim got into his car without looking back and slammed out of the parking lot. Conscious for the first time that rain was falling steadily, he forced himself to slow to a normal speed. For an instant he considered driving to the apartment building where young Willoughby lodged in bachelor splendor. Instead, he turned into his own street and climbed the walk-up stairs.

Not that he expected to find his wife's saturnalia going in the dawn, but he wanted the record straight. Besides, he had a final errand before he sought them out.

He was almost calm when he crossed the empty, smoke-haunted room to his chest of drawers and lifted the gun from its hiding place. From the moment he had stepped into the rain he had felt his resolve harden. He was ready to take over now, to give orders and demand obedience, whatever the cost. . . . *Alex would never know me tonight,* he thought—and snapped home a fresh cartridge clip as he continued to study the lethal weapon nested in his palm.

It was a Japanese automatic, one of the few souvenirs he had brought back from Asia—and he was adept in its use. Not that he intended to use it now—unless his hand was forced.

With the gun in his raincoat pocket he crossed to an open window and closed it against the storm. It was quite like Taffy, he thought, to go rushing into the night and leave her home open to the elements. . . . Not that this was really Taffy's home. She had yet to learn the meaning of the word.

Was it her fault entirely that this room might have belonged to any unattached female? Had he been a better husband, had he spent more time on tenderness and less on passion, could he have changed the girl to a woman, the woman to a wife? His fist closed on one of the carnival dolls. Watching the china skull explode as he flung it against the far wall, he moved toward the door.

The phone stabbed at his ears when he was halfway down the stairs, bringing him back in a rush.

"Dr. James Corwin?"

"Speaking."

"This is State Trooper Carey, Doctor. Your wife's had an accident."

The voice wiped out the red haze of hate instantly.

"Where are you, Officer?"

"Baltimore Parkway. She was southbound—in a car driven by a man named Thomas Willoughby. They jumped a guardrail, doing eighty."

"Go on, please." He knew what the next words would be. After all, he had spoken them often enough as an ambulance intern.

"She lived long enough to send you a message, Doctor. I've written it down."

There was a short pause on the wire. Jim could picture the scene in detail: the emergency phone beside the great trunk-line highway, the flare-lit pavement (clotted with police cars and ambulances), Willoughby's brick-red Triumph, collapsed like a toy crunched underfoot. . . . When the trooper spoke again his voice dropped into a solemn tone.

"She said, '*Ask Jim to forgive me. I couldn't help it. I never could—*'"

"Was Willoughby hurt?"

"He was dead when we got to them. We're taking the bodies to the Hyattesville morgue. Can you join us there, and make an identification?"

"Yes. I'll come."

"Know your way? It's still Maryland—just over the D.C. line."

"I know the way, Officer."

After he had replaced the receiver, Jim weighed the gun in his hand and considered raising it to his head. Then he put the urge aside and walked heavily downstairs to his car.

The Creole Belle

*T*HE *FREIGHTER* had almost cleared the levee. In another moment, New Orleans would begin dropping astern in the gathering dusk. Dr. James Corwin (his eyes still heavy from a restless nap) had just emerged from his cabin to witness the familiar maneuver. About to take a turn of the deck before the usual sundowner in the charthouse, he paused rigidly in his tracks. A dozen feet away, in the shadow of a lifeboat davit, Taffy was standing with her eyes on the receding shore line, her figure in sharp relief against the red glow of sunset.

In the past six months he had seen her often—in smoky barrooms, in the hotel lobbies where he had sought companionship whenever the *Creole Belle* had docked to take on cargo. This was the first time she had appeared on shipboard. Caught up in a familiar panic, he wondered if his mind was giving way at last. Then the girl bent forward to look down at the levee. He saw her face clearly (as he had seen all the others) and knew it was only the graceful figure and the shoulder-length blond hair that had created the illusion. This was just another pretty girl—a rarity, to be sure, aboard this rust-chip tramp, for the *Creole Belle* carried few passengers—and there was no reason for the sudden angry thudding of his heart.

"Lynn! Are you there?"

The voice came from the levee—or, to be precise, from the pier that had been the freighter's berth on her two-day stopover at New Orleans. Moving to the ship's rail, careful to keep the davit between them, Jim saw why the girl had turned—and why she moved even deeper into the shadow of the lifeboat.

Already the young man had reached the end of the pier, his hands cupped to shout again. In that light it was impossible to make out his features—but Jim was conscious of a crew cut, fullback's shoulders, an electric vitality that seemed to crackle against the freighter's side.

"Answer me, Lynn!"

The *Creole Belle,* completing her slow turn, had pointed her bow downstream. The engine room, picking up its signal for half speed ahead, began to hum on a deeper note as the vessel swung into the full thrust of the Mississippi. Still in her hiding place, the girl ignored the final shout. Only when the levee and the figure standing there had vanished in the dusk did she move into the light of a companionway and through a cabin door amidships.

Feature for feature, Jim thought, she could hardly be more unlike Taffy: only the tormented eyes were similar. But he was sure of this much. The girl the young man had called Lynn was fighting an inner demon just as Taffy had fought—as he himself had struggled so desperately these past six months. Now, feeling the beat of his pulses recede, he knew the worst of his own heartache was behind him. That six-month hiatus (spent mostly at sea) had accomplished its purpose. Perhaps he would never be heart-whole again—but he was ready to face tomorrow.

ii

Jim had signed on as a ship's surgeon, in the New York offices of the Kingsmith Line, on the advice of Alex Goldschmidt. The psychiatrist had been a wise counselor in the first black days after Taffy's death. Tonight—lingering at the rail to watch the sunset on the river—he could remember his friend's summation word for word:

"You won't believe me now, Jim. But you'll come out of this business stronger than before."

"How can I—when I let her die?"

"That's nonsense. You'd done all you could to save Taffy from herself."

"I hadn't even started."

"You loved her, Jim. *That* was a start. I'm going to be brutal—and tell you it should have been enough."

"You're wrong there, Alex. Taffy needed the sort of help I couldn't give. She'd promised to visit you on Monday——"

"Call it bad luck that I was away. Certainly it wasn't your fault you were on Disaster Alert that night."

"I was a doctor. I knew she needed psychiatric guidance. But I pretended her mental blocks weren't serious. I delayed taking her to you——"

"You're hurting yourself needlessly, Jim. Taffy's urge to prove her independence—even in another man's arms—was the controlling fact of her existence. In the end, it was stronger than her love for you. Doesn't that show you couldn't have helped her?"

"Alex, when I found they were headed for Virginia Beach, I was ready to follow—with a gun in my hand. I might even have killed them both."

"It was a natural anger. Most married couples wish death for their opposite numbers on occasion. Some even put the wish into action. I hardly think you'd have pulled the trigger, Jim."

"That's something we'll never know."

"You loved Taffy—and you did your best for her. But you aren't the kind of man who goes melancholy mad because he's loved and lost. Once you've pulled yourself together you'll start building on the ruins of this marriage. Meanwhile, I'd prescribe sea air—and a long, hard look at the future."

"I'm not too sure I *have* a future, Alex——"

"You mean because you lost the residency? That's the worst nonsense of all. You're a Lakewood graduate and a skilled surgeon with plenty of career ahead. All you need is perspective. My old man's a director of the Kingsmith Line. He'll open doors if you'll agree to go to sea as a doctor."

Hearing a step on the afterdeck, Jim turned away from the rail. Ted Malone, the radio operator who doubled as purser and passenger agent, had just emerged from his shack, an eyebrow cocked at its usual sardonic angle.

"Take a good look at New Orleans, Doc. It'll be a coon's age before we tie up here again."

Genial, intelligent (and cynical only on surface) Sparks Malone had made Jim welcome aboard from the start. He suspected this was because the radio operator had been an enlisted surgical technician in the war—and spoke his language. But he had been glad of that easy camaraderie at sea—and even more, in the stopovers at Deep South ports that had preceded the present leg of their voyage (the *Creole Belle*, after calls at Savannah, Pensacola and Mobile, was outbound for a leisurely circling of the globe via Central America and the Canal).

"See the new passenger, Ted?"

"You bet I did. I also heard her boy friend's mating call from the pier. Looks like she's got him neatly hooked—if she wants him."

"Where's she booked for?"

"Veracruz."

"This isn't the season for Mexico."

"Maybe she hopes he'll follow her if she doesn't run too far. It's happened before."

Jim let the observation pass without comment. "What's her name?"

"Lynn Thorndyke. Student from Glenville—a university town not too far north of here. She came aboard at the last moment and paid cash for her passage. Didn't say much about herself. Cute as they come, Doc—but a bit young for you or me."

"I guess you're right, Ted." Jim had made no mention of his wife's death—preferring the give-and-take of shipboard living to clumsy expressions of sympathy, however sincere. Freighter passengers were rarely young or beautiful—so the question of sea-borne romance had not yet been raised. "Shall we have a sundowner with the off-watch?"

The dinner gong sounded while they were drinking a tot of rum and water in the charthouse. The *Creole Belle* carried less than a dozen passengers—half of whom sat at the captain's table, while Jim and the mate did the honors at the other. Most of them were elderly folk enjoying an inexpensive jaunt around the world on retirement incomes. Even when the weight of his hidden grief had been most painful, he had found conversation with them easy enough.

Tonight, when the meal was over, he smoked a pipe in the lounge, then took a stroll on the deserted deck. The freighter, plowing between the channel markers on her way to the tidal reaches of the Mississippi, seemed suspended between earth and sky, to ride the glass-smooth current with no help from her propellers. Passing the door of Miss Thorndyke's cabin, he recalled that she had not appeared in the dining saloon. Perhaps the last-minute appearance of the boy on the levee accounted for her retirement. Had Sparks Malone put his finger on her evident malaise—a lovers' quarrel ending in flight, for which she was already sorry?

The door to the radio shack was propped open. On Jim's second turn aft Malone beckoned him inside.

"The Thorndyke girl just got a message," he said. "Even money says it's from the fellow who missed the boat."

"Isn't this a bit unethical, Ted?"

"Extremely—but I have my reasons. I took it to her cabin just now. Nothing unusual in the radiogram, you understand—he loves her, wants her back. But that girl bothers me, now I've had a real look at her. If you ask me, Doc, she's sick."

Jim looked at Malone sharply. It was not the first time he had respected the accuracy of the ex-technician's instinct.

"Did she complain?"

"She hardly spoke. Just thanked me for bringing the message. Then looked at it, like she didn't even want to slit the envelope. It was that look upset me. Afraid and dead, all at once—like an animal in a trap. I saw it in the trenches, and so did you."

Jim nodded soberly. He was remembering his own reaction, after his brief glimpse of Lynn Thorndyke—the way she had stood frozen in the shadow of the lifeboat, refusing to respond to the shout from the levee.

"If she needs help, why hasn't she sent for me?"

"They don't always send. Not when they're really bad."

"I'll stop by her cabin now."

Jim walked slowly forward, pausing at the rail to knock out his pipe, hoping that Sparks had guessed wrong for once. There was no light in Lynn Thorndyke's cabin—and he had a curious notion that it was untenanted. The feeling deepened after three knocks (each one louder than the last) failed to bring a response. There was a faint call inside when he rattled the knob and found the door was locked. After a longish pause, he heard the key turn and found himself facing the passenger, who had already moved forward to block the cautiously opened portal.

"I'm the ship's doctor, Miss Thorndyke. Are you all right?"

"Why shouldn't I be?"

She was wearing a cloth robe over her nightgown. Her face seemed ashen-pale in the faint light from the companionway—and her hair, in wild disarray, all but obscured her eyes. Even so, there was no missing the glow of defiance that filled them.

"You weren't at dinner," he said. "I only thought——"

"I'm all right."

"Sure you aren't ill? Convalescing, perhaps?"

"Quite sure. Thank you for asking." He saw a spasm of pain cross her face; her hand tightened convulsively on the knob, closing the door abruptly. He raised his hand to knock again, then let it drop at his side. This seemed more than an aftermath of a lovers' quarrel. As Sparks had said, the girl appeared to be badly in need of his services. Yet there was no way he could force an entrance if she refused to ask his help. Perhaps he had only witnessed another of the absurd self-dramatizations of youth.

He paced the deck before turning in, as was his custom. More than once he paused to listen at Miss Thorndyke's door, but no sound came from inside. When finally he settled in his own bunk, he found he could drop off instantly for the first time in weeks. Once again his slumber was profound, untroubled by Taffy's ghost.

iii

Jim slept late, as was his privilege when there was no sickness aboard. When he came on deck the *Creole Belle* had dropped the vast silt apron of the Mississippi delta astern and was plowing through a clean blue sea, on course for Tampico and Veracruz.

Miss Thorndyke, he learned, had not appeared for breakfast. The stewardess (a buxom Norwegian named Hedda Alving) reported that she had ignored her mid-morning knock, then refused to unlock her door.

"Did she sound ill, Hedda?"

"Her voice was weak, Doctor, now you mention it. Maybe she's only seasick."

"We'd best have a look, just the same."

With the stewardess in tow and a skeleton key from the purser's office in his pocket, Jim tapped discreetly on the panel of Miss Thorndyke's door. Hearing no response from within, he turned the key softly and stepped inside. The cabin was dark and unbearably hot—the porthole closed, its curtains drawn. The passenger lay on the bunk, apparently unaware of his presence. Even in the gloom he could tell at a glance that she was suffering acutely. When Mrs. Alving touched the light switch at his signal he saw that her face was marble pale, the lips devoid of color.

"What's wrong, Miss Thorndyke?"

The wide-open eyes continued to regard the ceiling without a flicker of the lids. He was about to repeat the question when the lips moved slowly.

"Leave me alone."

"You're obviously quite ill."

"I'll be all right," said the girl in the same dead whisper.

"We can't let you die without attention!" He had made his voice deliberately harsh, hoping to shock her from her apathy.

"No one can help me, Doctor. No one at all."

"Mrs. Alving and I can certainly try. Whether you agree or not, it's my duty to examine you."

The girl made no protest while he gave the stewardess his instructions. Nor did she stir when he returned with his medical bag and began his examination. Blood pressure, as he had anticipated, was dangerously low: the pallor of the lips and mouth membranes completed the picture of internal hemorrhage. By the time he had examined the abdominal muscles—and found them tense and diffusely tender—his diagnosis was complete.

"Your condition is critical, Miss Thorndyke," he said. "We must operate at once."

The eyes were still unwinking. When he repeated his statement they continued to look through him unawares.

"Do we have your permission?"

There was still no answer. As he repacked his medical kit he noticed the torn envelope on the cabinet, with the crumpled radiogram beside it.

BON VOYAGE DONT WORRY ABOUT MARY LOU
COME BACK SOON ALL MY LOVE
JAY

A quarrel and a flight—with the lady named Mary Lou as the bone of contention? It seemed a reasonable guess—but it had no importance now, and certainly no bearing on the present emergency.

"Miss Thorndyke," he said quietly, "I'm taking your silence as permission. The captain can authorize me to do whatever is necessary."

He had feared she would object, but the words drew no reply. Taking a syrette of morphine and atropine from his bag, he made the injection with Mrs. Alving's help. Still watching the girl carefully for some reaction, he massaged the opiate into the tissues with a gentle thumb.

"Stay with her, Hedda. I'll find the skipper."

Captain Evans, the ancient Welshman who was master of

the *Creole Belle,* had turned over his bridge to the mate. Jim found him in the radio shack, watching Malone and his junior assistant break down the last unit of the receiving set. The sender was already demolished, a mass of vacuum tubes and condensers spread in careful order on the operator's bunk. The skipper was observing the work with gloomy attention. Jim remembered (a bit tardily) that Captain Evans had given Malone permission for this breakdown and re-assembly if the morning weather report was fine.

"How soon can you send a message, Ted?"

"Three or four hours, with luck. What's up, Doc?"

Evans swore adequately when Jim had conveyed his news. "This was a portside job, Malone. *If* you'd kept off the beach and stayed sober." He turned to Jim. "Can you wait three hours, Doctor?"

"Not a chance, sir. It would be touchy enough, even if we radioed ashore for a helicopter."

"What ails the girl?"

"She's bleeding to death internally. From a ruptured ovarian follicle."

"Say that in everyday words, man. I'm not up on your lingo."

"Normally, one female germ cell breaks free of the ovary each month and is discharged into the uterus, leaving no damage behind. Sometimes the ovarian pocket continues to bleed. In this case the bleeding is copious. I've no choice but to stop it surgically."

"Is the operation dangerous?"

"Not in itself," said Jim. "It's the blood loss that's our concern. She'll die unless it's controlled promptly."

"Operate then, by all means," said the captain. "Thank God the sea is calm. Do we have the equipment?"

"We can manage, according to my inventory. Ted can give the anesthesia, unless he's forgotten what he learned in the Army."

"I can still drop ether, Doc," said the radioman.

"Ether's all we've time for, I'm afraid. The girl's already under sedation. The stewardess can assist—I hope."

"Is that wise, Doc?" asked Evans. "Using unskilled help in abdominal surgery?"

"Is there a physician on the passenger list?"

"Not this time."

"Then we must make do—or let the girl die."

Evans was already moving toward the door. "I'll order half speed ahead," he announced. "We'll roll less that way. Make it fast, Doc, before the weather changes."

"I've done this job in half an hour," said Jim. He did not add that he was laying himself open to trouble if anything went wrong in that half hour—though he was still within his rights, in this case, to operate without a signed permission. Lynn Thorndyke was twenty-two (he knew that much from the file card in the purser's office). Her next of kin, according to that same card, was her mother, a Mrs. Florence Thorndyke—evidently a widow or a divorcee, with no address given. The girl's occupation was set down as "student," with no address but the state university at Glenville. . . . Since they were at sea with a dead wireless, he was proceeding under a doctor's traditional rights—but the consequences of failure could still be dire.

The surgery of the *Creole Belle* had an adequate operating table: as Captain Evans had predicted, the ship rode steadily at half speed ahead. While curious passengers were herded forward, two seamen brought Lynn Thorndyke through the door. Thanks to the injection of morphia, the girl was now in deep sedation: Ted Malone poured his ether with a steady hand, while Jim painted the operative area and draped it with sterile towels from the small autoclave. When he was scrubbed and gloved he gave Mrs. Alving an appraising glance before calling her to the table. The stewardess had pulled on her own gloves with steady hands: she did not flinch as she arranged the towels under his direction.

"I'm making an incision in the lower mid-line," he said. "Keep her well under, Ted—but remember she's very weak."

The operation itself was fairly simple, and the approach he had chosen was free from any large source of bleeding. The scalpel moved swiftly to slit the abdominal wall and the peritoneum for a distance of several inches. The instant gush of blood, clotted and fluid as it was, was the final proof of his diagnosis.

Slipping a pair of retractors under the edge of the abdominal wall, Jim showed Mrs. Alving how to manage the instruments —holding them so they would tent both fascia and peritoneum slightly, and keep the blood from spilling out. Absorbed directly (once he had stopped the bleeding at its source) that blood would help the patient to regain hemoglobin. At Lakewood, of course, he would have drained the abdominal cavity by suction, mixed the whole blood with a citrate solution to prevent clotting, strained it through sterile gauze and reinjected it directly into a vein. Such an autotransfusion (an indicated procedure under ideal conditions) was clearly impossible here.

Reaching into the cavity with a gloved hand, Jim lifted the right ovary into the incision and searched its surface carefully for the telltale laceration that would spell out a ruptured follicle, the small global bed in which the germ cell grew to maturity. Convinced that the organ was whole, he restored it to place and brought the left ovary into view. A sigh of relief escaped him when he located the bleeding follicle bed: with the scalpel he removed a tiny wedge of ovarian tissue that included it.

In another moment, slender catgut sutures had joined the cut surface snugly. For extra safety, Jim waited three minutes by the wall clock to make sure the bleeding had ceased. Then, with the left ovary returned to the abdominal cavity, he sutured the peritoneum with a running strand of catgut and closed the initial wound with equally meticulous stitches. A final glance at the clock, after he had strapped on a gauze dressing, told him that Lynn Thorndyke had been under the anesthesia less than forty minutes.

From the first he had worked, quite literally, with one eye on the incision and the other on Malone and his ether can—but the radio operator had done a competent job. Not once had the patient's breathing shown the depression that would have indicated too great a depth of anesthesia. Now—Jim was happy to note—her blood pressure had actually risen a few points.

"A routine procedure, thanks to you both," he said gratefully. "She can go back to her cabin now; I'll stay with her until she comes out."

After he had injected a heavy dose of penicillin (a routine insurance to cover any possible infection that might have resulted from skimpy equipment and unskilled help) Jim stripped off his gloves. Once again he had fulfilled the first medical law, spelled out in textbook Latin as "Do no harm." By acting promptly he had saved the girl's life—yet somehow he doubted that she would thank him tomorrow.

iv

Jim's optimism, so far as his corrective surgery was concerned, bore instant fruit. Lynn Thorndyke was conscious by midafternoon, but he kept her drowsily relaxed under opiates until nightfall. Then (though he was obliged to resort to forced feeding) she was able to take a nutritious broth. Next morning he propped her in her bunk, as comfortably as though it were a hospital cot, and resumed the nutrition. Over the next twenty-four hours he remained with her constantly—save for a few hours of sleep when Mrs. Alving relieved him.

If his patient's physical recovery was rapid, her spirit seemed unwilling to return to anything resembling normalcy. As the hours passed he could see no lightening of her somber mood.

"You'll be out of bed by tomorrow, young lady," he told her the second morning after the operation. "That means two full days in a deck chair before Veracruz. Do you have friends in Mexico?"

"No one, Doctor."

"May I ask why you're going to Veracruz?"

"I didn't intend to get there."

The bald statement confirmed his worst suspicions. Her withdrawal to her cabin, her failure to seek medical care for a near-fatal illness had been deliberate acts of suicide. "You don't mean that, Lynn," he said, using her Christian name as though she were still a child. "I won't let you mean it."

"Why didn't you let me die?" Her voice had risen at last—and it was a child's wail, thin and piercing and forlorn.

"You're too young for that sort of surrender," he said. "Your life is just beginning."

So had Taffy's life been just beginning, he thought. . . . He had lost Taffy because he had found no way to keep pace with her hunger for experience. Lynn Thorndyke had chosen another road to self-destruction, but the goals had been identical—until he'd intervened. Here, at least, his help had come in time.

"We know you ran away from the campus at Glenville," he said. Their first radiogram (sent out after Malone had reassembled his transmitter) had brought that much information from the dean of women at the university. At the same time, they had learned that Mrs. Florence Thorndyke was Lynn's only living relation. At the moment, it seemed, she was traveling abroad and had neglected to leave a forwarding address.

"Tell me, Lynn," he pursued gently. "Is Mrs. Thorndyke your mother?"

"You might call her that," the girl said sullenly.

"How can we reach her?"

"There's no way to reach her. She never writes me."

"Who is Jay?"

"A senior—at the university."

"Is he in love with you?"

She turned her face to the wall. "I've told you enough now."

"You're *sure* there's no way to reach Mrs. Thorndyke?"

"When she puts me in college, she always goes abroad. I don't know where she is and I don't care."

"Do you realize this makes Captain Evans responsible for your immediate future?"

"I can manage my own affairs."

"The stewardess found less than twenty dollars in your baggage. It's obvious you're not really able to take care of yourself. So we'll have to help you."

"How?"

"You're emotionally disturbed, Lynn. You need medical help I'm not qualified to give. Let me send you to a friend of mine in Baltimore—one of the best psychiatrists in America. He helped *me* once. I'm sure he can help you."

"Suppose I don't want help?" But there was a subtle change in her voice, a faltering that raised his hopes. Of one thing he was positive: Lynn Thorndyke was aware of the nature of this illness and the direction it was leading her. It might mean that some deep inner urge wanted to shake off the incubus.

"Look at me, Lynn. You owe me this much—for saving your life."

"I didn't want you to save it," she insisted stubbornly.

He took her hand and pressed it gently. "Take my word—you've no right to make that decision. No one does."

"It's *my* life, isn't it?"

"Yes, it's your life," he said, with the image of Taffy still bright before him. "But I'm a doctor—and I can't let you lose it."

Her eyelids fluttered wearily, and she did not speak for a long time. Had it not been for the steady pressure of her fingers againt his own, he might have thought she slept.

"I'll go to Baltimore, Dr. Corwin," she said at last, "if it's what you want."

"It's what I want for you."

"All right, then. *Now* will you leave me alone?"

"I'll radio at once," he told her. "You can fly up from Veracruz."

Alex had sent a prompt reply. Lynn Thorndyke would be admitted on his service at Scripps until contact could be made with her mother. Air space was waiting at Veracruz: Jim had wired ahead for tickets—paying for them out of his own pocket, though it had taken nearly all his slender funds. It had already been decided that Mrs. Alving would accompany Lynn to Baltimore, then fly back in time to catch the ship at Panama.

At the quay in Veracruz, Lynn was well enough to walk to the waiting ambulance. Now and again she glanced through the window at the blur of adobe walls as they circled the Old

Town and bore down on the airport—but she seemed only partially aware of what she saw, as though this fleeting glimpse of Mexico was a blinding white nightmare beyond her ken. . . . A half hour later Jim stood at the airport barrier, watching her Constellation make its test run before the pilot set its course.

At the take-off he had glimpsed Lynn's face at a window: she had lifted her hand in a mute farewell just before the pilot gunned his motors. There was no friendliness in the salute: it was a gesture of dismissal. . . . And yet, turning away from the barrier with a heavy heart, he could not shake off the strange feeling that this was but a first step in a relationship whose end he could not foresee.

Ten days later, at Panama, Mrs. Alving brought the preliminary report from Alex Goldschmidt. The working diagnosis was a severe emotional disturbance—but Alex (who made no attempt to hide his concern) was positive that deeper involvements existed. . . . At Honolulu, his airmail letter confirmed Jim's worst fears. Lynn Thorndyke was suffering from schizophrenia, and the disease was in the progressive stage: she had reached the Scripps Institute just in time.

Alex's final report (which reached the ship at Genoa just before the long voyage home) was even more disturbing. Lynn's mother had appeared at the university in Glenville at the opening of the fall term, with the intention of enrolling her daughter one more time. When she had learned that Lynn was at the Scripps Institute in Baltimore and that she would be responsible for her bills, the woman had acted with dispatch. . . . Two days after a peremptory phone call to Alex, the Thorndyke family physician (a Dr. Cronshaw) had appeared in Baltimore. He had ordered Lynn's transfer to Leyden—a state mental hospital located near a village of the same name, about fifty miles from the university at Glenville, where she had been a student.

v

It was late winter when the *Creole Belle* reached her home port again: appropriately enough, a heavy sleet was falling over Brooklyn when Jim said his good-bys. Late that afternoon he was seated in Alex Goldschmidt's Baltimore office, strangely uplifted by the conviction that he had never been away.

"So my prescription worked," said Alex, beaming through his thick lenses.

"If you mean the freighter——?"

"You're on your feet again, Jim. You're ready to get to work. I could tell as much from your last letters. Now I'm sure."

"What's the fastest way to reach Leyden?"

The psychiatrist took the question without a flicker. "In this weather I'd take the Southern Railway," he said. "The best train is the Pelican. Sit back—you've plenty of time to reserve a berth."

"I've got to see Lynn Thorndyke, Alex. With my own eyes. She's worried me ever since I operated on her."

"Does she mean that much to you?"

"Don't ask me to explain it," said Jim. "I don't know what happened myself. I saved her life aboard that freighter—and I sent her to you. That should have been more than enough. But I can't seem to get her off my conscience."

"You know we did everything we could here at Scripps?"

"Of course."

"The psychosis developed too rapidly. None of our treatments gave any response."

"Do you consider the case hopeless?"

"She was in catatonia before Mrs. Thorndyke's doctor could reach Baltimore. Patients at that level do recover sometimes. In her case I'd say the odds against it are overwhelming."

"Did Dr. Cronshaw concur?"

"Entirely," said Alex. "He also said that Mrs. Thorndyke didn't have the funds to meet institute fees. In any event, I couldn't offer enough hope to justify the expense."

"Did Leyden take the girl without charge?"

"Yes. Her mother's a taxpayer in that state." Alex picked up a slim file folder from the desk. "Here's a case summary to date. You won't find it rewarding reading."

At Scripps, the record indicated, Lynn Thorndyke's condition had deteriorated steadily. Dr. Cronshaw had added an endorsement of the diagnosis—and his opinion that commitment to the state mental hospital was the only practical solution. A third report—on a mimeographed form sheet signed by a Dr. Kurt Frankel—acknowledged Lynn's arrival at Leyden. Pending a final evaluation of her condition, it stated, she had been confined to one of the locked wards.

"What sort of place is Leyden?" Jim asked.

"No worse than the average snake pit," said Alex. "And not a great deal better. Run on political lines, I'm afraid—with economy the watchword. I stopped off there last year, when I was lecturing in the South. The director's an old-fashioned hog with both feet in the public trough—but they do have a first-rate chief physician in Frankel." He looked at Jim thoughtfully. "Still want to make the trip—even though I tell you it's useless?"

"I can't help myself, Alex."

The psychiatrist nodded. "Compulsions are strange things. Who would know that better than I?"

"Are they always as obscure as this one?"

Alex smiled. "You don't think yours is really obscure, do you?"

"What do you mean?"

"You've needed a love object to replace Taffy. A girl was bound to turn up in time."

"Must you put things so coldly?"

"I don't mean to sound cold. Most widowers, regardless of their age, have the same impulse."

"Don't be a fool, Alex. I'm old enough to be the girl's father."

"Not quite, if I remember your birth date correctly. In any case, your ultimate intentions don't concern me now. The big thing is your loss of *both* grief and guilt—so far as your dead wife is concerned. By settling your interest on this girl you've found a reason for going on. Through trying to help her—even when your common sense tells you a cure is impossible—you'll be making sure your atonement is complete." Alex's face sobered. "Just be careful, Jim. Letting guilt drive you to a hopeless task could ruin your life."

It was like Alex to anatomize every emotion, thought Jim.

It was part of his trade to insist that all feelings (including love) were vulnerable to dissection. "Let's see if I follow you," he said. "You're insisting that Lynn Thorndyke has become Taffy in my mind. Now she's been stricken—much as Taffy might have been, had she lived through the accident—I have a second chance."

"Your psychiatry's improved over the past year," said Alex dryly. "I hardly thought you'd agree with me so soon."

"I haven't agreed. I'll admit that a superficial resemblance to Taffy attracted me the day Lynn came aboard the freighter. I've already said that I've become involved in her case, ever since I operated——"

"Precisely. You've identified this girl with Taffy. If you can save her, you're hoping she'll explain what drove Taffy to destroy herself. Judging by your report, they were both going at it in different ways—but the purpose was identical."

"You're right there, Alex. If Lynn hadn't been stricken in her cabin I'm sure she'd have gone overside."

"Then visit Leyden by all means. If you want it, there's even a job open on Frankel's staff."

Jim frowned. "Have you been playing *deus ex machina*?"

"I wouldn't hesitate for a moment," said Alex, "though I'm not exactly built like a Greek god. In this instance, Frankel sent me a personal note when he mailed us his report on Lynn. They're looking for a staff surgeon with some experience in neurology. You're well enough trained for the work, if you want it."

"Perhaps I'll give it a try," said Jim slowly. "At least I'd have a chance to do something about this compulsion."

Alex nodded briskly. "I've asked Frankel to hold the job open. If you like, you can accept it this afternoon by phone. Then, if I were you, I'd make sure of that berth on the Pelican."

"Did you tell Dr. Frankel of my interest in Lynn?"

"Of course not." Alex leaned forward, and his voice was earnest. "Let me repeat, Jim—don't go off the deep end for this girl. Don't let a natural sympathy run away with your judgment. In my opinion, she's almost certainly a hopeless case."

"I'll remember, Alex."

"And above all, be realistic about the conditions you'll find at Leyden. Life at such a place can be pure hell, if you lose your sense of detachment. So can advanced schizophrenia. Not a few doctors become psychotic while working in state mental hospitals—from sheer frustration, I expect."

Leyden

WHEN JIM tried to bring back his first impression of Leyden State Hospital (in contrast to what his mind had fashioned in advance), he knew this was an instance when imagination was more dire than reality. He had slept badly while his train roared through the Virginia Piedmont. During the long day, boring ever deeper into the pine barrens of the Gulf coastal plain, he had visioned a series of blank-walled donjons, echoing to the gibberish of the damned. In the midafternoon he had stepped down at the station of the hamlet that gave the asylum its name. Ten minutes later his taxi had crossed a tan-colored river and zoomed through a thicket of water oaks to breast the bluff on the southern bank—and the real Leyden burst into view.

At that distance the hospital might have been a college campus—with country-club overtones in the wide green lawns, the massed azaleas that flanked the central drive. The buildings were Georgian: red-brick walls drowned in ivy, white porticos aloof in the winter light. Jim noted a baseball diamond in a half circle of live oaks. There was a neat string of cottages that resembled a faculty row, a steepled chapel whose carillon was just sounding the hour. He was still gaping when the taxi ground to a halt at the main gate.

Here, for the first time, he noted the bars in the containing wall—an impregnable barrier, for all its discreet landscaping. Beyond, the windows of the halls were fitted with steel-mesh screens—and the uniformed attendant at the gate, though he seemed unarmed, was a guard nonetheless.

Stepping from the cab to hand his credentials to the guard, Jim saw the first patient—a woman who might have been thirty or sixty, in a shapeless Mother Hubbard and carpet slippers. She was squatting in the shade of the nearest portico: her eyes stared blankly into space, and she plucked endlessly at her body, like a monkey in search of lice. Save for this single figure, the lawns and buildings seemed deserted. Jim would learn later that he had arrived during a visiting hour, when nonviolent inmates were permitted to see relatives in the central hall under the supervision of the guards.

The taxi driver took the macadam roadway leading to the main building on two wheels: evidently he was anxious to drop his fare. As they passed the portico where the crone was squatting she spat furiously at a mudguard. The throb of the engine echoed from wall to wall. A dozen voices protested the intrusion from the barred windows—long-drawn howls that poured like ice water down Jim's spine, like the wails of dogs in pain.

At the central building he paid off the driver and carried his bags up the steps. Another attendant directed him to a corridor that branched from a central rotunda where visitors and patients sat in small, huddled groups and appeared to speak only in whispers. The near silence was more chilling than the babble he had expected. Yet it was appropriate to this bare, whitewashed room with its iron chairs and benches (stapled to the floor, like furniture on some hurricane deck). A nameless odor hung in the air like marsh gas—a blend of sweat, formaldehyde, and despair.

He tried hard not to stare at the inmates—though they seemed, in passing, only a trifle less drab than their visitors. Clearly, the face that Leyden turned to the state highway was only a mask.

ii

The corridor led to an anteroom, where a platoon of stenographers typed busily, surrounded by filing cabinets. In the facing wall a door held the legend he was seeking on an imposing brass plate:

THADDEUS MEEKER, M.D.
SUPERINTENDENT

No eyes had been raised at his appearance. Jim braced his shoulders as he moved forward to state his business to the nearest of the stenographers. Without a word of greeting the girl jerked her head toward the name plate.

"He's expecting you, Dr. Corwin. Go right in."

Taking the advice literally, Jim pushed the door wide and entered without knocking. At first glance he was overwhelmed by the contrast between the director's sanctum—and what he had so far observed of Dr. Thaddeus Meeker's domain. Paneled in pine, thick-carpeted, and prodigal of portieres and deep-cushioned chairs, the room had the sheen of easy living, a spot to loll in rather than work. The flat-top mahogany desk was bare of papers; the pillows on the couch beneath the windows bore the imprint of a body that had napped there but recently.

Meeker himself (strolling from an alcove that held a built-in bar) brought the scene into focus. The man was as big as his voice, and as overbearing: he went with this ostentatious luxury, body and soul. The eyes, Jim saw, were tiny, deep-set, and quick-reading. The three-hundred-dollar suit he was wearing fitted him perfectly. So did the shot glass of whisky in his freckled fist and the cigar smoke that wreathed him. . . . *Without retouching,* thought Jim, *you could step into a Nast cartoon and play Boss Tweed, right down to the simian grin.*

He suppressed a panic impulse to cut and run, as Meeker waved him to an armchair without offering his hand. "I'm afraid the train was late, sir——"

"Trains in this state are *always* behind time, Dr. Corwin," said the director. "See you don't follow their example."

"I'll try to keep my perspective, Dr. Meeker."

The headman of Leyden settled behind his desk and lifted a well-shod foot to the mahogany. "So you're the man Goldschmidt is touting as a brain surgeon. Ready to get into harness?"

"Yes, indeed. That's why I'm here."

Meeker shoved a humidor across the desk. "Have a cigar?"

"Thank you, no."

"They're Havana Uppmans—finest on the market. Smoke it later—I don't mind."

Jim accepted a thick, aluminum-cased cigar: it was hardly a moment to announce that he was a pipe smoker only. Again he tried not to stare when Meeker flipped the switch of an intercom box, using his toe as a lever. "Send Dr. Frankel here at once," he directed—and swiveled in the visitor's direction, making his tone less pompous. "Mostly, you'll find, your job is a round of splints and broken skulls. Now and then we have knifings—they *will* get hold of razors, God knows how. I'm also planning a program of skull punctures—how d'you pronounce the word?"

Startled, Jim kept his face bland. "Lobotomy?"

"That's the ticket. It's the real reason I told Frankel to hire you. Didn't Goldschmidt explain?"

Alex had not explained, Jim reflected—and with good reason: remembering his friend's deep disapproval of the operation, he could understand the omission. In a way he welcomed Meeker's bluntness. This might be his chance to prove the truth of the thesis that had so angered Dr. Anton Ziegler at Lakewood—namely, the superiority of transorbital lobotomy over Ziegler's own method.

"Is the operation in general use here?" he asked.

"Not yet. No one here has the training, and we couldn't afford a specialist just for that. You know the technique, don't you? That foreign fellow at Lakewood seems to be doing a lot of 'em."

"I'm familiar with the operation, Dr. Meeker."

"Confidentially, I'm expecting great things of it. Could you process fifty cases right away? Maybe even a hundred?"

"I think so—with the right equipment."

"Do you need a full operating team?"

"A few capable assistants will do. But it's still a surgical procedure."

"We've a fine surgery, right in the main building. You can have what you need, if it's within reason."

"Just what is your over-all plan, sir?"

"If I can believe Frankel, this operation turns lunatics into lambs overnight," said Meeker. "If it's done on a large enough scale at Leyden, we can cut down on attendants—at the same time we'll be getting more work out of our patients. It'll mean a lot to me, Corwin, if I can show we're reducing costs here. Every other nut farm in this state is yelling for more money."

"May I ask what your patient day-cost is at present?"

The director scowled at his cigar. "Two dollars was the last figure—and the hospital committee says it's too damned high. If your method works, we'll make some real changes here. Maybe we'll get the cost down to one-fifty a day——"

The office door swung open without ceremony. Instinct brought Jim to his feet as a tall, stooped figure loomed on the threshold. Even before Meeker could boom out an introduction, he guessed that this was Dr. Kurt Frankel, the medical chief. The face beneath the shock of white, untidy hair was surprisingly young, the mouth relaxed and humorous. Only the eyes (deep-set and sparkling) suggested that their owner had observed most forms of folly—and had long since pardoned the fools.

"This is a real pleasure, Dr. Corwin," said Frankel, with only the faintest of accents. His handshake was unhurried. His eyes, for all their sharp appraisal, welcomed Jim in a language he understood instantly. While the communion lasted, he felt his doubts slip painlessly away. . . . The reprieve was a short one, shattered instantly by the director's attack. Like politicos the world over, it was evident that Meeker could not endure silence.

"Dr. Corwin tells me lobotomy's feasible here, Frankel. D'you agree?"

Jim raised an eyebrow: so far, he had offered no positive endorsement of Meeker's plan. The chief physician did not appear intimidated by the director's bellow.

"Is it still your intention to cut the patient day-cost, Dr. Meeker?" he asked.

"Damn it, yes! Why else would I hire a specialist?"

"I've already protested. The present figure is dangerously low. However, if the committee insists—"

"It does insist," growled Meeker. "And so do I."

"Then we must comply, Dr. Corwin."

With no conscious effort Jim found he had moved to Frankel's side: there was an edge to his voice when he put his next question to the director. "Correct me if I'm wrong, sir," he said evenly, "but how can we possibly give maximum care at such a figure?"

He had expected an explosion—but Meeker only rumbled heavily, like a sleeping volcano. "Just do the operating, Corwin. I'll worry about the rest. I'll match the health record of my wards with any in the state—and we've useful jobs by the hundreds, right under this roof. It's all part of my occupational therapy program. Right, Frankel?"

"Dr. Meeker's therapy program is an ambitious one," said Frankel with the faintest of smiles. "So far it has suffered from a chronic lack of pupils—a condition I hope your surgical program will correct, Dr. Corwin."

The director was almost purring now. "I'm glad we see eye to eye, gentlemen." He offered Jim his hand for the first time. "Show our new staffer to his quarters, Frankel. If there's time before dinner, have someone take him through the wards. I want him familiar with our whole operation here."

"So do I," said Frankel softly.

"When can you schedule the first lobotomy, Corwin?"

Jim glanced at Frankel. "I'll need special instruments."

"Are they expensive?"

"A hundred dollars should cover everything."

Meeker let his palm fall heavily on the desk top—a sound, as Jim would discover, that signified a meeting was ended. "I've a special fund for such purchases. Give me a list in the morning and I'll shoot out a wire. Like I said, you're going to fit in nicely here. *Right, Frankel?*"

"I sincerely hope so, Dr. Meeker," said the chief physician. "Leyden can use a man with Dr. Corwin's training."

iii

Staff quarters for bachelors, Jim learned, were in a wing of the main building: the married doctors lived in the cottages he had mistaken for faculty row. Frankel led him down a bare, echoing corridor and opened a door at the end. The room was on the Spartan side, but the hospital bed looked comfortable enough. With books on the shelves and a cushion to soften the springs in the armchair, Jim saw it could be made livable.

Frankel sat down on the window seat and began to fill his pipe. "As you've observed, the luxury of our director's quarters does not extend to his staff wing. Will it disturb you if I speak candidly?"

"By no means."

The chief physician turned brooding eyes to the sweep of lawn outside the window. "My colleagues gather in the lounge before dinner, when hospital routine permits. You'll meet them this evening, *en bloc,* as it were. Meanwhile, since we are alone here, I'll take the opportunity to fill you in."

Jim settled gingerly in the armchair. "Do you mean the staff is spied upon?"

Frankel shrugged. "I have served in many hospitals. In Austria before the war—in various centers of England—now here. Regardless of the language we spoke, those of the administrative departments always suspected those of the professional. At Leyden one might say that such frictions are raised to the nth degree. You understand, I hope?"

"Perfectly. We had the same pressures at Lakewood."

"At Lakewood, I'm sure, the motivations were different." Frankel held up a detaining palm. "Since this is your first contact with a state hospital, I will not prejudice you in advance. Let me say at once that my staff does its best with the facilities at its disposal. Always, of course, there is the battle over money——"

"Does the director honestly believe he can justify a day-cost under two dollars?"

"He can and will–since he is answerable to the state capital and to the state Democratic organization. They call the tune –he sings on key. Next year, perhaps, if there are no false notes, he may be state director."

"No wonder he's so anxious to start my program."

"I see you are *au courant*, Dr. Corwin."

"It's hard to believe the state would give him such a promotion," said Jim. "After all, his only approach seems to be to cut costs–and cut again. Even a two-dollar rate is far lower than the national standard."

"Most state hospital directors are less concerned with curing mental illness than keeping within their budgets," said Frankel. "Remember, our patients no longer vote. The main purpose of the hospital board–and Dr. Meeker–is to spend taxes on people who appreciate it later–at the polls. By the way, are you a Democrat?"

"I'm afraid my political views are muddled."

"You've no objections to becoming one, I trust?"

"Is it that important?"

"All of us at Leyden vote the Democratic ticket," said Frankel. "I, too, saw the light–after I became a citizen."

Jim voiced the thought that had been in his mind since he'd met the chief physician. "Why did you come here? And why do you stay?"

"Leyden is my life," said Frankel simply.

"Surely–with your qualifications–you could do better."

The Austrian smiled. "Who told you that?"

"I didn't come here blindly. In Baltimore I looked up your record–in the *Directory of Medical Specialists*."

"So you know I'm a certified psychiatrist–and a psychoanalyst as well," said Frankel. "That makes me unique here. In fact, only two of our doctors beside myself can qualify as a psychiatrist–and neither is a specialist."

"With the degrees you've brought from Vienna, you could make a fortune in private practice. Why are you at Leyden?"

"I might ask the same question, Dr. Corwin. I won't—until you're ready to answer it."

Jim met the other's steady look without wavering. "My reason is valid," he said. "And I'm not slumming—no matter how I sound at the moment."

"I accept the rebuke," said Frankel slowly. "That was a Yankee trick on my part—answering one question with another. An Austrian Jew has no right to use it. Incidentally, that's one of *my* reasons for remaining at Leyden. America gave me asylum from the Nazis—life in place of death. I'm trying to repay the debt."

Jim said nothing, recognizing the depths of feeling the exchange had opened. Frankel spread his hands in a quick, explosive gesture before he spoke again.

"I'm afraid that was a bit hysterical," he said. "It isn't the whole truth, either. When I came to your country before the war I wasn't seeking a permanent haven. Now—for my wife and children, as well as myself—Leyden is the first safe home we've had. The schools are adequate. As a state employee I will complete my boys' education at the university for almost nothing. Perhaps I *have* settled for second best. I still feel I'm doing more here than I could outside."

"What can you accomplish—at two dollars a day per patient?"

"Enough—for most of our inmates. You see, Dr. Corwin, physical surroundings aren't so important as you imagine. We've over six thousand patients here. Most are hopeless cases. At least we can give them a refuge—a place where they're safe from the normal ones."

"Do you endorse lobotomy for these hopeless patients—as completely as Dr. Meeker?"

"By no means. I've seen far too few cases. At Lakewood you must have handled many."

"We did—but at O.R. level only. We saw them for a few days after the operation, of course—but only long enough to check setbacks. Occasionally there were exceptions." Jim spoke at some length of Ignaz Lavorsky. The man's history had had a reasonably happy ending: last month, he had risen to the post of chief ward attendant at Rocky Point.

Frankel nodded his approval. "For this individual, at least, lobotomy was a deliverance."

"The effects were still irreversible."

"Believe me, I have chosen patients for your program who have nothing to lose. Naturally, you have the right to screen them."

"I'll accept your choices, Dr. Frankel. I'm no psychiatrist."

"The name is Kurt, Jim—if you're really staying."

"You can count on that, Kurt. Already I can feel the challenge here."

"Good. Now we'll go down and meet the others. You'll find us a mixed lot, I'm afraid."

"How d'you mean?"

"For most staff doctors," said the Austrian, "a state mental hospital is a refuge."

"Just as it is for many patients?"

Frankel nodded—and rose from the window seat. "Often I ask myself if the reasons are too different. For me, it was freedom from persecution. For others on my staff—shall we be charitable and say it was escape from their own failures?"

"And for me?"

"Your reasons are your own, Jim. None of us will question them. Just remember that your colleagues here are the forgotten men of medicine. You'll find it a fraternity of sorts."

iv

The staff lounge (like Jim's own quarters) was shabby but comfortable—a roomy rectangle with a fine view of the clay-red river that bounded Leyden to the north. Since Dr. Meeker had suggested that the newcomer make his first tour before dinner, there was only time for a round of handshakes—and a dutiful repetition of the names the head physician intoned as they passed from man to man.

In all, there were six other doctors. Three were in training as psychiatrists. The others were men who had withdrawn from the stress of private practice. Tonight Jim found it impossible to sort out this elderly trio, all of whom had limp handshakes and seemed to wheeze through identical upper plates.

Of the three younger men, one was a saturnine fellow named Stuart Keegan. He spoke with a drawl oddly at variance with an explosive, restless manner—and what seemed a grudge against the whole family of man. Since it was Dr. Keegan's week to take charge after dark, he was still yawning from an all-day sleep. Jim learned that one doctor was on duty each evening from lights-out to dawn, with all of Leyden under his care. He, too, would be required to serve, once he was familiar with procedure. Meanwhile, it was his special task—whatever the hour—to treat any injuries inflicted on themselves or others by the more violent patients.

The second of the two younger doctors was a pink-cheeked boy named Ira Welles. Fresh from medical school, he seemed balanced on a knife-edge of self-doubt, and spoke brashly by way of compensation. The third student-physician was a dark-skinned man with a porcelain smile and intelligent (if somewhat bovine) eyes behind thick, perfectly round spectacles. He gave his name as Dr. Chandra Singh, and Calcutta as his birthplace. His manners were impeccable, and his clipped accent betrayed an English education.

Dr. Singh explained that each doctor had an equal number of wards under his care: while the post of surgeon had remained vacant, the Hindu physician had taken on several floors that would soon be Jim's domain. When he proposed himself as a guide through these wards Jim accepted eagerly—hoping that he would discover Lynn Thorndyke in this way, without revealing his special interest.

Crossing the lawns in the deepening twilight, forcing himself to shorten his long-legged stride to keep pace with Dr. Singh, he tried hard to keep his eyes (and his thoughts) from those files of barred windows ahead. Leyden had long since lost its resemblance to a college campus. Despite the cheerful, red-brick shell, he saw it for what it was—a backwater far from the great mainstream, a final haven for the doomed and damned.

The Hindu, he noted, was studying him covertly as they mounted the nearest of the white porticos. He spoke at random, to cover the rudeness of silence.

"I imagine this is a far cry from home?"

"No, Dr. Corwin. India is a whole world away—but conditions are not too different there. Our hospitals are crowded with the poor, just as yours are. True, we spend even less money for the sick—but the difference is one of degree."

"Why did you come here to complete your studies?"

"At the University of London, one of my professors was a friend of Dr. Frankel's. They had kept in touch, and my teacher recommended him. That was almost two years ago. I have found the recommendation justified."

"I can believe that. He seems a remarkable man."

"And a great teacher. I have learned much from him—and from Leyden. I fear that sounds cryptic now. In time you will understand."

Passing under the portico, they stopped before a steel door in the boxlike anteroom beyond. Singh selected a key from the chain he carried and turned the lock, exposing a second vestibule. Jim entered on his guide's nod. He saw that the Hindu was careful to lock the outer door before opening a second portal that gave to a long, tiled corridor. Instantly a din of voices assailed his ears, a demonic chatter that seemed pitched too high for human tongues. The stench that greeted him was overpowering, a nauseating miasma of sweat and excreta, visible as fog.

"This is a locked ward," said Singh. "Hold your breath. You will grow used to the stink in time—but never entirely."

Jim's visits to Rocky Point had not prepared him for this: it seemed impossible that patients could exist in such fetid air. Yet the guard who emerged from the chartroom seemed entirely at ease. He was a huge man with the build of a professional boxer, garbed in gym shoes and a uniform that had once been white.

"This is Adam Strang, our chief attendant in this building," said Singh. "Dr. Corwin is Leyden's new surgeon, Adam. He will soon be in charge here."

Strang thrust out a massive paw. Jim found that his handshake was surprisingly gentle.

"Welcome to Brown One, Doctor."

"Our buildings are named after former governors," explained the Hindu. "Each of them has three floors. Ground level is reserved for destructive patients. Less difficult cases are quartered above."

Jim forced his numbed mind to take in details. Two rows of cells flanked the corridor, with eye-level grilles in each door. From each cell came wailing. Here and there a grille shook under the impact of an angry fist. Singh moved calmly down the corridor, with the guard a step behind.

"You'll need time to place individual cases," said the Indian doctor. "Even I must rely on the attendants' charts—with five hundred patients under my care."

"Do you have nurses here as well?"

"A few. They can do little more than give special medications and keep track of the narcotics. At night we try to have at least one on call for every building—and two by day. In addition, there are two daytime attendants on each floor, and one by night."

Jim made a quick calculation. It was beyond belief that a single attendant could care for at least a hundred patients by day, and twice that number after dark. Yet he realized that conditions here were no worse than those in most state mental institutions. Leyden was probably only a trifle below average.

"Look inside this room, Dr. Corwin," said Singh. "It will do for a beginning."

Jim forced himself to peer through a grille halfway down the corridor. The cell was padded, and the single bulb in the ceiling was caged in wire mesh. There was no furniture but a pallet, which had been clawed to shreds. The naked, bony figure crouching in a corner seemed more ape than man. The skin, a fish-belly white, was smeared with filth: a mat of hair spread fanwise across the face, and the eyes that stared out of that wild ambush glowed like coals in a cave. Only those eyes were alive. The body, sprawled in corpselike abandon, scarcely seemed to breathe.

"I'll wash him again later, Dr. Singh," said the guard. "He had his bath this noon, too. Doesn't take old Enoch long to befoul himself."

Singh ran a finger along the chart. "This is Enoch Williams, a former pharmacist. Dr. Frankel listed him for lobotomy when he learned you were coming, Dr. Corwin."

"We never had a case this advanced at Lakewood."

"There are many such in Brown One," said Singh. They were moving on to the next cell. When they drew level with the grille, Strang grasped Jim's elbow and steered him firmly aside just as a white ball of spittle, propelled with bulletlike force, struck the far wall. The grinning face at the opening squeaked with childish laughter as they moved out of range.

"Hal's harmless otherwise," said Strang. "But he's a dead shot. "He'd have hit you between the eyes, Dr. Corwin."

At the next grille they looked in on another naked figure sprawled face down on the pallet. At first glance Jim was positive the man was dead.

"Catatonic stupor," said Singh. "Alternating with periods of mania. Last week he almost killed Adam's replacement."

The main section of the ward lay beyond—a vast, communal bedroom for less violent cases. Jammed as it was with cots, there was barely room for the narrow aisle that bisected it. Ragged blankets were folded at the foot of each bed. There were no sheets, and the mattresses were encased in tubes of stained canvas.

"Give these people sheets, and some of them would hang themselves," Strang explained. "Even so, they need watching all the time."

"Adam has just stated the first law of Leyden, Dr. Corwin,"

said Singh. "You must develop eyes in the back of your head. Above all, never enter this type of ward alone."

"Is *all* the hospital like this?"

"By no means. Perhaps I did wrong to bring you first to Brown One. Patients such as these make up less than ten per cent of our population. The others are docile enough. They are merely escaping from what we call 'outside.'"

They entered a porch, heavy with barred casements, that filled the whole rear wall of the building. Here the men who slept in the vast bedroom were sunning themselves. Most of them sat in attitudes of cowed sloth, their heads sunk low on their chests. A few were pacing in solemn circles as precisely as though they were following a pattern traced on the floor. Many were jabbering to themselves—or, more rarely, to each other. Most of the words were unintelligible. Here and there a four-letter obscenity was chanted endlessly. . . . Jim looked over the shoulder of an octogenarian who was gravely studying a comic book that he held upside down. Another was turning the pages of a magazine at dizzy speed, while he sang a revival hymn in a high, true tenor:

Throw out the lifeline!
Throw out the lifeline!
Someone is sinking today . . .

Across the porch, in a patch of sunlight just inside the rail, a boy whose face suggested the muzzle of a mournful beagle was doing push-ups in an endless series. His half-clad body, and the mat beneath him, were drenched in sweat. Adam Strang moved forward and tapped his shoulder gently. With a grateful grin the would-be athlete collapsed on the porch and seemed to fall into slumber instantly, his head cradled in his arms.

"This is Clint Prescott, Dr. Corwin," said the attendant. "If you're a baseball fan, you'll know the name. He was a twenty-game winner for the Orioles two years ago."

"Not *Iron Man Prescott*?"

"Remember how they sent him back to the minors when he lost his control? It was more than he could take. He came straight to us last fall after a month in the Sally League." Strang looked down at the sleeping boy, who had already begun to snore lightly. "For some reason, he thinks I'm the Orioles' manager—so he takes orders. It's a lucky thing. Otherwise, he'd do those push-ups until he fainted."

Jim had cheered the Iron Man after several of those twenty victories. It was incredible that the two-hundred-pound athlete (whose fast ball had had pin-point control) could shrink so quickly to this half-naked wreck. . . . Somehow, this picture of youth blighted in its flower was more tragic than anything he had witnessed so far.

"Is *he* down for lobotomy, too?"

"Yes, with your approval," said Singh. "Even though he's mostly nonviolent. Dr. Frankel wants to try the operation on a few patients at this level."

"He's drenched in sweat. Shouldn't he have a pajama top?" In his mind's eye, Jim was watching Clint Prescott (magnificent in a fresh uniform, his windbreaker draped on his pitching arm) striding from the bull pen to thunderous applause, to save yet another game for the Orioles.

"He'd only strip it off," said Singh. "It's part of his illness—shedding all reminders that he's a man."

When they moved down the porch, a few of the patients approached, attracted by the sight of the Hindu's white coat. *Doctor, can I speak to you a minute?* was the usual query. To each, the dark-skinned physician gave the same answer, *A little later, I'm busy now.*

"Never stop to talk on the ward," he advised. "You'll get nothing else done. Let them come to your office for consultation, if you like. Even that can be an intolerable burden."

"Surely there's some therapy that gets results."

"Dr. Frankel believes in electric shock treatment for the more hopeful cases. You'll find our machines in constant use. Our record here with shock is the best in the state."

"What about personal consultation? I thought talking out was the best method."

"We try to use it with more acute cases—particularly in the earlier stages of their illness." Singh made a brief, inclusive gesture. "For *these* it is a waste of time. Some have been here for twenty years. The longer a mental patient is ill—the harder it is to help."

They left Brown on that note, crossing the lawn to an identical building that stood just within the retaining wall. "This is Lovell, the women's ward," said the Hindu. "It will be your responsibility, too. Dr. Frankel feels that those of us who are in training should work with both sexes."

"But I'm not in training."

"You'll find the prescribed course will fit in easily with your regular routine. In fact, the two are interchangeable."

"It's something to think over——"

"Stay here three years and you'll be eligible for certification in psychiatry," said the Hindu. He fitted a key into a lock and swung back another steel door, to engulf them in another nightmare wave of stench. This time the shrieks that rang down the corridor seemed even more deafening.

"We are now in Lovell One," said Singh. "The female violent ward. Generally speaking, our women are apt to be less destructive than the men. Unfortunately, they are sometimes far more vocal. Follow me, Dr. Corwin."

Jim shook off his unspoken dread. "Surely this *can't* be worse than Brown."

Singh paused, with one hand still on the automatic lock. "What was the most shocking case in Brown? I'm asking you to react personally—not medically."

"Iron Man Prescott, I think."

"Naturally. You remember young Prescott as a man. At the moment the others seem no more than animals."

"I'm afraid that's all too true," said Jim ruefully. "It's a highly irrational approach for a doctor."

"But a natural one," said the Hindu. "That is why I'm afraid a real shock awaits you. We have a former patient of yours in this ward—a girl named Lynn Thorndyke."

v

Hesitating confusedly in the anteroom, Jim tried not to stare at his guide: at the moment, Singh bore a remarkable resemblance to Aladdin's djinn, waiting to lead him down a predestined path. The Indian doctor had shown uncanny ability to penetrate his thoughts—but this final revelation bordered on the occult.

Then, in a flash, the truth struck home: the secret he had guarded so carefully was no secret at all. When Lynn was transferred from Scripps, Alex Goldschmidt had obviously sent a complete medical resumé to Leyden—including the operation performed aboard the *Creole Belle*. "I'd heard she was here," he said quickly. "Dr. Goldschmidt told me in Baltimore."

"Judging by the report he sent us," said Singh, "the operation you performed at sea was barely in time. It must be bitterly frustrating to save a patient with the scalpel—then lose her to a locked ward."

"Is her prognosis that desperate?"

"See for yourself. I was trying to prepare you—not dramatize the situation."

Again a steel door shut behind them and the automatic lock clicked home. The long, tiled corridor beyond seemed identical with Brown One—only the screams issuing from the cells suggested that these inmates were female. . . . In the chartroom, two white-clad women were counting narcotics as calmly as though they were both stone-deaf to the cacophony. The larger of the two (a Junoesque figure, with biceps that would not have disgraced a weight lifter) Singh introduced as Mrs. Foster, the ward attendant. The other was presented as Janet Moore, the assistant head nurse—a graying, birdlike woman with striking blue eyes and a warm smile.

"Welcome to bedlam, Dr. Corwin," she said. "Think you can take it?"

"I'll admit it's a bit strange, so far."

"Like having a nightmare—and waking up to find it's real?"

"You've stated the case perfectly."

"You'll grow hardened to it." The nurse turned to Singh. "What's he seen so far?"

"The ground floor at Brown One."

"Why bring him here, then? Take the poor man to his dinner. This is only more of the same."

"I want him to see our Sleeping Beauty, Miss Moore."

"She's still in coma."

"So much the better," said the Hindu. "I've told him he won't enjoy the experience."

"He'd enjoy the disturbed state still less," said Janet Moore. "I'll join you as soon as I finish this inventory."

Jim followed Singh down the corridor, glad that he had been largely ignored in this brisk exchange. His heart, which was already beating fast, seemed to choke his throat when the Indian doctor paused at the first cell on the left and fitted his key to the lock. When he stood beside Lynn Thorndyke's cot at last, he felt the crushing weight of a frustration that seemed more than he could bear.

He had expected some visible mark of her ordeal—an emaciation just short of death, perhaps even a scar or two. The girl on the cot in the small, whitewashed room had all the serenity of sculpture—and the same icy aloofness. Common sense told him that she lived and breathed, but his first glance did not confirm it. Now, with frightening clarity, he saw why Alex had warned him against emotional involvement. *You were a fool to come this far,* he told himself. *A greater fool to sign on at Leyden—to pretend you can help her.*

He turned from the cot, hoping that Singh had not guessed how deeply he was hurt. The Hindu spoke quickly—his odd, precise English suggesting that his sentences had been formed in advance.

"The first time it is encountered, Dr. Corwin, the collapse of the psyche can be a heartbreaking thing. Still, it is a phenomenon we must face if we're to seek its cure."

"Then there *is* some hope?"

"Schizophrenia is nearly always a self-created hell. Patients have emerged from it—given a strong enough reason."

"You mean she's inflicted this condition on herself?"

"Exactly. In many minds there is a sense of uselessness, the conviction that one is unwanted, the guilt complex that goes with failure. Normally, ego gratification at some level destroys these phantoms. On the other hand, they can be nurtured by parental neglect, rejection of love—every cruelty that man has practiced against man since the Stone Age. It is my guess that Miss Thorndyke suffered from such pressures in childhood. In adolescence, perhaps—when they grew still stronger—she lacked the strength to conquer them. As a result, she has come to this."

Jim turned back to the cot. As she lay there, the girl still suggested a medieval saint, carved on the marble lid of some cathedral tomb. But now his slowly clearing brain took in other details. He saw that her cheeks were rouged, her full lips scarlet. It should have been a jarring note. The truth was, he found the make-up both poignant and natural. It suggested that she had returned here from some gala—and had stretched on the cot for the briefest of naps.

"Mrs. Foster puts on the rouge when the patient is in stupor," said the Hindu. "I should forbid it, I know—but it seems harmless. In this setting she reminds one of an orchid in a swamp. Just to look at her is a refreshment of the heart."

"How long do these stupors last?"

"Sometimes for weeks. When the disturbed phase begins she is like some beast defying its captors." Singh sat down beside the bed to test the girl's pulse. "You may think me fanciful, but to me *this* is the real Lynn Thorndyke. The pure spirit, untouched by the special hell she can't escape in her waking moments. Or is that too mystical a concept?"

"Not for me," said Jim. "Don't forget, I saw her before her breakdown."

"How did she strike you then?"

"Like innocence escaping the furies."

"Only she didn't escape, Dr. Corwin. If we could only call those furies by name—and exorcise them!"

Jim remembered the boy who had pursued Lynn to New Orleans, the radiogram with its unexplained reference to Mary Lou. Were these the demons that had hounded Lynn to the brink of suicide? And what was the role of the mother who—by the girl's own admission—had all but abandoned her?

"Isn't there some way to show her where she failed—and how to fight back?"

"You are forgetting a basic obstacle, Dr. Corwin," said Singh patiently. "This is an advanced case, with just two phases. Either the patient is in coma—as you see her now—or she's fighting us with all her strength. In either phase the psychiatrist is helpless."

Jim shook his head slowly. "I'm shockingly ignorant when it comes to mental disease," he admitted. "Including schizophrenia."

"Freud defines the disease as a narcissistic withdrawal," said Singh. "It is a regression deeply involved with a weakening of the basic will to exist, to accomplish, to prove one's self a man —or a woman."

"Down with the Super Ego? Up with the Id?"

The Hindu smiled. "You are not so ignorant as you pretend, Dr. Corwin."

"I can't define the Super Ego exactly."

"Shall we call it the mind's finest flowering, the dynamic that can make *homo sapiens* resemble a demigod? The Id plays Mr. Hyde to that Dr. Jekyll. It is the beast that hides by day, the atavism that defies civilization and all its ways." Singh rose from the bed and looked down at the patient. "At this moment, Miss Thorndyke seems a seraph chained to earth. When the stupor passes, however, her mind will again become a servant of the Id."

"Completely?"

"Vestiges of the Ego—even the Super Ego—are still present, of course. But they are now so disorganized that they have become willing partners in her break with reality." Singh tossed up his hands. "To turn from the mystical to the clinical—schizophrenia is no more than a largely incurable regression. One of its most striking features is the patient's complete lack of capacity for transference—the *sine qua non* of analytic treatment. Therefore, in the opinion of most specialists, including Dr. Frankel, psychotherapy is largely ineffective."

"Suppose she does become rational again. Wouldn't it help to have her life story on hand as a point of reference?"

"Yes, Dr. Corwin—it would help greatly. Whenever possible, we assemble a complete background history on each patient. In Miss Thorndyke's case we've had little firsthand information—with her mother abroad and no other relatives available."

"Have you written to the mother?"

"Yes—via the family doctor. She has ignored our letters so far."

"Perhaps some questions could be answered at the university."

"Only last month Dr. Welles talked with the dean of women—and with several of the students. His report's been put on file."

"I want to read it."

"Dr. Welles's notes are not too revealing."

"At least they're a start. I intend to supplement them, if I may."

"The girl will be under your care," said Singh. "You've the right to proceed as you wish."

"Within safe limits, of course."

"What harm can questions do?" said the Hindu. His eyes turned to the marble-cold figure on the cot. "*She* can't be hurt."

vi

Thorndyke, Lynn —— (Female) —— Lovell One

(Preliminary investigation of case history, based on visit to campus of State University, Glenville, January 29th, last.)

Undersigned talked with Louise Pearson, dean of women, with several of patient's classmates, with Professor Fabian Blake, head of the Fine Arts Department, the subject in which patient was majoring.

While not unpopular, patient kept much to herself. As senior, exercised privilege of rooming alone. Worked long hours in her art courses—mostly at her painting, in which, according to Professor Blake, she showed unusual talent. Several canvases, still on exhibit in student gallery bear him out.

(N.B.: suggest Dr. F., or someone competent to judge, study these canvases for clues to derangement. In most of them, patient employs techniques—wild whorls, sunflower bursts, drowned suns, etc.—reminiscent of later, manic work of the Dutch artist Van Gogh.)

Jim sat propped against the pillows on his Spartan bed, the gooseneck lamp twisted so the light fell directly on the file folder which lay open on his knees. He was forcing himself to read Dr. Ira Welles's report slowly, to ponder every fact in the light of what little he already knew of Lynn—and Lynn's enigmatic past. So far, the facts supported the vague sketch he had formed of her life story prior to her illness. It was right that she should mingle but little with her fellow students, that she should live alone—and those long, slim hands were made to hold a paintbrush. . . . *If Jay was her lover,* he told himself, *they loved in secret. If love had driven her mad, it was right that she should express her torment on canvas.*

While the patient had no roommate, several girls on her dormitory floor remembered her well. Though I questioned them closely, they insisted that she had seemed "normal" at all times. Without an exception, they were deeply shocked to learn that she was now an inmate of Leyden. (Typical quotes follow.)

Sylvia Warner: "She was quiet but nice, a real lady.

A good student, the kind who's modest about her grades. No visible beaus, but she didn't seem to mind."

Laura Townsend: "We sat together in chapel. She always seemed devout. Never joined any of the dormitory arguments about sex and its place in college life. Was good at tennis, but went out for no teams. In my opinion, she lived for her art."

Hope Hollins (graduate student in psychology): "She was a bit intense at times, a still-waters-run-deep type—but that seemed to go naturally with the artistic temperament. Remarkable is the only word for her paintings—she had genuine talent. Maybe it *was* only the expression of her inner torment—or its catharsis. I'm sure she had an unhappy home life (or, maybe, no home life at all), but she wasn't the kind to talk about it. Maybe art wasn't enough of an outlet. If she'd had just one *friend*—and opened up—it could have made all the difference."

Dean Pearson's file report, made after standard interviews in patient's freshman year, gives an I.Q. of 125, good co-ordination, a determination to succeed on all academic levels. Grade-A attention in class, meticulous paper work. Some of her professors noted a certain tension when patient was called on to recite.

Her secondary school record was above average, though not markedly so. During her high school years, patient resided with an aunt (since deceased) in Louisville (Ky.) while her mother traveled abroad. Patient's father (whom her mother divorced when patient was thirteen) was a wealthy lawyer. He died in mysterious circumstances a year after divorce, when car he was driving overturned.

Jim turned the page in the file folder, with a sigh that mingled impatience and a certain pity for the dogged efforts of Dr. Welles. So far, the report was moving in a sluggish circle, touching on clue after clue, without exploring in depth.

Even so, a definite pattern was emerging. The tragedy of the home broken in early adolescence. The father's probable suicide, the rich-bitch mother (who, it seemed, was rich no longer). Here, in short, was the vicious circle that had isolated Lynn Thorndyke from the world of the wanted, from children who took their parents' love for granted. . . . Then, too swiftly, the high school years in the home of a relative, the frightened withdrawal at the university, the practical compensations of good grades, the chance of a career in art. What had come next—to drive her into headlong flight? What was Jay's role in the mystery—who was Mary Lou?

> Clearly, the mother's coldness, her refusal to grant patient anything resembling a home life, is a contributing factor in her trauma. Girls in her dormitory report an even more marked withdrawal in the week preceding her abrupt departure from Glenville. Prior to this, they also report that she was often absent for long periods in the evening, returning at the last possible moment before lights out. When questioned, patient's reply was always the same: she had "worked late on her painting" in the studio.
>
> Mother should be contacted again for clues. She can be reached via the family physician, Dr. Leonard Cronshaw, 1407 Cedar Drive, Louisville, Ky.

The report ended on that suggestion. Staring at the neatly typed sheet, Jim could see why Mrs. Thorndyke had ignored all queries so far. From what Alex had said in Baltimore, it was evident she had put Lynn's case in the hands of Dr. Cronshaw when she realized the disease was probably incurable. It was unlikely that she would prove co-operative at this late date. Particularly when the only questions he could ask would underline the damning fact that she was (at least in part) responsible for her daughter's breakdown.

Forcing his mind, he took up a pen and began to sketch the letter he would have written, had Lynn's mother been a normal parent. Five minutes later he had abandoned the effort. What could one say to a woman whose existence had been devoted to the gratification of her own appetites, who had fled the cares of parenthood from the start?

For the present, he told himself, he would ignore Mrs. Thorndyke. Beginning tomorrow, he would open his own sleuthing with a visit to the Glenville campus. The clock at his bedside already hung on midnight. His hand was on the light switch when the phone rang softly. The voice on the wire was both weary and competent.

"Dr. Keegan speaking. We've had trouble in Brown One. Can you meet me in the surgery?"

"Have you brought the patient over?"

"He's on his way. It could be serious."

"I'll be down at once."

Years of interning had trained Jim's hands to assemble an operating suit in a fraction over a minute. Following the gloomy staircase that led to his special domain, he could almost welcome the interruption. So far, his investigation of the mystery that was Lynn Thorndyke had simply dead-ended. There was no logical reason why his luck would improve tomorrow.

The surgery was compact and well equipped: tonight, with its lights blazing, it was a beacon of brilliance in the pitch-dark flank of the main building. Two attendants had already arrived with the patient on a wheeled stretcher. Keegan, looking grumpier than usual in a fresh white coat, was taking the man's blood pressure.

"One-twenty over eighty," he said. "The injury may not be so severe as I thought—but that's a bad cut over the right temple." He indicated the taller of the two guards, a beefy man with a scarred face and an odd look of hostility in his close-set eyes. "This is Jack Hanley, our head attendant. He'll tell you how it happened."

Jim nodded to the man and moved forward to test the patient's pulse. It was slow and strong. The injury, as Keegan had said, was extensive—a deep gash in the scalp exposing the bone, and matted with dried blood.

"Shall I send for a nurse?" Keegan asked.

"We can manage between us, if you know where things are," said Jim. "Was the injury self-inflicted?"

Hanley came a step nearer: his scowl dissolved in what could only be called a smirk. "This fellow's pretty active, Doctor. We had him in a jacket all last week. Maybe we let him out too soon."

The second attendant snorted a wordless affirmative, and Jim felt sure the man was choking down a laugh. Clearly this was a situation that Keegan could explain later. His job at the moment was to patch a head wound—and make sure that its results had not been too serious.

Keegan had already brought a sterile suture tray from the cabinet: while Jim scrubbed his hands he shaved the area round the wound and cleaned it. The cut was bleeding freely again when he approached the table to swab it with antiseptic. There was no reaction from the patient, a sure sign that his blackout was complete. Thanks to that inertia, it was a simple matter to probe beneath the scalp until he had assured himself there was no fracture. A dozen stitches were enough to close the wound: Hanley came forward at his nod to hold the patient's head while he applied a bandage.

It was a routine procedure, finished within ten minutes. With a flashlight Jim examined the pupil reflexes of the eyes after he had made a quick neurological check. The pupils seemed to react a bit sluggishly to the light—but there was nothing to indicate that the patient's coma was anything more than the end product of a simple concussion.

"How long ago did this happen?"

"Close to an hour," said Hanley stolidly. "It took us awhile to get a stretcher over to Brown One. He'll be all right, Doc. These nuts are hard to crack."

"Maybe—we'll have to see." Jim kept his anger in control when he saw that Keegan had accepted the impertinence. "Can we keep him under observation until morning?"

"If you like," said the other doctor. "We've a couple of emergency rooms on this floor. Will you stay with him, Jack?"

"I reckon so," said Hanley grudgingly, "if it's an order."

In the emergency room the patient was transferred to a cot; the attendant pulled a chair beside it and settled there. This time there was no mistaking the hostile look he threw at Jim.

"Like a snack before you turn in, Corwin?" asked Keegan. Again he seemed to take Hanley's manner in stride. "I'll look in on this fellow later."

In the staff dining room there was a tray of sandwiches, and coffee simmering on a hot plate. Keegan filled two cups and dropped into an armchair with a cavernous yawn.

"I snooze here when I can," he said. "Which isn't often, as you can imagine." He bit into his sandwich with relish. "One thing you can say for this mausoleum, the food's first-rate. It's the only item that Meeker shares with his staff. Believe me, if it weren't for Frankel, I'd have pulled my freight years ago."

"Dr. Singh tells me he's a fine psychiatrist."

"One of the best, for my money—and just as good a teacher. Deserves a lot better than Leyden, but he's one of those dedicated coves. Are you, by any chance, two of a kind?"

"So far," said Jim cautiously, "I'm only here to learn."

"You'll join the head shrinkers in time. I figured as much when we met."

Jim was not sure he liked Keegan. There was a hard gloss about him that repelled friendship in advance. For the present he felt he must shift the conversation to safer ground.

"D'you think that head injury is serious?"

"Probably not," said Keegan. "Concussion's the most likely diagnosis."

"An extradural hematoma can form fast, if you aren't watching—and it can kill even faster."

Keegan yawned again even more cavernously. "I almost hope there *is* a kickback this time. It'd do my heart good to hang something on Hanley. He's been riding much too high."

"Are you telling me the man was slugged?"

"Of course. It's Hanley's favorite way of cooling off an excited patient. Usually he's smart enough to use a soap sock."

"What on earth is a soap sock?"

"A cake of laundry soap crammed into the toe of a sock and swung like a blackjack. It can knock a man cold and not even leave a bruise."

"I thought slugging was against the rules."

Keegan shrugged. "That doesn't keep it from being an everyday occurrence. Some of our attendants, like Adam Strang—you probably met him this afternoon—are good Joes. The rank and file are close to idiot level themselves; no one but a moron would work for the sort of pay they draw. Even so, the turnover's too damned high for efficiency. If we made 'em mollycoddle the patients—particularly these disturbed cases—we'd have no strong-arm help at all."

"I'd heard of such conditions," said Jim slowly. "But I only half believed the stories."

"Don't get the idea that Leyden is beyond the pale. Actually it's better than some state asylums I've worked in. Frankel sees to that. But there's bound to be slugging, even in the best."

"What happens if this patient dies?"

"Nothing."

"You mean there'd be no investigation?"

"Sure they'd investigate—that's the law. But it'd be a whitewash. Just another nut that banged his head and killed himself. The coroner wouldn't even leave the county seat."

"What about Hanley? Can't he be punished?"

Keegan put down his cup. "I'd better give you the real lowdown, Corwin: it'll save you steps later on. Jack Hanley's brother is Big Al Hanley—chairman of the County Democratic Executive Committee, which makes him boss-man in these backlands. Big Al is also high up in the state organization. Meeker is bucking for the mental health commissioner's job, so he's staying in good with Al. Besides, Jack is the hospital collector."

"Come again?"

"I'm referring to the party's cut in your salary. Amounts to about one per cent, payable to the Glenville Democratic Club. But it all siphons into the same pot."

"Is Meeker part of that setup, too?"

Keegan's sleepy eyes opened wide. "How else would the super of a state hospital rate imported Havanas and bonded bourbon? Or a chauffered Caddy and a girl friend I'd give a month's pay to be making right now?"

"Are you referring to Miss Kendall——?" Lisa Kendall was the head nurse at Leyden, a generously endowed brunette whom Jim had met at the end of dinner. He remembered Miss Kendall's eye (which could only be described as roving) and the overlong pressure of her fingers when they shook hands.

"Lisa's the director's dish, all right," said Keegan. "Don't try making time in that quarter, though. Meeker has too many spies around."

"How did he get this job? Has he special medical qualifications?"

"Between us, he wouldn't know a dipso from a paretic. He leaves that part strictly to Frankel. They tell me he was just a G.P.—and a bad one at that—until his relatives up in the capital began to play the old wire game. Believe me, Corwin, there's nothing like family connections in the South." Keegan rose reluctantly from the armchair. "Will that do for the first lesson?"

Jim grinned. "Thanks—it's more than enough for tonight."

"I'll tell you more later, when I'm sure no one can listen in," said the other doctor. "Right now I must get back on my rounds if I'm to finish by daylight."

"I'll look at the head injury again before I turn in."

In the recovery room Hanley was craftily asleep but wakened so expertly on Jim's entrance he had no excuse for a reprimand. There was no sign of complication in the patient, but he vetoed the attendant's suggestion that he be wheeled back to the ward. This, after all, was outside the brute's domain, and Jim felt that the man would at least be safe until morning. . . . Back in his room, he was oppressed with a sense of futility so great that he felt his head swim. He needed all his powers of concentration to strip off his clothes and fumble his way to bed.

Six hours later the alarm clock wakened Jim from a dreamless sleep that had brought no real refreshment. The breakfast bell had sounded before he could dress and hurry to the dining room. Keegan was already at the table, staring glumly at an empty coffee cup.

"Sorry to begin your day with bad news," he said. "But we lost our patient."

Jim looked at him in stunned amazement. "Why didn't you send for me?"

"There wasn't time. He seemed all right when I looked in. Jack said he'd been moving about a bit, so I figured he was coming out of it. At five he fell apart all at once. Convulsions only lasted a few minutes. I couldn't have gotten word to you. I was too busy holding him down."

"It sounds like an extradural hemorrhage. A craniotomy might have pulled him through."

Keegan shook his head. "He went too fast–no one could have saved him." His eyes narrowed as his weary voice went on. "Incidentally, you can forget our talk last night. I've a tendency to exaggerate when I'm tired—"

"I'm afraid I don't understand," said Jim.

"I've investigated this fellow's case," said Keegan in the same tired tone. "He had a seizure and slipped on the floor of his cell. Smacked his head against the floor."

"Will the coroner accept that?"

"He already has. We don't waken Meeker when someone dies this early–so I called him myself. I've just signed the death certificate."

"There's to be no inquest?"

"The coroner said not. Took my diagnosis without question, as he's done before. Meeker will add his name to the report later: it's on his desk now. As I say, he doesn't like to be wakened early–nor does Miss Kendall."

Jim took his place at the table. Last night Keegan had told him the truth. This morning he was lying–and it was the blandness of the lie that disturbed him most. Yet, if the other doctor had cleared the death with the coroner, what could he gain by demanding an inquest, save an enemy on the hospital staff?

"What about the man's family?"

"There wasn't any. File folder says he was picked up off the streets in d.t.'s. We're delivering the body to the university medical school."

"That makes the wrap-up easier, doesn't it?"

Keegan took the jab with aplomb. "I'll give you one more bit of advice, Corwin. Don't begin feeling sorry for these derelicts—or you'll find yourself buying your own ticket to the bird cage. Remember, most families with inmates at Leyden consider them already dead. More often than not they're *glad* to hear their relatives are ready for burial."

"I still wish you'd sent for me."

"Don't worry—no one will question you now."

"Why should they?"

"You're a brain surgeon. You saw a man with a head injury and didn't operate. A few hours later he's dead. *I* don't blame you, God knows. Meeker might, if he wanted to make something out of it. He won't—now the guy's signed out."

There was no threat in the casual words, yet Jim could hardly miss their implication. For his own good he had been warned to hold his tongue: by exhuming this case, so to speak, he'd only be exhuming the fact that he might be partly responsible. Actually, he had followed hospital routine in putting the patient under observation—and the blame, if any, lay on Keegan for his failure to call him. Yet Keegan's story was airtight too.

"Very well, Doctor," he said. "The case is closed."

As he spoke he leaned back to accept the plate of ham and eggs an orderly had just brought from the kitchen. Tired though he was, he was a little shocked to find his appetite was excellent. . . . Less than twenty-four hours after his arrival, was he already inured to the routines at Leyden?

Weeks later (when his initiation was complete) he came upon the dead man's hospital record quite by accident—and noted the diagnosis under which it had been filed:

Pneumonia, with cerebral complications. Died in convulsion.

Dean Louise Pearson had been cold at first, after she had granted Jim a rather grudging interview. Clearly she felt this second visitor from Leyden was wasting her time. Her manner changed when he reminded her that he had known Lynn Thorndyke before her collapse—had, in fact, exchanged radiograms with the university while aboard the *Creole Belle.*

"Forgive me if I seemed brusque, Dr. Corwin. I understand your curiosity now."

"It's far more than curiosity. The girl is still my patient. I'm hoping you can help me to find a cure."

"*I*, Doctor?"

"It is evident she suffered a traumatic experience here at Glenville. Perhaps this wasn't enough in itself to bring on her present condition: that has been a long time developing. However, I think you'll agree she didn't run away without a reason."

"You've seen her record." The dean sounded aggrieved, as though Lynn Thorndyke's illness—in some bizarre fashion—threatened her reputation as an educator. "If she'd confided in me—or her faculty adviser——"

"People in Miss Thorndyke's condition seldom confide in anyone," said Jim. "What's her adviser's name?"

"Mr. Fabian Blake. He heads our Fine Arts Department. At the moment he's conducting a class. You may see him when it ends."

"Wasn't he her favorite teacher?"

"The girl kept constantly to herself. If she had preferences—in teachers or friends—she never revealed them."

"Didn't you find that a cause for concern?"

The dean took off her spectacles and gave Jim the first smile of the interview. "Youth's an odd time, Dr. Corwin. My business here is to keep it in line. Naturally, with Lynn's record before me, I could see she was throwing chances away. I could hardly suggest she date a classmate now and then—or go out for something besides her art. After all, I had no cause for complaint. Her grades were far better than average. Until she ran away she never broke a rule——"

"But you *did* feel she wasn't normal?"

"No girl is normal if she's unloved, Doctor. This one wasn't even wanted."

"Did you ever meet her mother?"

"We met each fall—when the new school year began."

"Would you care to express an opinion of her?"

The dean's smile vanished. "She was one of the coldest women I ever knew—and one of the most self-centered."

"Yet she came to Glenville each fall to make sure her daughter was settled?"

"Her husband's will insisted she do so."

"You've seen the will?"

"Only the stipulation that affected the university. When Mr. Thorndyke died, his lawyer was instructed to forward it to me." The dean shrugged, as though answering an unspoken question. "Apparently he set great store by education. He left a bequest of fifty thousand dollars to our building fund—providing Lynn took her degree here. When that condition was met, Lynn and her mother were to receive similar amounts."

"In other words, Mrs. Thorndyke had a fifty-thousand-dollar stake in her daughter's graduation?"

"Yes, Doctor—to put things bluntly. That's why she called on us each September."

Here, at least, was one important clue to the girl's breakdown—and the mystery that surrounded it. It was all too evident that Mrs. Thorndyke (believing Lynn's illness to be incurable) had shipped her to Leyden as casually as a gambler whose horse has lost a vital race.

"Would it help if I wrote to Mrs. Thorndyke?"

"She's washed her hands of her daughter," said the dean. "I doubt if she'd answer your letter."

"Not even if I held out some hope of Lynn's recovery?"

"Does such a hope exist, Dr. Corwin?"

"It exists in my mind," said Jim firmly. "Otherwise, I could hardly call myself a doctor." He got to his feet as a bell clanged outside the office door. "May I see Mr. Blake now?"

"Of course. You should find him in the studio. Fine Arts Building, just across the quad."

The campus walks were teeming with students when Jim emerged into the afternoon sunlight. Crossing the quadrangle, he glanced covertly at a dozen young faces and wondered if he dared stop for questions. Here, after all, were Lynn Thorndyke's classmates: some of them were sure to remember her. He put down the temptation, telling himself that his visit with the dean had raised more problems than it had solved. When he climbed the steps of the Fine Arts Building he wondered if his next interview would be more rewarding.

Professor Fabian Blake, in a sky-blue smock, was working at a canvas when Jim entered the empty studio. The head of the Fine Arts Department was a tall, leonine man who suggested a dozen professions rather than the artist: only the smock and the open-toed sandals betrayed him. He put down his palette as Jim entered—and welcomed him with an expansive gesture when he had stated his errand.

"A tragic loss, Doctor," he said. "Come into the gallery—I'll show you her paintings."

The gallery was a long, skylighted corridor whose walls were only partially filled with pictures. Fine Arts, Professor Blake explained with a grimace, was one of the best endowed faculties on campus—and one of the least attended. Most of his students were girls, coasting to an easy degree in a major that required little application.

"Lynn studied with me because she loved painting," he said. "So, I'm thankful to say, do a few others. The teacher's life is frustrating at times. It also has its rewards. Here is one of them."

He paused before a group of canvases that occupied a special niche between two tall casement windows. Jim knew they were Lynn's work without asking: unschooled though he was in techniques, he felt their impact instantly. Dr. Welles's report had done them less than justice. He had mentioned the tortured whorls without speaking of the vitality that burst from every brush stroke. Here, indeed, were drowned suns, and flowers whose petals seemed to drip blood—yet the flowers lived in their canvas prison, the suns seemed ready to burst like meteors. The comparison to Van Gogh had been an apt one, he reflected—but Lynn's style was her own.

"I see you feel them too," said Professor Blake. "I hoped you would."

Jim nodded soberly. "They explain a great deal, don't they?"

"Believe me, these canvases are the work of a master in the making. Lynn had yet to find herself in oils. Her brushwork is uninhibited. The composition leaves much to be desired. But I could see her advance with each day we worked together. Given another year she would have found herself."

The teacher settled on a bench, across the way from the paintings. Jim sat beside him, careful to put no premature questions. If the dean had been on the reticent side, it was clear that Fabian Blake was overflowing with memories.

"Doctor, when my classes are behind me, I come here often to sit by these canvases and study them. As my assistant once said, they speak a language all their own: the triumph of the life force over death. Of course, words are quite useless to describe a painting: all one can do is chatter technique. Jay was aware of that, when he made the remark."

"Did you say *Jay*?"

"Jay Thompson, my assistant. Do you know him?"

"I've heard the name," Jim said quietly. "Is he here now?"

"Jay graduated a year ago. At present he's studying in Paris—at the École Nationale. He's returning for the fall term, to take his doctorate. A fine young man and a born teacher. Sometimes I think he understood Lynn even better than I."

"Were they good friends?"

"Lynn was not one to make friends easily. Let us say she was an apt pupil, he a patient instructor."

"You're sure they were nothing more to each other?"

"No, Doctor—now you mention it. Is that why you're here, to uncover a hidden romance?"

"I'm here to restore a patient to health, if I can find the

means," said Jim. "Perhaps you can help me. If not, I'm sure Thompson can."

Professor Blake listened attentively while he told of his meeting with Lynn, of Jay Thompson's appearance on the levee, and of the radiogram that Lynn had received just before her collapse.

"They painted here after hours," he said. "But then, so did several others who loved their work. When they put their brushes aside, I'd have sworn they went their separate ways——"

"Who is Mary Lou?"

"I can't be sure; it's a common name in the South. But there *was* a Mary Lou Donelson in Lynn's class. I remember the name, because Jay was engaged to her during her senior year." Professor Blake, whose eyes had been on one of the paintings, turned to Jim with real concern. "Have I said something to trouble you, Doctor?"

"Don't tell me they're in Paris together?"

"Far from it. She broke off the engagement and married someone else. A man named Lee Morison—one of the best horsemen in the state. The families were delighted, I'm told——"

"How can I reach Mrs. Morison?"

"The Morison estate is ten miles west of here—on Route Eighty. It's called Far Hills. D'you have a car, Doctor?"

Jim rose and held out his hand. "I have a car, Mr. Blake—and thank you very much indeed."

"I hope I've been of some help."

"You've helped greatly. Don't be surprised if I call on you again."

The car to which Jim had referred was actually a Leyden ambulance—the same that had been used to deliver the body of last night's patient to the morgue of the university medical school. It was hardly the ideal vehicle to approach Far Hills, a vast, neo-Grecian pile at the end of a driveway that seemed to wind on forever from its fieldstone gatehouse. Mrs. Morison's house, Jim reflected, was worthy of a Natchez pilgrimage. So was the handsome Negro butler who received him on the Ionic portico. . . . So, for that matter, was Mary Lou Morison herself, a svelte flower of the South with a coquette's smile and flawless manners. She welcomed him to her living room with genuine warmth.

Lee Morison, it developed, was riding in a horse show. His bride, who had sprained a knee in the last drag hunt, had been getting through the afternoon as best she could. She was delighted to have a caller—and an excuse to order drinks.

Yes, she remembered Lynn Thorndyke perfectly. An odd, intense girl who might have been pretty if she'd been taken in hand—but what could you do with a classmate who lived for her painting? At least, until she met Jay?

"Did they fall in love, Mrs. Morison?"

"So Jay told me. He was nice about it, and quite miserable. You see, he'd made up his mind to marry *me*—and he couldn't quite bring himself to take back his pin."

"I understood you were engaged."

"Nothing formal, just an understanding." Mary Lou dimpled over her highball. "You see, Doctor, being pinned in this corner of the South only means *engaged* to be engaged. I liked Jay. He was fun to be with, a wonderful dancer. But I couldn't be sure he wasn't marrying me for my money. He was a very ambitious boy: he wanted to go on from art teaching to collecting. Eventually he planned to open his own gallery—with what he thought was Donelson cash. I could hardly tell him that the Donelsons were long on ancestors but short on capital——"

Nursing the drink his hostess had generously poured, trying not to let the white-and-gold splendors of her drawing room overwhelm him, Jim thought swiftly as the smooth, fluent voice went on. Mary Lou Morison, he gathered, was already a little in her cups. She was also a thoroughly nice girl, with a prattling spirit and no visible reticence.

"Tell me this, Mrs. Morison. Did Lynn think your engagement to Jay was serious?"

"*Everything* was serious to Lynn Thorndyke, Doctor. She

was that kind of girl. When Jay was teaching her to paint she held him off at first; when she found herself falling in love she made him meet her in secret. At least, that's the way *he* told the story."

The triangular tension was taking form now. At the apex the handsome young art instructor (a decent enough boy, though something of an opportunist). At one corner Mary Lou Donelson (a *femme du monde* from the cradle) playing a canny game of beaux, wearing Jay's pin while she stalked her eventual prey. In the other corner Lynn Thorndyke, who had never dared to date a man before, much less fall in love. . . . With different characters the situation might have had comic aspects. Here it had ended in tragedy.

"Believe me, Doctor, it was the most clandestine romance that campus had seen. When Jay told me, I couldn't believe my ears at first. I haven't told a living soul to this day. Doesn't that prove a woman can keep a secret?"

"Please don't think I'm prying, Mrs. Morison. I've a reason for every question I ask. Did you give Jay back his pin, ever?"

"Of course I did, the week before exams. I even pretended to be brokenhearted, so he'd have some idea of what he was missing." Again the mistress of Far Hills dimpled—and rose to freshen her drink. "He was still quite nice about it all. Said that Lynn couldn't live without him—and hoped I'd forgive him for jilting me."

"Did you?"

"Of course not. Why should I let him get off so lightly? I walked out with the last word—that's a woman's privilege. Told him not to be surprised at *anything* I might do. Then I jumped in my car and drove to Loon Lake. I'd just been invited there—to spend the weekend at the Morison lodge: it was the last big party before exams. I didn't tell Jay. I wanted him to be miserable, until Monday at least——"

The rest of Mary Lou's story was a comedy of errors that somehow failed to end happily. There had been aquaplaning at Loon Lake, and water skiing. An expert at the latter, Mary Lou had outdone herself in jumping and running the slalom course.

Lee Morison (the man she had long since decided to marry) had been dazzled by her skill. It was sheer bad luck that a final slalom had spilled her in the center of the lake—where she had almost drowned before help could reach her.

A pulmotor had been rushed to the scene—and for a while her life had hung in the balance. That evening a rumor had spread on the campus that she was dead. Evidently it had reached Lynn only a few hours after Jay had told her of the broken engagement, and of Mary Lou's tearful departure. . . . Lynn had left Glenville that same night on the express to Atlanta. From Atlanta she had flown direct to New Orleans and boarded the *Creole Belle.* Jay, in hot pursuit, had just failed to overtake her with the tidings that Mary Lou was safe and sound.

"Dr. Corwin, did she run away because she thought I'd committed *suicide*?"

"Isn't it a logical deduction?"

"I didn't mean to hurt *Lynn*—really and truly. I just wanted to punish Jay."

"Please don't blame yourself, Mrs. Morison."

"When I heard she'd had a breakdown, I was brokenhearted. She *is* getting well, isn't she? That's why you're here—to clear up this silly mistake once and for all?"

"I came to clear things up," said Jim soberly. "What you've told me may help eventually. I've no way of reaching the patient."

"Don't tell me she's honest-to-goodness *insane*, Doctor."

"At the moment Lynn Thorndyke seems a hopeless case. The fault isn't yours. Her flight from the university was the culmination of a disorder that had been years in building. In other words, her psychosis was already present when she fastened her affections on Thompson. You might call that fastening a last-minute compensation——" Jim paused, wondering how much of this lecture on elementary psychology was reaching Mary Lou. "When Lynn was a student at Glenville, I doubt if she was capable of giving real love—or receiving it. You might say the boy is well out of an impasse."

When he climbed into the ambulance for the last time that

day, he knew Mary Lou would keep his visit a secret. The cold breath of Leyden State Hospital had brushed the doorsill of Far Hills, however distantly. Mrs. Morison's recoil had been instinctive.

Had Jay Thompson made his own recoil, obeying the same reflex that separates the well and the sick? There was but one answer to that question—and Jay himself had made it. Obviously he had done his duty (as he saw it) with the dispatch of his radiogram from New Orleans. Pondering the disadvantages of marriage to so obvious a misfit as Lynn Thorndyke, he had simply returned to Glenville, taken his degree, and made his escape to Paris. Who could say he had acted unwisely—now that Lynn had vanished into a locked ward at Leyden?

Long before the ambulance swung into the hospital gate, Jim had dismissed the boy from his mind. With Lynn's file folder before him once again, he put together his own notes of the day on his portable typewriter and found them anything but meaningful:

> Patient was born to easy circumstances. Elder of two children (a brother died in infancy).
>
> No lack of security. A total lack of love? Father's place in picture?
>
> Child of broken home, patient remained with mother. Father died shortly after separation. (Suicide?)
>
> Last parental tie severed when mother went abroad. Ego nourished, for a time, by success at painting. Belated fumble at romance with Jay Thompson. Chance at happiness broken beyond repair by patient's flight.
>
> Clear guilt complex here—thanks to mistaken belief that Mary Lou Donelson had died of broken heart, with patient herself as cause. . . .

He put the notes aside with a sigh that combined weariness and despair. Until he could talk to Lynn's mother, he told himself, he would only be running in circles: the fact that Jay Thompson's relation to the girl was now crystal-clear only deepened the gloom that shrouded her origin. Shocking though the news of Mary Lou's supposed suicide had been, he was convinced that it could not, in itself, have caused Lynn's hagridden flight from the university, to say nothing of her mental collapse. Rather, it must have been the spark that had triggered a long chain reaction, whose beginnings stretched into the past.

This time it was easy to compose a note to Mrs. Thorndyke, requesting that she appear at Leyden. Without the slightest compunction he suggested that her daughter might recover, with the proper therapy, but that such therapy could begin only with her help. It was a dangerous game, he knew. The odds seemed worth the try.

Fifty thousand dollars was not a sum to be surrendered lightly. So long as Lynn's case had seemed beyond salvage, Mrs. Thorndyke had been willing to bury her in Leyden. He was sure she would give him what information she could, if the choice lay between life and death.

viii

Next morning the weekly staff conference was held in the lounge. At Dr. Frankel's suggestion Jim sat down with the others, though he had no patients to present.

In the ordinary hospital routine, Dr. Singh had explained, new patients were seen by the admitting physician during the admission period each day and were questioned briefly in order that a tentative diagnosis might be made. They were then assigned to the ward that suited their condition. During the next few days, basic lab tests were run; the physician in charge took the history and made a detailed examination. If the patient posed an unusual problem, he was interviewed by Dr. Frankel, who might suggest further exploration, such as an encephalogram or brain-wave test if an organic disorder seemed the root of the trouble.

Finally, when the examinations were finished—but never

more than a week after admission—the cases were presented at a staff conference for final diagnosis and discussion of treatment, if other than simple domiciliary care was to be administered.

Staff conferences were attended by all the doctors, including Meeker. Today, however, the director was at the state capital on business. Lisa Kendall, looking even more poised then usual in a crisp white uniform, moved briefly through the lounge to say a civil word to each man present before she drifted away on business of her own. Again her hand seemed to rest in Jim's for an extra interval, as she put a few sympathetic questions: remembering Keegan's warning, he wondered if she had been told to sound him out. He watched her trim figure vanish through the door with real relief. Lisa Kendall was a type all too familiar to his intern days, and he could only pray that he would be spared her teasing allure in the future.

This morning the first case was Dr. Singh's. He got up and faced the group, sorting his notes as he moved.

"My patient is a twenty-two-year-old female named Susie Learoyd," he said in his precise English. "By profession, a waitress. Her parents are rural storekeepers from River County. Susie complains that people are hatching plots against her and destroying her reputation with their gossip. She was committed when she threw a cup of coffee in a patron's face because she said she could read his mind. At night—and sometimes by day—she hears voices threatening her with punishment for her sins. These include an affair with a married man—which continued for some time, until she discovered he was not, as he told her, a widower. Since then, she has felt that her adultery was unpardonable. Attendance at an evangelist's service only made her more conscious of her sin—and exaggerated the voices."

"What about family background?" asked Frankel.

"Both parents work in the father's general store at River Crossing. Originally they were farm folk"—Singh paused with an apologetic smile—"what are known locally as red-necks. People of shallow educational opportunities, and deep religious feelings amounting at times to mania. Mr. Learoyd is a hard worker. He has little time for churchgoing. Mrs. Learoyd, however, is a constant penitent at revival meetings. When her daughter consented to join her cult she was delighted——"

"Is Susie an only child?" asked Welles. A stenographer's notebook was open before him. He was taking Singh's report almost verbatim, with copious annotations of his own.

"There is one younger brother, who is the mother's favorite. Patient does not admit envying the boy—but envy is still apparent. Both, in the mother's own words, were 'well brought-up.' Patient, whose I.Q. is only sixty, did poorly in school and left in eighth grade to work in the nearby commercial town of Seaverville. In school and later, she preferred being by herself to playing with other girls. She shunned boys until she was grown—in fact, until the incident which seems to have precipitated her condition. Before that time she kept much to her room, where she played the same records endlessly, and read motion-picture and the so-called 'confession' magazines."

"I gather you've seen the family," said Frankel.

"Only the mother: the father could not leave the store for an interview. She believes the illness is a punishment sent from God because Susie refused to join the church when a child. She does not know of the affair with a married man."

"Bring Susie in," said Frankel.

The girl walked into the room with an attendant at her elbow and was given a chair. She was pretty in a superficial way, with white skin that seemed transparent and the general air of emaciation so common among families of her class. Her eyes roved vacantly: already, after two days at Leyden, Jim had seen that identical, empty look on a hundred faces.

At a nod from Frankel, Singh took his place in the semicircle of chairs. The head physician settled at the interrogation table with a notebook before him.

"How are you, Susie?"

"All right, I reckon." The girl's voice was without inflection. It seemed to come from a slight distance, as though she had only half heard the examiner's query.

"Do you like it here?"

"No, sir, I don't."

"Why not?"

"Shut up and fingerprinted, like I did some crime? Why would I like it?"

"Have you committed a crime?"

"I guess so. Ma says it was a sin against God to stay away from church."

"Is she right?"

"I reckon so."

"Do you know why you are here?"

"I guess I'm crazy. This is the nut farm, ain't it?"

"This is a hospital, Susie, and we're here to help you. But you must tell us all about yourself."

"Ain't much to tell. That fellow in the restaurant was saying things about me——"

"Aloud?"

"In his head—but I heard 'em. So I threw coffee in his eyes."

"Are you sorry for what you did, Susie?"

"I dunno. I reckon so."

"What was this man saying in his head?"

"That I was bad—did bad things. Like going with a married man." Her voice rose a little. "I told the doc all about it. That one there—the foreigner."

"But that's all over, isn't it?"

Susie was breathing hard now, and her mouth was tense. "Sure it's over: I told him off proper, soon as I found he was married. I ain't no Jezebel, to go running after men."

"We all know that, Susie," said Frankel gently. "Nobody is accusing you of anything wrong."

"*They* are. They won't let me alone."

"Who are they?"

"The people out there. They try to use electricity on me. They watch me on TV——"

"You've been on television, Susie?"

"*They're* on TV—no matter what program I turn on. They watch me, right out of the screen."

"Do they speak to you?"

"Sometimes. They want to make me bad—but I won't let them."

"I'm sure you won't. Not after we've helped you."

"If you really want to help me, turn me loose."

"Not until you're well, Susie. You're a sick girl now."

"I could take care of everything—if they'd only let me be."

"Who are they?"

"I told you. People. Children."

"The children of the man you were going with?"

"Them—and others. But I won't let them hurt me." Her face had taken on a sly look. "They don't know it, but I got powers to stop 'em."

"What kind of powers?"

"Just powers."

"Who gave them to you?"

"God."

"When did you get this gift?"

"When I was first received in Christ." Her voice was strident now. "Like Brother Radford said when he was preaching. If you have faith, God will give you power to overcome your enemies."

"Do you possess such powers?"

"Yes, Doctor. I ain't used 'em yet. When I do, you can't hold me here. With God's help I can walk right through these walls. Nobody can stop me."

"We don't want to stop you from doing what's best for you, Susie," said Frankel gently. "We want to show you how to live like other people and be happy again. You want that, don't you?"

"I reckon so."

"Will you let us help you, then?"

"If you want. I don't mind."

"Good. We'll start by giving you some treatments to make you better. Just trust us—and I think you'll soon be well."

"All right." The voice had sunk to a sullen mutter. "Can I go now?"

"Yes, you may go."

When the attendant had taken Susie out, Frankel turned to Dr. Singh. "What's the diagnosis, Chandra?"

"Schizophrenia, certainly," said the Hindu. "I would like to think of it as a simple case, in a developing phase—but there are elements of paranoia already present."

"Excellent. Will the rest of you gentlemen give your views?"

The vote was generally in agreement. When it was Jim's turn to speak he shook his head. "I'm hardly qualified to express an opinion," he said. "But Dr. Singh's diagnosis seems accurate to me."

Frankel nodded. "In a way, this is a textbook case," he said. "I think it merits comment, since it illustrates the disease process on simple lines. We have, first, a girl of limited intelligence in a home characterized by a narrow—in fact, almost a medieval—outlook. The father is a small businessman, probably with little interest or understanding of his children: evidently he has left them to the mother. She, too, is warped—overstrict, an obsessional personality type with strong religious convictions. Following the birth of her brother, the girl undoubtedly suffered a feeling of rejection much stronger than is usual among elder siblings. In this case, she considered herself rebuffed by her mother."

Welles spoke without lifting his eyes from his notebook. "Perhaps she was correct in that assumption, sir. Doesn't the obsessional type of woman frequently concentrate her affections on the male children in her family?"

"A good point, Dr. Welles," said Frankel. "Certainly Susie buttoned up her reactions through childhood—probably hating the brother and distrusting others because she feared other rebuffs. When she became a woman and faced the problem of satisfying a woman's normal desires, she felt the same need to withdraw from reality for fear of being hurt. She followed this pattern for some time—existing in a closed circle, finding release in such make-believe as movies, television, aphrodisiacal records, confession magazines. When such a girl falls in love she generally goes overboard completely. The discovery that her first real love object was married, therefore, was shattering. The wound was simply too much for her."

Singh held up his hand. "Might one say that, for a brief period, Susie let herself be a woman—the thing she had hesitated to do in the past—and that the effort ended in disaster?"

"You're right, Doctor. Thereafter she has simply taken the easiest way—and shut all her unresolved conflicts from the conscious part of her mind."

"Does that mean her desires are now expressed in the form of other people—who, as she says, are 'working against her'?"

"Exactly," said Frankel. "In Susie's case, a mythical something *she* cannot dominate exercises absolute control over her. It is the essence of schizophrenia—the epitome of the 'split personality,' so-called. Of course, that mythical something is only the part of her personality she will not admit to consciousness. Naturally she considers it an alien, an independent being: it must be distorted to justify its existence."

"Can you call the illness itself a compromise?" Jim asked.

"That's just what it is," said Frankel. "A compromise with reality, an outlet for the patient's emotions she could never voice otherwise. Since Susie can't tolerate the tension her own urges cause, she attributes them to this second self who is trying to influence her—what the Germans call a *doppelgänger*. In this case, and in the worst sense, her alter ego."

"Is it not true," asked Singh, "that some schizophrenics describe their voices as a person—who even tries to love them?"

"So they do," said Frankel. "That's because they need love so badly they search for it within themselves. The *doppelgänger*, at least, will never rebuff them as the world has done."

"What about treatment?" asked Jim.

"What would you suggest, Dr. Corwin?"

"Can't the patient be led to see where her troubles began? Surely psychotherapy is indicated—or, perhaps, outright analysis?"

"Both are important," Frankel agreed. "In this case they may even be vital. If we had time, a trained analyst might lead Susie back to the roots of her trauma. But I'm afraid we would fail, even if such treatment were feasible. One deterrent is her limited mental capacity. Another is the fact that the schizophrenic clings to his symptoms as an escape from the hard decisions that await him outside the domain of his illness. Where we have so many patients we must compromise. In this case it means shock therapy."

"Can you hope for a cure that way?"

"Probably not," said Frankel. "And yet, in Susie's case, I think shock will break up the particular emotional pattern in which she's trapped. We may even send her home in time with some understanding of her difficulty. But the illness is almost sure to recur when another crisis comes." He closed the file folder and rose to face the group. "Will you vote for EST, gentlemen?"

Seven hands were raised in assent—Jim's a trifle reluctantly. "Wouldn't you say the sooner the better, Dr. Frankel?" asked Keegan.

"Yes, Doctor. You all saw the evidence of beginning excitement at certain points in my questioning: Susie is certain to become highly delusional and disturbed in the near future. Dr. Singh will give the first EST this afternoon." Frankel turned to Jim. "Later, Dr. Corwin, if the pattern seems beyond reversal, we may call on you. Lobotomy, as I see it, is our last resort in such cases. Do you agree?"

A last resort—and a cruel one, thought Jim. But he did no more than nod assent as the next case was presented. At the moment he was a man in a dark room, groping for an object he could not quite name—though he could sense its fearful contours clearly.

That afternoon Jim made his rounds of the wards without Singh's aid. Thanks to the attendants, and the entries on each chart, he found he could handle the work without too much fumbling. For all his surface efficiency (his years at Lakewood had paid priceless dividends here), he still felt lost in the welter of delusions, hallucinations, and bizarre symptoms so many of his patients presented. . . . Midway of his chores in the women's ward he felt his brain reel with weariness. It was a relief when the head physician joined him on the stair—just as he was bracing himself for his descent to the wailing inferno of Lovell One.

Fresh from an afternoon in the shock room, Frankel looked almost as exhausted as Jim.

"Singh tells me that Lynn Thorndyke's in stupor again," he said. "Mind if I have a look at her?"

"On the contrary," said Jim gratefully. "I've been nerving myself to ask your opinion."

Alone, he might have lacked the resolve to unlock Lynn's door. With Frankel beside him it seemed natural to enter the shadowed room again. The girl lay as he had left her, rigidly immobile, her apparently sightless eyes staring unwinkingly at the ceiling. Her chart indicated that she had been tube-fed twice daily since the stupor began. It was clear that Lynn Thorndyke's body, despite its pallor, was in perfect health. Yet Jim could not shake off a primitive fear in her presence—the conviction that she was truly dead, that this tiny, white-walled cell was an actual tomb.

"A most amazing case," said Frankel. "I hope it hasn't already driven you to despair."

"Is that what Dr. Singh told you?"

Frankel smiled. "Chandra said nothing—beyond reminding me that this girl was once your patient. It must be a heavy blow to find her here. Incidentally, what did you learn at Glenville?"

The Austrian listened in meditative silence while Jim repeated his findings. "Do you see any pattern in those notes you made?" he asked.

"Not yet."

"And yet, a pattern certainly exists." Frankel held up a detaining palm before Jim could speak. "I won't attempt to trace it for you now. Not until we've more data. It was an excellent idea to write Mrs. Thorndyke. Obviously, the woman's a monster of selfishness. But I'm sure you've struck the dominant chord in her nature—money."

"Do you think she'll pay us a visit?"

"Definitely—once your note reaches her. Few of us are stronger than our appetites. If I read her history correctly, Mrs. Thorndyke's penchant for travel abroad is surpassed only by her greed."

"Perhaps it was cruel of me, luring her with a forlorn hope," said Jim. "But I won't rest easy until I've learned what brought Lynn here."

"Don't waste pity on Mrs. Thorndyke," said Frankel dryly. "Remember, it's the cash she's after: her daughter's health is secondary. As for the mystery—I'm as eager as you to solve it. You understand, of course, that no amount of information can aid us—unless we can reach Lynn's mind and help her unburden herself?"

"After forty-eight hours in Leyden, I'm beginning to understand all too well."

Frankel looked down at the motionless girl. "If you've had a chance to examine the record, you know we used the standard approaches," he said. "Treatment with insulin is rare these days, since it's so difficult to administer—but we tried it. For a while I told myself it was helping, but it was only wishful thinking. In a few days she'd slipped back to—what you see before you. EST was no more effective. We discontinued it after a week, lest we do permanent damage to the brain. If all else fails, would you consider lobotomy?"

"I wouldn't hear of it!" Shocked by his own vehemence, Jim forced himself to speak in a normal tone. "Such a decision isn't mine. But I'd resign sooner than operate on Lynn."

The Austrian put a hand on Jim's arm. "Did you realize I brought up Susie Learoyd's case this morning for your benefit?"

Jim nodded dazedly. His mind was still numbed by the picture Frankel's words had raised. "Were you making a comparison between that girl—and Lynn?"

"In a sense. People like Susie can be helped, to a point. They can be sent back to their own little lives—and you can dismiss them from your mind, knowing you've done what you can. Even when you fail, you can wonder whether they aren't better off with their fantasies. But with someone as gifted as Lynn the waste can be heartbreaking."

"You've seen her paintings?"

"I spent an hour in the gallery the last time I lectured at Glenville. Art is my relaxation—and my greatest love, next to medicine. I speak with authority when I say this girl is a genius. What does a doctor do next—when he sees what a patient could give the world, and finds his hands are tied?"

Again Jim forced himself to answer calmly. "Proceed to the next case, I suppose—and never stop hoping."

"Good—I knew you'd say that. Meeker's in Atlanta for the weekend. He phoned to say those special instruments you ordered are on the way. Shall we schedule your first operation for Monday?"

"I can't start too soon, Kurt." Bewildered as he was by the long, grinding day, Jim was glad to turn back to a branch of medicine that had tested his skill and proved it. As they moved to the door he fought off another wave of giddiness and steadied himself against the wall, feeling the probe of Frankel's eyes. "Don't mind me, please. I'm learning my job too fast for comfort."

"Are you sure you're all right?"

"Quite. I'll soon adjust myself."

"Don't push too hard, Jim: I've been studying psychiatry for thirty years, and feel lost at times."

"I still can't wait to begin."

"Stop by my office after dinner. I'll leave a copy of *Brill's Lectures* on my desk. They'll do to launch you."

Frankel was gone with the words—walking with his odd, jerky stride, pausing for a moment to speak to the attendant before he vanished through the anteroom. It was only when the steel door closed that Jim realized he had offered himself as a pupil—and had just been accepted.

ix

By noon the next day the instruments for Jim's projected operative program had been unpacked and ranged on a special tray in the surgery. After consultation with Frankel, he scheduled four patients for Monday—starting with Enoch Williams, the former pharmacist.

The file informed him that Williams had suffered a complete breakdown almost ten years ago. For most of that time he had been confined to the same cell. Too destructive to mingle with the inmates, he had enjoyed no contact with his kind—save for the attendants who brought his food. The other operative cases had similar histories—frowsy, dirt-crusted veterans of Leyden who required constant vigilance, lest their unpredictable rages destroy them, as well as others in their reach.

Heavily sedated, Williams was brought to the operating table in the surgery, his drowsy thrashings controlled by the wise hands of Adam Strang. His jungle mat of hair had been shorn, his face scrubbed. No other preparation was necessary. The conjunctival sac of the eye (through which the probe would be inserted) was normally sterile, thanks to its constant bath of tears.

Janet Moore, who would handle the few instruments Jim required, exchanged a smile as she drew on her gloves.

"Looks almost human again, doesn't he?" she asked. "Think you can prove it, Doctor?"

The probe Jim had selected (a leucotome resembling the ice pick originally used for this type of surgery) lay ready on a sterile towel. Dr. Singh bustled in cheerfully, pushing the EST machine before him—a squarish box on wheels with an instrument panel worthy of a space ship: for this operation, electric shock served in lieu of anesthesia. At the surgeon's nod, a second attendant came forward to help strap the patient to the table. Jack Hanley (glowering as usual in the background) stood ready with a mouth gag wrapped in cloth. A second nurse was busy at the table's edge, smearing electrolyte jelly on the flat metal conductors now plugged to the machine via insulated wires.

The Hindu flicked a switch on his instrument board. "Ready when you are, Dr. Corwin."

Jim glanced round the room. Frankel had just come in to observe. He was a trifle startled to note that Meeker stood behind the chief physician, peering intently over his shoulder. Jim wondered how many years had gone by since the director of Leyden had witnessed an operation. The practice of medicine, as opposed to its profitable manipulation, was something Dr. Thaddeus Meeker had long since abandoned. Of that much he was sure.

"Ready, Dr. Singh."

"The machine is set for three hundred milliamperes, in two tenths of a second," said Singh. "I will give two shocks, a minute and a half apart. You may then start the lobotomy."

The assistant nurse, holding the electrodes in gloved hands, stepped forward and pressed them firmly against Williams' temples. At the contact, despite his sedation, the patient began squirming wildly, an automatic revulsion at a procedure his instincts had already recognized. Adam and his helper anchored the man's limbs to the table, and Hanley slipped the mouth gag between his teeth. At that precise moment, Dr. Singh pressed a button on the panel. The room filled with a low, vicious humming as the current surged through the patient's brain.

Williams' body stiffened, toes extended until the feet pointed almost directly downward, back arched like a taut longbow. Ankles and wrists strained at the cuffs so violently that the guards were hard pressed to keep him on the table. Foam sprang to his lips. Again and again his muscles were racked with convulsive spasms, shaking his human anchors until their own teeth rattled. Jim was already familiar with this form of torture. As always he felt he must cry out against the degradation of this man's body, even though the torture was intended for his benefit.

Then, as suddenly as it began, the current subsided. Williams lay inert under the attendants' grip. Singh was studying a stop watch. For a few seconds it seemed that the patient had ceased to breathe. Then he began inhaling in great, snoring gasps.

"Apnea, thirty seconds," said the Hindu. He made a note on the pad attached to the machine, recording the period of respiratory cessation—called apnea—that always followed electric shock. The attendants, who had relaxed their grip, did not leave their places. At Singh's nod, they snapped to their former pose. Once again the humming filled Jim's eardrums. As the second spasm abated, he held out his hand for the leucotome.

Adam Strang circled the table to place a palm at each of the patient's temples. Ordinarily, Jim knew, the deep coma that followed shock treatment would last long enough for him to complete the transorbital lobotomy—at least on the left side, where he had chosen to make his first entry. Those powerful hands were clamped to the patient's skull as insurance, in case of unlooked-for spasm.

Again Williams began his snoring intake of air. Jim moved to the head of the table. Tenting the left eyelid with a gauze sponge, he lifted the leucotome in his right hand, and spoke for the benefit of both team and observers.

"You can see that this probe is graduated into centimeter marks along the shaft," he said. "The depth to which it is inserted is usually seven centimeters from the edge of the eyelid."

He was already working the point of the leucotome into the conjunctival sac that surrounded the eye here—a simple technique, horrendous though it might seem to the layman. Then, setting the point firmly, he drove it through the thin layer of the eye-socket roof.

"I have now penetrated the bone—at a point opposite the pupil, two centimeters back of the frontal sinus. As the instrument is pushed deeper in this plane, it enters the frontal lobe. Entry is made about three centimeters from the mid-line—some two centimeters behind the frontal pole, at the end of the lobe itself."

It was a textbook reading, but he gave it as solemnly as he could—knowing, without raising his eyes from his work, that Frankel had bent forward to watch. His hands moved easily, steadying the eye socket as the instrument thrust deeper.

"I have now reached a depth of seven centimeters. By moving the instrument laterally, through a range of about fifteen degrees, and then medially in the same direction, I will sever the connections between this part of the frontal lobe and the thalamus, where the more primitive brain centers are located." While he spoke, his right hand was deftly carrying out the surgery he had just described. There was no reaction or resistance in the soft brain tissue—and only a little from the small puncture in the eye socket.

"With the handle of the instrument in the lateral position," Jim continued, "I will now make a deep frontal cut—elevating the handle until the shaft lies nearly parallel with the orbital plate. From this position the handle is returned to a plane parallel with the mid-line and then withdrawn."

The leucotome glided smoothly from the depths of the patient's skull. Still tenting the eyelid, Jim watched the tiny opening he had made in the conjunctival lining. There was no sign of blood to indicate a vessel had been injured. . . . When he looked up, he found that Frankel was still watching intently. There was no sign of Meeker.

Jim stood back to let the nurse repeat the routine of the electrodes. Again the painfully thin body on the table arched in convulsive spasms while the current was applied; there was the same collapse, followed by deep-toned snoring some thirty seconds after the final convulsion. Sure of his timing now, he moved to enter the right eye socket, repeating the exact procedure he had used in the left. The surgery completed, he glanced at the wall clock. The entire operation had taken less than twenty minutes.

There was a moment's pause before the next patient was brought to the table. At a nod from Frankel, Jim left his place and entered the anteroom. Meeker was standing at the window, puffing on his cigar.

"Congratulations, Corwin," he said, his ferret eyes snapping. "That was a remarkable bit of surgery."

Jim exchanged a glance with Frankel. He knew that the head physician was chuckling inwardly at Meeker's praise for an operation he had not troubled to watch—and certainly did not understand.

"The procedure is simple enough," he said. "What happens later will tell the story."

"Williams' reaction will be favorable," said the director. "So will the others—I feel it in my bones. You're making history here—don't think I'm not grateful. What do *you* say, Frankel?"

"As Dr. Corwin has just remarked, time will tell," said the Austrian.

Meeker seemed unaware that science had just administered a rebuke to greed. "See he has everything he needs," he ordered. "This investment will return dividends, gentlemen—for us all."

"We won't require much," said Jim. "Postoperative care is routine. But I'd like a complete record on each patient, in case we decide to report them in the literature."

"Consider it already done," boomed Meeker. "Dr. Frankel will concur, I'm sure. We've a fine record at Leyden, and I want everyone to know it." He left the room when Lisa Kendall appeared in the hall to say that a long-distance call awaited him. . . . This, Jim realized, was as close to praise as Meeker would ever come. He looked inquiringly at Frankel.

"That's probably Dr. Damphier on the phone," said the head physician. "The state hospital director. Our own man's a bit heavy in the tail—but he can move fast when need be."

"Don't tell me he's *already* calling this program a success?"

"You can be sure he's laying the groundwork. Just as he'll claim every ounce of credit if you do succeed."

Jim shrugged. "Let him—so long as he gives us a free hand."

The three remaining cases were finished without difficulty. Like Williams, they were moved to recovery rooms in the surgery. The following morning Jim felt it was safe to return them to their wards. As he had expected, the change in each case was already noticeable.

These, he reminded himself, were the incurables of Brown One. For years they had been dangerous problems, so far as everyday care was concerned. Now, twenty-four hours after lobotomy, they were sleeping in cots again—and their slumber was deep and natural. In their first period of wakefulness, three of the four had entirely lost their tensions. The fourth patient (an eighteen-year inmate) relapsed briefly, cursing the guards and denying that he had ever had an operation. Then he, too, slipped into the profound relaxation that was the most striking feature of postoperative behavior.

On the second day, Jim ordered all four cases from their beds. Under the watchful eyes of the attendants they were made to bathe, dress, and feed themselves. For years they had refused to follow these simple routines. Now they accepted orders with a docility that was both heartening and pathetic. By the fifth day, all four were eating with excellent appetites and were able to perform dressing and bathroom functions unaided.

Enoch Williams, whose progress was especially marked, was gaining weight at an amazing rate and had already asked for a newspaper. The demon-ridden skeleton which Jim had seen that first day at Leyden was now a docile little man with myopic eyes and perfect manners. Watching him puzzle over the headlines from a world he had left more than ten years ago, he felt this was magic made visible.

After his success with this first quartet, Jim was forced to select carefully from the host of patients presented by the staff. Working closely with Frankel, he went over each case in detail before scheduling surgery. Since the reports on lobotomy indicated that advanced schizophrenia—particularly among the elderly, who had become entirely disoriented over the years—seldom improved with any permanence, such cases could only make the final report look poorer by their presence. On the other hand, there was the dramatic recovery of Williams (who, after a fortnight, was able to work in the hospital pharmacy) as evidence that few cases could be classed as incurable. Medical logic, in these first weeks of trial and error, fought a losing battle with the evidence before his eyes. It was difficult indeed to deny the benefits of surgery to any who might be helped.

Operations were now scheduled at three-day intervals, whenever staff conferences did not intervene (Jim noted, with secret amusement, that Meeker was attending these meetings regularly, with a stenographer beside him). The task of selecting patients was a formidable one, and postoperative inspection was arduous. Both Jim and Frankel were determined to make their records foolproof. From the start they had devised a special form on which the attendants could make daily notations and thus obtain a behavior profile of individual patients.

Four weeks after his operation on Williams, Jim crossed his fingers on his first tentative conclusion: transorbital lobotomy seemed far safer than the more extensive procedure Anton Ziegler had used at Lakewood. True, a few cases developed convulsions—but none to a dangerous degree. Some turned into literal robots. These were quiet creatures who did as they were told, performed any task they were assigned, ate when they were herded to the dining room, dressed themselves on command—and seemed, even in their most wakeful moments, to be sleepwalking. . . . Jim could only look on such cases with an emotion that mingled resignation and dismay—but he was quick to note that Meeker made no real distinction between these perambulating zombies and Enoch Williams.

All of them, in the director's view, were useful—and the disturbance in the locked wards had decreased at an amazing rate. With many of these former incurables now added to the work force (and the others far easier to manage) the turnover of attendants had also decreased sharply.

Had Meeker been given his way, Jim would have staged daily operations and doubled the number of patients who came to the table. But he was adamant in his refusal to accept cases where he felt nothing would be gained. Here, as he had expected, Frankel supported him.

x

Five weeks after his arrival at Leyden, Jim met the Austrian in his office for the first definite evaluation of a half hundred file folders on patients who had submitted to lobotomy. So far there had not been a single fatality—though both doctors were aware that this record could not possibly be continued. The literature on the operation was now fairly extensive. Yet no observer had been able to explain why a few patients still died following the procedure, regardless of the approach employed.

Frankel turned the last chart face downward on the desk and reached for his pipe. Intent on detail, they had spoken only in snatches through the long, meticulous checking. Jim drew a deep breath before he asked the inevitable question.

"What d'you think, Kurt?"

"First—and perhaps most important—you've been working much too hard."

"I won't deny it's been a grind."

"How much sleep do you average?"

"Five to six hours a night. I've been studying a lot."

"So I've observed, Jim. You've learned a great deal since you came here."

"Mostly from you."

The Austrian smiled. "I'd like to believe that—but I know better. Mostly you've learned procedures firsthand. I can tell by your comments at staff meetings. One thing you *haven't* learned—to stop driving yourself."

"I've had my days off. I played seven innings of baseball yesterday."

Jim touched the palm of his left hand gingerly. One of his off-hour duties was the coaching of rival baseball teams organized among nonviolent inmates. Yesterday, when the regular catcher of the Browns had pulled a muscle, he had gone into the game to backstop Clint Prescott. The former star of the Orioles (who seemed to have staged a complete recovery after his operation) had pitched a no-hitter, using nothing but a fast ball and an occasional change of pace.

"I watched that game," said Frankel. "Not that I'm an authority on your national pastime—but even on the diamond, you seemed to be working rather than playing."

"It was important to make sure Clint won."

"I wish you could have delegated the job."

Jim knew he was flushing. This was no time to tell Frankel that he had kept constantly busy for one dominant reason—

work and more work was a sure antidote to the hard, overriding fact that the problem of Lynn Thorndyke's illness remained unsolved. Inured as he was to the banshee howls of Lovell One, it had chilled him to the marrow yesterday when he made his tour of that ward—only to realize that the girl had emerged from her stupor again and had joined the demonic chorus. Mrs. Foster's calm acceptance of the fact had added nothing to his peace of mind. This, she had reminded him, was only the other extreme of the cyclic pattern Lynn had followed since her admittance. . . . A panther screaming defiance from its cage could not have been more inhuman than this snarling creature when she had flung herself headlong against her cell door in a vain effort to claw her way to freedom.

Until he had forced himself to witness that manic frenzy, it had seemed logical to close his thoughts to lobotomy so far as Lynn was concerned. It was another matter now. He knew he possessed the power to bring her from darkness to light, after a moment's sleight-of-hand with a leucotome. Did it matter too much if the light proved murky—when each day was bringing the girl closer to the point of no return?

"Sorry, Kurt," he murmured. "I'm one of those fellows who aims for bedrock. Until this program has paid off, I *can't* settle down."

"You won't be much help to us if you fall ill. We need you badly at Leyden, Jim. As a doctor, not a patient."

"Do you feel the program has proved itself?"

"Not with only fifty histories. We'll need hundreds before we reach a true verdict. But I'll say this now—for a certain type of illness, your probe is a godsend."

"Incidentally, when are these fifty cases going home?"

The head physician frowned. "I fear there's a stumbling block at the gate."

"Meeker?"

"Our director is primarily interested in a work force here. Or what he calls occupational therapy."

"There's damned little therapy in running a laundry mangle, or hoeing corn on the farm."

"I agree with you there. But if we start releasing too many inmates, the other hospitals will begin dumping their worst cases here. From Meeker's viewpoint, more patients mean more expense—his *bête noire.*"

"Don't tell me you're backing him?"

"Passively I suppose I am." Frankel rose abruptly and moved to a window. From where he stood, Jim knew the head physician had an unobstructed view of the small, neat cottage that had been his home for nine years. He recalled his visits to that haven—the delicious meals Frankel's plump Viennese wife had served in the tiny dinette, the two stalwart boys who were growing to manhood as American citizens. It was easy to understand the older doctor's reluctance. Havens of any sort had been rare in Kurt Frankel's life. He had every reason to cling to this one.

"Sorry if I sounded off, Kurt."

Frankel turned. "I'm glad you did. I haven't asked myself that question for some time. And I *have* supported the system here—for want of a better."

"I'm sure you had good reasons."

"One of them—the greatest—is the fact that Meeker allows me elbow room. So long as I give him lip service, I can do as I like. Believe me, that's a priceless boon. Other hospitals in the state aren't nearly so fortunate."

"So I've been told."

"I can speak firsthand, Jim. I've talked to other doctors at psychiatric meetings. Most of them are so tied down by red tape they hardly have time to see the patients."

"Don't forget your school for psychiatrists," Jim reminded him. "Isn't that worth something too?"

"I've sent some good men into outside practice," the Austrian agreed. "Don't think I'm unhappy as a teacher. But I still can't find an answer for the question you've asked me."

"I had no right to ask it."

"As a doctor you had every right. Why should we stand by and let Meeker cut costs? It's axiomatic in state hospital work that more money means more patient care—and there's never enough of either. But if I started demanding funds, I'd only stir up discord, maybe destroy a system that runs adequately, after its fashion. Let's admit that a few dozen people are kept in Leyden because they fill a bed, do some necessary work—and cause no trouble——"

"Are you sure it's only a few dozen?"

"Very well. Suppose this lobotomy program creates a hundred harmless slaves for Meeker's work force—or even more. You must admit most of them are content. Some, like Prescott and Williams, are slowly improving themselves. We'll restore them to society in time. A few more will follow later. In all honesty, I think we should keep the others where they are."

"I can agree—to a point."

"Have you any idea what the average ex-patient from a mental hospital must endure when he returns home—the isolation, the suspicion, even the downright abuse?" The Austrian went to his desk and balanced the stack of file folders on his palms. "*We* know how much these poor devils have improved. Their families don't. In most cases they'd seem useless misfits."

"Surely we can prove otherwise."

"Jim, there are some rules of society you'll never change. I won't say these people are better off at Leyden, working for Meeker. You can't deny they're safer."

A week later Jim was still brooding over the head physician's words after he had paid his daily visit to Lovell One. There was no change in Lynn Thorndyke's condition. His ears rang with her imprecations when he left the ward. Today his only consolation was the cable in his pocket: it had reached him that morning, announcing the return of Mrs. Florence Thorndyke from abroad—and the fact that she was honoring him with a visit.

The following day, the cyclic pattern of Lynn's illness repeated itself—and she lapsed again into stupor. Jim was pacing the walk outside the women's ward when he was aware of Frankel's gaunt silhouette, hurrying along the driveway that led from his cottage to his office door. Normally he would have permitted the older doctor to follow that path undisturbed. Today he called a greeting.

Frankel listened with his familiar, quiet intentness while Jim sketched the latest setback in Lovell One.

"You're about to ask a favor," he said. "I can tell by your voice. Out with it."

"I'll be seeing Mrs. Thorndyke soon," said Jim. "As you know, I've great hopes for that meeting."

Frankel nodded. "With luck, we may get a complete picture of what caused Lynn's illness. We've yet to find a way to reach her mind."

"Kurt, there *is* a way to reach her. Have you ever tried a sodium cyanide injection in cases of this kind? I saw Alex Goldschmidt use it in Baltimore—on an identical case."

"The results are never permanent, Jim. Basically it's only a stimulant to respiration."

"At least it would tell us whether her mind has deteriorated."

"So it would."

"May I try it, while she's in stupor?"

"I've a half hour to spare," said Frankel. "Let's give the injection now."

Jim had made his request spontaneously—only half hoping it would be granted. He had never expected this prompt acceptance. But he had no choice, now that Frankel was marching across the portico. Singh was on the ward, checking tomorrow's list of operations with Janet Moore. The nurse went at once for a syringe and an ampule of the drug. . . . Jim knew he was trembling as he turned the key in Lynn's door. If the sodium cyanide revealed an already deteriorated psyche, he would have no choice but lobotomy—if only to make sure Lynn did not injure herself permanently in one of her manic rages.

The girl was lying on her cot once again, much as he first remembered her—immobile as a statue and quite as lovely. He felt his vision blur a little when he bent to take her pulse. *Kurt's right,* he told himself angrily. *You've been working much too hard. It isn't like you to admit defeat in advance.*

Janet Moore came in with the instrument tray. She glanced

at Jim inquiringly, while she lifted the towel for their inspection.

"Will you inject, Dr. Corwin?"

"No, Miss Moore. Will you take the syringe, Dr. Singh? I want to be free to question her."

He thrust his hands into his pockets and moved to the head of the cot—hoping the others had not noticed how badly his fingers were twitching. No one spoke while the Hindu began injecting slowly. . . . Jim kept his eyes on the plunger of the syringe—reminding himself that the vial of sodium cyanide was diluted well below poison level, and how brief the patient's reaction had been in Baltimore.

Lynn had not stirred under the needle. Save for her quiet, even breathing she showed no outward sign of life.

Frankel broke the silence. "In a moment, respiration will appear to cease. Then—if her reaction is normal—it should increase markedly."

Recalling the astounding change he had witnessed at the Scripps Institute, Jim held his own breath as it repeated under his eyes. Bit by bit Lynn's breathing quickened—and, with each intake of oxygen, her cheeks grew pinker. Before, her beauty had been, at best, a wan thing, shadowed by death in the making. Now she seemed vividly alive—far more alive than the girl he had known so briefly aboard the *Creole Belle.*

"She's waking up," Singh whispered.

The girl's eyelids fluttered as the Hindu spoke. In another moment the intense blue eyes Jim remembered so well looked up at the four faces above the cot as calmly as though she had just emerged from normal slumber. It was a tranquil look, unclouded by doubt. Her lips framed a smile of greeting, before she spoke in the barest of whispers.

"Hello, Dr. Corwin."

He heard his own voice respond, and rejoiced in its steadiness. "Hello, Lynn. How did you know my name?"

"You've been my doctor—for over a month."

"Why haven't you spoken to me before?" She had not mentioned their meeting aboard the freighter—nor did the omission surprise him. The *Creole Belle* was now part of the unplumbed past.

Lynn had frowned at the question—but her smile, when it returned, was peaceful as before. "I'm not sure, Dr. Corwin. Something wouldn't let me speak."

"Do you know Dr. Frankel? Dr. Singh? And Miss Moore?"

"Of course. Dr. Singh was in charge here before you came. You're the new surgeon—who has helped so many people."

"How did you know that?"

"Miss Moore and Mrs. Foster speak of you often."

"Will you let me help you too?"

"With the operation?"

"No, Lynn. By talking of the past—as we're talking now. By learning why you're ill—and taking the cause away."

"If you can."

"You want to get well, don't you?"

"Yes. I must go on with my painting."

"Is that the only reason?"

"I—suppose so, Doctor."

He noticed the slight hesitation and hurried on. "We'll help you to paint, Lynn. I'll get you brushes——" His eye went to the syringe in Singh's hand. The position of the plunger told him it was empty.

"I'd like to paint again, Dr. Corwin——" The last words were slurred—and the rise and fall of her breast had slowed perceptibly. Across the cot, Frankel was already shaking his head in warning.

"*Lynn!* I want to go on helping——"

"I'll let you know—when I'm ready."

The words were barely uttered: he wondered afterwards if he had imagined them. This was the voice of a patient already under anesthesia, about to fall asleep. Jim bent forward to ask one more question and saw it was useless. Once again the girl's face and body had assumed their familiar, masklike rigidity.

He forced himself to meet Frankel's eyes. Despite the older man's warning he had been half convinced he could keep Lynn rational, once the injection had roused her. Now, he felt nothing beyond the crushing weight of his failure.

"At least we know her mind hasn't broken permanently," said Frankel. "That could mean a great deal."

"How—when we can't reach her for more than a moment?"

"We may find a way, Jim."

"Not with cyanide, that's evident." He nodded his thanks to Janet Moore, and stumbled through the door. The treatment, experimental at best, had its dangers. Their meager gains could hardly justify a second injection of so toxic a drug.

Frankel stayed close beside him until they reached the anteroom door. "At least you've seen one thing clearly, Jim. Her need to escape reality is still overpowering. Far too strong for her rational mind to cope with." He rested his hand on Jim's arm momentarily, then turned away.

Jim made no effort to follow, though his chores were ended until tomorrow. Instead, he stood irresolute at the door of the chartroom, torn between the urge to return to Lynn's side and the irrational desire to admit defeat and flee. His brain whirled in an effort to choose between those alternatives. . . . Curiously, when Singh emerged from the ward he seemed to be whirling too—a plump white top that threatened to spin off into the blue. Jim put out a hand to bring his friend to earth—and found he was clutching thin air, on the edge of a pit that had opened mysteriously in the floor.

When he came to his senses his forehead was resting on the chartroom table. Janet Moore was behind him, steadying him in the chair. He found he could lift his head to accept the glass that Singh was offering. He recognized the sharp odor of ammonia, the flat, alkaline taste.

"You didn't quite keel over," said the nurse.

"Not quite," said the Hindu cheerfully. "I caught you in time. *Now* will you admit you've been overdoing?"

Frankel had prescribed a thorough checkup and a week in the staff infirmary. Jim had not argued too strenuously. He was convinced that his illness was not serious. But it had been sheer luxury to submit to the ministrations of others, to sleep the clock around and waken to watch the telecast of the Yankee-Braves game in Miami, now that spring training was under way in Florida.

On the fourth morning of his enforced rest period, Frankel and Singh came into his room together.

"Will I live, gentlemen?"

"For quite a while," said Frankel with a smile. "Once we've brought down your blood pressure."

"*Blood pressure?* Mine's never been high."

"It was one-eighty over a hundred ten when you were admitted here."

"I can't believe it."

Frankel handed the chart to Singh. "Give him our prognosis, Chandra," he said. "And our prescription. You're our specialist in internal medicine."

"Rest has brought the reading down to one-sixty over one hundred," said the Hindu. "But there's no doubt about it, Jim. Over the past few months you've worked yourself into a mild case of essential hypertension."

Now that he thought back, Jim saw there was no arguing the verdict. The severe neck pains and headaches that he'd suffered from lately completed the picture. The attack of vertigo had been only a final warning.

"You mentioned a prescription, I believe?"

"I'm going to put you on Rauwolfia. In my country, it has been used for centuries to ease tension."

Rauwolfia. Jim had seen the word in medical journals—though he could not pin down its meaning.

"Isn't that some kind of root?"

"It comes from a plant that grows in India. Pharmacologists

have isolated the active fraction—a drug called reserpine. So far, the use isn't widespread. But in cases like yours, where there's been no permanent damage, the results have been remarkable."

"Does that mean I can resume work?"

"Within limits," said Frankel. "Doing one man's job, let us say, instead of three."

"I promise to behave," said Jim. "When do I start?"

"I've brought the first dose with me," said Singh.

As the Indian doctor had predicted, the effects of the drug were remarkable. By the next day, Jim noted a definite lessening of the malaise that had pursued him, the slow, angry throbbing at his temples when his mind turned to Lynn. It was a strange effect—quieting, but with none of the drowsiness that accompanied ordinary sedatives. Indeed, he could not recall when his mind had seemed more alert, his critical faculties sharper. . . . This, Singh explained, was a standard reaction—and insisted on continued bed rest.

On the third day after the drug was started, Jim's chart showed a thirty-point drop in blood pressure, confirming the Hindu's belief that there had been no permanent change in the circulation.

"Does this mean I can discontinue the drug?"

"By no means," said the Indian doctor. "We'll keep the dosage constant for at least a month. Does it bother you at all?"

"I can't remember when I felt better. It's a curious sensation—as though actual weights were lifting from my brain. Even when I think of Lynn—and how we've failed with her."

"The effect certainly involves a lessening of tension."

"How? By calming the emotions that cause it?"

"So we Hindus believe. Rauwolfia has been a panacea among us for countless years. Native doctors will grind the crude root to a powder and use it to relieve many illnesses."

Jim smiled. "Just as back-country housewives once used foxglove as a remedy for dropsy?"

"The story of Rauwolfia is even more romantic. One legend has it that the mongoose chews the leaves of the plant before attacking a cobra. Such tales are fanciful, of course. Yet they contain a grain of truth."

"More than a grain, Chandra—if you'll consider me an example. For my money, it's the discovery of the age."

A few days later, when Singh had permitted him to leave his bed, Jim found himself badly in need of the calming effects of reserpine. The Atlanta paper that arrived with his breakfast tray was folded back to the page devoted to regional news. In the place of honor was a three-column cut of Dr. Thaddeus Meeker. Beneath it, a fat black headline stood out boldly:

> LEYDEN DIRECTOR ANNOUNCES
> WONDER CURE FOR THE INSANE
>
> Dr. Thaddeus Meeker, director of Leyden State Hospital, revealed today that, in line with his policy of keeping treatment for his patients abreast of latest medical developments, a new operation is bringing amazing results in his so-called "violent wards."
>
> "Transorbital lobotomy" is the name of this new technique. It was described by Dr. Meeker as absolutely safe, and remarkably effective in restoring disturbed patients to a normal routine.
>
> Thanks to the operation—it was performed recently on some fifty "hopeless" cases—Dr. Meeker believes many mental patients will, in future, "find the road back much less arduous."
>
> "Our fifty cases," he continued, "have been thoroughly rejuvenated. Most of them are now working happily in the occupational therapy rooms of the hospital. One, a former druggist named Enoch Williams, who had been a Leyden inmate for nearly ten years, is now presiding in the hospital pharmacy. Others, who (like Williams) were confined for their own protection, now have ground privileges and work full-time on the hospital's model farm."

Dr. Meeker heard of this dramatic new cure for mental illness while attending a medical meeting in Washington. He immediately instituted it at Leyden —where, in his own words, "it is already revolutionizing the treatment of our patients." He described the actual operation as "the sectioning, by means of surgery, of nerve tracts in the brain that seemed to transmit impulses causing breakdown."

The patient's intelligence, Dr. Meeker said, is not affected.

Hearing Frankel's step in the hall, Jim tossed the paper aside without reading further. The Austrian chuckled as he picked up the chart.

"It's a good thing Chandra isn't here to take your blood pressure," he said. "We might note a relapse—what's called blowing your top."

"I won't blow mine, Kurt. Did Meeker tell you about this interview?"

"I wasn't even aware he'd visited Atlanta."

"The whole article is a distortion of the truth. Lobotomy is no 'wonder cure.' Many clinics—Scripps, for instance—refuse to use it."

"The public doesn't know that."

"So the story is just another political dodge."

"Naturally. Already it's brought Meeker a long step nearer to the job he really wants at the state capital. You've noticed he mentioned his firm belief that the operation would eventually halve our day-cost at Leyden."

"I didn't read that far."

"He's returning today. I'm going to protest his failure to mention your name."

"Don't, Kurt. I'd rather not be identified with a program that's still premature."

"Perhaps you're right, at that," said Frankel. "It was still rank injustice, leaving you out. Whatever lobotomy's done for us here, it's your contribution."

"The operation itself deserves no publicity: it requires little skill."

"You're taking this well, Jim." Frankel's voice was far less bitter now. Jim realized that the head physician had sent in the newspaper deliberately. In its way, that headline had been a final check on the powers of reserpine.

"Don't tell me you have *more* bad news?"

"One other item, I'm afraid. Your favorite patient is doing her best to break out of her cell."

Jim half rose in his chair, then settled back with a sigh. The expected drumbeat at his temples had not come, even now. *Thank God for Rauwolfia,* he thought. *At least I can think clearly, without cursing fate.*

"Did the cyanide injection bring on the change?" he asked quietly.

"I think not. Catatonics tend to follow these patterns. Unfortunately, this is the most violent relapse we've recorded."

There was no need to complete the psychiatrist's unspoken thought. Jim shook his head slowly: he was still amazed at his *sang-froid.*

"The answer's no, Kurt—if you're asking me to consider lobotomy for Lynn Thorndyke."

"We'll carry on as before, then. Will you be ready to resume your operative schedule on Monday?"

"If you like I'll start tomorrow."

"Monday will do nicely," said Frankel. "I'll hold Meeker at bay."

That same afternoon, Jim was not surprised to receive a visit from the director—with Lisa Kendall, as always, a few discreet steps in his wake. Meeker was in a booming good humor.

"I hear you're better, Corwin. That's good news for our violent wards."

"Much better, Doctor—thanks to reserpine. I'm resuming our program on Monday."

"Did you see the story I gave the Atlanta papers?"

"I did."

"Miss Kendall tells me I let myself go a bit. Do you agree?"

Jim met the head nurse's eye—and kept his face straight with an effort. "I agree emphatically. Fifty cases is not a very large series."

Meeker's voice hardened. "It's enough to show what the operation can do. Why, we've saving three hundred dollars a month on Williams alone. Always had the devil's own time keeping a pharmacist in the drug room until you got *him* in shape. Now it runs like a clock."

"I'll grant you Enoch Williams has made a remarkable recovery," said Jim. "He should be able to go home soon."

"That's a yes-and-no judgment, Corwin. The little fellow is happy here—right?"

"So Dr. Frankel says."

"While I was away, I had Miss Kendall call his wife. What'd she tell you, Lisa?"

Miss Kendall spoke precisely, her full lips still tightened in an on-duty smile. "Mrs. Williams feels her husband should stay, so long as we're willing to keep him. She has a younger man in charge of their drugstore now, and he's doing a good job."

Jim held his tongue: watching Meeker in action, even through a mouthpiece, had its special fascination. "I suppose we can't release him without her consent," he said at last.

"Not unless Frankel will certify him as cured."

"Anyone who's suffered a mental illness can relapse," said Jim. "No patient can be pronounced well until he's had a chance to adjust to home conditions again."

"Granted, Corwin. I still think we should wait awhile on Williams. By the way, I hope you weren't upset that I didn't mention you in my interview. It seemed a bit premature."

"I'm glad you didn't, sir."

"Why? Don't you want to be famous?"

"The results are still inconclusive. One hundred cases is the very least number I'll require for a final estimate. Dr. Frankel and I agreed on that this morning." Jim braced himself for a tongue-lashing that did not come. Instead, Meeker grinned broadly.

"Sounds all right to me."

"After a hundred operations, we'll make an official report in one of the psychiatric journals."

"That's good horse sense. It helps the hospital to have staff papers in print."

"Let's hope the report is favorable—with the state commissioner about to retire."

Despite her decorum, Lisa Kendall permitted a giggle to escape her lips. Meeker guffawed, like an actor picking up a cue. "Don't miss much, do you, Corwin?" he said, in the same hearty tone. "I didn't mention it, while nothing was definite—but I *am* in line for the job. Make your report a success, and you can move right up with me."

"How, Doctor?"

"Let's say your next fifty operations turn out as well as the first set. Once I'm in the saddle I can create a special job for you. One that'll take you into every mental hospital in the state to operate on similar cases. You'd be a damned important man before it was over."

When the director had left, Jim realized that he had not answered—and wondered if Meeker had taken his silence as acceptance. There was no doubt that he had been offered a bribe, along with a blueprint for his future actions.

Once again he blessed Singh for the medication he had prescribed. Even with the calming effect of reserpine he was still cold with rage when Jack Hanley stopped by for his usual visit. It seemed appropriate that the gorilla-muscled attendant should collect his weekly contribution just then for the county Democratic club—the organization that claimed Jim as an automatic member, along with every doctor on the staff.

The following Monday (when his discharge from sick bay was official), Jim felt in perfect health. When he began his rounds again it cheered him mightily to note how glad the patients were to see him. Even when he unlocked the doors of Lovell One he could assure himself he was prepared for the worst.

Mrs. Foster joined him while he was checking the latest—and most depressing—report on Lynn. The Junoesque attendant had accepted him as a friend. He knew she would answer today's questions truthfully.

"Is Lynn really this low?"

"Never saw her worse, Doctor. I put her in hot packs when I can—which isn't often, with a whole ward to run."

Jim had long since realized that a kind heart was encased in this lady-wrestler's body. The hardheaded affection Mrs. Foster gave her charges was reflected in their obedience: time and again he had marveled at the way even the most violent cases quieted under her touch. Ever since his operation on Williams he had wondered what she thought of the program.

"Tell me truly, Mrs. Foster. In my place, would you schedule a lobotomy for Lynn?"

"It'd be the last thing I'd use, Dr. Corwin."

"What's your opinion of the operation?"

"Do you want a snow job or the truth?"

"Say what you think, please."

"I'd operate in some cases. Never on Lynn. Not if she has a prayer of getting well."

"I'm glad we agree, Mrs. Foster."

"Use it on the old stagers, if you must. Most of 'em were born without a brain. Any change inside their skulls is an improvement. But leave the younger ones alone. The ones who still have hope. Don't turn *them* into sheep, Dr. Corwin."

"You have to admit the sheep are easier to manage."

Mrs. Foster chuckled. "I'm not speaking for the staff, understand. Most of 'em love the way you're changing things here. 'Specially on the farm—and downstairs in the laundry."

"You mean—because sheep don't mind working?"

"Put one of 'em on a mangle, Doctor, and she'll stay with it for hours. They're working twenty locked-ward cases down there full time—and crying for more."

"At least it saves money for the state."

"Maybe, Dr. Corwin. And maybe not."

"What does that mean?"

They were alone on the ward, but Mrs. Foster moved to shut the chartroom door before she spoke again. "I've a niece in the business office, Doctor. She sees the reports that go up to the state capital. Costs haven't gone down one nickel."

"But they're bound to, with almost fifty patients working! Why, Enoch Williams alone is saving the state a three-hundred-dollar salary every month."

"Not the *state*, Doctor—or the taxpayer."

"Who, then?"

"I'm not saying, when I can't swear to it. But do you pay Big Al Hanley every week, same as the rest of us?"

"Yes."

"Well, lots of other money here siphons off the same way, you can count on that. Maybe that's why our director drives a Cadillac, and gives his girl friend a mink cape on her birthday. Don't let on I told you that, please. Like I said, I can't prove it."

Jim tried to shut off the sudden anger that gripped him. It was hardly news that Meeker had lined his pockets at Leyden. Still, there was a certain irony in the fact that a special operation (planned for purely humanitarian ends) had contributed to that same fund.

"Perhaps I should discontinue the program," he said. "I've half a mind to demand an accounting."

"Don't you do it, Dr. Corwin. You'll only lose your job and get nowhere. This kind of graft was invented when the first politician was born. The machine couldn't run without it."

"I'll take your advice this time," said Jim evenly. "And I'm glad you spoke your mind about Lynn. It's helped me to think more clearly. Shall we have a look at her?"

For all his new-found calm, he needed a moment at the grille before he could bring himself to unlock the girl's cell. He noticed that one of the walls was smudged from floor to ceiling (at his suggestion, Singh had brought Lynn a set of finger paints in the hope of distracting her). The empty tubes were scattered about the floor in the wildest disorder. Evidently she had begun a landscape of sorts, then rubbed it out.

"She painted by the hour before she relapsed," said Mrs. Foster.

"Too bad she couldn't have a canvas and brushes."

"She might have harmed herself, Doctor."

Lynn lay face down on the cot in apparent slumber—a pose Jim had long since learned to distrust. He turned the key and stepped inside the cell. The click of the lock brought the girl to her feet. With a single leap she reached the far wall, her fingers arched like claws. Mrs. Foster had already moved to his side, her shoulders braced for the expected impact. It would not be the first time Lynn Thorndyke had flung herself upon her doctor, tooth and nail.

Jim spoke as easily as he could. "Hello, Lynn. Do you know me?"

"Go away!"

"I can't, Lynn. Not until I've helped you."

"Will you let me out of here?"

"Not until you're well."

"You'd open that door—if you really *wanted* to help. You've no right to keep me here."

"We're your friends, Lynn. Don't you know that?"

"Oh no, you're not. You're just like the others." With an odd, scurrying gait, the girl crossed to the paint-smeared wall and raised herself on tiptoe—as though straining to touch an invisible object.

"Why do you do that, Lynn?"

"Can't you see I'm reaching?"

"For what?"

"For my nerves. Once I get my nerves back I'll break down that door."

"It's been like this since Friday," Mrs. Foster whispered. "Reaching for her nerves, so she can get out."

"I'll find them too," Lynn Thorndyke screamed.

"Where do you want to go, Lynn?" Jim asked.

"Away from *them*—and you."

"Why me?"

Her face changed, grew almost sly. For that moment, she might have been Susie Learoyd. "Because they paid you to get me. But I'll fool you—just wait and see." Her voice was trailing into gibberish. All over the ward a chorus of harpy voices answered her.

"Stop it, Lynn! Control yourself!" He moved toward her.

"Don't touch me! I'll kill you if you touch me!"

Taking her by the shoulders, he shook her gently. The contact seemed to break the skein of her hate: while the shock lasted, the fury left her face and she stared up at him with a trembling mouth and tear-filled eyes. Then she tore free of his hands and backed to the nearest corner: her fingers were arched again, like the claws of a cornered cat.

"Leave her be, Doctor," whispered the attendant. "I'll clean up here later, when she's quieted down."

Jim nodded and left the cell. For a moment he paced the corridor, ignoring the imprecations spat from a half dozen grilles. Now he knew the worst, he felt strangely detached from the horror he had witnessed. When Mrs. Foster joined him in the chartroom, he was calm enough.

"She may be better tomorrow, Doctor."

"Let's not delude ourselves," he said. "She's regressing steadily. The charts prove it, and so does her behavior."

"At least she's painting now and then. I brought my camera. If she does another wall, I'll snap it for you in color. The last one she did was beautiful—like a paradise without people."

A paradise without people, Jim thought. There was little comfort in the phrase. Could it be that Lynn's painting, in this manic state, was an escape of another sort? Did she paint landscapes without people because she feared mankind? He did not put the questions into words. Mrs. Foster had told him all she could.

xii

When he had finished his last tour of duty, Jim turned into the door of the pharmacy. Enoch Williams was hard at work behind the ground-glass partition of the drug room, his snow-white pompadour rising neatly above the eyeshade he was wearing.

"It's good to see you back, Dr. Corwin." The greeting was part of that picture of belonging—the murmured civility of a worker who has found his groove.

"The reserpine you dispensed for me did wonders, Mr. Williams."

The pharmacist's eyes lit up. "I've been reading about that drug. Sounds like something out of *The Arabian Nights*."

"It's been just that for me."

"Dr. Singh got me a *Materia Medica*, and some books on the history of pharmacy. As a young man, I'd planned to teach pharmacology. Of course that dream ended when I married." Williams spoke with an odd detachment—as though the *I* were a being from another universe. "I've traveled a rough road, Doctor—but I don't regret the journey. My wife's been provided for—better than most."

"You have your own pharmacy, don't you?"

"The best in Ellenville—and she's doing a fine job running it. Not that I didn't do well myself, before I was taken." The little man's voice rang with pride. "I'll grant you I worked long hours, but I got results. The doctors did their best to stump me with prescriptions, but I've yet to read one I can't fill."

"Would you like to go back?"

The face beneath the eyeshade went tense. For an instant the eyes held a ghostly reflection of old fires. Then Enoch Williams smiled warmly—and the brief glimpse of a brain attacked by fear and uncertainty was gone.

"I don't rightly know about going home, Dr. Corwin," he said slowly. "I'm comfortable here. I can handle this job. But when I think of running my own store again——"

"We realize these things can't be rushed, Mr. Williams. And we can certainly use you here."

"It's good to be useful again, Doctor. And I *am* getting better fast. I'll be ready for the outside before long."

Jim did not pursue the subject. It seemed wiser to take his

leave at once. In the doorframe he looked back. Williams was carefully separating a layer of powder into equal squares before putting each of them into a capsule. With the counter between them, and the spill of light on that snow-white pompadour, he resembled a rabbit, rising on cautious haunches in its burrow.

That evening, smoking a pipe with Dr. Singh in the lounge, Jim reviewed the day's cases one by one, to bridge the gap caused by his absence. The Hindu sighed at the mention of Williams.

"His wife's in no hurry to have him back, Jim, and Williams doesn't want to go. If we sent him home now, he might relapse completely."

"Surely a case of this kind proves that lobotomy doesn't remove basic conflicts? That it merely cuts them off from the *feeling* part of the personality?"

"Ask Dr. Frankel. He'll tell you there's no real cure for mental disease—except to reorient the personality through psychotherapy." The Hindu was speaking in his precise textbook manner: with a flick of brown, aristocratic fingers he dismissed all other argument in advance. "It's the blank wall we hit every day at Leyden. Before his operation, Enoch Williams had retreated into madness to escape the intolerable burden of living. Today, he's hiding behind our drug counter."

"Will we ever lure him out?"

The Indian doctor smiled. "If you'd met his wife, you'd see why he prefers to stay there. She's a type all too common in your American matriarchy—the sort who simply work their men to death. Of course, overwork is only part of his trouble. I'd say that the real cause of his breakdown was his endless, fruitless search for love. Again, I blame America for his failure."

"That's not fair, Chandra."

"I think it is. You Americans have been so prosperous—so eager to become even richer. Regardless of his station, each American father wants his son to have a better life than his own. But that wish is born from pride, not love. As a nation, you are fast forgetting how to love one another."

"Isn't that a thundering oversimplification?"

"Is Enoch Williams wanted? Or did his wife marry the best drug business in Ellenville—and devote her life to making it bigger?"

"Don't tell me you're against ambition."

"Not if ambition serves good ends. In Williams' case you see what happens when it gets out of hand."

"Can you say things are truly different in India?"

"Much different, Jim. Many of my people are starving, it is true—but not for lack of affection within their families. Here, in what should be the most secure country on earth, you have starvation of the soul. Why else would you lead the world in psychosomatic disorders—and in mental illness?"

"The evangelists say we've lost touch with Christ."

"Perhaps you have. Primitive man was in constant touch with God. In modern life we tend to forget the everyday participation of God in our affairs. Man-made machines supply man's every want: his self-esteem is boundless. And yet he has never been more afraid—because his self-esteem has no lasting base. With no faith outside himself, he feels he is doomed."

"What's the remedy, Chandra?"

"Teach your children to love God—whatever His name may be. To *know* that God cherishes them as persons. But remember this: such knowledge can flourish only in a warm family relationship, where it's second nature to be loved and wanted. Such children have a real chance to grow into men and women. When a crisis comes they've a reserve of strength to surmount it."

"What of the others—like Lynn?"

"In her case there's a basic cause which you've yet to uncover. But I don't doubt that she, too, has suffered from the lack of love. If this boy called Jay Thompson had really cared for her——"

"I think he did, Chandra."

"We don't know how deeply. In all events, it was a guilty

love, on her side. She believed that her happiness was based on another girl's misery—that she'd driven the other to suicide. But these are only surface facts. The real cause lies deeper in the past. In the childhood pattern, when the girl was turning into a woman."

"So we're back to psychotherapy as our solution."

"It is the only sure method. To uncover *all* the facts, from the start. To learn how and why Lynn Thorndyke's personality turned inward to feed upon itself. How else can we restore her Ego until it takes command once more?"

"Even if we could reach her personality—would such a program be possible here?"

"No, Jim—and that's the tragic thing about modern psychiatry. In private practice it's concerned chiefly with neurotics—and has little to do with real mental illness. Psychoanalysis, in the same field, is limited almost entirely to the well to do. At the state-hospital level we're deluged with people in desperate need of such treatment—and we can do little more than lock them up. When someone of Dr. Ziegler's stature introduces a program of lobotomy you can hardly blame Dr. Meeker for trumpeting its virtues to the skies."

A few days later, Lynn's mother arranged for her long-awaited interview (via a phone call from Atlanta).

Jim had braced himself for this first contact with Florence Thorndyke; he had expected everything from tears to a tongue-lashing. But the woman's voice was subdued. Her concern seemed entirely genuine.

"It's good to hear your voice, Dr. Corwin: the director at Leyden speaks highly of you. Before you say anything, let me tell you I feel sure you've done everything you can for Lynn."

Jim hesitated as he accepted the compliment. It was only natural that Mrs. Thorndyke should speak first to Meeker—yet a warning bell was ringing in his brain.

"So far," he said carefully, "we've been able to do very little here. We've no real idea how to proceed—until you give us Lynn's whole picture."

"Her whole picture, Dr. Corwin?"

"The emotional background. The life story. When can I talk to you?"

"I'm willing to arrange a date, if you feel it's any use."

"I do, Mrs. Thorndyke. In fact, your contribution could be vital."

"You frighten me a little. Am *I* about to be analyzed?"

He kept his voice coldly professional. "All I'll ask are the facts to round out Lynn's case history. With those facts at my disposal I hope to discover a lead that will help me cure her."

It was an impromptu statement, and he made it deliberately. Even if Lynn were in condition for treatment, he had no qualifications as a psychotherapist so far. Yet he felt instinctively that this was his only approach.

"I'll do what I can, of course," said the well-modulated voice on the telephone. "Shall we meet in Atlanta?"

"Unfortunately, I'm on a full-time schedule here."

"Then I must drive down to Leyden." The voice seemed a trifle annoyed now. "I'll call back to arrange a date. I've a great many friends to see here."

"I'm at your disposal, Mrs. Thorndyke. Just remember this is important."

"*Must* I come to the hospital, Doctor? Can't we meet in the village?"

"There's a hotel. I'll call on you there."

"I won't have to see my daughter?"

"Of course not. At this time it would only distress you both needlessly."

He hung up on that, convinced that he had handled the situation well enough. An image of the woman persisted—a tall, patrician creature with built-in good manners and a belief in her own essential rightness no man could shatter. When they met in the town of Leyden a week later (the date had been twice postponed) the real Florence Thorndyke was even more disturbing.

At first glance she seemed hardly older than Lynn, and almost as lovely—a porcelain doll who had managed to pass through the world with her bright paint unsullied. Here (he thought swiftly) was a lady, in the manner born. The sort of lady a man could spend his whole life protecting, and feel the sacrifice was inevitable. . . . It was only when they were seated in one of the hotel wall booths (appropriately enough, she had chosen the bar of the Jefferson for their meeting) that he noted the crow's-feet around her eyes, the hard lines of her mouth, even when that mouth was smiling.

"What will you drink, Doctor?"

"I'm afraid I'm on duty."

"Does that mean *I* can't have one?"

"Not if it will make things easier."

Jim sat back, watching her covertly while she summoned a waiter—and ordered a double bourbon in a way that did nothing to destroy her status.

"Don't keep me in suspense, please," said Mrs. Thorndyke. "Can Lynn really be cured of this nervous breakdown?"

He managed to keep down a grimace at the euphemism. "Perhaps—if you'll help me."

"I'm her mother, Dr. Corwin!"

"I want you to answer my questions. No matter how irrelevant they seem."

"Of course. I know how you analysts work."

Again he stifled the impulse to reveal the truth about himself. This was no time for half measures. "First, I must say that your daughter's very ill indeed."

"So Dr. Meeker has told me. It must have come from her father's side. *I'm* a Burford, Doctor—the Virginia branch. No one in my family was the least bit abnormal."

"Mental disease isn't always inherited," said Jim.

"Surely it doesn't develop from thin air."

"The causes are usually set up in childhood. I'm afraid we'll have to go into that angle pretty thoroughly."

"Lynn had the best of everything—always."

"Including a happy youth?"

"She was always moody and introspective. Try as I might, we were strangers to each other."

"Mrs. Thorndyke, some of the things I'm about to ask may seem embarrassing. I hope you'll bear with me——"

"In all my life I've done nothing by which to be embarrassed. You may ask me what you like."

"Your marriage ended in divorce, I believe. Can you tell me why?"

"My husband was a self-made man, Doctor. He was also an egomaniac who thought only of himself. I learned as much before we'd been married a month."

"Why didn't you leave him then?"

"A child was on the way—my daughter."

"You had another child later, didn't you?"

"A boy called David. He was born when Lynn was nine."

"Was he born without love?"

"Of course. You see, Dr. Corwin, I wasn't just trained to be a Burford. I was taught to be a wife, that I might become a mother." Mrs. Thorndyke had spoken with weary politeness—and quite without rancor. Taking notes rapidly, Jim wondered what problem play had inspired the last line.

"When did your son die?"

"At the age of thirteen months. When Lynn was eleven."

"Can you recall the circumstances? Don't leave out a thing, no matter how irrelevant it sounds——"

An hour later he was well into a third notebook and the woman was still talking—in the same even voice, with only an occasional flash of malice.

What struck Jim most forcibly was Mrs. Thorndyke's refusal to admit the smallest blame for Lynn's plight. From her earliest childhood, it seemed, the girl had brought unhappiness upon herself by her cold withdrawals from the sunshine of her mother's love. . . . Later, when the father's demands had proved unendurable, the mother had sought a divorce, for simple self-preservation. Naturally she had demanded and received complete custody of her daughter—in the vain hope that they might finally arrive at some *modus vivendi,* once she had removed herself from her husband's monstrous shadow.

"Forgive me for returning to a painful subject, Mrs. Thorndyke. But are you *sure* Lynn disliked her baby brother?"

"Intensely. When he was born, she went to my husband and asked that he be put up for adoption. When he died, she didn't shed a tear——"

"Did your husband love the baby?"

"It was more than love. Had David lived, he'd have inherited the practice. Most men rejoice in the birth of an heir—but my husband's devotion was pathological."

"But you say he was also devoted to Lynn?"

"More than was good for her. If ever a child was spoiled by her father, Lynn was that child. Obviously she had to take a back seat when the boy was born——"

"Afterwards, did her father restore her to favor?"

"He did. Emotionally he was a weakling. *I* could never pardon her for hating her brother as she did. He was more magnanimous."

"At the time of your divorce—did she come with you willingly?"

"Not until I'd convinced my former husband it was for the best."

"May I ask what argument you employed?"

"The natural one—that a daughter's place is with her mother. She gave in—when her father advised her that she had no real choice."

"Then it was her *father* who convinced her?"

"You may put it that way, if you insist," said Mrs. Thorndyke. "The girl was not yet of age. No court in this state would have refused me custody, if he'd forced me to press the matter."

"But isn't it true that Lynn was closer to her father than to you?"

"Perhaps it was one of the secrets she kept from me. In my opinion, she never loved anyone."

"Isn't it also true that your ex-husband—if only to avoid tension after your divorce—surrendered the child in the hope she'd choose *him* after she came of age?"

"It's quite likely. In his way, my husband was just as crafty as my daughter."

"Did you allow him to see her after the divorce?"

"Our agreement stipulated that they could meet alternate Sundays. Usually he was away on business. Now and then Lynn availed herself of the privilege—if you can call it that."

"How often would you say they met?"

"A dozen times, perhaps."

"This is the most painful question of all, Mrs. Thorndyke. In your opinion, did your husband commit suicide?"

"He killed himself, Doctor. And that's not just an opinion."

"On what do you base that statement?"

"On a letter. Would you care to read it?"

Jim opened the letter Mrs. Thorndyke lifted from her purse. Here, he realized, might be the last missing piece in the puzzle.

"May I make a copy?"

"Keep the original. *I've* no use for it."

He read the note carefully. Lynn's father had typed it on a single sheet of paper. His signature, slashed across the bottom with a firm hand, hardly suggested a man who had taken leave of life—but the intent of the letter itself was unmistakable.

> Florence:
>
> When you read this I shall be dead, by my own hand. With luck, I hope, it will seem an accident.
>
> Now that David is gone, now that you no longer even pretend to love me, Lynn is all I have. Or all I *had*—to put my failure in the proper tense.
>
> Things might have been different had Lynn stayed with me after our divorce. Quite naturally, you insisted she go to you. I had hoped to change her decision someday. Now, it seems, the effort is beyond me.
>
> When my will is read, you will find I have provided for Lynn's education in a rather special fashion. That, at least, is something you cannot take from me.

"What do you make of it, Dr. Corwin?"

He came back to the woman in the wall booth. Lost in his musings, he had half forgotten her presence—now that she had told him all he needed to know.

"It leaves no doubt of suicide," he said.

"Naming Lynn as the cause, of course."

"Did you tell her that?" he asked quickly.

"How could I help it?"

"Then *she* read this letter?"

"It seemed only fair—so she would know the real reason her father died."

"How did she take it?"

Mrs. Thorndyke shrugged. "As she took every crisis in my life. Coldly—without a word of pity."

"Has anyone else seen this letter?"

"I felt it should be my secret—and Lynn's."

"Why give it to me now?"

"I'm a woman of my word. I promised to answer all your questions. Obviously you would wonder how my husband died—and why."

Jim hesitated, with his eyes on the closed notebook. Eager as he was to escape, he could not afford to antagonize Mrs. Thorndyke now. "Did you go on as before—after his death?"

"Of course. He'd been less than a shadow to me, while he lived. Why should I mourn him?"

"Was there an inquest in connection with his death?"

"No, Doctor. It was reported as an accident—on a mountain road."

"Even then you kept the letter to yourself?"

"We Burfords harbor no weaklings in our ranks. Not even by marriage."

"One last question, Mrs. Thorndyke. When I visited Dean Pearson at the university, she told me of your husband's unusual bequest. How did you interpret it, when his will was read?"

"As his way of striking back from the grave. It was a virtual order to keep my hands off Lynn—and Lynn's education."

"You felt you should obey?"

"It was his dying wish. How could I do anything but respect it? Once I'd registered her at Glenville I felt I'd done my duty."

"Is that why you severed all other ties?"

"She never wanted me, Dr. Corwin. Why should I want her?"

Why indeed? thought Jim. The question still echoed in his brain on the drive back to the hospital—long after he had watched Florence Thorndyke's beige-colored convertible vanish on the long, ruler-straight road that led to Atlanta.

Florence Thorndyke's own course, he reflected, was much like that road: it had always pointed straight to the gratification of her desires. Her husband had understood her perfectly. His will had made certain that this monstrous woman (who was a mother only in the crudest biological sense) would trouble Lynn no longer. In the circumstances, the lonely, hagridden man had decided a fifty-thousand-dollar bribe was not excessive.

Dismissing his taxi at the gate, Jim walked across the hand-tailored lawns of Leyden, breathing deep of the balmy spring. For the first time he had the illusion of homecoming. Compared to the airtight cosmos where Florence Thorndyke ruled as undisputed queen, the world of the mentally ill seemed strangely normal. . . . His first impulse was to go to Frankel with his findings—but he vetoed the idea sternly. Lynn's case was his special preserve: until he had some hope of its solution it was a responsibility he could not share. Instead, he climbed the steps of Lovell One for a glance into her cell, a daily ritual that had become almost second nature.

Only yesterday Mrs. Foster had scrubbed the cell walls clean. This evening Lynn was crouched on her heels, with a dozen tubes of paint before her, smearing a wall with huge, cloudy symbols. Nearly every foot of space was covered with these strange hieroglyphs: at first Jim could discover no logical pattern. Then (as though blinders had dropped from his eyes) he caught a recurring motif of green and blue, a meadow arched by a cloudless sky. When he moved closer to the grille he saw that Lynn had included a figure in this landscape for the first time.

"What do you make of it, Doctor?"

It was Mrs. Foster, whispering like a conspirator at his elbow. He spoke without turning, conscious only of the vast lifting of his heart. The child who played in that green meadow (he was repeated on each of the four walls) was indeed an answer from heaven.

"It's David," he said.

"David?"

"Her brother. The rival she tried to hate—and couldn't."

"You must be a mind reader, Doctor. That's what *she* called him when she began to paint."

The girl on the floor, feeling their presence at last, rose from her work. Without a word she moved from wall to wall, smearing the images with both palms. Only when the last stroke of paint had been hopelessly muddled did she fling herself on the cot, arms folded on her breast and knees jackknifed to her chin. It was the pose of the infant *in utero*, the ultimate withdrawal to the one sanctuary untouched by life.

There were no screams this time, no further awareness of the faces at the grille. Lynn Thorndyke, so far as her conscious mind was concerned, was safe in the womb of time.

xiii

Three weeks later, when their tally of lobotomy patients had passed a hundred, Frankel and Jim put every avoidable task aside to prepare their report. The manuscript that emerged was a weighty one—and Jim realized it would scarcely be intelligible to the layman. Yet it was a real labor of love. Admitting his prejudice against the operation, he could hardly gainsay the results.

One general conclusion was evident. Immediately after lobotomy, the vast majority of the patients followed the same course. For sometimes as long as a week they seemed to lose the tensions that had accompanied the excited phase of their illness. By contrast they appeared stuporous, sometimes even confused. At first they were indifferent to externals. At this stage it was necessary to care for them, much as a nurse might watch over a growing, but somewhat doltish, child.

As this period waned, a few of the patients became noisy and overexcited. In rare cases they seemed more destructive than before. The others slept much of the time—waking easily, but dropping back whenever stimulation ceased. Compulsory exercise periods, including courses in self-feeding and other guidance in matters that separated man from beast, were used to break this pattern: in over ninety of the hundred cases, this was the turning point. During the second week (sometimes even earlier) these patients ceased to vegetate and became self-sustaining in matters of food and hygiene. About this time they also accepted whatever work was offered them—and performed it well after a few hours' training.

The best results—as Jim had expected—were achieved among patients who had been most violent before the operation. Nearly all such cases were now fairly well-adjusted entities in the sheltered hospital routine. Most of them (Williams was a fair example) were quietly sociable and well pleased with their lot—though here again the major characteristic was a peculiar flattening of the personality. A small percentage seemed entirely well—cheerful, relaxed, and eager to converse on such topics as current events.

Seven of the hundred patients showed disturbing symptoms: any unpleasant trait that had formerly dominated the personality was accentuated. As a rule, lack of self-consciousness was a feature of such histories, along with a complete absence of consideration for others and a facetiousness that was almost infantile. It was this inability to experience adult emotion that worried Jim the most: to him, it would always be a tragic loss. He was forced to admit, however, that the loss did not seem to trouble the patients, not even those whose rehabilitation had been least successful. In fact, they appeared to enjoy boundless self-esteem.

Frankel stacked the bulky manuscript and tucked it into an envelope for mailing. The paper had already been accepted for publication by one of the psychiatric journals to which he was a regular contributor.

"It seems that lobotomy makes them less than men—and more than brutes," he said. "I suppose we'll have to call that the final verdict."

"I'd prefer a more positive conclusion."

"I *am* being positive, Jim—by the standards we're forced to use here. What's the one, dominant cause behind these breakdowns?"

"Collapse of the Ego and the Super Ego?"

"Yes—to put it in the simplest terms. These people tried and failed—and couldn't endure the world's rejection. Their dreams were boundless, their achievement nil." The Austrian stared down at the closed envelope. "You realize, of course, that only a hairline separates such unfortunates from you or me?"

Jim smiled. "Shall I quote Dryden to you—on the thin partitions that divide great minds from madness?"

"The fact remains: regardless of brain power—or its lack—one needs strong moral muscles to endure failure, or to run against the herd. Look around you. How many of our fellow citizens are concerned with the things *we* consider essential to mental well-being? Idealism, dedication to one's work, appreciation of the arts, the pleasures of philosophy, the give-and-take of real conversation?"

"Say ten per cent, to be charitable."

"Call it five," said Frankel, "and you'd be nearer the mark."

"Are you suggesting that these hundred schizos belong to such a minority?"

"No, Jim. But they *thought* of themselves as superior beings—and found refuge in fantasy when they discovered their error. As you just said, that's the root cause of their illness. Few of us can face the vast gulf that lies between romance and reality, and remain wholly sane. Perhaps we're doing them a favor to cut them off from such hopeless effort."

"How can you be sure you aren't destroying genius in the process? A man's imagination and his creative and intellectual functions always go hand in hand. As a psychiatrist, you can't deny it."

"You've a point there, of course."

"Suppose you could subdivide *homo sapiens*—as exactly as a prism divides the color spectrum, from ultraviolet to infrared. Using imagination as a standard—and ultraviolet at the short end of the scale. Let's put the pragmatists there as a subspecies. The men who exist without dreams. The dull fellows who do their jobs like robots, who have no real life of the intellect, let alone of the spirit——"

"The bulk of humanity, in other words."

"If you insist on so harsh a judgment, Kurt. We don't get many such people here as patients—since most of them exist, from birth to death, with no real tension whatever. There's no conflict in their psyches between *can* and *might have been*. Inadequacy, which drives the average neurotic mad, is a word they never use——"

The Austrian smiled. "Don't lose your prismatic simile, Jim."

"Let's move down the color scale, toward the infrared end of the spectrum. You'll find people here with varying degrees of imagination, an increasing creative and intellectual drive. As you approach infrared, you find yourself moving into the company of the artists, the philosophers, the builders. Men with a vision of what this world might be, if we could find peace within ourselves, if we could *really* learn to love one another. Almost without exception such men pay a high price for that ability to imagine. Usually it's paid for in nervous tension, in blind conflict with the everyday. The strong ones smash through to achievement. The real infrareds go over the brink as madmen. Or sometimes they're called madmen in their day —and *still* go on, to write the history of tomorrow."

"Where d'you draw the line?" asked Frankel.

"No one can," said Jim. "Sanity and insanity are words that have no place in science—though we use them for want of better. Many of us straddle the line without admitting it. Just to round out the simile of the color spectrum—let's call that line the division between the *visible* infrared and what's beyond the reach of the optic nerve."

"The difficulty, of course, being in the point of view," the Austrian agreed. "Some optic nerves are stronger than others."

"Then sanity and insanity are relative concepts. It depends on who's doing the judging."

"Precisely. That's why no psychiatrist would use such terms clinically. Better doctors than I have tried to find an all-inclusive label: in every case they've come a cropper on the rock of human behavior. What's considered perfectly normal in one society is damned in another—and in every case it's the individualist who suffers. In our own century, unfortunately, the concept of normality is constantly contracting. Nothing is more dangerous to a healthy personality than a growing urge to conform."

"Could that be why we're having so much mental illness?"

"I can't think of a single factor that contributes more."

"Then civilization itself is the creator of its own breakdown?"

"And of its eventual destruction," said Frankel. "Unless we reverse the trend. In the ideal society, the urge to conform would not be an essential element, but an infrequent accompaniment. The tendency to whipsaw all society into robots who work, think and eat alike is hardly an end product of intelligence. On the contrary, it's the most abject form of surrender—the urge to take the easiest way, *despite* one's intelligence."

"Chandra thinks we're losing our sense of kinship with the Divine in the process," said Jim.

"And so we are. It's happened to every civilization since Egypt."

"Shall we include these lofty pessimisms in our report?"

"And fail to conform as doctors?" asked the Austrian, with a chuckle. "We'd be the laughingstock of our profession."

"Can't a doctor also be a philosopher?"

"Not if he's wise. Let's be content with the obvious fact: we've rescued one hundred members of our species from the slag heap. Let's take credit for that—without reminding our colleagues that this operation does not enrich society an iota."

Jim found he could join in the older doctor's bitter mirth. "I suppose our concluding sentence is strong enough, at that."

"Quite," said Frankel. He quoted from memory. "*'We do not feel that lobotomy is, in any sense, a cure. It does, in selective cases (marked by considerable tension and overactivity associated with mental illness), allow the patient to resume a useful life again.'*"

"Meeker will scream like a mink when he reads it."

"I think not, Jim. Just between us, our director's an opinionated idiot. He is also one of those wise fools who keeps an ear to the ground. The people *he* wants to convince don't read *The Journal of Clinical Psychiatry*. They merely vote—and make up legislative committees. As long as he keeps them on his side, he won't trouble himself about our conclusions. Wait and see."

Frankel's prediction proved true. Meeker made no objection to the paper, despite its conservative approach. But he did pounce on the over-all figures, which proved beyond a doubt that the majority of Jim's patients had become reasonably efficient workers. The result was a second interview (this time on a national wire service), with the director of Leyden as the star performer. Again the facts were crudely distorted to make lobotomy seem a universal panacea—and Meeker its all-wise dispenser:

SURGERY FOR MENTAL DISEASE
MAY REVOLUTIONIZE TREATMENT

Results of the first hundred lobotomy operations for serious mental illnesses at Leyden Hospital promise a revolution in the treatment of these disturbing conditions, Dr. Thaddeus Meeker, hospital director, announced today. Dr. Meeker based his conclusion on a long and painstaking series of such operations undertaken by staff members at his direction. Patients selected for surgery were, in almost every case, among the most violent of the "locked-ward" cases. Without exception, their condition had been heretofore considered hopeless.

Now, most of those so treated are completely recovered from their delusions. Seventy-eight in all are living normal lives, working normal hours at carefully supervised tasks within the hospital walls, and responding in every way to the demands of society.

"If future experience bears out this exhaustive preliminary study," said Dr. Meeker, "it will give physicians in mental hospitals a vitally needed tool in treating the mentally ill." Based on the initial experience of these first hundred operations, he added, the program at Leyden is now being stepped up markedly, as the life-giving process is used on an ever-expanding list of patients.

Frankel read this piece of tailored journalism to Jim in his office. They had expected just such an announcement from the director, but the blow was no less numbing. Read at its face value, the story seemed a blanket endorsement of the operation.

"We can hardly issue a denial," said Frankel. "Even if the general reader was in the habit of reading denials. I'm afraid the damage is already done." He riffled a stack of letters on his desk. "Here's the first result—over fifty requests for lobotomy, in a single day, from relatives of inmates."

"We needn't accept all of them."

"Your judgment is still final—as of now," said Frankel. "I'm sure Meeker will keep his hands off—unless he's really pressured. Here's an example of what I mean." He took a letter from the stack and tossed it across the desk. Jim recognized Florence Thorndyke's handwriting instantly.

"At least Lynn's mother reads the papers," he said.

"I gather she was in Europe when Meeker gave out his first interview. Now she's demanding lobotomy for her daughter."

"But the woman's whole purpose is to send Lynn back to the

university," Jim protested. "She must realize the girl could never graduate *after* this process."

"The story doesn't mention that possibility," said Frankel. "I doubt if Meeker was aware of it when he saw the reporters."

"Has he read Mrs. Thorndyke's letter?"

"We've already had it out, Jim. I stated our side—as strongly as I could. Explained that a patient's higher mental processes are nearly always destroyed in lobotomy. I also insisted that Mrs. Thorndyke get an accurate blueprint of the procedure—and its probable consequences. I'm afraid he only half listened."

"I'm going straight to his office, Kurt."

"You're a bit late for argument. The director took off this morning—on a month-long tour."

"Where can we reach Mrs. Thorndyke?"

"Through her family physician. She's gone abroad again, and he has the final decision. But I'm afraid he's already sold on Meeker's cure-all."

"I'll resign before I operate."

"You can keep your job awhile longer, Jim. I've persuaded Dr. Cronshaw to give us six weeks more."

Jim smashed his fist on the desk. "It isn't fair. The hell of it is, Lynn's seemed a trifle better recently."

"I'll grant you her finger painting's a hopeful sign. In time she may have rational periods when she'll respond to therapy. But we could hardly break her basic problem down in six weeks—even if she were fully co-operative tomorrow."

"What shall we do, Kurt?"

The Austrian tossed up his hands. "Nothing, Jim—unless you can produce an overnight cure." A phone burred at his elbow and he turned to pick it up. Watching his face, Jim knew that trouble was piling up again, even before he recognized Singh's familiar high-pitched voice on the line.

"Sorry to harp on my favorite topic," he said apologetically as Frankel hung up. "I realize Lynn's just one of many——"

"At the moment she's our most important patient," said Frankel crisply. "Get over to Lovell as fast as you can run. She just broke out of her cell."

xiv

Afterwards, when he tried to piece out the events of the next half hour, Jim could not quite remember that headlong run from the main building to the women's ward. Singh was already on the portico, giving orders to a half dozen attendants—and Janet Moore was distributing bull's-eye lanterns. On all sides the grounds were alive with lights, as the searchers beat the bushes in precise patterns. Escapes from a locked ward were rare at Leyden—but the methods for tracing an escapee were as precise as a fire drill.

Taking his place in that pattern as naturally as a soldier on parade, Jim picked up the story in snatches. An untrained attendant had been trusted with Lovell while Mrs. Foster was on her supper hour. Making her rounds, she had noticed the wall paintings in Lynn's cell—and, thinking the girl asleep, had rashly unlocked the door for a closer view. Lynn had whipped out in a flash, locking the woman inside with her own key. . . . Apparently she was familiar with the outside watchman's schedule, probably from listening to his passing at night. Knowing just when he would check the portico of Lovell (and well aware that he would never hear the attendant's cries for help in the usual midnight cacophony of the ward), she had waited in the anteroom until his lantern winked by. Then she had simply vanished in the darkness.

"She's still in hospital clothes," said Singh. "Without regular shoes she can't get too far."

"Think she'll try the north wall?"

"She might."

They were already approaching the barrier. The outer wall itself, designed for such a contretemps as this, was unclimbable. However, a new service gate had just been cut in the northern side—and part of the scaffolding still remained. Reviewing the geography of the hospital while he ran, Jim realized that this impromptu ladder was in clear view from Lynn's cell.

"Have the state troopers been notified?"

Singh, trotting a dozen steps behind, shouted a denial. "Dr. Frankel said we could wait—until we're *sure* she's outside."

"I'm with him there." Jim darted his torch into an azalea thicket. There would be no choice but a state-wide alarm, if the present search was fruitless. It was unlikely that Lynn would get far outside, or that she would cause trouble for anyone but herself. He could still hear the first radio broadcast perfectly, and see the morning headline:

MANIAC ESCAPES FROM STATE HOSPITAL

Lynn Thorndyke was no maniac, he was convinced of that much. In cases like this, the label was applied without distinction. . . . Not that labels would matter too long, if she reached the state road beyond that wall. The two-lane pavement was heavily traveled at all hours. He could imagine Lynn trapped there, confused by the roar of motors, and rushing into a path of headlights like a helpless moth.

The image faded before it could take coherent shape, as he saw the flashlights converge on the ghostly scaffolding just inside the gate. Already those white probes of light had picked out the crumpled form in the rubble. With a shout of relief he pocketed his own torch and rushed forward to lift Lynn in his arms.

A glance assured him that she was not severely injured, though it was evident that she had fallen while attempting to climb the scaffold. Blood oozed from a shallow abrasion above the hairline of her left temple. He could not be sure if she had been knocked senseless by the fall, or merely relapsed into catatonia under the strain of fear. The fact that her body was naturally limp suggested the former.

"I'll send for a stretcher," said the Hindu.

"I can carry her myself, Chandra."

Under the lights in the surgery, Jim found no broken bones; save for the scalp wound, there was no sign of another abrasion. While he waited for Frankel's arrival he made a thorough neurological check, if only for his own peace of mind. It confirmed his first tentative guess that Lynn had slipped on the scaffolding—and had suffered, at worst, a slight concussion when she fell into the rubble.

He was dressing the wound at the girl's temple when the chief physician hurried in. Knowing what Frankel would be saying, he kept his eyes on his work.

"She got off easily, Kurt," he said, as he wound the last spiral of bandage. "Nothing but a light concussion—if it's that serious. The unconsciousness may be a defense reaction."

"That seems a reasonable diagnosis," said the older doctor. "Still, we'd better watch her closely. I'll put one of the attendants on special duty with her."

"If you don't mind, I'll take the duty myself," said Jim. The presence of Jack Hanley in the doorframe had reminded him—all too vividly—of the patient he had lost his first night at Leyden. He could not believe that Lynn's case was that serious—but he was reluctant to leave her side.

"Shall we keep her here or move her to the ward?"

"She can be taken back safely now. I'll stay in her room until she becomes conscious again."

Frankel did not speak while the attendants transferred the inert form from table to litter. Walking at Jim's side, he seemed a little aloof from the white-clad procession as they crossed the lawn again and took the walk that led to the women's ward. The aloofness persisted when he paused on the portico of Lovell and reached for his pipe. Pausing in turn on the top step, Jim braced himself for what he knew was coming.

"You realize what this means," said Frankel. "I won't spell it out."

"Of course, Kurt. Meeker will insist on a lobotomy the moment he returns."

"Can we refuse him?"

"I'll resign before I'll perform one."

"If she had scaled that wall, the first passing car could have killed her. What choice is there—if we expect to keep her alive?"

"I won't argue. Clinically I don't have a leg to stand on. But I won't give in, even now."

"Sure you want to sit up with her tonight?"

"I couldn't rest until she's conscious again."

Frankel nodded. "Just do one thing for me. Keep that blood pressure down with an extra reserpine tablet."

When Jim entered the ward, the guards had already placed Lynn on her bed. Mrs. Foster was in the act of clothing her in fresh hospital pajamas. The girl was breathing quietly now. Save for the bandage at her temple, she might have just dropped into a peaceful slumber.

"It's past your check-out time, Mrs. Foster," he said. "I'll lock myself in—with my own key."

"There's a cot in the chartroom, Doctor. I'd be glad to stay until morning—now the ward's quieted down."

"I won't have you doing extra duty. Besides, I'll want to keep checking her pulse and blood pressure."

It was a ready-made excuse—and they both knew it. When the door had closed on the attendant, Jim moved to turn the emergency lock. Then he sat down at the bedside and buried his face in his hands. There was no avoiding the fact that he had failed here—as disastrously as he had failed with Taffy. Once again he had done little more than stand by helplessly, while a woman he loved moved down the road to madness. Lynn's wild dash for freedom was the final event to drive that conviction home.

Alone with her in the cell, he let his flashlight pick out bits of her painting on each of the four walls. By daylight, those whorls of color had possessed a special beauty. He had persuaded himself that they were art, in its purest form. Viewed in this cold midnight, he saw they were only the outward, explosive evidence of dementia.

The ward seemed oddly still, after the uproar that had followed the girl's escape. Only a single voice broke the quiet, the cackling laughter of a hebephrenic far down the corridor. The sound was typical of the final phase of schizophrenia. He knew the patient well, a crone who had occupied that same cell for a quarter century, her mind so pitifully darkened that both he and Frankel had ruled out lobotomy on the basis of the case history alone. . . . Even if Meeker should yield, had he the right to doom Lynn to that same slow extinction?

He could feel his own mind waver, as he continued to torture himself with that dilemma. Remembering Frankel's order, he took the vial of reserpine from his pocket. The flashlight picked up the dosage, written on the label in Enoch Williams' copper-plate hand. *One Tablet With Meals*. . . . He had never used the medication at this hour. Acting on impulse, he uncorked the vial and swallowed not one, but two, of the whitish pellets.

The reaction was swift; with his stomach empty, the drug was absorbed into the bloodstream quickly. Almost in a matter of minutes he felt the first subtle easing of tensions in both body and mind. Before a half hour had passed, he knew he would accept the verdict of fate; within the hour, he could tell himself that not even this heartbreaking problem was insoluble. . . . Then, out of the black pit of his despair (now that he had risen safely above it), came the rocket-burst of inspiration, a thing so simple he could only wonder at his former blindness.

He sank to the floor beside the cot and pillowed his head on his folded arms. Weary though he was, he had no need of sleep. . . . When he glanced again at his watch, he was surprised to find it was almost morning. While he had floated between sleep and waking, his inspiration had been a formless thing. Now, with dawn at the barred window, it took on concrete form, like day breaking through the dark barrier of the night. This was the therapy Lynn Thorndyke so desperately needed. This was the Leyden miracle.

Lynn was still asleep when he heard Singh's key in the lock. Brimming over with his plan, he needed an iron effort of the will to keep from shouting it. Instead, he got quietly to his feet.

"Let's waken her, Chandra—if we can. I could use some breakfast."

He shook Lynn's shoulder gently. Singh, poised on the far

side of the cot, repeated the gesture. On the third try, the girl's eyes opened and stared up at Jim blankly.

"Does your head hurt, Lynn?"

She continued to stare as a whispered negative formed on her lips. For a second he could almost believe that her fall had shocked her back to lucidity. Then he saw the fear deepen in her eyes as the dark pupils contracted. In another instant she had flung away from him—so violently that she would have tumbled from the cot, had not Singh moved to steady her.

"Go away! Why won't you leave me alone?"

A few hours ago he would have left the cell with a heavy heart. Now, with his new-found inspiration to sustain him, he shrugged briefly and turned to the door.

"Meet me in the dining room when you've examined her, Chandra," he said quietly. "I've something to discuss that can't wait."

xv

Two cups of scalding coffee restored Jim's well-being completely—but his mind was still racing when Singh entered the staff dining room. Deep in thought as he was, he did not even notice his friend until the other physician sat down at the table.

"Since we're colleagues," said the Hindu, "I'll ignore the slightly glazed eye. Just remember that daydreaming is the first symptom of dementia."

"Forgive me, Chandra. I'm coasting on the aftereffects of two reserpine tablets I took last midnight."

"*Two* tablets, Jim?"

"Kurt felt I needed them." Jim knew his voice was shaking: he forced himself to slow down, to make his statement calmly. "Do you recall the first time you gave me the drug? When I was recovering from that spell of vertigo?"

"I recall perfectly."

"Exactly what did you say about the root from which reserpine is derived?"

Singh put down his teacup, and spoke with his usual precision. "The root of *Rauwolfia serpentina* has been used by Indian doctors for centuries. Particularly for the relief of mental tension——"

"*Mental* tension, Chandra?"

"What are you driving at?"

"If it served that purpose in India, why can't it be used at Leyden?"

The Hindu was staring openmouthed. "Have I, by any chance, been a bloody fool?"

"I was the fool," said Jim. "You were only repeating legends. I could feel the effects of the drug on my own body—and mind. I *knew* what it could do."

"Are you implying that reserpine saved you from a crack-up?"

"It saved me from something—I don't know what just yet. Go on: tell me more about Rauwolfia."

"It's a common belief in my country that a man who's deranged will lose his madness if he eats slices of the root. In the Bihar dialect of India, the name of the root is *paglakadawa*. Literally translated, that means 'madness cure.'"

"The active principle of Rauwolfia—reserpine—must be many times as potent. Can't we use it *here*—as a 'madness cure'?"

"Cure is a big word." But the Hindu's usually placid eyes were blazing now: Jim knew that he had caught fire from the question.

"As an aid, then. There's no denying that a strong dose of the drug—such as I took last night—lifts the mind outside itself, relieves it of all pressure. Ten minutes before I swallowed that extra tablet, I was willing to call quits on Lynn's case. Thirty minutes later I was above and beyond my worries—and calling myself a fool for an easy surrender."

Jim slapped the table with his palm. "If reserpine helped me, it can help others. Who knows? Once tensions are dissolved, once a patient's mind is free of its manic state, we can use everything in the book to keep it free—maybe even a short form of psychoanalysis. The patient himself will help: that's the vital point. Every sick brain has a core of normality that's ready to fight for survival——"

"Save your arguments, Jim," said Singh. "I'm with you all the way. Reserpine is surely worth a trial. When Dr. Meeker returns I'll ask for a stock of the drug. At the moment, there's hardly enough in the pharmacy to fill your own prescriptions."

"We can't wait for Meeker. He'll insist on an immediate lobotomy the moment he hears Lynn tried to escape. I've got to show improvement *before* he gets back."

"Lynn's an extreme case. As such, she's hardly a fair test of the drug. Suppose you administer reserpine—and it fails. If I know Meeker at all, he'll turn thumbs down on the whole idea."

"I still say we can't wait. Another thing: if the drug does help her, we must prove it isn't an accident. Say, an affect-effect from her concussion."

"How can you be sure?"

"By treating other serious cases with reserpine. And giving another group a placebo—something that looks like the drug but isn't."

"We haven't enough in stock."

"I'll stop taking it for a while."

"As your medical adviser, I'd have to veto the idea."

Jim smiled. Now that his plan was taking shape, he felt the last of his doubting vanish. "Consider your veto overridden. Williams can set up the medication this morning. I'll take five patients from my wards, including Lynn. You can select five from yours. We'll want the most disturbed cases: this must be an all-or-nothing test run, something even Meeker will believe. At the same time we'll each pick five patients who will get the placebo."

Singh tossed up his hands in a gesture of dazed acceptance. "You take my breath away, Jim. Already—as you Americans say—I feel myself out on limbs."

"'Nothing ventured nothing gained' is another saying that's pertinent," Jim reminded him. "How soon can you have your guinea pigs ready?"

"As soon as you produce the drug," said the Hindu.

Fifteen minutes later, Jim was outlining his plan at the pharmacist's counter.

"I can make the placebos from milk sugar," said Williams. "But we've no more than two hundred reserpine tablets in stock. They won't last long among ten patients."

"What's the procedure when we order new drugs? Who approves the requisition?"

"Dr. Singh—in the case of the reserpine. It was a special medication, and only a little was needed."

"I'll sign a new requisition now. This time, make it a thousand tablets. You'd better order them from Atlanta, by wire."

"We've never placed so large an order."

"We're going to need still more, if this idea of mine proves true."

"I think it will, Dr. Corwin."

Jim looked at the little pharmacist in surprise. "You've heard of it elsewhere?"

"I've always tried to keep up with new discoveries in pharmacy," said Williams. "But there was never time at the store. When we first put you on reserpine, I wrote to the manufacturer for literature. You knew, of course, that the crude root was widely used in India. Doctors there have prescribed it in a large number of mental cases. They reported that it was of great merit."

"Why didn't you tell me?"

"I thought they could be mistaken. After all, they were using the crude root of Rauwolfia, not the pure alkaloid. There were also two preliminary reports in this country—made direct to the manufacturer. A psychiatrist in Boston has used it to quiet disturbed patients. And a Dr. Ferguson in Michigan also advised its use in mental disease."

The realization that he was not a true discoverer dampened Jim's spirits only a little: pioneering, in this case, was less important than the fact the drug had proved itself elsewhere. Signing the requisition hastily, pouring the entire stock of reserpine into a single vial, he hurried to the chartroom of Lovell One. Janet Moore had just arrived for her morning check. She held up a detaining hand before he could speak.

"Don't tell me we're in for a lecture," she said. "We deserve one—after last night's shenanigans."

"Last night is behind us, thank God. I'm here to change the program of medication. We're starting Lynn Thorndyke on reserpine, along with four others. The toughest cases you can find."

The nurse opened the order book. "Write it down, Dr. Corwin. I'll see it's carried out."

"I've been taking a milligram daily—but I want to hit these people hard. Let's put them down for three milligrams. Can Mrs. Foster persuade them to swallow it?"

"They'll take what she gives them—including paraldehyde. What's one more pill in *their* lives?"

"In Lynn's case, I want a five-milligram injection, intramuscularly. Daily, for at least a week. We've less time to show results with her."

The nurse took off her spectacles and studied him with narrowed eyes. "I don't speak out of turn often, Doctor. But do you know what you're doing?"

"Of course. I'm taking a one-way street—and praying it doesn't dead-end on me."

"You've made a good start here, Jim Corwin. Everybody likes you—and you've already learned more about psychiatry than most residents ever do."

"Thanks for the back-scratching. What's the tie-in with reserpine?"

"Only this, Arrowsmith. With your brains—and what Kurt Frankel can still put into 'em—you'll pass the psych board exam next year like a breeze. That means a free ticket to the gravy train. I don't have to tell you what a good man can make in private practice. Why risk losing all that—just to save a girl from lobotomy?"

"It seems you've been reading my mind, Janet."

"You mean the heart you're wearing on your sleeve."

"So I'm taking a chance with Lynn—and the others. If the

test backfires—if just one of our patients has a bad reaction to the drug and dies—I'm the goat. I'll admit it, freely."

"And you'll still gamble your reputation?"

"Yes, Janet. Because I believe—and hope—it's more than a gamble."

"Get about your business, then," said the nurse. "I'll see that the medications go through." She picked up the order book and turned away: the catch in her voice had betrayed her. "Damn you anyhow, Jim Corwin. Why did I have to be an old woman before someone like you came along?"

Janet Moore was as good as her word. In Jim's wards, as well as Singh's, the reserpine treatment went into effect with the passing of the next meal trays. At Singh's insistence, neither of them knew which of the ten patients were receiving the drug—and which an exactly similar tablet whose sole ingredient was milk-sugar. Lynn, of course, was the one exception, since her case was special.

The program was announced at the next staff meeting—in a routine way, as an experiment suggested by Jim's own reaction to the drug. As he had foreseen, there was no enthusiasm among the other doctors for what—to them—seemed a radical departure from routine. Nor did he urge them to launch a similar program in their wards. Both he and Singh preferred to work with a small group of patients, on whom exact records could be kept.

When the meeting broke, Jim lingered to talk privately with Frankel. The head physician's expression was almost grim.

"Tell me now, Kurt, if you don't approve."

"I approve entirely—for the patients. You're going about this in the only sensible way. It's you I'm worried about, Jim. You've a great future in psychiatry: I'll stake my own reputation on that belief. Don't let it slip through your fingers at Leyden."

"Do you expect our experiment to fail?"

"If it does, you might fail with it. Not just at Leyden. In your own spirit."

"I won't go off my rocker again, Kurt. That's a promise."

"You're in love with Lynn Thorndyke," said the Austrian. "I've watched it build—from the moment you stood at her bedside and heard her speak your name. We know *why* you've been trying to save her—to balance your conscience for the loss of your wife——"

"Isn't that my privilege?"

"Only if you don't tear yourself apart—in case you fail one more time. The loss of a career is too high a price."

"Meeker can wreck me overnight, Kurt. I'm aware of that."

"So can adverse publicity. The spotlight's about to swing toward Leyden again. Investigating mental hospitals is always smart politics. Normally, it will come next year. One of those committees from the legislature, armed with typewriter and camera. Something like this could bring them to our doorstep tomorrow."

"Suppose the test run's a success—and we let Meeker take the credit again?"

"He'll remain your enemy—simply because you started a program without consulting him."

"We opposed him on lobotomy and won our point."

"That time you were the only surgeon available for the operation—and Meeker was too ignorant to give us an argument. This business with reserpine is something his witch doctor's brain can grasp. If it fails, he'll rattle his voodoo gourds and drive you from the compound."

"And if it doesn't?"

"In that case he'll sell himself with the drug—just as a circus barker sells swamp-root tonic."

"So I'm under a cloud, no matter what happens?"

"You'd notice the shadow now," said Frankel, "if you weren't so detached."

"In my place, would you act differently?"

"No, Jim—but I still feel for you. You'll have my backing when the showdown comes. But I can't promise what that will be worth."

xvi

During the first three days of the injections, there was no apparent difference in Lynn's behavior and not a ripple of change on her charts. Jim felt his heart grow heavier with each passing hour, as he saw the worst of Frankel's predictions justified. Then, on the morning of the fourth day, his telephone rang just as he had finished dressing. Singh's voice was almost a shout in his ear.

"Come over to my ward, Jim. I've something to show you."

The Hindu was waiting at the anteroom door, his key chain dangling from one hand, and a chart in the other.

"You'll remember this patient, I'm sure. Mrs. Rhoda Stanley from Ellenville?"

Jim nodded, as his eye ran down the chart. The woman had been discussed at a staff meeting three weeks ago. "A relatively young schizo, wasn't she?"

"Young—and dangerously violent," said Singh. "The symptoms date back less than six months. Before the birth of her first child."

The chart, Jim noted, was a model of its kind. Electric shock and insulin had both proved negative. For the next month, Mrs. Stanley had spent most of her waking hours in a strait jacket. A footnote stated that she had been the first patient on Singh's list for the test run.

"We'll look in on her now, Jim. You must see it to believe."

The woman's cell was halfway down a corridor echoing with the shrieks and imprecations of patients in all states of dementia. Singh turned the key in the lock and stepped back. Four days ago, when Jim had made the rounds of this ward with the Indian doctor, Rhoda Stanley had been a sweat-soaked harridan, rattling the bars of her grille in a frenzy that all but wrenched her arms from their sockets. Today, in a spotless hospital gown, she was seated on her cot in an attitude of quiet waiting. Her blond hair, freshly washed and combed, surrounded her pretty, heart-shaped face like an aureole. The eyes she raised at the two doctors' entrance were friendly and unwavering.

"How good of you to visit me, Dr. Corwin."

Remembering the notations he had just read, Jim took the hand the young woman offered him. He knew that he was staring, as though he were seeing her for the first time.

"Mrs. Stanley, would you be hurt if I admitted I can't believe my eyes?"

"*Hurt,* Doctor? It's the finest compliment I've ever had. Not that I deserve any credit. It was the medicine Mrs. Foster gave me."

Jim sat down beside the cot. Try as he might, he could not leave off his staring. Here, at last, was visible evidence that the effects of reserpine were not figments of his brain.

"You're sure it was the pills that helped you, Mrs. Stanley?"

"What else? I began to feel better, almost from the moment I took the first tablet." She turned to Singh. "You remember how Mrs. Foster made me swallow it, Doctor? I was in the jacket that day. She pried my jaws apart."

Jim regained his poise. "Can you describe how reserpine affects you?"

"It's a strange feeling, Dr. Corwin. As though I were relaxed, in the softest bed there was—and *studying* myself. Seeing the things that troubled me, for what they really were——"

Jim and Singh exchanged glances. He, too, had experienced an identical reaction from the first tablet—a separation, so to speak, from every earthly care.

"If I can just keep on, Doctor. Staying outside myself. Thinking things out. I know I'll be ready to go home soon—to my husband and our baby."

Jim risked a shot in the dark—one which Frankel would never have approved. "Then the medicine helps you to see why you were troubled?"

He caught Singh's frown, and knew that the Indian doctor shared his fear of such a head-on approach. But Rhoda Stanley answered with only the barest of pauses.

"Yes, Doctor. It *has* helped me to understand. By taking me outside myself—if you can put it that way. By letting me *see* myself as I really am. When I married, I was a pretty girl—and extremely vain. Jeff and I didn't want children right away: we both pretended we couldn't afford it. That wasn't true, of course. I was afraid having a child would spoil my figure. That a baby in the house would cut down on my dancing——"

"Many young wives have those fears, Mrs. Stanley."

"So I've discovered—the hard way. I hated Jeff, when they said I was pregnant; I hated the baby I was carrying." Her voice was quite calm, as though she were speaking of an enemy she had long since pardoned. "It was even worse, after my little girl was born. You might say there was a battle going on inside me. Between the part of me that wanted her—and the part that wouldn't grow up. The wrong part won that battle—and landed me in Leyden."

"It doesn't have control any more?"

"Not while I can stay outside myself. When I see how mean and spiteful that part of me was, I can *laugh* at it. I just can't believe it could cause all this trouble."

Jim got to his feet, blinking to clear his vision. "Thank you, Mrs. Stanley. You don't know how much you've encouraged me."

"Dr. Singh tells me you thought of this treatment. So I owe everything to you."

"You owe me nothing. It was Dr. Singh's countrymen who discovered this drug. They used it—when the rest of the world was too scientific to know what they had."

In the hall, with the cell door closed on Rhoda Stanley, Jim looked at Singh for a moment without speaking.

"Do you believe me now?" asked the Hindu.

"I'm trying hard."

"In the bazaars at Calcutta," said Singh, "I've seen fakirs raise men from the dead. As a child I believed the trick was real. You might call this a return from the dead. Only it has actually happened."

"There's a factor we've overlooked, of course. Reserpine may have nothing to do with Rhoda Stanley's recovery. She *could* be on placebos, you know."

"I hadn't thought of that."

"My records are in Lovell," said Jim. "Let's cheat a little and see if she's been taking the drug."

The record sheets were in a locked drawer of the chartroom. Jim felt a surge of relief when he saw that Mrs. Stanley had been on reserpine from the start.

"What about the other nine on your list, Chandra?"

"There's been a marked change in more than half of them. Seven in all, to be exact. In every case, they've quieted down."

"You're getting the usual placebo reaction with a few, then?"

Singh nodded. In trials of this sort, tablets whose medical content was nonexistent often appeared to produce an effect. In this case, as Jim had expected, some of the ten patients had reacted to the milk-sugar pills—simply because a reaction was expected by their own flawed minds.

"We're still feeling our way, Chandra," he said. "Don't forget it."

"Not with Rhoda Stanley."

"One case doesn't establish a diagnosis. We know improvement has taken place—but we can't be positive that reserpine is the cause."

"There's no news on Lynn, I gather."

"Results are negative so far," said Jim. "Several of my other patients are improved—and Mrs. Foster insists that Lynn is quieter. Of course, that could be only an aftermath of her fall."

"Your own reaction to the drug wasn't marked for almost a week."

Again Jim looked hard at the Indian doctor. "Do you really think that Rhoda Stanley's a herald from heaven, telling us we've won?"

"I do, Jim. And I can't wait to see Dr. Meeker's face when you inform him that lobotomy's outmoded here."

"He won't like it, Chandra. We haven't scheduled an operation for nearly a week."

"Perhaps we never will."

After Singh had returned to his own chores, Jim opened Lynn's folder—which contained enlargements of the color snapshots Mrs. Foster had taken of her cell-wall paintings. Once again he studied them minutely, seeking for the gleam of returning sanity he had found (or imagined) in her first tentative sketch of the boy in the meadow. He was still poring over the strange whorls—and wishing his medical studies had left room for a grounding course in art—when Mrs. Foster put her head in the door.

"You'd better have a look, Doctor. Lynn's at work—for the first time since her fall."

He was on his feet instantly, reminding himself to walk on tiptoe at the door to Lynn's cubicle. A glance through the grille told him that she had already covered a whole wall with her finger paints, and had begun work on another. The finished painting was familiar, a repetition of the meadow she had sketched before her attempted escape. This time, however, a girl was standing beside the boy. There was another significant change. In the earlier painting, the human figure had been almost tiny in proportion to the landscape: this, Jim knew, was in character, since the true schizophrenic usually draws or paints people smaller than they really are. Today, both figures were in balance with their surroundings—the girl a slender silhouette in a pinafore, the boy a chubby two-year-old.

On the facing wall, a new landscape was taking shape with incredible swiftness as Lynn's hands flew to their task. This scene, too, was rural—a pasture with cattle drowsing beside a pond, a cluster of farm buildings beyond. Intent on her task, the girl did not seem conscious of her visitors—nor did she look up when Mrs. Foster lifted her camera and snapped the finished painting.

"What do you make of it, Doctor?" the attendant whispered.

Jim pointed to the chartroom: they moved back to the doorframe, well out of earshot. "Remember her mention of David—a baby brother?"

"Yes—the one that died in infancy."

"She's just painted him on the east wall—as he would have been if he'd lived. The girl, of course, is herself."

"Would you call it a clue to her condition?"

"I'd go beyond clues, Mrs. Foster. I'd say it suggests an approach that might have taken months of psychotherapy to uncover."

"Will you tell her, if she'll listen?"

"Not now, I'm afraid. Telling a mental patient how his disease came about is usually the worst form of treatment. They only refuse to accept the fact, then distort it into new symptoms."

"What's the value, then?"

"The fact that she's painted herself and her brother—and made them life size—is proof that she is groping back to the memory of the life they had together, however short it was. The fact of his death is a definite part of her illness. She must see it plainly, in her own way. Besides, we both know what would happen if I told her now."

"Sorry, Doctor. I'm trying hard to catch up."

"She'd only destroy the painting—as she destroyed the others. It's important that she let it stay awhile."

"Will you risk talking to her now?"

He nodded. "Let me go in alone. I'm sure it'll be quite safe."

Back at the cell door he let the key turn softly in the lock and stepped inside. The girl did not appear to notice the creak of the opening door. Even when he moved beside her, she did not raise her head from her work. Rejoicing in the depth of her concentration, Jim did not speak until she had sketched in an earth dam at the end of the pond and settled on her heels to study the effect.

"It's beautiful, Lynn," he said. "The best you've done so far."

As he had feared, her body went rigid when she noticed his presence—but she made no move to destroy what she had just painted.

"Did I startle you?" he asked. "I'll go away if you like."

She did not speak, but he saw the tension melt from her muscles as she wiped her fingers on a cloth. This, too, was a sign of improvement. During his other visits she had merely smeared her hospital gown—or her hair-matted forehead.

"Go on, please. I'd like to watch you."

Her right hand trembled, then steadied as she reached for a plastic paint bottle. In a few deft flashes of her fingers she sketched a pine tree on the high ground above the pasture. Others followed swiftly, until there was a whole grove of dark-green trees, in perfect balance with the farmhouse blocked into the lower corner of the painting.

"You must have seen such a place, Lynn—to paint it so exactly."

"It was our farm," she said, in a small, cowed whisper. "We spent the summers there."

"Did you enjoy those summers?"

"Yes. Once I caught a fish in that pond. Then I was sorry for him—and put him back."

"Did you go to the pasture often?"

"There was a haystack beside the barn," she said. Already, the conical shape of the tightly stacked hay was taking shape against the sky. "I used to climb to the top—and make myself a nest. When I was there—I pretended no one could find me."

"Why did you want to hide, Lynn?"

He saw he had said the wrong thing. Her hand had closed on the plastic bottle so violently that a long, brown tongue of paint oozed to the floor.

"I won't tell you," she whispered. "I won't tell anyone."

"Forget I asked you, please."

"Mother scolded when I got my dress dirty," she said. "She told me I was being common. Like Jenny."

"Who was Jenny?"

"The hired man's daughter. We played together, but Mother didn't know."

"Why didn't she like Jenny?"

"Jenny wore overalls, like a boy. I wanted some of my own. One day I put on Jenny's, and Mother caught me. She made me wash with laundry soap. Not in the bathroom. On the back porch, in a tub. Then she whipped me."

"You never talked like this, Lynn. Why are you doing it now?"

"Painting the haystack made me remember."

"Can't I help you?"

"Not yet, Doctor."

"Are you still afraid of me?"

"Yes." The whisper was low and tense now. "You're making me say too much. Go away! *Please* go away!"

The brief moment of insight was gone. He could only make things worse by pushing her further.

"All right, Lynn, I'll go," he said gently. "Just remember—I'm trying to help you get well."

As he spoke, she had backed to the wall with one of those flailing gestures he knew so well. But she had not raised her voice. Instead, the trembling lips were innocent as a hurt child's—and the tears that welled from her eyes were a tribute to a time she had found and lost again.

xvii

Frankel's face brightened that afternoon when Jim stopped with his first report.

"We're on the threshold of something," he said. "Let's hope we can give it a name."

"I think we're proving this drug can split the rational intellect away from its delusions. There's no doubt that Mrs. Stanley has made the break. So far, I can't say as much for Lynn."

"Mrs. Stanley has been here less than six months, Jim. Her history is far simpler than Lynn's. Be patient with the girl—she may end by surprising us all."

"As of now, I've less than a month to be patient in. All this week I've been expecting a blast from Meeker. He must be getting reports from Lisa Kendall."

"Maybe we can fire a blast in return, if it seems necessary," said Frankel. "In his absence, I've been acting head of Leyden. I've even gone over some of his accounts. They make revealing reading."

Recalling his talk with Mrs. Foster, Jim pricked up his ears. "How did you manage to unscramble them?"

The Austrian sighed. "I've just enough bookkeeping skill to recognize that our friend the director is a brazen thief. Of course I've known as much ever since I started here. I thought it was only the usual, garden variety of graft: *quid pro quo* deals, kickbacks from contractors—"

"Thief's a label that won't always stick, Kurt."

"True. I can't prove it from the books: they're much too cleverly rigged. Just to take a case at random: how long has Williams been in the pharmacy?"

"Close to three months."

"There are vouchers in Meeker's files, right through to the present. All of them are drawn for the pharmacist who left us last year. Is Williams getting a salary?"

"To my knowledge, not a penny."

"Then the money has gone into Meeker's pocket. Another thing, our day-cost per patient—so far as the books say—is about what it was six months ago."

"It *can't* be. Not with eighty lobotomy cases working full time here."

"The bills on the state treasury are the same. In this case, I don't think Meeker would dare to keep it all. He must have arranged a split with Big Al Hanley. Most of the accountants at the capital are on his payroll."

"Isn't there some way to pin this down?"

"I'm a doctor, Jim. Not a detective."

"Mrs. Foster has a niece right in Meeker's office. We can trust them both. Why not try a little low-grade snooping?"

"It's playing with dynamite."

"Didn't you once say we needed dynamite to blast him out?"

Late that night, Jim recalled the exchange with Frankel as he was passing the lighted door of the drug room. It did not surprise him to find Williams hunched over a book at his counter. It was the little man's custom to read there, far into the night—even when there could be no possible call on his services.

"What's the book this time, Enoch?"

"It's still *Materia Medica*, Dr. Corwin. I can remember when I knew whole chapters, almost by heart. Quite a bit is coming back." The pharmacist took an invoice from his file and spread it on the counter. "I'm glad you dropped in. You can initial this shipment and give me a head start in the morning."

Jim glanced over the invoice. It was addressed to Leyden from a pharmaceutical house in Atlanta, a local branch of one of the great drug manufacturers. A note requested receipt for a thousand tablets of reserpine, which had just arrived by air-mail express.

"That was fast work, Enoch," he said. "Our supply must be running low."

"I'm watching the supply, Doctor: trust me for that." Williams took off his eyeshade, and Jim saw that his forehead was knotted in a frown. "I don't like to ask this but—now we've ample stock, could you put *me* on the drug?"

"Of course—if you feel the need of it."

"You took me out of the wards, Doctor, and I'm doing the work I love. But I'm still not quite what I'd like to be. The same worries come back, and the same fears. The only difference is, the operation's pushed 'em back to where I can keep control. I'd like to have that drug here—in case I need a helping hand."

"Prescribe a course for yourself, by all means. Three milligrams a day is standard."

"It's all over the hospital what it's done for Rhoda Stanley. And the Thorndyke girl—they say the things she's painting are out of this world."

"So they are, Enoch," said Jim. "We're preparing a series of colored photographs—to use later, in a paper Dr. Singh and I are writing on reserpine."

"After we've run our series, you mean?"

"When we've enough cases to make an evaluation. I'm afraid it'll be some time in the future."

"In that case, you'll need a real stock of the drug," said Williams. "Why don't you write direct to Atlanta—and ask them to back a clinical trial? It's common practice, when they're testing new products."

"That's a first-rate suggestion, Enoch. This is a strange field for me: I'd never have thought of it."

The pharmacist beamed with pleasure. "Here's a carbon of the invoice, Doctor—with the name and address."

"Do you need anything in town? I'd like to do something to show my appreciation."

"*I'm* the one to show appreciation—after what you've done for me."

"I mean it. Will you let me know?"

"My wife sends me a five-dollar bill each month," said Williams. "It covers my personal needs. She sent me a radio too, on my birthday. I tune in on the world news—when I can stand it. When I can't, I read *Materia Medica.* Now that you've put me on reserpine, I'd call myself a happy man."

Jim went out after a hearty exchange of good nights, hoping that he didn't sound the hypocrite he felt. At least he had the first item in a dossier that might hang Dr. Thaddeus Meeker someday. The knowledge gave him confidence—a few days after his council of war with Frankel—when he entered the director's office after a chilly summons by telephone.

Meeker was fresh from his travels: a bottle-green Bavarian hat rode on his forehead and an expensive ulster still draped his massive shoulders. Evidently he had pounced on the phone before he could settle at his desk. Jim sniffed the air before he took the visitor's seat, and noted that the aroma of bourbon was richer than usual. If Meeker had needed a drink before their meeting, it suggested he was unsure of his ground. So did his preliminary rumblings, while he flipped through the weekly hospital report.

"Dr. Corwin, I can hardly believe what I'm reading. Has my staff taken advantage of my absence to soldier on the job?"

"Work has gone on as usual, I'm sure."

"Not on my lobotomy program. If I'm to judge by this report, you've been taking a vacation at state expense."

"On the contrary, Doctor: I've never been busier. Dr. Singh and I have been launching a new treatment."

"From where I'm sitting, you don't look like a pioneer."

Jim kept his temper. So far, he knew, Meeker was throwing his punches at random. "It *is* a new technique, sir—though I can't say I invented the process. It's been tested both here and abroad. If it succeeds at Leyden, we can dispense with lobotomy entirely."

Meeker bounced up from his chair—so violently that the absurd green hat cocked over one eyebrow. "*I'll* decide when a proven method is to be discarded, Corwin. Is that clear?"

"Quite, sir. I might add that Dr. Frankel has approved the project."

The director controlled himself, with an apparent effort. "What's this treatment called?"

"So far, it has no formal name. Essentially, it's a method of easing tension in our violent wards with reserpine."

"The drug you've been taking for high blood pressure?"

"Yes. It has already been used, with considerable success, to combat mental disease."

"As I recall, it's damned expensive. How are you getting it?"

"I've ordered a thousand tablets from Atlanta."

"At what price?"

"The quoted figure was around two hundred dollars."

Under that tip-tilted hat, Meeker's jowls had already turned a rich purple. He raised a fist skyward, and Jim braced himself to counterpunch. Instead, the fat fingers uncurled, to busy themselves with an Havana Uppmann.

"You placed this order without my approval?"

"The situation was urgent, sir. Particularly in the case of Lynn Thorndyke."

"Miss Kendall informed me of her attempted escape," said Meeker. He seemed a trifle calmer, now that his head was wreathed in the most expensive of cigar smoke. "Do you know the hell I'd have caught if she'd climbed that wall?"

"Of course. That's why I started her on the drug at once."

"You had her mother's permission to perform a lobotomy. That would have settled matters once and for all."

"Dr. Frankel agreed the operation was contraindicated," said Jim patiently. "Her family doctor granted us six weeks to help her with other methods."

"Very well, Corwin. Have your say with Miss Thorndyke—pro tem, at least. Placing wholesale drug orders in my absence is another matter. I'm disapproving this shipment. Tell Williams to send it back."

"Most of it has already been used, Dr. Meeker."

"Send back the rest, then."

Their eyes met and held. Jim kept his voice quiet as he fired the first shot in his own attack.

"Won't you even listen to the results we've obtained?"

"My job is to run Leyden as cheaply as I can. Suppose I *did* let you use this medication. What would it cost per month?"

"We're planning to handle a series of fifty cases—now we've established our test run. Five hundred dollars should cover them."

"Six thousand a year? Have you lost your mind?"

"All I'm asking is the chance to run a decent series. We'll have definite results long before the year is up."

"Meanwhile, you plan to stop a treatment that costs nothing. Don't deny those operations have saved us money here."

"Dr. Meeker, it isn't my job to check your bookkeeping. But can you prove that the patients on your work force have cut the budget?"

Meeker had turned to the bar. At Jim's last question he stopped dead, in the act of reaching for a glass. When he spoke again his small eyes were guarded, his tone almost wheedling.

"Money isn't the only yardstick we use here, Corwin. Cures are important too—and the best care available within our budget. Certainly that means not wasting funds."

"Is it wasting money to help people? *Really* help them?"

"You've that much confidence in your new procedure?"

"I think its possibilities are beyond belief."

"Suppose your patients do improve? Won't they be like diabetics—needing the drug the rest of their lives?"

"Dr. Frankel hopes not; it's something we've yet to investigate."

"Meanwhile, there's no cash available to run a clinical test that may fail. If our costs go up, without results, we must explain to the legislature. Have you ever testified before a state hospital committee? I can assure you it isn't a pleasant experience—if you're on the defensive."

"It's possible I can obtain the drug—for a while at least—at no cost to the state."

"In that case I'll withdraw my objection."

"I'll call Atlanta at once. Perhaps they'll make a special dispensation to back a new product."

"Make your call, if you insist. Meanwhile, we can't stop our lobotomy program. I'll expect it to continue as before." Meeker's voice trailed off as he lit a fresh cigar: this, Jim recognized, was only a rear-guard action.

"Some of the cases we'd considered for surgery have already responded to reserpine."

The director shrugged, and opened a file folder at random. It was a way of signaling the end of an interview. "I want my patients quiet, Corwin—and able to work for their keep. How you obtain these results doesn't concern me too much."

"Meanwhile, will you write to Mrs. Thorndyke—telling her we hope to cure her daughter by other means?"

"If you insist." Meeker feigned absorption in the papers before him. Taking his cue, Jim left the office—with the heady certainty that he had found the weakness in the director's armor.

In his room again, waiting for his phone call to Atlanta to go through, Jim wrote out a check for two hundred dollars and clipped it to the invoice for mailing. Come what may, he thought, this will pay for the testing of Lynn Thorndyke.

The voice in Atlanta belonged to a Dr. Arthur Small, regional manager of the Runyon Pharmaceutical Company, distributors of the drug. From the first words, it was more than cordial.

"I've a copy of your recent invoice before me, Dr. Corwin. May I ask where you first heard of reserpine?"

"From a Hindu colleague here at Leyden."

"Have you seen any preliminary reports?"

"Frankly, no. We plan to run our test as an independent experiment."

"May I ask what inspired it?"

Dr. Small listened with respectful, purring affirmatives while Jim described his own cure, his decision to extend the same medication to the wards—and the results of the test run.

"This is extraordinary, Dr. Corwin. The manufacturer, as you may know, has branches abroad. Our opposite numbers in Europe have been testing reserpine for some time—comparing its effects with those of chlorpromazine. Both drugs are beginning to be used abroad. We've also encouraged several mental hospitals to test them over here. Rockland State, in New York, to name just one. Clinics in California and Massachusetts——"

"May I ask the results?"

"They've been staggering. As conclusive as your report on Rhoda Stanley. Naturally, we're still in the process of checking, before we make them public. Do I gather you've been using reserpine mainly with patients scheduled for lobotomy?"

"With a few exceptions, yes."

"Our preliminary tests seem to indicate that reserpine—and, perhaps, chlorpromazine—will eventually do away with lobotomy as treatment for schizophrenia. Perhaps with shock treatment as well. Supposing this first series you are planning is successful—will you continue?"

"That's why I'm on long distance, Dr. Small. There are difficulties here at Leyden—mainly financial."

"Can you be specific, Doctor?"

"This is a low-budget institution, supported entirely by state funds. Our director has told me he cannot order an expensive drug like reserpine, if it's to be used on a test basis. I've sent my personal check for the first thousand tablets. In the future I'm hoping you can give us some kind of discount."

"Will Leyden pay the lower cost?"

"Frankly, no. I was planning to handle it myself—if I could."

There was only the briefest of pauses in Atlanta. "That won't be necessary, Dr. Corwin. Not if you can set up a really conclusive procedure for testing the effect of the drug."

"At the moment, I'm using the double-blind method, with an equal number of placebo tablets."

"There's none better, in my opinion. How many patients can you test as a start?"

"I was planning on fifty for the first run."

"Could you handle a hundred?"

Jim made a quick mental check. He and Singh had at least a thousand patients each under their care. Of these, well over two hundred could be classed as disturbed. It would mean endless, drudging work to check and tabulate the effects of the drugs on so large a number—but it could settle the future of reserpine at Leyden, once and for all.

"We can handle them, Dr. Small," he said firmly. "Providing *I* can meet the expense."

"There will be no expense, Doctor. Until further notice, I'm putting you down for ten thousand tablets a month—gratis—for a clinical trial. Will that be sufficient?"

"Wait till I get my breath," said Jim. "Did you say *ten* thousand?"

Small's voice boomed with laughter. It was the conspiratorial mirth of the businessman extending a gambler's hand to the man of science and rejoicing in the contact. "Believe me, it's to our advantage to prove the worth of reserpine in American medical circles. I don't have to tell you how important it is to keep accurate records."

"We're using a three-milligram daily dosage. Supplemented with intramuscular injections for those who can't take it orally at the start."

"That's standard procedure. I'll put through your order for the drug today. It should reach you within the week."

"I can't begin to thank you properly, Dr. Small."

"*You* are doing us the favor, Doctor. We've been desperate to find capable men who'll run tests under controlled circumstances. Yours may well be one of the most conclusive projects."

Ten minutes later, at a rendezvous in Frankel's office, Jim detailed the results of his afternoon's campaign to the head physician and to Singh. "Part of my mind tells me I'm still dreaming," he said. "I suppose you might call it the result of luck and boldness."

"With the medical proof still to come," said Frankel dryly. "Meeker gave in today, because he doesn't want a knockdown fight with me—and a call from the state committee—before he has time to cover his recent banditry. Give him another month and he'll be demanding concrete results—or your heads."

"I can handle a hundred cases—if Chandra will help."

The Hindu nodded happily. "You can count on me, Jim. It's logical to run the test in our wards. That way, the others can act as our controls."

"You'll have to set up detailed records," Frankel warned.

"We've profile charts worked out now," said Jim. "I can run off a hundred copies on the mimeograph tonight."

"What about the ward attendants? Fellows like Jack Hanley, for example? It'll mean extra work."

"And quieter wards," said Jim. "Jack has already congratulated me on that detail. He can't back down now."

"One thing more, Kurt," said the Hindu. "This is your province, not ours. Assuming we can bring these hundred patients to the point where we can communicate, our whole psychotherapy program must be stepped up enormously. Can we count on our staff?"

"If you two fellows will do your part," said Frankel, "I'll bring the others in line. Group work seems indicated, if the program's really successful. That should spread the load evenly." He lifted a detaining palm, before either of the younger doctors could speak again. "For the present, let's stop counting our chickens—until we *do* get results. Don't forget there have been other promising treatments in psychiatry."

Jim did not stir as the head physician took a yellow-backed journal from his bookcase. It was like Frankel to be cautious, and he respected that caution. Yet he could not help but smile inwardly as he detected the note of excitement under the Austrian's professional pose.

"Keep a tight rein on us, Kurt," he said. "I'm sure we both need it."

Frankel was turning the leaves of the ancient pamphlet. He read, in an odd singsong that was almost a parody of the medical-school lecturer:

> Patients showing marked habit deterioration—such as soiling, wetting, destructiveness—become more cleanly, less destructive, and better able to care for themselves. Patients given to outbreaks of violence, with a tendency to assault both guards and doctors, become much better adjusted to their environment. Following treatment, their activities are more easily directed into useful channels.

He tossed the journal on the desk without comment. Glancing at the date, Jim saw that it had been published in 1926. The article described the action of certain bromide compounds on the mentally ill.

"Make haste slowly, gentlemen," said Frankel. "Forget Meeker and all outside menaces. I'll protect you—as long as I can. The big point is that *other* drugs have given promise during the last quarter century—from bromides to amytal and pentothal. There's just one ideal treatment—to return the patient to reality on a *permanent* basis."

"Or at least to institute treatment that will bring him back," said Jim.

"If reserpine or chlorpromazine can do that much, I'll endorse them. If they do not, they'll have no lasting benefit in psychotherapy. In fact, for the long pull, they could do more harm than good. I'm already convinced that reserpine will make our job easier by quieting our patients. The danger is that it may lull *us* into false security. Keeping a man drugged is no answer to his problems. Not if the drugged state obscures the true reason for his breakdown. Obviously, you'll never let that happen at Leyden."

xviii

For the next eight days, Jim and Singh got what sleep they could—most of it in snatches. The technical difficulties of starting a hundred patients on reserpine (and a second hundred on placebos) were staggering. The profile charts Jim had devised proved more complex than he had anticipated, and required much revising. So did the system of issuing the medicine from the pharmacy, and the matching of Williams' records with Janet Moore's, who had been assigned the all-important task of riding herd on the actual administration of the drug at ward level.

After the first week, however, the system began to mesh all down the line, from paper work to clinical testing. In the first department the little pharmacist proved an invaluable ally—as well as a walking demonstration of the strange powers of reserpine. Since he had put himself on a three-milligram dosage he seemed to become more alert with each passing day—and more confident of his abilities at the prescription counter. Best of all, he was losing the diffidence and withdrawal that had persisted even after his operation.

Jim was careful to keep up a restricted schedule of lobotomies—since there was still a reservoir of hopeless cases that had been ruled out in advance as candidates for the drug. At this stage he wanted to stay clear of Meeker at all costs. There was the ever-present danger that the director might blunder into print with a premature account of the experiments before Frankel was ready to announce his findings.

Halfway through the second week, the effects of the medication were apparent in every ward. Almost without exception, the patients who had been put on the drug were quieter and more co-operative. Here and there (as the charts proved with detail that could not be denied) a case duplicated Rhoda Stanley's. Her almost complete recovery was still the brightest spot in the series. Thanks to Frankel, Jim had arranged her outright release from Leyden for a trial visit with her family.

As both Jim and Singh had expected, many of the patients on placebos had also improved markedly in their behavior. In each of these cases it was necessary to keep a painstaking check on their daily routines. Reactions of this sort were characteristic of the highly charged emotional reserve that was so much a part of mental illness, and remained so suggestible to outside stimulus. In every case (and this, after all, was the proof Jim was seeking) the improvement was more apparent than real. After a brief flare-up of "normality," these patients lapsed into their former states.

When the experiment was two weeks old, Jim could note tentatively but exultantly that better than fifty of the hundred patients on reserpine had been soothed out of their disturbed phases—enough, in many cases, to permit the first tentative analysis that was the *sine qua non* of this pioneering venture. Lynn Thorndyke, unfortunately, was not among that percentage.

After her first sharp improvement (when he had stood before her painting and talked with her for a moment as friend to friend) she had seemed to regress rather than to move forward. True, she was no longer disturbed, and Mrs. Foster reported her easy to control. But the lethargy that gripped her, along with the apparent hopelessness (though it had had no verbal expression so far) troubled Jim almost as much as her former ravings. Had he yielded to Meeker and performed a lobotomy, he told himself sadly, results could hardly have been more negative.

At the end of the first fortnight, he asked that both Frankel and Singh join him in consultation. Lynn was examined at length in her cell. Her answers were dutiful and showed a certain limited contact with reality—but Jim could read his own disappointment in the eyes of both doctors, long before the interview was ended. Later he made his own notes on the chart and worked hard to control his despair. Lynn, after all, was but one of a hundred items in an experiment that had already paid dividends. He had no right to rail at fate, simply because a particular prayer had gone unanswered.

"The first response was so dramatic, Kurt. I can't understand what's happened since."

"Certainly she's improved since our last examination," said the head physician.

"Don't pretend you aren't as unhappy as I."

Singh put a hand on Jim's sleeve. "Be honest with yourself, my friend. Are you sure you haven't been too anxious with her, ever since you came to Leyden?"

"I'll admit it freely, Chandra—but time is so short now."

"Meeker's just left on a political fence-mending expedition upstate," said Frankel. "I think he'll keep his promise—when he said you'd have six weeks to show real improvement."

"More than half the time is gone."

The Austrian rubbed his chin as he flipped the closely annotated pages of the chart. "It's almost as though she'd changed from a schizoid to a depressive. Could *that* be a kickback from the drug?"

"We've had a few such reactions in my wards," said Singh. "I've been treating them with caffeine, and brought most of them out."

"The reaction seems deeper with Lynn," Frankel observed.

"We've had that too," said Jim. "In several instances there's been retrogression after the first improvement. All of the other cases have been taken off the drug."

"You've used caffeine as a corrective in Lynn's case?"

"For three days. The results seem negative."

"Why not try something stronger?"

"A real cerebral stimulant might backfire."

"The fact remains, this is an emergency. If her state's unchanged when Meeker returns, he'll insist on a lobotomy—and I'm afraid he'll be justified."

"I could use dexedrine," said Jim. The stimulant, he knew,

usually had powerful effect on the cerebral cortex. It might be the jolt Lynn needed to rouse her.

"In conjunction with the reserpine?"

"I can't let up on the dosage, Kurt—not while there's a ray of hope."

"It's agreed, then. Prescribe dexedrine, and we'll look in on her again in a few days."

The dexedrine was given at once—by hypodermic, to enhance its effect. While he was waiting for Miss Moore's first report, Jim put in another call to Dr. Arthur Small in Atlanta. The regional director was delighted with his over-all report.

"What's the hitch in this one case, Doctor?"

"The girl seems depressed rather than disturbed."

"Have you tried stopping the drug?"

Small listened attentively, as Jim described his difficulties with Meeker—and the fact that Lynn's mother had given her permission for a lobotomy.

"Dexedrine may be indicated," he said, "though I doubt it. Let me do a bit of telephoning around the country. I'll be in touch with you tomorrow."

Early next morning, after an unusually trying night on the wards, the phone in Jim's room jabbed him out of the first deep slumber he had known in weeks. Small's voice, however, soothed away his resentment: it was evident at once that this business-scientist had news.

"Take a new lease on life, Doctor," he said. "Your Miss Thorndyke's not at all unique. At least three clinics have reported identical setbacks after an extended course of reserpine. In several cases the regression was succeeded by even more violent disturbance."

"God forbid that should happen here."

"It doesn't sound likely, when you consider the time lapse. You'll be glad to know that in nearly every similar case—where the attending physician has had the courage to continue the drug—the final stage has been a relatively quiet one, amenable to various forms of psychotherapy. Only two out of twelve were forced to discontinue reserpine entirely."

"Is the continued use of dexedrine indicated? So far, she hasn't responded."

"I may have another lead there, Dr. Corwin. Our research department has been working for some time on a drug that seems to have great stimulative powers in such cases of depression. It's still in the experimental stage—but all we've learned so far suggests it's quite safe. The studies made abroad are particularly promising."

"Is this drug available?"

"We haven't released it officially—but I'll send you a supply by airmail. The chemical label is phenidylate: we'll give it a trade name later when it's proved its worth. I'd suggest a dosage of ten milligrams several times each day."

"We'll use it exactly as you recommend, Dr. Small."

Jim felt his heart lift as he hung up the phone. A glance through the window told him that Dr. Frankel's cottage kitchen was already lighted. The Austrian (who kept early hours) always left his latchstring out. . . . Hurrying across the wide lawn that separated the homes of the married doctors from the main building, he cocked an attentive ear toward the wards. At this hour, when the shifts were changing and the inmates were ending their morning meal, the air was usually hideous with their din (food, in violent wards, acted as a stimulant to the tongue, precisely as liquor raised the decibel level of a cocktail party). Today, there was no mistaking the difference in the uproar from the other wards, as contrasted to the relative quiet of the four shuttered wings that housed the cases on reserpine.

Frankel, still in his bathrobe, was standing at his electric stove in the act of pouring out the thick chocolate for which his kitchen was famous. He smiled at Jim, and reached for a second cup.

"What's the good news this morning?"

"We've another trump card after all. At least, I hope we have."

The Austrian nodded his approval as Jim repeated the conversation with Dr. Small. "Perhaps it will turn the trick," he said. "Even if there's no immediate response, I wouldn't feel too badly. After all, the difficulty with Lynn may be psychic—with you as the chief troublemaker."

"I've had a bad night," said Jim. "Don't hit me where it hurts."

"That means you've noticed too," said Frankel. "Yesterday, for example—when the three of us were questioning her—it was apparent that Lynn was far more tense with you. When you allowed Singh and myself to approach, her whole body relaxed."

"It was even worse before the reserpine."

"You're familiar with the phenomenon of transference in psychoanalysis, aren't you?"

"Fairly. Don't ask me for an exact definition."

Frankel shrugged. "No one has tried to pin it down precisely. You might call it state of trust—and attachment—that the patient develops for the therapist. Not so oddly, it usually works best when the analyst is a member of the opposite sex."

Jim kept his eyes on his cup. "I hope I'm not too far ahead of you."

"Perhaps you haven't caught up. One of the fundamental conflicts that bring on schizophrenia is the inability of the patient to handle normal sex urges. You're a handsome man, Jim—with an air that is attractive to many women. Am I still clear to you?"

"If you are, I won't admit it."

"Sometime in the course of her treatment, Lynn has been attracted to you as a man. Who can say when? Aboard the *Creole Belle*, perhaps—when she was on the very brink. Or during that brief moment of sanity when you brought her back with the cyanide injection. She has probably been fighting your attraction ever since. Simply because it brings to the front impulses she was unable to handle in the first place—when she still lived among the sane."

"If that's true, I've no right to continue treating her."

"Correction, Jim—it may be the most compelling reason why you should."

"Now I've really lost your drift."

"Don't forget there can be both a positive and a negative

transference. The latter usually predominates at the early stage of analysis. Only when it's replaced by the positive element do you begin to get results. It's quite possible that you're on the edge of such a turnabout—particularly if phenidylate can bring her out of this depression."

"Let's see how well I understand you," said Jim slowly. "At present she hates me because she's attracted to me physically—and such an attraction threatens her emotional immunity. Later, if I play my cards, I *may* use that same attraction as a means of breaking through to her."

"You have stated the case exactly," said Frankel. "First, you must break the shell that separates her from reality. Next, you must use your knowledge of her past to expose the roots of her illness and destroy them."

"With reserpine as the bridge to unite us?"

Frankel nodded. "If the bridge is strong enough—and always providing you can change the nature of her transference."

Jim breathed deep before he spoke. "If that chance comes, I'll do my best," he said. "Somehow, I thought *you'd* take over, once she was ready for therapy. I'm still afraid it's more than I can handle."

"No, Jim. I'm convinced that you're a born psychiatrist, one of the few it's been my privilege to train here. Keegan, Welles, and Singh are run of the mine."

"Not Chandra, surely."

"He's a cut above the others, and a grand fellow: when he returns to India he'll be a leader in his field. But he lacks your ability to get to fundamentals. Like so many Asians, Chandra believes that time is a dream—and man himself but a puppet of the gods. You can't expect a doctor of his background to take the individual too seriously: in his country, life has always been a weed."

"Perhaps I lean to the other extreme with Lynn. Doesn't that disqualify me from treating her? A physician who's gone overboard for his patient should turn in his license."

"Not at all—if you keep your emotions in control. And I'm

convinced you can—now. I couldn't say as much when you first came to Leyden."

"Very well, Kurt. I'll carry on—and pray this tandem of reserpine and phenidylate gets results."

"If it doesn't, Jim, something will turn up later. Think of Ehrlich—and the six hundred and five compounds he tested before he discovered salvarsan. If reserpine fails in every possible combination, there'll be other drugs. Chlorpromazine, perhaps—or some compound that isn't even in a test tube, so far. I'm convinced we're on the verge of a great advance in psychiatry. Remember how we started using penicillin during the war? In those days it was touchy stuff—nothing like so effective as the present derivatives. Drug treatment for mental disease may be in the same early stages——"

"Even so, our record shows something to cheer about—if the results hold."

"They'll hold, Jim. And I'll tell you more. The ones who failed to benefit may have had an idiosyncrasy for the drug—something that happens at every level in clinical practice. Even if Lynn never responds, even if we lose her to Meeker, reserpine will prove its worth."

Jim nodded soberly. "Thanks for putting me straight. I was thinking like a medical student."

"Don't apologize for that. A lot of our discoveries came about because a medical student with a bright mind asked a professor a question he couldn't answer—and started *him* thinking. It's a process none of us should forget—especially professors."

xix

The phenidylate tablets arrived the following morning, and Jim took them to Lovell without pausing for breakfast. Lynn was put on a three-tablet dosage daily—and, lest the new drug overstimulate her, he ordered the dexedrine injections discontinued. Since a half dozen of Singh's patients were exhibiting similar but milder depression patterns, he rationed the bottle with his colleague's wards, in order to establish a control on the drug.

This time there was little chance to build up anxiety. The next morning, when he made his rounds in the women's ward, Mrs. Foster was beaming.

"The medication brought her 'round, Doctor."

"She's out of the depression?"

"Overnight. She's been painting since dawn."

He risked a quick glance through the grille of Lynn's room. The girl was on her feet, painting a landscape on the southern wall, her slim figure in bold relief against the glow of morning at the window. He could sense her new vigor instantly. Save for the fact that she was using finger paints, she might have been a working artist busy in her studio. He drew back quickly, before she could note his presence, and returned to the chart-room, where the attendant awaited him with a triumphant smile.

"If you want to talk to her, I'm sure she'll respond."

"Let her go on with her work. I don't want to break the pattern."

"Do we continue the phenidylate?"

"By all means—as long as it helps her." This, he reflected happily, was an improvement that even Meeker could recognize. "How's the rest of the ward, Mrs. Foster?"

"It's still hard for me to believe, Doctor. Women who haven't put a sentence together in ten years are acting like folks again."

"Let's hope the improvement continues."

"Can you keep on getting the medicine?"

"Until we've completed this trial run, at least. Eventually, of course, the state will have to foot the bill."

"The legislature can be pretty bullheaded about hospital costs, Doctor—to say nothing of the director himself."

Jim glanced sharply at the attendant. It was not the first time Mrs. Foster had spoken out against Meeker. "Won't we be cutting costs—if we can start sending people home?"

"And cut the work force? You know Dr. Meeker better than that."

"Enoch Williams wants to go home. I signed the application yesterday."

Mrs. Foster sniffed. "D'you know why? Because his wife caught that bright young assistant of hers with both hands in the till. Now, if you please, she needs a husband again. So she writes to Dr. Meeker, asking that he be released."

"I think it's worth risking."

"Maybe—I won't argue. Anyway, Dr. Meeker won't approve the application."

"Not even now? He hasn't a single valid reason for keeping Enoch here."

"Then he'll invent one."

Jim would recall the observation later. Today, with his heart singing over the dramatic change in Lynn, he could put it from his mind as he finished his tour of the wards. When that chore was behind him, he stole a few moments to confer with Singh. The Indian doctor's report on the virtues of phenidylate matched his own.

Planning his visit deliberately, Jim put off his call on Lynn until the end of his working day. When he entered Lovell for the second time, he was prepared for the look of revulsion he expected to find in her eyes. His talk with Frankel had been a needed corrective. Understanding the cause of the girl's persistent antagonism, he could meet the challenge squarely—and hope for the moment when unreasoning hate would turn into acceptance.

This time the change in Lynn was even more startling. During the day Mrs. Foster had washed and waved her hair, and given her a light summer dress to wear in place of the shapeless hospital uniform. When Jim unlocked her door, she was standing with her back to the window, studying details in the half-finished painting. At his entrance she shrank back with a frightened gasp—precisely as she had done in the past. But there was no bitterness in her eyes when she faced him. He spoke quietly, careful to keep the room between them.

"Good evening, Lynn."

For a moment he was certain that she was about to lapse into the mutism he knew so well. Instead, her lips moved slowly.

"Good evening—Dr. Corwin."

"You're much better, aren't you? I'm glad you're painting again."

For the first time he risked a look at her work—fearful even now that she might rush forward to destroy it. When she held her ground, he ventured a step nearer. This time, he saw, the wall painting represented a section of a college campus. There was no mistaking the ivied walls, or the white cupola of the chapel in the background. Lying beneath a tree was a stack of books—and, bent above them, a girl who could only be Lynn herself.

"Is it Glenville?"

"I think so, Doctor. I'm not sure."

"May I stay and talk awhile?"

The girl moved to the cot and sat there with her hands in her lap. He felt a lump rise in his throat at her artless grace, the visible evidence of her lack of tension. Her voice was part of that new picture—low, controlled, with only a ghostly overtone of her old anger at his presence.

"If you like, Doctor."

"Does it make you happy to paint?"

"I suppose it does—a little."

"Do you know why you've improved so much lately?"

"The tablets did it. The reserpine. Mrs. Foster said you'd ordered them for me."

Bless Foster for that, he told himself. *It's made you part of the pattern that spells out sanity.* "They've done wonders here at Leyden," he said carefully. "When we saw they were helping you, we gave them to others. Some of them are even going home."

He caught the wary gleam in her eye and realized that he had pushed her too far. "Home, Doctor? What is *home*?"

"Never mind, Lynn."

"Are you sending me away too?"

"Not until you're ready. Just remember, what we've done for

you so far is only the beginning. We can do much more—if you'll tell us what troubles you."

She did not meet his eyes: instead, she continued to stare down mutely at the inert hands in her lap. But he was sure that the brief flare of tension had faded. "Will you let us go on helping, Lynn?"

"Yes—if I can."

"You aren't afraid of us?"

"No, Doctor." Only by the shape of her lips was he sure that she had spoken.

"Would you like to go into the open ward with the other patients? Not now, of course—but when you're better?"

"Perhaps—when I'm better."

"Out there you could use water colors and brushes."

"I'd like that."

"Tell me about your work at Glenville. You were a fine arts major, weren't you?"

"I think so."

He dared to press the point. "You loved painting, didn't you?"

"Yes, Doctor. I worked hard at it, until——"

"Until you got sick?"

"I remember now. The day I first did that scene." She gestured vaguely at the whorls of paint. "Culpepper Hall—and the chapel——"

"Did you always do landscapes?"

"Mostly. Even when I began working in oils."

"But there's a girl in this painting." When she did not reply to this, he risked another question—warned in advance by the sudden tightness of her lips. "She looks like you, Lynn. Why is she alone?"

"There wasn't anyone with me. There never was."

Remembering his visit to Glenville and what he had learned of Jay Thompson and Mary Lou, Jim chose his words with care. "On a college campus? It's usually a busy place."

"Not for me."

"Then you painted yourself alone because you *felt* alone? Even with people all around you?"

He could see the question break through her reticence as tangibly as though an invisible wall had crumbled between them. The tightness left her mouth, until she was almost smiling. Her voice, though it was still only a whisper, was charged with a sudden animation that set his heart leaping.

"How did you know that, Doctor?"

"*I've* felt that same way often, Lynn. Everyone does at times."

"Not as I did."

"Most of us can't help being lonely."

"Sick people?"

"Ordinary people, Lynn—like your classmates at Glenville. The friends you wouldn't put in the picture—because you felt *you* were the only lonesome one."

It was the first time she had opened her eyes wide in his presence, the only time she had dared to meet his own eyes without flinching. "Is that really true, Doctor? You aren't saying it to make me feel better?"

"I'll never lie to you, Lynn. You know that in your heart."

She nodded slowly—and her eyes did not waver. "Yes, Doctor. I guess I do."

"Do you remember the day we injected cyanide, here in this room? When you wakened—and talked to us for a moment?"

"I'm remembering now."

"You weren't afraid of me then. Why have you been afraid until today?"

"I don't know."

"Think, Lynn. Was there a *reason* to be afraid?"

He watched her mind take hold of the idea and test it cautiously. Even now there was none of the tension he had expected the question to generate. "I can remember I was afraid," she said. "But not why."

"Doesn't that fear seem a bit foolish now?"

She smiled then. "Yes. I suppose it does."

"Can you begin to look back at that fear—and see it was quite needless?"

"I—already have, Doctor."

"When, Lynn?"

"When they began giving me the drug. First in the needle—then in tablets. Before, there was just one me—now, I can get outside that old me whenever I like. Ask it questions, the way you're asking now. *Make* it answer——" She broke off, as though the effort to complete the thought was beyond her. "It didn't last, though—that breaking away. Lately, I've felt I was back where I started."

"That was only the depression the drug causes in some people. The new medicine Mrs. Foster gave you yesterday took care of it——"

"I still feel closed in, a little."

"You'll lose that feeling, too, as time goes on," he promised her. "But I want you to remember one thing, no matter what happens. You've nothing to fear from me. I'm here to help you, like the others. Will you promise?"

"Yes, Doctor. I'll promise."

He turned to the door then—afraid he might outstay his welcome. "You'll soon be running out of walls here. Tomorrow I'll see about getting you some water colors and drawing paper."

"Mrs. Foster told me you ordered the finger paints. I want to thank you."

"Just keep on improving, Lynn. That's all the thanks I'll need."

"I'll try, Doctor."

"I know you will—now we're friends."

Hesitating with a hand on the door, he feared she would make no response to this final offer. Then, with a wan smile, she put out her hand and let him take it in his own. At first the hand was limp—but he felt a faint returning pressure before he released it. The contact reminded him of his first day in an operating room, when he had picked up a freshly delivered infant and felt the tiny fist close round his finger.

"Good night, Lynn."

"Good night, Dr. Jim."

It was the name many of his patients used, but it was the first time she had spoken it. There was a blind trust in its utterance. It filled him with the greatest happiness he had ever known.

xx

Dr. Meeker returned to Leyden a full two days ahead of schedule—and once again Jim was summoned to his office, long before the news of the unexpected arrival had spread through the wards. It was now full summer, and the air-conditioners purred discreetly at each window. The director, Jim observed, had switched from bourbon to a tall gin and tonic to honor the changing season—but the tilt of his cigar was unchanging.

"I see you've approved Williams' request for discharge, Doctor. Aren't you taking a good bit on yourself?"

Recalling Mrs. Foster's warning, Jim kept his voice mild. "Isn't that one of my functions, sir?"

"On what do you base your opinion?"

"He's improved steadily since his operation; I believe he'd get along well at home. His wife wants him back—and his business needs him."

"A month ago he was content to run our drug room. Why the change?"

"In his case, I'd say that reserpine finished what surgery began. I've noted a similar reaction pattern in a few other patients—but his is the most remarkable."

"What happens if he discontinues the drug?"

"He needn't—for the present. He can get reserpine at wholesale rates. As a pharmacist he knows how to handle it. Besides, his home town is only a short distance from Leyden: he can return for checkups."

Meeker's heavy face settled into a frown. "Corwin, is this a grandstand play to prove the value of a newfangled treatment?"

"Mr. Williams asked to leave, Doctor."

"D'you realize what it will cost to replace him?"

"What's more important—saving a pharmacist's salary, or releasing a patient as cured?"

"How can I know he's *really* cured?"

"In the case of mental illness, there's no absolute certainty. There is also no better final testing than the return of a patient to society full time."

"If I meet this request, there will be twenty other letters on my desk tomorrow. What becomes of my labor force then?"

"We have plenty of custodial cases at Leyden. Half the population of our wards is beyond rehabilitation."

"And useless as workmen."

"You can always admit new cases from the waiting list."

"Damn the waiting list! It takes six months to process a new patient. Meanwhile, my day-cost skyrockets."

"Surely it's to Leyden's credit to show we're discharging patients."

Meeker stamped into his bar for a refill. This, too, was a familiar tactic. Like an actor after an exit to the wings, it was the director's custom to return with a brand-new attack on the scene. His voice was deceptively gentle as he settled at his desk again.

"Dr. Corwin, you've been with us long enough to know the facts of life here. Believe me, they're also true of every institution of this type. At the state house, the important thing is *not* how many patients we release from Leyden—it's how cheaply we can lock in the ones we have. Do we speak the same language so far?"

"I'm afraid not—but go on."

"Lobotomy's a means to that end. So, perhaps, is this medicine you're guinea pigging. At least, I'm told your wards are quieter. That means I can cut down on attendants, if the cure works all the way. Can you assure me it'll stick—once the medication is stopped?"

"We've no such assurance at the moment. In fact, we haven't used the word *cure* so far."

"I thought not. That's the trouble with you idealists—you won't look ahead. Will the manufacturer go on supplying drugs indefinitely?"

"We can hardly expect that, sir. The company's only real concern is the clinical tests we're running. Once those results are established, we'll have to place orders at wholesale rates."

"Not if it costs more to run Leyden with the drugs than without them."

"Even if I've demonstrated that cures are possible?"

"Even then, Corwin."

Jim stared into the bland, faintly smirking face across the desk. Hard though it was to believe that anyone could be so callous, he knew that Meeker meant every word. To his mind, the patient day-cost was the only yardstick that mattered. Jim was sure the legislature used the same standard of judgment. Like the average, unthinking voter, the solons at the state house might authorize a drive for mental health, or weep without shame before their television screens when a popular actress was saved from madness by modern psychiatry. In their book, a sufferer from mental disease was still someone to be locked up, as a protection for society.

"May I ask a statistical question, Dr. Meeker?"

"By all means."

"Last year the records show that you admitted three hundred and six patients—into a hospital population of over five thousand."

"We admit patients whenever space is available. The rate's been roughly the same for ten years."

"In that time you discharged three hundred and ten to the custody of relatives—with just twelve certified as cured."

"Believe me, Corwin, those figures will compare with the average institutions."

"Suppose just a little more was spent on each patient—enough to provide an adequate supply of drugs like reserpine. You'd have a higher cure rate, and more discharged as improved——"

"And still more to process. Every jail in the state is on my waiting list."

"At least, more sick people would be hospitalized."

"Not with a legislative committee poking into my books to see why I can't run Leyden more cheaply."

"I'm not concerned with the legislature, Dr. Meeker. I'm not even concerned with the patient day-cost. My job, as I see it, is to help as many patients as I can."

"What are you asking me to do? Change the whole system here so you can keep your ideals burnished?"

"I'm asking you to admit that a man's life is worth more than a taxpayer's vote. At the last session, the legislature authorized a two-hundred-thousand-dollar appropriation to build a new mansion for the governor. Each year it puts millions into new office buildings for civil workers—complete with air-conditioning and recreation rooms. Surely the state can spend a little more—and keep our drug room stocked."

Meeker drained his glass. "I won't say you're wrong, Corwin: I don't want to sound like a human cash register. Perhaps we can buck the system later, if the drug really proves itself. Meanwhile, you must hold down costs. That's an ultimatum."

"You've no objection to my continuing the test run—so long as it's free?"

"None whatever. But I want Williams kept in the pharmacy—at least for the present."

So we're back to Williams, thought Jim. *Back to the three hundred dollars you pocket each month to spend on Lisa Kendall.* Aloud, he said only, "To save a salary, Doctor? Or to save the man himself?"

Meeker shrugged. "Have you ever worked in private practice?"

"Only in hospitals," said Jim. Already, he could sense what was coming. "I can't count my service in Korea—or eighteen months as a ship's surgeon."

"*I* was in practice for almost twenty years, Dr. Corwin: it didn't take me long to discover that medical idealism, to be effective, must also be practical. Williams has staged an amazing comeback—I'll admit it. But he's still a mental patient."

"He needn't be forever."

"Let me finish, please. Suppose we let him go back to Ellenville. It isn't a large town. As I remember, it has only two drugstores. Of course the home folks will welcome him at first.

They'll drop in for a chat at the shop, same as always. But once the excitement's over they'll start having afterthoughts. How many prescriptions have you filled in your time?"

"Nothing that wasn't elementary."

"I was a drug clerk before I went to medical school. When a patient takes a dose of medicine, he must believe the doctor prescribed correctly. He must also be sure that his druggist followed the prescription. I don't have to remind you that many medicines are outright poisons, if they're taken in too large a quantity."

"The same is true of table salt."

"Suppose you're a citizen of Ellenville. You take a doctor's prescription to Williams' pharmacy. You and Williams were fellow Rotarians before he went to Leyden. You're glad he's back, of course, want him to get ahead. Now, let's say that this medicine's something to take with meals. Next time you pour out a dose at lunch, a friend at your table asks what you're taking. 'A tonic,' you say—and gulp it down. 'Did you know that lots of tonics contain strychnine?' asks your friend, who happens to be a joker too. 'Isn't that a poison?' Maybe you get a little pale at that, before you pull yourself together. 'Not when the prescription's filled out right,' you say—but you won't be human if you aren't remembering that Williams was crazy once. Next time you open that bottle, even money says you pour it down the sink, get a second prescription from your doctor, and go to the *other* drugstore in Ellenville."

"Aren't you being a bit dramatic?"

"Like hell I am. Know what a prescription business means to the average small-town druggist, Corwin? It's usually his major source of income—particularly when he's an old-fashioned apothecary like Williams. Suppose he goes back home again and fails. Can you assure me he won't break down again?"

"You know I can't."

"Then is it *fair* to send him back—and undo all we've accomplished?"

"Perhaps not, Dr. Meeker. The point's still arguable."

"Not if it puts Leyden's reputation on the line. That's why

I'm refusing to release him at this time—and you can be sure I'm acting for *his* sake. Not just to save a few dollars."

"As you wish, sir." Jim knew he was surrendering far too easily.

"Tell you what I'll do," said the director. He was almost genial, now he had won his point. "How long has Williams been on reserpine?"

"A few weeks."

"Let's re-evaluate the case in another month or so. Maybe he can make the outside after all—if he continues to improve." Meeker handed Jim the application. "Meanwhile, I'm afraid he's just where he belongs. Will you tell him—as kindly as you can?"

Despite his inner rage, Jim could not help marveling at the man's effrontery. Meeker had just vetoed a decision of his own staff. It was his job to explain that veto to the patient—particularly a patient who had proved as valuable to the hospital as Enoch Williams. Yet he had tossed the task into Jim's lap—with no choice but acceptance.

"It's a job I don't relish, Dr. Meeker."

"You can do it better than I, Corwin. He's grateful to you. And he'll believe you, when you give him the real reason."

When Jim entered the drug room, he found Enoch Williams deep in one of the books Singh had loaned him. A glance at the pharmacist's pale, indoor face told him Williams had guessed his errand.

"Don't blame yourself, Dr. Corwin," he said, when Jim had repeated the gist of his visit with Meeker. "You did what you could, I'm sure."

"The director has the last word, Enoch. He may be right."

"Do you think I'm ready to go outside?"

"Definitely. But Dr. Meeker has a way of bludgeoning opinions he doesn't share."

"This morning I was sure I'd be going home. Do you know what changed my mind?" Williams dropped his voice. "It was next month's salary requisition. When his secretary brought it here for me to sign—I *knew* he'd never release me."

Jim felt his hackles rise. "What's this about a salary requisition?"

"I was speaking of the pharmacist's salary at Leyden, Dr. Corwin. I believe it's three hundred dollars a month. Dr. Meeker suggested I donate that sum to the welfare fund."

Thanks to Frankel, Jim already knew that Meeker had written off the pharmacist's salary under another name. He had wondered how the director would cover his tracks.

"Does Dr. Meeker administer this welfare fund?"

"So his secretary told me. Hadn't you heard of it?"

"I'm a bit behind the times on front-office procedure, Enoch."

"Dr. Meeker said my three hundred dollars would help everyone at Leyden. He felt I *owed* it to the hospital—after what it's done for me. I couldn't very well argue—could I, Dr. Corwin?"

Turning to leave, Jim forced himself to put a final question. "What kind of drugstore do you operate in Ellenville?"

"An ordinary small-town shop. Main and Jackson. It's called the Sugar Bowl."

"Does that mean you have a soda fountain?"

"Best in town. We carry a good line of sundries, too. Last year my wife put in a lending library."

"What about prescriptions?"

"We do a fair business—but I can't call it our mainstay. There's a pharmacy in the new Medical Arts Building. It gets most of the doctors' orders."

Jim's fist beat a soft tattoo on the counter, as he forced his anger under control. One thing was certain: Meeker had hoodwinked him as brazenly as he had robbed Williams of his pay.

The pharmacist pushed back his eyeshade with a chuckle. "I see your drift, Dr. Corwin—can't say as I blame you. I've plenty of friends in Ellenville—but they still might worry, with an ex-mental patient filling their prescriptions. A nephew of mine is graduating from pharmacy school this June, I'd always planned to take him into the shop. The minute he has his diploma, my wife's putting him behind our drug counter."

"I've let you down, Enoch—badly. If you like, I'll fill out another application now."

Williams shook his head. "I'll put on pressure elsewhere. Maybe even in the state house. I've a brother-in-law in the legislature, you know."

"Ask his help, by all means."

"My wife will do the asking, now that she really wants me back. That's one thing we can count on."

In his quarters again, after a grumpy half hour in the staff dining room, Jim was still fighting the urge to confront Meeker and damn him as he deserved. Early afternoon was the patients' rest period—and it was the doctors' custom to use these hours for a siesta of their own. For his part, Jim had fallen into the habit of reading at his desk. Today, the toadlike image of the director continued to intrude between his eyes and the pages of *The Interpretation of Dreams*. He had just flung the book across the room when Dr. Keegan thrust a cautious head through the door.

"Still letting off steam, Corwin?"

Jim forced a laugh, and retrieved the volume. "Sorry. That wasn't meant for you."

"I'll give you two to one Meeker was the target."

Since their first meeting in the surgery, Jim and Keegan had talked but little. Knowing that the saturnine physician was far more friendly with the director than the other staff members, Jim had made no effort to break through his watchful aloofness. Wondering if this visit had a hidden motive, he was careful not to speak his mind.

"Obviously, you've heard of our argument over Williams."

"Argument's hardly the right word—when you're discussing Meeker." Keegan ambled easily into the room, accepted a cigarette, and refused the offer of the armchair. Instead, he perched on a corner of the desk and looked with distaste at the stack of fat tomes Frankel had assigned his staff as required reading. "If you're up to *The Interpretation of Dreams*," he said, "you're a fast reader."

Jim established himself in the armchair, with a certain defiance. "Did you come to make this a study hour?"

"Hardly. I *am* sticking out my neck—which is something I don't do often." Keegan flipped the door shut with a practiced toe. "Think you could use a few words of advice?"

"I'm sure of it."

"Corwin, I haven't forgotten the day you joined this happy family—and the midnight lecture I gave you. Somehow, I don't believe it's penetrated."

"I remember every word."

"Which means, of course, that you refuse to believe things at Leyden are as hidebound as I said. I can understand that—because I was like you once. A freewheeling do-gooder, who meant to set the medical world on fire—and distribute the blessings of psychiatry into the bargain. Fortunately for my future, I got into state-hospital work early."

"You've had an excellent chance to learn here."

"Sure I have—and I've made the most of it. I've been smart enough to stick to routine and avoid the high hurdles. In a few more months I'll pass the psychiatric board exam. So can you—in time—if you'll stop riding for a fall."

"If you're referring to Williams and his discharge——"

"Did you honestly believe you could sign his release, and make it stick?"

Jim shrugged. "Not now. I've learned that much, the hard way."

"How badly do you want that certificate in psychiatry next year?"

"Enough to slave for it."

"Has it occurred to you that you'll never even take your exam without Meeker's approval?"

"Why should he keep me out?"

"Two reasons. You challenged his authority by thinking for yourself. First, when you started this program with reserpine, and again when you signed Williams' release. From the start he's known you're ten times the doctor he'll ever be. Which means he'll continue to hate you—unless you learn to play down your brains and take his guff without gagging." Keegan rose from the desk and stretched out on the bed with a long sigh. "My advice is short and sweet. Stick to your wards—and *never* ask questions about the rest of the operation."

"Like the man who died in the recovery room my first night here?"

"A perfect example. Still think that was an extradural hemorrhage, brought about by slugging?"

"I'm sure of it—and so are you."

"The death certificate read differently. I know what was reported to me, Corwin—nothing else. The patient was in confinement: Jack Hanley says he was unconscious when they found him. Maybe he butted his head—it happens every day. Maybe he tried to climb the wall and fell——"

"It was a soap sock, and Hanley used it."

"Maybe Hanley *was* careless. It still isn't part of the record."

"But the patient died——"

"Mental patients are always dying from things we can't control. Let a schizo get a hot appendix—what happens next? He clams up or goes into stupor. Before that, he's been complaining of everything in the book—so how do we know he's really sick? We can't give five hundred patients a daily physical. Why, I've seen 'em in the terminal stages of pneumonia—without even running a fever."

"At least we can *try* to help——"

"Don't mistake me, Corwin. I wish I had the courage to run your present program. But you'll admit it's a tricky business. Reserpine has a powerful effect on the blood pressure. It was used for that purpose, long before this mental-disease gimmick came up. Suppose one of your human guinea pigs goes into circulatory collapse tomorrow? Early in the treatment, before he's rational enough to complain? He could die before you picked up a symptom."

"We've been watching that angle carefully."

"With two hundred test cases? It could hit any moment—and you'd never be the wiser, until it was too late."

"Are you suggesting we stop this run?"

"Far from it. You've got something big by the tail—it might even make you famous."

"It can also break me at Leyden tomorrow."

"Not necessarily—if you have friends to cover your tracks. Just keep your nose out of Meeker's affairs and you can have that help." Keegan had seemed to drowse as he spoke. Now he opened one eye and closed it in a pointed wink. "End of sermon, Corwin. Have I made my point?"

Jim hesitated. It was evident that the other doctor had come as an emissary from Meeker: he could almost believe that his motives were sincere. And yet, still smarting from his defeat at the director's hands that morning, he was in no mood to back down openly.

"Everyone must do what seems best to him," he said.

"And *for* him," said Keegan. "I'm older than you, my friend—and I've been through the mill. Hick medical school in Kansas—insurance practice all through the Midwest—contract surgeon at a miner's co-op in West Virginia. I've cut out gang-war bullets in Chicago and done my share of abortions on the side——" He closed his eyes again, and a smile softened his thin, careworn countenance, giving him the look of a bogus cherub. "Don't say I'm boasting, please. Just see me as I am. The day they handed me my diploma, I was looking out for Number One. Now that I'm about to call myself a soul doctor, I intend to do the same—at a hundred bucks an hour. I'd advise you to follow my formula."

Five minutes later, when Keegan had departed to finish his nap in his own quarters, Jim was ready to admit that most of his advice was sound. Viewed in its proper perspective, the case of Enoch Williams was only a straw in the wind—but it was also a warning that he had gone too far. Like Frankel, he told himself, he must learn to stay within bounds, if he meant to achieve his purpose here.

True, his test run with reserpine had been blessed with luck: the fact remained that death could strike there without warning. In large doses, the Indian drug-root did have a marked lowering effect on blood pressure. . . . No treatment of this sort was immune from perils. Even today, patients were struck down now and again by penicillin—because, in some fashion not yet understood, they had become sensitized to the drug.

What if such a fatality occurred at Leyden—and Meeker seized it as an excuse for his dismissal? Once he was outside the hospital walls he would be helpless to aid Lynn Thorndyke, in the event of another collapse.

Knowing Meeker, he was certain the director would hit back with the handiest weapon if his authority was threatened. Only an idealistic fool would attempt to fight back barehanded. Nothing (not even his fears for Lynn) would induce him to abandon his reserpine program, since he was battling here for a principle that transcended individuals. For the present (even as Frankel) he was prepared to stay on his wards, so long as he was given a free hand there.

Lynn's personality—like a flower that had languished too long without sun—had only begun to unfold, to respond to his attempt to reach its essence. It would still need careful nurture before the petals opened fully.

xxi

When the test run was a month old, Jim and Singh presented their findings at a weekly staff meeting.

The presentation included interviews with several patients, Lynn among them. Jim had hesitated to include her in the hearing, though she had now been working some ten days in the open ward. His fears were soon dissolved. The girl was shy when she sat down with the doctors, and her responses were made with lowered eyes. But there was no mistaking her lucidity and her determination to give a clear account of her condition.

After Mrs. Foster had taken Lynn back to the ward, Singh

wheeled in a projector and exhibited the series of colored photographs the attendants had made of the girl's painting. (Later, the two doctors intended to use them as the basis for a paper they had promised *The Journal of Clinical Psychiatry.*) Jim sat back during the exhibition, permitting his colleague to outline this aspect of Lynn's case history.

"These photographs are most revealing," said the Indian doctor. "They show how the drug acted to remove the repressing effects of the disease process on a natural talent. Even in the period of setback preceding Dr. Corwin's use of phenidylate, it is evident that the personality of the patient, was, so to speak, unshackling itself."

As he spoke, Singh flashed the last of the slides on screen—a water color Lynn had completed three days ago. "In this painting, regressive influences are almost entirely absent. It contains not one human figure but several. The figure representing the patient, which has remained constant throughout, shows a decided tendency to mingle with its kind. Best of all, the proportions are professional, without a trace of the distortion that marked the earlier efforts."

Keegan was the first to speak when the lights came on. "Does this mean Miss Thorndyke is well, Corwin?"

"Far from it," said Jim. "As you saw just now, she's eager to improve herself. But she still holds back from complete communion with her kind."

"She's in the open ward."

"True—but she feels sheltered there, with Mrs. Foster always present. Even so, she keeps mostly to herself and works constantly at her easel."

"Then there's still a barrier between her and society?"

"Definitely. You might say she's like a chick about to emerge from the egg. She'll peck her way out—on her own timetable. We can't hurry her."

"Have you set a target date for the breakthrough?" asked Dr. Welles.

"In psychiatry, Doctor," said Frankel gently, "we can't set target dates. The wounded mind rarely heals as predictably as the human body." He smiled at Jim, as Welles dived into his notebook. "Have you anything to add, Dr. Corwin?"

"No, sir. I was hoping you'd sum up for me."

Frankel got to his feet and rested an elbow on the projector. "All of you must realize what we owe Dr. Corwin," he said. "Had it not been for his concern over the patient you just saw, this program might never have begun at Leyden. He is not a pioneer in the use of reserpine, but he is among its first users. And I suspect the test we are running here is one of the most important of its kind, so far."

"Surely it's not yet conclusive," said Keegan.

"Not yet, perhaps. But the possibilities are limitless. What you've just seen, in these colored slides, is a graphic pattern of the mind of every patient who responds favorably to the drug. I'll go a step beyond that, Dr. Keegan. In my opinion, what's shaping up here, among our relatively active cases, may not be merely a palliative but a cure."

Ira Welles looked up. "May we use the term *cure* in connection with definite mental disease, Dr. Frankel?"

"Three months ago," said the Austrian quietly, "my response to that question would have been negative. Thanks to reserpine, I'm prepared to reverse my opinion." He paused to look hard at young Dr. Welles, who still sat with his pencil in mid-air. "Let me state the psychotherapist's problem in the simplest way. The best we've done, so far, is to help the patient adjust to the stress of his immediate situation. If the adjustment is complete, he reaches a point where he can respond thereafter in a normal manner——"

"But there's no norm in the psyche."

Frankel smiled. "True, Dr. Welles. But the psychiatrist must sometimes invent one. As a yardstick, if you will, to contrast with the regressive character of mental disease. As of yesterday, only the patient's own resurgent ego could dominate the conflicts that made him seek refuge in regressive behavior. Now—and remember, I'm speaking hopefully, on the basis of this test—it actually seems possible to *remove* those conflicts with reserpine. As drastically, and as completely, as penicillin removes a streptococcus from the bloodstream."

"Can you tell us how the drug operates, Dr. Frankel?"

"So far, we've no definite idea," said the head physician. "It's my guess that it exerts a calming effect upon the lower thalamic centers—what we call the more 'primitive' portions of the brain. In so doing, it may have a controlling effect on some of mankind's more atavistic impulses." He turned to Jim and the Hindu. "Unless that's too fanciful to suit you."

"Would you say that reserpine attacks and subdues the Id?" asked Singh.

"As a psychiatrist," said Frankel, "I can't give a definite answer. I can't even tell you that what Freud called the 'Id' is localized in any particular portion of the brain. Since its impulses are the least controlled of all human drives, we assume it inhabits the more primitive centers. There's no doubt whatever that reserpine slows down the Id impulses. Or that it lets the patient see those impulses clearly. Not as threats to his security—but as maverick urges he can now control."

Welles, who had been writing at a furious pace, lifted his hand for attention. "May I restate that, Dr. Frankel? *Reserpine, in acute cases of schizophrenia, may actually give the patient control of the Id drives in his personality—a control he should have learned as a child, in the usual course of his development.*"

The Austrian shook his white-maned head, but his eyes were twinkling. "You're pushing me into textbook jargon, Dr. Welles. Yet you're not far from the mark. Mind you, this seems true only in acute cases. Where the reaction pattern is more definite, we will probably never teach the patient to adjust completely. But we *can* make him realize that those bogeymen are not so terrible as he thought."

Keegan held up his hand. "Doesn't all this mean that reserpine is just a supersedative?"

"On the contrary," said Jim quickly. "Bromides, the barbiturates, and paraldehyde calm the patient by putting him to sleep. The effect of reserpine is quite different. It's true that our test cases appear to sleep a great deal—but they can be aroused at will. Invariably they are alert and mentally clear, not dull and 'drugged' as is the case with the barbiturates. Because of this, they can be talked to and reasoned with at any stage of their treatment. This bears out Dr. Frankel's statement that reserpine is an adjunct to psychotherapy. All ordinary sedatives hinder it."

"That's hardly true in narcosynthesis," Keegan objected. "We've proved right here at Leyden that pentothal relaxes a patient's higher centers. So completely, in fact, that a painful episode can be brought into consciousness—and relieved in catharsis."

"You're right, Dr. Keegan," said Frankel. "Unfortunately, pentothal is seldom effective in schizophrenia—since, as a rule, a patient's condition is not brought on by a single disturbing experience. The Id, in other words, is an elusive villain. Often the Ego itself is its most willing shield."

"What of cases that seem rational for extended periods—and then regress?" asked Keegan.

Jim spoke up. This was a point that had concerned him deeply in the early stages of the test run.

"The question's still open," he admitted. "We all know that some schizophrenics appear, quite literally, to cure themselves—at least for a time. On occasion, the disease disappears entirely, never to return."

"That's the exception, rather than the rule," said Keegan. "Regression's the usual pattern." He reached for the thick dossier that detailed Lynn Thorndyke's history. "To take an extreme example, here are your notes of an experiment you conducted with Miss Thorndyke—an injection of cyanide that caused her to become lucid for a few moments, though she was deep in catatonic stupor. You can't deny that her subsequent lapse into an excited state was a violent one——"

"I don't deny it," said Jim. "All the experiment proved was that her mind had not deteriorated beyond salvage. Today you saw how far she's moved toward recovery."

"Perhaps. The fact remains that schizophrenics *are* subject to abrupt turns for the better—just as they are for the worse.

I'm wondering if you're stepping up a normal swing with reserpine. If a later relapse may still be inevitable."

"When we discontinue the drug?"

"Precisely," said Keegan—with a triumphant glance at Frankel.

Once again, the head physician faced the group. "I think we've an interesting parallel here with insulin," he said. "We all know that massive doses are needed to restore the sugar metabolism to normal when a patient is in an acute diabetic condition. Later, a far smaller dosage keeps him in perfect balance. The same pattern has repeated itself in this test run. Certainly it's possible to taper off the reserpine as a patient becomes more rational. In time, perhaps, the medication can be discontinued entirely. Or used only in periods when the patient is subject to mental stress."

"You still haven't proved it reaches the underlying disease condition," Keegan persisted.

"I can't agree," Jim put in quickly. "And I think Dr. Frankel will bear me out. Miss Thorndyke and her paintings are the most striking proof to date. You saw the dramatic change the moment reserpine was started. Naturally, the reaction of the true artist is more sensitive than the average patient's—but the connection seems unmistakable."

"Isn't the effect more marked in early cases—such as hers?"

"The test run shows marked benefits in three out of four early cases. On three-year patients the rate is still fifty per cent. With still older cases, it's far lower—with a few exceptions, like Enoch Williams. With the burnt-out ones, of course, there's usually no effect at all."

Ira Welles had picked up a fresh notebook. "What of such conditions as depression and melancholia?"

"Reserpine affects these afflictions in proportion to the degree of excitement," Singh said. "It quiets the patient, without producing the curative effect that's so marked in schizophrenia. But since shock therapy has proved remarkably effective in combating such disorders, it seems unlikely that the new drug will replace it."

"Will it replace shock treatment in schizophrenia?"

"I can give you only a tentative answer," said the Hindu. "In general, any case that responds to shock therapy will respond even more positively to reserpine. In fact, many patients who did not respond at all to shock have been greatly helped by the drug."

Dr. Frankel rose to close the conference. "I'd suggest a vote of thanks to our two innovators," he said. "Even though I must warn you that you'll all be taking on more work—when we begin our group-therapy program."

xxii

Two weeks later (so remarkable was the advance in Lovell One) Jim was able to organize the first group-therapy team. At Frankel's suggestion it was kept small at first—a dozen women (all of them reserpine patients) whose case histories suggested a definite interest in art. Lynn Thorndyke had been chosen as their teacher, since her own improvement had been sure and steady. Jim had not hesitated to outline the plan in her presence—and to ask that she superintend the distribution of water colors and easels.

Janet Moore had been selected to keep a wary eye on the first painting class after the easels had been set up on the north porch of the women's ward—but no discipline was necessary. Busy as he was, Jim had found no time to look in on the experiment until it was well under way. He had expected a grotesquerie, featuring amateur daubs. Instead, he found a dozen intent students, each working happily at her easel. The subject (a bowl of fruit) had been repeated with varying results. But even to his untrained eye there was no mistaking the depth of interest.

The teacher, he noted, was quite as absorbed as her pupils, moving from easel to easel with words of encouragement, pausing now and again to guide a hesitant hand. Lynn was wearing a paint-daubed smock today: her hair, knotted into a pony tail, glowed in the sunlight like a golden pennon. When their eyes met, her smile was a reward—and a reproach—for all his doubting.

He drew back into the shelter of the doorframe, to stand beside Janet Moore. The nurse was surveying the scene with folded arms—and an expression in which amazement and delight fought for precedence.

"Can you believe it, Doctor? They've been working like this since breakfast."

Jim saw now that the entire open ward had congregated farther down the porch to watch the painting class—save for the hopelessly deteriorated patients, who still remained on their benches, staring into space as they did for all their waking hours. Among the curious were a number of women he had tentatively scheduled for reserpine, once the test run had ended. Many of these harmlessly deranged patients were aping the women at the easels—some with scraps of paper salvaged from the reading room, others with castoff bits of cardboard.

"Take a bow, Dr. Corwin," the nurse whispered. "You've earned it."

"Don't give *me* the credit. It goes to reserpine and phenidylate."

"Drugs can do just so much. Man does the rest."

"Aren't you being a trifle mystic, Janet?"

"I'm referring to the teacher—not to her class."

"I won't argue about Lynn. Whatever happens to the rest of this program, she's still the Leyden miracle."

"Miracle's a slippery word, Dr. Corwin," said the nurse. "It should be used sparingly."

"What are you driving at?"

"Ever hear of love?"

"Echoes—now and then."

"It's still the best medicine our Creator ever made."

"Are you suggesting I'm in love with Lynn?"

"And vice versa."

Jim did not trust himself to speak at once: instead, he turned away, feigning a profound interest in the nearest canvas of the art class. *I've loved her since the* Creole Belle, he thought. *It's too much to hope that Lynn loves me. That's a miracle too big for Leyden—or for heaven itself.*

"Well, Doctor?" said Janet Moore. "Does silence mean assent?"

He found it was an effort to speak naturally. "Sorry—I'm afraid I was daydreaming."

"And well you might, with the evidence of your handiwork before you. Have you ever seen anything prettier?"

"She's returned from the dead," he said quietly. "As literally as anyone can make that journey. Do you suppose that gives her an added bloom?"

"Never mind the smoke screen, Doctor. I know *you're* in love: I saw your face just now, when you were off guard. Why shouldn't she love you too?"

He met the challenge almost gruffly. "Lynn won't be the first patient to imagine she loves her doctor."

"I've worked with the mentally sick all my life," said Janet Moore. "I've yet to see an upturn until they shook off their strait jackets of self-pity and began loving others. That was Lynn's turning point—when she found you were a man, not just her doctor. A man who needs to receive love, as well as give it."

"This is a mental hospital, Janet—not a lonely-hearts column——" He broke off as Lynn hurried across the porch to join them, grateful that the interruption had come in time.

The girl's cheeks were glowing. It was not the flush of the neurotic, but the whole-souled joy that comes only from participation. He felt his heart rise in answer: this (he told himself) is your greatest test. From this day forward, you must begin your retreat to the wings. If Lynn Thorndyke is to complete her journey back to life, she must learn to walk alone.

"Isn't it wonderful, Dr. Jim?"

"Uncovered any geniuses?"

"Three of those twelve are real artists. The others will be good Sunday painters in a month."

"That's a fine score for any teacher, Lynn."

"Believe me, there's no greater thrill than discovering talent."

"Did you know *you* had a talent for making people happy?"

The girl's eyes had not left his face since she joined him in the doorframe. "Not until today," she said softly. "I'm afraid I've been too busy thinking of myself."

"You're glad to be working in the open ward? You want to go on?"

"There's nothing I'd like more."

"Would you care to move here for good?"

Her face clouded, and he read his answer there in advance. Lynn, for all her surface poise, was far from a complete recovery. So long as she clung to the solitude of her own cell, so long would she cling to the rocklike strength he represented. It was good to know he was still needed—even as he recognized the importance of breaking that dependence.

"Lovell One is my home," said Lynn. "It's the only one I remember."

"You'll find a better one soon."

"Perhaps—when I'm stronger. Please don't make me go until I'm ready."

"Of course not. You've time to spare."

"I'll come here each day and teach my painting class. If you wish, I can take a second group. They're all my friends: we understand one another." The girl turned impulsively to the nurse. "Miss Moore knows what I mean."

"She's right, Dr. Corwin," said the nurse. "Already, she's worth more than a dozen attendants to me."

"Have it your way, then," said Jim. "We'll organize a second class tomorrow. But you must promise me one thing first, Lynn—to share my next day off. We'll go outside together."

The color was high in the girl's cheeks, but her eyes did not waver. "I'd love to, Dr. Jim—if you think it's wise."

"Let's plan on next Friday," he said. "I'll bring steaks and roasting ears. We can have a real cookout." Watching Lynn move back to her class—in answer to a call for help from one of her students—he felt he had handled himself well enough.

"Is *that* what the doctor ordered?" asked Janet Moore. "Or is the doctor covering his tracks?"

"One more question in that vein," he said, "and I'll pull rank on you."

"What are you going to do, Jim Corwin? Let the girl down gently—and ease out of her life by degrees?"

"Isn't that sound strategy?"

"Why not marry her—and cure her at your leisure?"

"For one thing, we're at least ten years apart."

"Six. I looked up both your ages."

"Never mind our ages. I'm a broken-down widower. Lynn's on the threshold of life—with a talent that can take her to the summit. My job is to get her out of Leyden before the fall term begins at the university. She can still get her degree, if she puts in a semester of hard work. The dean has promised me as much."

"So Lynn must carve out her future with her own hands," said the nurse. "Is that your prescription—minus the Freud?"

"Can you think of a better one?"

"I've given you *my* prescription. It's too bad I can't force it down your throat."

Walking out of the ward with his best poker face, Jim told himself he had been wise to leave so promptly. He could hardly explain (especially to a spinster like Janet Moore) that love is a word of many meanings. Or that sacrifice, in some form, must always be its keynote. . . .

"Wake up, Jim—you're sleepwalking!"

He paused in some annoyance, aware that Singh was waving from a crosswalk. "Sorry, Chandra. What's up?"

"The operator is paging you. You've a visitor in the main building."

"Thanks—I'll stop by."

A young man was seated in one of the stiff-back chairs that lined the rotunda walls. Even before he rose and held out his hand Jim recognized the broad shoulders, the too-handsome profile. Jay Thompson's crew cut was a bit longer after a year in Paris: there was depth to his dark eyes, and the clasp of his hand was firm with purpose. In essence, however, this was the same boy who had made the despairing run down the New Orleans levee.

"How is Lynn, Doctor?"

"On her way to a cure, I hope." Jim sat down in a facing chair. Now that the boy had turned up at Leyden, he realized that he had expected the visit, was even prepared for it.

"When can you release her?"

"Soon, I hope. It depends on Lynn herself."

"I'm fresh from a year's study in France, Dr. Corwin. Got into Glenville only yesterday: I'm teaching art this fall term."

"So I'd heard from Professor Blake."

"Dean Pearson says there's a chance Lynn might enroll again."

"There's an excellent chance—if her improvement continues."

"May I see her now?" The boy flushed a bit under Jim's steady gaze. "Or wouldn't that be wise?"

Jim hesitated—wondering how far he could confide in Jay Thompson. "I'm afraid this isn't the time or place," he said. "That doesn't mean you can't help later."

"I'll do anything, Dr. Corwin. Please believe me."

"You might explain just what happened between you."

The boy's flush deepened. Once again Jim realized that this was one of the handsomest young men he had ever seen. It was easy to understand how Lynn had fallen in love with him. Easier still to guess how small an effort it had been (on Jay's side) to return that love.

"On the way to Leyden," said Jay, "I stopped at Far Hills for a chat with Mary Lou Morison. She's briefed you pretty thoroughly, I gather."

"So she did. Were you in love with Lynn?"

"Enough to break an engagement with Mary Lou—and ask her to marry me."

"And you love her still?"

"Would I be here if I didn't?"

"I could make several replies to that question," said Jim. "The first is the most obvious. Why didn't you come sooner?"

"Dr. Corwin, I saw Mrs. Thorndyke in Paris last year. She told me Lynn's case was hopeless."

"So it was—a year ago."

"When she ran away from the university, I did my best to stop her. At the time, I figured everything was over between us."

Studying Jay Thompson carefully, Jim saw that he was entirely sincere. From his viewpoint, the part he had played in Lynn's debacle was an innocent one. At the university he had offered himself to a love-starved girl in good faith. He could never have foreseen that their brief affair (Jim wondered if "affair" was too strong a word) would have this outcome.

"Dr. Corwin, if I could have helped, I'd have come back at once. If I thought for a minute she had still *wanted* me——"

"I don't blame you for staying in Paris," said Jim. "At the time, your presence might have done more harm than good."

"Does Lynn know that Mary Lou's alive and well? And that she's married to the man she wanted all along?"

"Not yet. So far, it hasn't been feasible to bring her that close to reality."

"I don't follow you, Dr. Corwin. If she knew she was blameless, wouldn't it clear up everything?"

"Perhaps—if she found out in her own way." Jim hesitated, troubled by the boy's honest bewilderment. "It's difficult to explain to a layman—but illusions, to the mentally ill, are often more important than facts. Until a few weeks ago Lynn was very ill indeed. Part of her illusion is the feeling she's unwanted. It's based on repeated rejections in her childhood——" Again he paused, as Jay Thompson's frown deepened. . . . *You were never unwanted,* he thought. *You'll never imagine the torment of loneliness Lynn endured.*

"*I* wanted her," said Jay. "I was ready to marry her. Why did she run away?"

"Because of Mary Lou. And an even deeper illusion. A belief that she couldn't love one human being without causing the death of another. Does that seem fantastic to you?"

"Fairly, I'm afraid."

"It's still a basic cause of her illness. Here at Leyden we're helping her to live those illusions down. She's wanted here.

She's beginning to feel really useful—perhaps for the first time in her life. Our next step, of course, is to prove she can find these same rewards outside. Finally, we must destroy her greatest illusion—the belief she caused the death of others. But it's something we can't *tell* her. She must discover it—in her own mind."

"Couldn't you say I'm back in Glenville? And that I'll marry her the moment she's ready?"

Looking into the boy's earnest eyes, Jim made his decision. Proof of Lynn's innocence awaited her on the campus at Glenville. So did the future her talent so richly deserved. A happy marriage would round out the pattern; it could make her life complete. Did it matter if Jay had learned of the bequest that awaited her on graduation? There was no need to spell out the fact that some marriages are based on pity as well as love. Or that a fifty-thousand-dollar legacy would go a long way toward financing an art teacher eager to branch into other fields. . . . Lynn (to put the matter bluntly) stood with one foot already outside Leyden: she was ready to make the final step that would assure her return to normality. If his own love was real, he had no right to delay that step another moment.

"First, we must test her reaction to Glenville itself," Jim said carefully. "If it's favorable, perhaps you can appear next. When does the fall term open?"

"Wednesday, Doctor."

"I gather you'll be on hand then?"

"From the start. I'm helping Professor Blake organize the fine arts curriculum."

"This Friday I'm treating Lynn to a picnic—a kind of trial run. I'll take a chance on her reactions and go by way of Glenville. We'll have a look at the campus, for a starter. If her response is good, I'll bring her to the gallery—let her see her paintings again, talk with her old professor. If she's still undisturbed, we'll let her know you're back from Paris——"

Hearing his voice go on, he could read the answer to his plan in Jay's face. Already (as he could see too clearly) the boy had cast himself in the role of Lynn's savior. Who was

Lynn's doctor to veto that natural impulse, when it fitted his therapy perfectly?

"Let me get one fact straight, Dr. Corwin," said Jay. "Lynn *could* remember me—if she wanted to?"

"Of course. The whole thing's locked away in her mind. She'll bring it out when she's ready. Once she's made that effort, it will prove she's strong enough to cure herself. *Then* we can tell her what really happened at Loon Lake."

"Perhaps we could go there," said Jay quickly. "The three of us, I mean. I don't want to horn in too soon——"

"We'll see about that, after she's visited the campus. Remember, the decision must be hers, if it's to have any real value."

When the boy had departed, Jim sat without stirring. As a psychiatrist in the making, he told himself he had done right. Yet an instinct he could not define warned him that this was a dangerous game, that he was a fool to surrender Lynn so soon. Rising at last to return to the wards, he moved with a leaden heart. The picnic he had visioned so gaily had turned into an excursion of quite another sort.

xxiii

They had planned to borrow Frankel's roadster for the drive. When that ancient car developed engine trouble, they were forced to use a spare ambulance instead—with Jim at the wheel and Lynn (gay in a summer dirndl) at his side. The picnic hamper was stored in the ambulance proper, along with the grill for the cookout.

Jim had wanted to hire a car, rather than use so official a conveyance: he felt it was an unfortunate link with the past. But Lynn had insisted they take the ambulance.

"You've spent enough on our picnic now," she told him with smiling firmness. "Dr. Frankel has said we could have the ambulance for the whole day. We'd be foolish not to use it."

During the hour-long drive she had chatted happily on a dozen topics—all of them relating to the art-therapy classes, which had absorbed her more with each passing day. There had been no apprehension in her manner as they roared down the state highway—nor did she seem curious about their destination. When they passed the gateposts of Far Hills, Jim had been tempted to mention Mary Lou—and had held his tongue in time. . . . Now, turning the ambulance into the tree-arched drive that led into the Glenville campus, he made the first casual mention of his plan.

"We've hours to spare for the picnic, Lynn. I thought we'd swing through the university for a moment."

"Whatever you say, Jim." Outside the hospital he had insisted she use his given name. "I'm enjoying every minute."

"We might even visit awhile with Professor Blake. Then we'll go on to our cookout."

"Have you picked a spot?"

"It's a choice between Loon Lake and the river. Which do you prefer?" Watching her covertly, he felt relieved when he noted no sign of tension. Naming the place where Mary Lou had suffered her near-fatal mishap had been a calculated risk.

"Why not the lake, Jim?"

"Fair enough. It's just off the highway to Leyden—so we can stay that much longer."

They were crossing the campus now, and he was forced to drive slowly: the bell tower in Culpepper Hall had chimed the hour and the crosswalks were crowded with students. Again he observed with relief that Lynn was studying the laughing young faces with perfect serenity.

"Do we *have* to see Professor Blake today, Jim?"

"If you don't mind, I think it's important."

"Why?"

"It's time you made plans for your future. I want you to set a date for your return to the campus."

"Do you think I'm ready?" she asked quickly.

"The moment you really want to be."

"I don't want to leave you, Jim. I never will."

He spoke patiently, while he parked the ambulance in the driveway of the Fine Arts Building. "Learning to do without your doctor is the final phase of your cure. It's time you began it."

The girl smiled up at him: her voice was part of her manner. "Are those doctor's orders?"

"They are," he said firmly. "You *do* want to continue your painting, don't you? Take your degree in art—and find a teaching job?"

"It was what I wanted—before."

"What do you want now?"

"To stay at Leyden, Jim. And help people there—as you helped me."

"You can come back to Leyden as a teacher, if you wish—after you've taken your degree. With special training, you'd do twice the job you're doing now."

"Could you arrange it, Jim?"

"I'll speak to Dr. Frankel tonight. It's a promise."

They mounted the steps of Fine Arts. He felt Lynn stiffen for an instant just outside the tall, fanlighted doorway, as though a ghost had crossed her path. Then, as he stood aside, her chin lifted and she went in—marching straight down the center hall and turning as though by instinct to the picture gallery and the alcove where her own canvases hung.

"Do you remember when you did those paintings?"

"I'm trying, Jim. I'm trying hard."

"Don't be afraid to remember."

"I'm not afraid," the girl said slowly. "It's coming back now—in bits and pieces."

"Do you recall how Professor Blake encouraged you?"

"I'm beginning to, Jim." Her eyes were glowing now. He sat beside her on a marble bench, certain that this was a happy omen.

"He's a fine teacher, Lynn. He wants you back."

"Does he, really?"

"I'm sure you'd enjoy working here again. Do you remember your fellow students?"

"A few."

"An instructor named Jay Thompson?"

It seemed quite logical that Jay himself should appear at that precise moment, shepherding a group of students from classroom to studio: dangerous though it was, Jim could welcome the testing. He had felt Lynn go taut at the mention of the name. Then, as the boy himself came forward, she shrank back —precisely as a child might shrink at the approach of a menacing stranger. The withdrawal was brief. Jim saw that her conscious mind had already taken over—forcing her to accept Jay's hand, with a strained smile of recognition.

"Am I intruding, Doctor? I hope not. How are you, Lynn? You look wonderful."

"I feel wonderful—thanks to Dr. Corwin."

"Is it true you're coming back this fall?"

"I'm not sure." Lynn was already on her feet.

"Professor Blake hopes you'll make it. So does the dean."

"Dr. Corwin and I were just going——"

Jim stood beside her with a hand at her elbow. Her brief moment of poise was gone, he saw. He could sense her effort at self-control as tangibly as though an electric current had coursed from her body to his own. . . . Jay, he observed with dismay, was still unaware of the trouble he had caused.

"Still having that picnic, Dr. Corwin?" he asked breezily.

"We are—if you'll excuse us."

"Good-by, Jay," said Lynn. Her voice was taut as a violin string tuned beyond its pitch. "We're going to Loon Lake—it's a long drive——"

"You can make it inside an hour. I'm going out later for a swim. Perhaps we'll meet at the pavilion."

The exchange, stilted as it was, seemed almost natural when contrasted to Lynn's departure from the gallery at a gait that could only be described as a flight. It was not quite a run: enough of her self-control remained for that. . . . On the steps she forced herself to pause and breathe deep before she hurried into the quad, taking the first path that opened before her. Jim had kept abreast of her, slowing her headlong pace with a discreet hand at her elbow. With each stride he could see her tension lessen. He knew she was safe, long before they paused beside a lily-bordered fountain, in the midst of a leafy maze that shut off the campus entirely.

When she spoke, her voice was still taut—but the fear was gone.

"Did you plan this, Jim?"

"Not *that* way."

"I'm sorry to cut and run. Meeting him so suddenly threw me off. It made me remember too much too fast."

"I can see that now, Lynn."

"You wanted us to meet later, didn't you?"

"Yes. I brought you here today, hoping you'd revisit as much of your past as you could endure. The paintings first. Then Professor Blake. Then, if you were ready, Jay Thompson."

"You must think I'm a dreadful coward."

"Not at all. You must return in your own way."

"Jim, am I still crazy?"

"Of course not. Something just got the better of you once. When you're ready, we'll talk it out. Whatever it was, you'll find it's as curable as an inflamed appendix. And as unimportant—once you're rid of it."

"It won't be that simple, I'm afraid."

"There's a cause for everything, Lynn—including mental illness. Bring that cause into the open and you can destroy it."

"Walk with me awhile, Jim. Before we go back to the car. I'll be good."

She put her hand in his while they followed the margin of the fountain: as he had feared, the fingers were still icy cold. They walked for a while without speaking, taking a path that led to the far side of the quadrangle. Another bell had sounded in Culpepper Hall, and the walks were deserted once more.

"You knew Jay was part of the cause, didn't you?"

"Yes, Lynn. Ever since I saw him at New Orleans."

"I'll tell you all about him later. After I've fought it out. Just don't leave me until I do."

"You can always find me when you need me. Never forget it."

"Having you beside me just now saved me from going to pieces. You don't mind if we put off seeing Professor Blake?"

"Another day will do. There's plenty of time."

"Shall we drive to Loon Lake now?"

"We can go somewhere else, if you prefer."

"You mean—because Jay is going there to swim? I don't mind meeting him a second time."

"You're sure?"

"I won't be a coward again. It was seeing him without warning that upset me."

The hand in his own was warm and trusting now. He knew she would follow his lead, no matter what the suggestion.

"Did you ever picnic at Loon Lake before?" he asked.

"I always wanted to. But I was too busy when I was on campus."

The admission told its own story. Loon Lake (as Jim had long since discovered) was a trysting place for Glenville students—and, though strictly out-of-bounds after dark, it was used round the clock by the more raffish of the undergraduates. . . . Glad that the girl was making her first visit in his company, he wondered if her story today might have been different, had she dared to break a few campus rules.

Sliding beneath the wheel of the ambulance, he let his eye rove up the façade of the Fine Arts Building. He had a brief glimpse of Jay Thompson, framed in the window of the gallery. He guessed that the boy had observed their every move—and knew his guess was correct when Jay lifted a hand in an elaborate conspirator's signal, then vanished from the casement. . . . Three minutes later, swinging the ambulance through the university gates, Jim glanced back—and was more angered than surprised to see a cream-white Jaguar leave the parking lot behind Culpepper Hall. The figure at the wheel was Jay, though his face was now obscured in racing goggles and a crash helmet.

Jim took the twenty-mile-long road to the lake with a wide-open throttle. The Jaguar hung easily on their trail, zooming at each curve like a white-winged bird. Despite their own speed, Jim was positive the boy could have passed them with ease, had he been so minded. Instead, Jay was idling a good four hundred yards behind them when the ambulance swung into the winding road that led through pine grove and high meadow to the lake shore. Silently, Jim cursed their pursuer and his persistence. Lynn, he was sure, had seen quite enough of this former sweetheart—for one day, at least.

If the girl realized they were being followed, she gave no sign. Her self-possession seemed complete as she leaned forward eagerly for her first glimpse of the serene blue water.

"We should have brought bathing suits," she cried.

"If you like, we can rent them at the pavilion."

She shook her head. "Let's drive on, where there aren't any people. Today I'll settle for a charcoal-broiled steak and a few hours of sun."

They were already skirting the pavilion grounds, with its outdoor dance floor and boat basin. Since this was a weekday, the place was almost deserted, save for a fishing party boarding a motorboat at the dock's end. Jim swung into the road that led to the low bluffs bordering the lake shore to the west. The Jaguar, he noted, had stopped at the bathhouse door. Evidently Jay had no intention of pursuing them further. . . . *Perhaps I've misjudged the boy,* he thought. *He may only be standing by, in case Lynn asks for him.*

He forgot Jay quickly enough as his senses yielded to the wild beauty of the vista that opened before them. Dense thickets of cedar and water oaks had already blotted out all evidence of man's handiwork, save for the rutted track they were following. On the right, the lake gleamed like a burnished mirror in a frame of wooded isles. Ahead, an unspoiled forest shut off the western horizon.

"I hope we'll have this end to ourselves," he said. "It's a different place on weekends, I'm told—when the college comes out for picnics."

"Aren't there a few lodges on the north shore, Jim?"

"I believe so," he said cautiously. "The owners keep them well hidden. They enjoy their solitude—just as we're enjoying ours." He did not add that it was from one of these hidden bays that Mary Lou had begun the water skiing race which had almost ended in her death.

"Pick your spot," said Lynn. "And pick it soon—if you're half as hungry as I."

"It's your party. I'm only your chauffeur-cook." This, he told himself, was the final test. If Lynn chose to picnic beside the water, it would prove she had put her nightmares behind her—including the mishap he had so carefully left unmentioned. . . .

"Here, Jim!"

She was pointing to a bit of meadow, shaded by a grove of pines and sloping gently to a sandy beach. With a singing heart he braked the ambulance sharply at the edge of the low bluff.

They unpacked the picnic things in contented silence. While Jim gathered dry wood as a base for the charcoal fire, Lynn bustled from car to meadow, spreading a blanket for their tablecloth and unwrapping the two choice *filets mignons* Jim had filched from the well-stocked larder at Leyden.

"I like steak rare," she said. "What about you?"

"The rarer the better," he said. "Charred on the outside, juicy underneath."

"And I think corn is much better roasted than boiled."

"I agree—all the way."

"We're of one mind on everything, then," she said contentedly. "From food to my career. Sit beside me while the fire burns down to coals—and we can talk."

Settling on the blanket at her side, he controlled a powerful urge to take her in his arms.

"What's the subject, Lynn? Past or future?"

"The past, first," said the girl calmly. "That's why we came to Loon Lake, isn't it? To talk about Jay—and Mary Lou?"

"Yes, Lynn. If you're ready."

"You know what happened here, don't you? Why Jay followed me to New Orleans? Why Mary Lou drowned herself?"

Weighing his words, Jim took her hand. The throb of a motorboat engine, coming up fast behind a wooded point, had distracted her for the moment: he could bless the interruption, since it gave him time to collect himself.

"Mary Lou didn't drown," he said slowly. "Will you believe that, for a start?"

"Is that what Jay's radiogram meant?"

"What else could it mean?"

"If she didn't drown—why didn't he say so?"

"Perhaps he didn't choose his words very well."

The motorboat was in full view now, a smartly varnished Chris-Craft with a towline and a water skier in its wake. Lynn got to her feet abruptly and shaded her eyes against the sun glare. With a sinking heart, Jim knew she had already recognized the figure on the skis. In swim trunks, Jay Thompson's resemblance to an Apollo cast in bronze was more marked than ever, his bearing just as confident.

"Where did *he* come from, Jim?"

"From the pavilion, I suppose. Apparently he hired a launch to show off his skill."

The Chris-Craft roared past the bluff in a wide arc: the man at the wheel (a Negro in yachting cap and jersey) waved a greeting. Jay, intent on an intricate slalom turn, did not look up until the launch had swung into open water. Then he, too, lifted his hand in a gay salute.

"Did you plan this between you?" There was panic in Lynn's tone now, a strident anger Jim recognized instantly.

"No, Lynn. Word of honor."

"Then it's his idea. And she *did* drown herself. I'm sure of it now. *He's skiing over her grave to prove he doesn't care——*"

"That isn't true, Lynn!"

"It's too late to lie, Jim. Much too late——"

Tears rained from her eyes as she wailed the words: with a single demonic gesture she lifted both hands to her hair, shredding it about her cheeks in wild disorder. Moving swiftly, Jim was barely in time to stop her headlong dash toward the bluff. He saw the reason for her terror when he turned again to the lake. The speedboat was making a long half circle, far out from shore. The towline dragged from the stern. There was no sign of Jay Thompson.

"He's drowning too!" Lynn screamed. *"Because of me!"*

The voice raised echoes on the far shore of Loon Lake before it died to a childish whimper. The girl gave a final, agonized glance toward the lake, before her knees buckled in a dead faint. Again he was barely in time to catch her in his arms.

Jim heard a shout from a distance. Pausing with one foot on the ambulance step, he saw that Jay was swimming toward the Chris-Craft with long, easy strokes. Evidently he had capsized after his incautious salute, forgetting that a slalom run, on water skis, demands the skier's undivided attention. Just as evidently, he had needed a moment underwater to free himself from his tangled equipment, and Lynn, unable to see him, had been sure he'd drowned. It was now too late to convince her that this near catastrophe, like Mary Lou's, had had a happy ending.

Her faint had not been really that, Jim knew. Actually, she had lapsed (via the familiar withdrawal pattern of her illness) into the catatonic state that was her refuge from reality.

"What happened, Doctor?"

The launch was nosing the shore line now. The skier had jumped to the bank and was scrambling toward the meadow. Jim did not trust himself to answer the shouted question. Instead, he stretched Lynn carefully on the wheeled cot inside the ambulance.

"Did she faint? So help me, I was only clowning—"

Jim turned, with one foot on the ambulance step. "It wasn't the best time to clown, Thompson."

"I only wanted to show her that water skiing isn't dangerous. It seemed a good idea."

"Not when she's convinced it caused the death of Mary Lou."

"Didn't you tell her the truth?"

"You didn't give me time."

"Tell her when she comes to, then."

"Unless we're lucky indeed, she may never waken again."

"You mean she's dying?"

"Yes, so far as the world is concerned."

"Doctor, you've *got* to bring her back!"

The boy's frightened eyes shocked Jim back to his own duties. When he spoke again he had mastered his anger.

"If you can handle a Jaguar, you can drive this ambulance," he said. "Get under the wheel and take us to Leyden—as fast as you can."

xxiv

Jay's driving had been inspired—but a flat tire had delayed them. It was almost dark when they roared up the hospital driveway.

Throughout that headlong journey Jim had sat beside the wheeled cot with Lynn's hand in his, talking to her gently in the hope she would lift from her dazed immobility. Instead, he had detected a steady increase in the tension of her body, sure proof that she was moving into the deeper stupor of true catatonia. It was a heart-rending admission, but he made it calmly. Jay Thompson's melodramatic play acting had undone his months of therapy in a twinkling. He would need drastic means to repair the damage—if it were even possible to do so.

At the emergency entrance, Jim glanced at his driver while Lynn was being removed from the ambulance. The boy sat slumped over the wheel. Now that he had brought Lynn to the sanctuary of Leyden, he seemed exhausted.

"The car pool's behind the main building," Jim told him. "After you've parked the ambulance you can wait in the rotunda."

"Isn't there something more I can do, Dr. Corwin?"

"Say a prayer, if you can."

In the recovery room Jim placed Lynn's rigid form on a cot, in the radius of the droplight, and picked up the phone. To his relief, Janet Moore answered from the supervisor's office—but two further shocks awaited him as he gave her his orders. Frankel's car had been repaired, and the head physician had taken his family for a weekend in Atlanta. And Keegan, not Singh, was the doctor in charge tonight.

"Will you ask Dr. Keegan to come to the surgery at once, Janet. I'm badly in need of advice."

"He'll be there right away, Doctor. So will I."

While he waited, Jim forced himself to be calm with a deliberate effort while he considered (from every angle) the desperate stratagem that was taking form in his mind. Occasionally he threw a hopeful glance at Lynn—but she remained rigid on the cot. The wide-open eyes stared up at the ceiling without the slightest flicker of the lids; the hair that framed her ashen forehead was still a jungle of gold. He bent to smooth it into a more orderly pattern—and was still running a comb through the finespun strands when Keegan came into the room, with Janet Moore behind him.

The other doctor's reaction was entirely in key—an instant disclaimer of responsibility. "I was against this trip," he said sharply. "My objection will be on the record."

"If we've failed with Lynn, the failure's mine," Jim admitted.

"This may ring down the curtain on your whole program."

"Not if I can get her out of stupor."

"What chance have you? All you can do is lock her up again and let things take their course."

"I won't do that, Keegan. A few hours ago we were planning her return to the university. She can still go, if you'll give me a hand."

"Don't be a fool, man! Her collapse proves this drug therapy can accomplish nothing permanent. Granted, she *seemed* better—so long as she was hospitalized. It didn't mean she could take the outside again."

"She was almost over the barrier," Jim protested. "I know the pattern of her basic conflict now. With proper timing I can still help her retrace it."

"That's wishful thinking. Obviously her regression occurred the moment she faced reality." Keegan turned to Janet Moore. "*You* know the case is hopeless—even if he can't see it."

The old nurse shook her head. "Not if Dr. Corwin says different."

"What would *you* suggest, Dr. Moore?"

"That you stop shouting and listen."

Keegan tossed up his hands. "All right, Corwin. What's your newest panacea?"

"Phenidylate. It brought her out of the depression. I believe it will serve the same purpose now."

"Phenidylate—to break a catatonic stupor? And risk shocking her into a still worse condition?"

"You've used metrazol—and EST. Why not this?"

"I won't endorse the experiment. It's too long a chance."

"So was reserpine," said Jim curtly. "If we hadn't risked its use, this girl would still be in a locked ward."

"She'll be back in one tomorrow." Keegan's eyes had narrowed as he spoke. Reading the agile mind behind them, Jim felt that he had made his decision. "What do you propose to do?"

"Intravenous injection. Will you get an ampule, Janet? There's a whole tray in the drug room."

"She's your patient," said Keegan, "so I won't countermand your order. But I'm making a notation on the chart that I advised against the injection. If she fails to respond, you'll have to explain to the director."

Janet Moore bustled in, with a tray wrapped in a sterile towel, as Keegan stalked from the surgery.

"Will you need an attendant, Dr. Corwin?"

"No, Janet." Now that he had won his first battle, Jim was strangely calm. "I'm counting on her waking from this stupor before the catatonic pattern is re-established."

Wiping the area just in front of Lynn's elbow with alcohol, he pushed the needle through the skin, feeling the soundless click as it penetrated the bluish wall of a vein. Blood spurted into the barrel of the syringe. With his left hand he flipped the loop of the tourniquet free. Across the cot the nurse lifted the girl's wrist to count the pulse beat, as Jim began the slow injection of phenidylate into the bloodstream.

Looking down at the mute, still form of Lynn Thorndyke, he could not shake off the memory of their first encounter at Leyden. The fact that she had lapsed so quickly into the same state (as Keegan had observed with such cruel clarity) seemed a shocking proof of failure. Five minutes later, when Janet Moore remarked that tension was lessening, he let his free fingers close on Lynn's left hand and was amazed at the sudden lack of rigidity. . . . *It's now or never,* he thought—and eased the pressure of his thumb on the barrel of the syringe.

"Do you hear me, Lynn?"

There was no answer from the still form on the cot. The lips (set in a taut, bluish line) seemed immobile as ever—but he could have sworn he felt an answering pressure from the fingers within his own. His thumb tightened again on the syringe, sending a full cubic centimeter of the drug solution coursing into the vein.

"Bend her arm, Janet—if you can."

The nurse raised Lynn's arm, bending it easily at the joint. When she released her grip, it dropped to the cot again as naturally as any sleeper's disturbed in normal rest.

"She's coming out, Doctor—no doubt about it. God help us if she starts to climb the walls——"

He felt his heart turn over at the thought, then forced his mind to settle on the business at hand. The syringe was still three quarters full: he stepped up the tempo of the injection.

"Lynn, you'll be all right this time. But you must try to help us——"

The bluish lips quivered as their tension eased—and the barest whisper escaped them. "I know, Jim—I know."

"You needn't be afraid any more."

"I killed Jay, too."

"Jay wasn't even hurt. He swam ashore a moment after you fainted."

"You're saying that to make things easier——"

"Have I ever lied to you, Lynn?"

"No."

"If I say that Jay Thompson's alive and well, will you believe me?"

"I'll try."

"Take it on faith, Lynn. *Jay is alive.* He drove us here in the ambulance. There's nothing to be afraid of: you don't need to run away again."

Her eyes opened—and he brought the light a trifle closer, until he could look into their blue depths. No cloud dimmed their serenity now, thanks to the deep relaxation of the drug. He wondered if he dared to go further and finish the dialogue he had begun on the lake shore. Clearly the injection had brought on something like narcosynthesis—a condition where the patient's waking restraint upon thoughts (and their verbalization) was wiped clean away. It was medical wizardry in itself, a short cut no less amazing than the effect of reserpine. The chance might never come again.

"This fear of death, Lynn. And your power to cause death. You *must* see it has no reality."

"If you say so."

"Forget Jay for the moment—and the mistakes we made today at Glenville. Go back to the beginning, when this fear was born. You remember that, don't you?"

"Yes. It was David."

"Tell us about David, Lynn. Miss Moore and I would like to know."

"He was my baby brother. I hated him. I wished he would die, so I could be first again with our father."

"All of us wish that at times. It's part of being a child."

"But he *did* die—when he was only a year old."

"It wasn't your fault. It couldn't have been."

"Did *you* ever wish for a brother's death?"

"A hundred times. In my heart—and out loud. It's something children can't help."

Across the cot, Janet Moore spoke tersely. "I had a pretty sister. Hated her like poison—and still do."

"What came next, Lynn? When you got your father back?"

"I didn't keep him long. Mother divorced him. He wanted me to live with him afterwards, but she wouldn't let me. She said it was unnatural for a girl to desert her mother."

"Did you want to go to him?"

"Very much—but I was afraid to show it. I—didn't want to hurt my mother. Even when I was sure she didn't love me any more."

"Did you see your father—after the divorce?"

"Only a few times. Then *he* died too. Mother said I was the cause. She showed me a letter——"

"Did the letter say you'd caused his death?"

"Not in so many words. But mother said that's what it meant."

"It wasn't true, Lynn. Your father died because he couldn't live with the failure of his marriage. *You* didn't cause that failure. All you did was remind him of the happiness he might have had—if your mother had been different. If she'd had the patience, and the tenderness, to make a home for you."

"She said I killed them both! First my brother, then my father. She said she wanted no part of me. That's when she sent me to live with my aunt——"

Hearing the quiet voice go on, sensing the rising confidence that vibrated in its depths, Jim saw that he was confirming a pattern he would have needed months of intense search to uncover. Unaware of his special knowledge, Lynn was picking up his cues with all the trust of a child. . . . The cause of that response was a blend of stimuli: the effects of the reserpine, counterpointed by the phenidylate—with the aftermath of the shock at Loon Lake a part of it. Together they had forged a key to open the secret places of her heart.

"There was insurance money for my education," said Lynn. "Mother sent me to Glenville: she couldn't help herself. I was a success there. I had something to be proud of——"

"Your painting?"

"It opened the doors to another world. I was happy—for a time. Until I looked around me and found I was still alone."

He felt her fingers close tightly on his as he watched the tears roll down her cheeks.

"How could you be alone, Lynn? You had Jay."

"It was wrong to love him."

"Wasn't your love returned?"

"I think so. He couldn't show it openly."

"Why not?"

"He was engaged—to Mary Lou Donelson. They'd planned to marry when he graduated. She had all the beaux she needed—but she still wanted Jay——"

"And you hated her for wanting him?"

"I'd never been in love before. I'd never even had a friend. I wished she'd die, so I could have Jay. Then he broke the engagement—and she drowned herself."

"Mary Lou didn't drown, Lynn. Today she's married to the man she really wanted."

"Don't make up another story. I couldn't bear it."

"Have I ever lied to you?"

"No, Jim. I'm *trying* to believe you."

"When you heard that Mary Lou had drowned at Loon Lake—was that why you ran away? The reason you came aboard the freighter? The reason you hated me—when I wouldn't let you die in your cabin?"

"I didn't deserve to go on living."

"Because you wished your brother dead? And blamed yourself for your father's suicide? And what you *thought* was Mary Lou's drowning?"

"I knew I was a monster—with the power to destroy people just by hating them."

"All of us have wished for that power, Lynn. It's a human failing. It isn't right, of course. We seldom think right when our thoughts get twisted."

"Mine have been twisted so long."

"Do you see now how easily they come untwisted? Once you *know* you can't hurt people by wishing them dead?"

She looked at him steadily. "I understand when you explain it, Jim. How could I be such a fool?"

"Call it a bad conscience, if you like. It'll do as a name for the thing that's tortured you. Always remember it was lying—from the start. You didn't harm your brother—or your father. And Mary Lou didn't drown at Loon Lake—any more than Jay drowned today. I can prove it."

Janet Moore left the surgery at his nod: he knew she would go straight to the rotunda where Thompson waited.

"It's too bad you were alone when these things happened," he said. "Particularly the accident at Loon Lake, when you ran away. If you'd talked to me aboard the *Creole Belle*, as we've talked tonight, you wouldn't be at Leyden now. If you'd trusted me, instead of hating me——"

"Why did I hate you? When you were only trying to help?"

"You'd lost your connection with reality. The voice in your subconscious was too strong to shout down. It can never trouble you again."

"We won't let it—will we, Jim?"

"*You* won't let it, Lynn. We've proved that tonight."

"I could never have done it alone."

Janet Moore had returned, and the boy stood beside her; both of them had paused in the shadows outside the warm cone of light that fell upon the cot. With gentle fingers, Jim disengaged the syringe from Lynn's arm and got to his feet.

"I want you to sleep awhile now," he told her. "Jay is here to say good night."

The boy stepped forward at his nod. Jim felt his heart contract, gripped by a triumph more precious than love. He stepped back, out of the cone of light, as Jay knelt at the bedside to kiss the girl's pale cheek. For an instant her eyes rested on Jay's face, as though she could not quite believe what she saw. Then, with a drowsy smile, her hand lifted to stroke his cheek gently, before she closed her eyes and slept.

Pattern for Tomorrow

RIPPING the last page of his report from the typewriter, Jim ran in a fresh sheet and began to reconstruct the final paragraph. The spring night was insistent at the open window. He ignored the invitation—forcing his mind to concentrate on the words he had written so slowly—and with such a deep glow of pride:

Final Case Summary

> Since her release from Leyden eight months ago, patient's recovery and her adjustment to society have been complete.
>
> Periodic checkups thereafter have revealed no trace of former trauma.
>
> The discontinuance of all medication, as of January 1st, has produced no ill effects.
>
> Patient has made herself well—through dissolving, and expelling, by her own conscious mind, the Pandora's box of evil spirits that had found asylum in the dark corners of her brain.
>
> This—in collaboration with the patient—is a clean-cut victory for reserpine.

He removed the page without a reading, and folded it into the loose-leaf notebook that held the voluminous case history of his favorite patient. Closing the cover on the record, he told himself that the last tie binding them was severed. For a moment he stood at his window and stared out at the April moonlight on the lawns of Leyden. Then he flung himself on his hard hospital bed, prey to the greatest desolation he had ever known.

ii

Frankel stacked the thick sheaf of typescript, and smiled at Jim across the desk.

"It's a brilliant summary, my friend," he said. "From first to last it does you credit."

Midway of their final grueling test with reserpine—and a comparable testing of chlorpromazine, which the manufacturer had been happy to supply without fee—the two doctors had fallen into the habit of these weekly meetings in Frankel's office. The business of the day, as always, was the comparing of results, both in the wards and in their long uphill battle with Meeker. The patient, point-by-point check of Lynn Thorndyke's dossier had been the last item on the schedule.

"As cases go," said the Austrian, "I won't call this one a classic. Your procedure was too radical for the books, I'm afraid. But there's no question that the girl's cure is permanent—so far as the word can be used in psychiatry."

"Lynn did most of the work—with the help of the tranquilizer."

The head physician grimaced. "*Tranquilizer!* I'm not sure I like that term."

"It's come into general use, I'm afraid."

"It has the smell of the lamp about it—or should I say the advertising business? Like so many labels, it may promise more than it can deliver."

"You'll have to admit that our results here are astounding."

"So astounding, my friend, that I'm beginning to worry a little. Remember, psychiatry is my livelihood. Now that I've given you carte blanche you may put me out of business—in favor of the pharmacists."

"That day will never come," said Jim. "And I'm willing to admit that our success with Lynn was blind luck. Look back at the night I brought her out of catatonia—and used narcosynthesis to identify the destructive forces in her personality. If I'd known their real strength—or had the knowledge of psychiatry you've given me since—I might have been afraid to turn those forces loose. Fortunately, she had enough strength on the other side to defeat them. It won't be that easy with the next case."

Frankel nodded. "Your approach *was* an oversimplification of the problem. With thirty years of Freudian techniques behind me, I'd never have attacked so blindly."

"I was desperate, Kurt."

"And you succeeded. If we'd known Lynn's whole story, I'm sure we'd have found other factors to produce a psychosis of such depth. However, she's accepted what she's learned about herself—that's what really matters. As the philosophers say, she's crossed the bridge of living into life. Few human beings in our time are so fortunate." Frankel rose from his chair and swept the air with a familiar, explosive gesture. "Nor are many patients blessed with such a doctor."

"Don't call *me* a hero," said Jim. "I'd made a near-fatal blunder at Loon Lake. I was only trying to correct it."

"Six months ago—when I certified Lynn as cured and she returned to the university—you were heartbroken. Why didn't you marry her, Jim?"

"Because it was essential that she break every tie. With this hospital—and with me."

The Austrian sighed. "Analysts face the same problem with most female patients. I'll say this for you. When you did make the break, you covered yourself beautifully. Even I was deceived—for a time."

"Look at the future through *her* eyes, Kurt. Naturally, she was grateful to me. Her plan to come back here and teach art therapy was part of that gratitude. Thank God she's said no more about it, now she's back at the university. I *can't* ask her to share my life here—not with Meeker's ax hanging over my neck."

"I won't deny your situation here is precarious," said the head physician.

"Besides, she's earned a chance to do really big things with her painting. And as Jay Thompson's wife—if she wants that."

"I gather Lynn's setting the Glenville campus on fire this time."

"She's led her class since mid-term," said Jim happily. "And she hasn't missed a party or a dance—thanks to young Thompson. To me that proves my decision was the right one."

"Undoubtedly—if *you* can endure the loss."

Jim looked into Frankel's eyes. "I'll muddle through, Kurt—thanks to what you've taught me."

"Does that mean you'll stay on here?"

"So long as you can hold off Meeker. If he does ax me, I want you and Singh to promise you'll finish the job."

"Meeker won't make a move until this last test run is finished. We can count on that much."

"Why? So he'll have enough to hang me?"

"Perhaps we can stage a lynching bee of our own, if he forces the issue," said Frankel grimly. "Meanwhile, he's playing a waiting game—because he has no choice. He can't deny we've improved psychiatric practice here enormously—thanks to your methods."

"Those same methods have cut into his graft—and cut deep."

"So they have—by reducing the number of patients suitable for lobotomy. A year ago, when the operation was in full swing, he had visions of living like a sultan here—with a thousand robots on his work force. Reserpine has canceled out that pleasant fantasy. He'll hate you to his dying day for introducing it at Leyden. But he won't lift a finger—until he can prove your methods are too expensive to be used permanently. Or until he catches us in a real mistake."

"He can't sit tight indefinitely," said Jim. "The committee is due to inspect the whole hospital in May."

"By May we'll be ready with our findings. They could make us famous, Jim."

"Maybe I was wrong to hold out for a trial run with chlorpromazine," said Jim. "Dr. Small wanted comparative tables; it seemed too good a chance to miss."

"I'd have settled for the lesser prize," said the psychiatrist. "Aren't you glad to have that extra data?"

"Of course," said Frankel. "It bears out what I've said all along. The history of these drugs—which the public insists on calling tranquilizers—is duplicating the story of the sulfas. Remember the first trial runs of sulfanilamide?"

"All too well. It killed bacteria, all right. Occasionally, it also turned a patient blue."

"Then we had sulfapyradine, the drug that really stopped pneumonia."

"And sulfathiazole," Jim put in. "It did everything *both* the others had done."

"Plus some tricks of its own," said Frankel, warming to a favorite topic. "Later still, we had sulfadiazine. And, of course, penicillin. A wonder drug in its own right—once we'd learned how to purify it and doctors had the courage to give man-size doses. I've said this before, but it bears repeating: the doctors of the mind are standing on the same threshold today. Here at Leyden we've proved beyond question that we can handle acute schizophrenics with a combination of chemical agents. Why not assume that a whole new arsenal of drugs is waiting for us now in test tubes? Ready to control mental illness, in *all* forms and degrees?"

"Amen," said Jim.

Frankel looked up sharply—as though he had not expected such quick agreement. "We must still keep our perspective. It's one thing to convince a dedicated scientist of our results—and quite another to sell them to the state hospital committee. Drugs costing what they do, you'll never make this program stick at Leyden without a special appropriation. The minute we have to pay for them, Meeker will begin howling—and half the legislature will join the chorus."

"What chance do we have with the committee, then?"

"I wouldn't dare guess, Jim. As usual, it's a house divided, and each man's pulling for votes. That's why they always make these tours in the late spring, a few weeks before the primaries."

"Do you have their names?"

"And their records," said Frankel, with a thin smile. "A friend at the state house keeps me up to date. The one unknown element is Enoch Williams' brother-in-law. He's been needling Meeker—to find out why Enoch *still* hasn't been released."

"Won't that work in our favor?"

"Possibly. It depends on how he uses his authority—and how fast Meeker counterpunches." Frankel took a list from his desk drawer and circled a name. "In any event, when you sit down across the table from the Honorable Sam Wylie, give him an extra-careful look. He's the youngest member of the legislature this session. So far, no one's quite sure what he stands for, beside himself."

"Who's the chairman?"

"A fine old southern gentleman named Garvin Rogers. His family's been in politics ever since the carpetbaggers pulled out. Rogers is the sort of anachronism who still keeps slaves on his plantation—and calls them share croppers. Oddly enough, he also tries to be fair." Frankel dismissed the name with a hopeless shrug. "Then we have Dr. Damphier, the state commissioner of health. He'll sit with Meeker, as the law requires——"

"What will he vote for?"

"Justice—only he doesn't *have* a vote. Damphier's a fine doctor, though a bit old-fashioned. Too good for his job, in many ways. There'll be a doctor on the committee itself—that's also a state law. Someone from the university medical school. It's a reasonable hope that he'll be impartial." Again the Austrian checked the list. "Harrington and Bell are both ciphers from the mountain counties: *they'll* vote with the chairman. The man we'll really have to watch is Virgil Stobbs. He's a killer on horseback."

"I've heard of Stobbs."

"He's been hitting the headlines regularly. The Stobbses are one of the oldest families in the state. Emotionally the whole clan is living in the last century—but don't undervalue their brains. They're smart as steel traps: the sort who fight progress by pretending to speak in its name. Virgil Stobbs is their spokesman: he knows every trick in the lawyer's book. Right now his hobbyhorse is economy in government, at all levels. He hopes to ride it into the Senate."

"You're making our chances look pretty gloomy, Kurt."

"Only to give you an objective view. Meeker *must* suspect we've a line on his thimblerigged bookkeeping here—to say nothing of his outright thievery. He probably figures I'll keep my own mouth shut, to save my job——"

"You mustn't get involved, Kurt. No matter what happens."

Frankel waved the objection aside. "I've sat back too long, Jim. Even if it ruins my future here, I can't let your work be discredited."

"How can Meeker discredit it? The facts speak for themselves."

"As an experiment, yes. Not necessarily as standard procedure at state-hospital level. The drug cost, as I've said, is the big stumbling block. That, in itself, could prejudice the committee at the start."

"It'd be in character for Meeker to stress that angle."

"This time I think he'll avoid a showdown—never mind how bitterly he hates you. Spelling out our economic situation just now might uncover the rackets he's been running here—to the public's benefit. He knows by now you'll never go back to wholesale lobotomies. He's afraid to fire you outright; that way you could go to the newspapers and demand an investigation. My guess is that he's working on some scheme to smear both you and the drugs when you testify before the committee. If it works, he'll force you to resign under a cloud. Then he'll hire a surgeon who's less scrupulous about using a leucotome on people's brains."

Jim shook his head slowly. "Using sick people for political graft is a new low, in my book," he said. "It makes you shudder for the future."

"Leyden's an exception, Jim—and a glaring one. It's our duty to expose it, but the job won't be easy. Meeker will probably stay in the background, and let Virgil Stobbs throw the punches. Remember, anything that resembles progress—and doesn't line the pockets of the state machine—is fair game to his kind. One bad break on our side and he can score a knockout."

"At least we know the enemy's name."

"But not the kind of punches he'll be using. If I were you, I'd brush up on my boxing between now and May."

iii

Ten days later, in the midst of a morning-long inspection of Lovell One, Jim had cause to remember Frankel's warning.

With Singh's assistance he was checking the cells in the locked ward one by one, to make sure that the orderlies had done an adequate job of whitewash. In this case, the whitewash was quite literal—part of the job of furbishing that Meeker had ordered, in anticipation of the hospital committee's arrival. . . . It was, Jim reflected, a signal proof of the tranquilizer program's success that barely a half dozen cells in the locked ward were occupied. Most of the former inmates (now useful members of the hospital work force) were laboring beside the regular attendants to push through the herculean job of making all Leyden neat as a child's pinafore.

Jim was still congratulating himself on those wide-open doors when the phone rang in the chartroom. To his surprise, he heard the booming voice of Jack Hanley when he picked up the receiver. The hospital politico had been assigned to the truck farm this morning, with a selected gang of workmen, to hand-tailor the peanut vines, which had spread like a jungle after heavy spring rains. At least three of the committee members were farmers. It was reasonable to expect that they would spend more time in the bean rows than in Frankel's office.

"Lester Clark just keeled over, Doctor. They brought him to the surgery."

"I'll be there at once." Clark was from one of Singh's wards, a particularly violent case whose response to reserpine had been slow but definite. That morning, he remembered, the patient had complained of a slight indigestion: on Singh's order he had been excused from his usual chores. . . . Wondering why Hanley (after a hard forenoon in the fields) had volunteered on the case, Jim had the reason instantly. The burly guard was Meeker's official spy in the men's wards. Clearly he was hoping to smell out trouble.

Hanley and Mal Orcutt (an orderly who was another of the director's watchdogs) were bringing an oxygen tent into the surgery when he entered. Janet Moore was already on hand. The patient was stretched on the emergency cot: his lips were ashen, his breathing shallow. At Jim's arrival, the nurse opened a blood-pressure gauge and wrapped the cuff around Clark's upper arm.

Hanley spoke up with unusual briskness. "I got in from the pea patch early, Doctor: thought I'd take a look at Brown before lunch. This fellow was complaining of stomach pains yesterday. We put him on soda tablets this morning and told him to hit the sack. In the open ward, where he could yell if he needed help. Like you see, all he could get out was a fair-sized groan——"

Jim nodded, without raising his eyes from the stethoscope he had applied over the artery constricted beneath the cuff of the sphygmomanometer. There was only a faint sound—one he could not measure accurately. It appeared to be around sixty, a dangerously low pressure. It was obvious, too, that the heart was laboring.

"How's he look to you, Miss Moore?"

"I'm afraid it's terminal, Doctor."

"You'd better call Dr. Singh. Clark's from his ward."

"He's on his way here now."

"Have you brought his chart?"

"It's on the stretcher. He's been improving slowly on reserpine; Dr. Singh doubled the dosage yesterday." The nurse turned as the Hindu came puffing through the door; Jim stepped back from the cot and handed him the stethoscope.

"Looks as though he's *in extremis,* Chandra. His blood pressure's so low I can hardly detect it."

A moment later, with his own examination ended, the Indian doctor nodded his agreement. "It's coronary thrombosis. No doubt about it."

"Could the drug have brought it on? The chart says you doubled the dosage yesterday."

"Clark's response was entirely routine," said Singh. "And the dose is within recommended limits."

"Let's take an electrocardiogram and be sure."

The oxygen tent was in place now. Jim continued to stand aside while the attendants turned the valves. Across the room Singh and Janet Moore were adjusting the portable electrocardiographic apparatus. The machine was an ancient one, equipped with a quartz-string galvanometer. This sensitive instrument recorded the action currents in the heart itself—photographing the movements of the string upon a strip of film. When this was developed, it gave the attending physician a permanent graphic record of the heartbeat.

As the flow of oxygen hissed beneath the plastic tent, there was some slight improvement in the patient's pallor, but little in his general condition. When the switch of the electrocardiograph was flipped, a faint, moving shadow appeared on the recorder as the galvanometer string began its vibration. Even now, with the film undeveloped, one could note that the heart's action was ominously weak. The pattern of its beat was barely visible, so feeble were the action currents produced by the muscle itself.

"The voltage is almost nonexistent," said Singh.

"Record it, if you can."

Again Singh flipped the switch of the machine. The low purr of the motor filled the room as it turned the long roll of film. From where he stood, Jim could see that the amplitude of the galvanometer's swing was diminishing steadily. He took the stethoscope from the Hindu and returned to the patient's side.

"No pulse at the wrist, Doctor," said Janet Moore.

"None at the chest either, I'm afraid."

Jim leaned forward for a moment more, listening carefully above a heart that had already stopped. When he lifted his head at last, there was no need to pronounce the formal verdict.

"The heart has ceased to beat," he said. "Mark it at two thirty-five on the chart, Miss Moore, and bring us a death certificate. What happened on that film, Chandra?"

"I'm afraid the movements of the string were too slight to record. We'll need a post-mortem, to establish the exact cause of death."

"His people live in Ellenville," said the nurse. "Shall I call for permission?"

"No need to bother," Hanley volunteered. "I know Clark's wife. She'll never sign a p.m. permit."

"Why not?"

"Belongs to one of them hell-roaring sects—the kind that heal with snakes. Did her damnedest to fight us off when we came to collect Lester—after *he* tried to brain her with an ax."

"It's still worth trying," said Jim. "I'll make the call myself." He picked up the wall phone. Two minutes later, with the widow's harpy screeches still in his ear, he hung up with a bitter smile.

"Looks like I was right," said Hanley. He was leaning in the doorframe, with his eyes on the cadaver—looking uncomfortably like a slovenly butcher between jobs. With a flush of resentment Jim remembered that he had taken in every detail of the examination—including the discussion of causes.

"It's quite possible we committed the wrong patient," he said. "Mrs. Clark tells me her family will sue the hospital if we lay a finger on her late husband. Then she ordered me to call Melcher's Funeral Home."

Jim shook his head. After nearly two years at Leyden, he had yet to summon the coroner. Had he made such an earth-shaking request today, he was sure Meeker would have vetoed it instantly. "We can make a final diagnosis on the evidence we have," he said. "You agree that it's acute coronary thrombosis, don't you, Chandra?"

The Hindu cleared his throat—an odd, rasping sound in the

silence. "That is certainly the presumption—in the absence of confirmation by electrocardiograph."

Jim wrote the diagnosis on the death certificate, and signed it. At the wall phone, Janet Moore was already calling the undertaker in Ellenville. Hanley and Orcutt came forward without awaiting orders and transferred the body to a litter. The former avoided Jim's eyes while he eased his burden through the doorway, but he was humming faintly as he vanished.

"I believe that cretin enjoys the sight of death," said the nurse. She took up Lester Clark's chart, made a final notation, and departed for the record room. Singh sat at the foot of the empty cot with his brows creased in a deep frown. It was a rare expression for the Hindu, whose face was usually placid as a harvest moon.

"Jim—could it have been the reserpine?"

"Was there any adverse effect yesterday?"

"Only the indigestion. Otherwise he was improving steadily. In another week I would have certified him for the work force."

Jim wheeled the machine into its corner. "I can't believe it was the drug. An autopsy would give the only certain answer, of course—since the ECG failed us—but we'll never have it now."

At his day's end—still troubled by that gnawing doubt—Jim sought out Frankel in his office and told him the whole story.

"All the symptoms of coronary thrombosis are there," said the chief physician. "The apparent indigestion, the strangled cry and collapse, the cyanosis at lips and fingernails. What else does it spell out?"

"The side effects of an idiosyncrasy to a drug, perhaps?"

"Suppose Clark had not been on reserpine. Would you have considered any other diagnosis?"

"No, Kurt."

"Then why are you so concerned?"

"I can't put it into words. Let's say the uncertainty weighs on my conscience."

"It shouldn't—with the evidence at hand. Isn't it time you got rid of your sense of guilt, Jim?"

"What does that mean?"

"You've sent Lynn Thorndyke back among the living. Didn't that banish your wife's ghost for all time?"

"I thought so," Jim said quietly. "My blood pressure is normal, despite the pace we've been hitting. Three months ago I discontinued reserpine entirely——"

"I'm aware of all that. The fact remains, you're something of a rarity these days, a completely honest man. Such inflexible integrity can play hell with any brain."

"I'm still wondering why Clark died."

"You must learn to live with failure if you intend to go on here, Jim. You paid your debt—if there ever was one—when you saved Lynn. Suppose Clark *did* collapse because of the drug? It was a chance we took when we started the program—hoping its benefits would be greater than the drawbacks. You've proved that much a hundred times over."

iv

"Mother doesn't worry me," said Lynn. "From what you've just said, I no longer worry her. Doesn't that make us even?"

Jim took back the letter he had just handed her. Mrs. Thorndyke had written it in England. He had received it at Leyden, two days after the collapse of Lester Clark. Troubled as he was by the event (and the fact that Meeker had accepted the death certificate with no comment whatever), he had treated himself to this afternoon off duty—and what he assured himself would be his final visit to the university campus. . . . The letter was excuse enough. Even though he was fairly certain of her response, it was important that he test Lynn's reaction to its contents.

The girl had been hard at work in the library when he arrived, but she had put her books aside to join him. By unspoken agreement they had crossed the quad to sit beside the fountain. Lynn was wearing the standard campus garb today—Bermuda shorts and a pullover. In the library, behind an imposing pair of horn rims, she had been a typical student. Here, in the bright May sunlight, she seemed to take on maturity like a new garment. In all their meetings she had never been more vibrantly alive.

Crossing the quad, Jim had fallen back a pace to watch her as she moved down the path to the fountain. Of late (when he permitted himself the self-torture of these visits to Glenville) he had taken to storing away such pictures. Now, seated beside Lynn on the grass, with his back resting comfortably against the bole of a huge live oak, he admitted willingly that his visit had been needless.

True, the girl's memory of her mother was one of the few elements in her past he had left unexplored: looking through Mrs. Thorndyke's letter, he had felt he must make sure the silver cord was cleanly severed. In Lynn's presence, such doubts were absurd. After the battle she had fought and won, she could face any crisis—including the fact that her mother had just chosen a second husband.

Dear Dr. Corwin:

Dean Pearson's latest report on my daughter has just reached me. As I gather, she is now recovered from her *crise des nerfs*—and fully restored to her place in society. The dean also tells me that Lynn is certain to graduate—and that she has so informed my solicitors. Which means, of course, that the university, Lynn, and myself will receive our stipends in due course, as provided by my late husband's will.

I am taking this means of expressing my gratitude for the way you have rescued my daughter. When I met you at the Jefferson Hotel in Leyden, I had made up my mind to spare myself nothing, if a full recital of the facts would aid you in treating her. Apparently my candor has paid handsome dividends.

Next week, I shall be marrying Lord Geoffrey Plowden, of Windon Hall, Sussex—the ninth baronet of that line. Since he is a recent widower, the ceremony will be private, with formal announcement reserved for a later date. As Lady Plowden, I plan to devote most of my forthcoming inheritance to the restoration of Windon, which has been in a state of disrepair since the war. Once that labor of love is accomplished, I intend to settle permanently in England.

Since you have done so much for me—will you do one favor more and break this news to my daughter? I am sure she will bear up under it. After all, she is now independent of me financially—as she has always been in other respects.

Cordially,
Florence Thorndyke

Folding the letter into his wallet, Jim reflected that each word was in character—including the dismissal (in quite needless French) of Lynn's illness and the ringing insincerity of the closing lines.

"Lady Plowden will sound very impressive," he said cautiously.

Lynn nodded her agreement, with a tranquil smile. "Poor Mother: I hope she'll stop being lonely, now she's joining the British aristocracy. Her initiation is costing all of fifty thousand dollars, that's obvious." There was no bitterness in her tone and no hint of satire: she had simply stated a fact, for what it was worth. Searching her face carefully before he answered, Jim was sure that Lynn Thorndyke understood her mother completely. With that knowledge, she had learned pity as well.

"Loneliness is a disease for which there's just one safe cure," he said. "You must find *someone* to trust, to confide in. I'll join you in praying that Plowden fills the bill. Up to now, it's evident she never trusted anyone but herself."

"It was part of her background," said Lynn. "No family in America could be good enough for a Burford. Least of all the Thorndykes."

"Perhaps she'll find her equal in Plowden."

"If she does, it's the one thing that will save her." Lynn put a hand on Jim's arm. "Did you think this news would upset me?"

"Not really. But I wanted you to have it without delay."

"I knew last week, Jim. Dixie Welch, who rooms on my floor, just flew back from an exchange scholarship in England. She got the story firsthand."

"Sorry if I'm a tardy courier——"

"Mother had ceased to communicate directly years ago. It hurt me once: I don't mind a bit today. You see, Jim, I realize she's afraid to meet me face to face—and admit what a failure she's been."

"What about your own wedding? Will you send her word before—or after?"

The girl's eyes were without guile—though she just escaped dimpling when she spoke. "How would you advise me?"

"It's your province, not mine," said Jim carefully. "But I think I'd return evil with good and send a formal announcement."

"I'll take your advice, Dr. Corwin: it's been excellent so far." Her voice was grave, but her eyes were smiling now, along with her lips.

"Have you set a date, Lynn?"

"It isn't definite yet. But I think I'll be married the week I graduate."

He forced himself to answer steadily, "May I wish you every happiness?"

"You gave me happiness, Jim—when you helped me to get well."

"Getting well is only the beginning, my dear."

"Do you think I'm ready to marry?"

"Of course I do."

This time there was no mistaking the dimple. "I've your permission, then?"

"And my blessing."

The deep tone of the chapel bell announced a new hour—and a new class in the making. Jim got to his feet and held out his hand. "I'll say good-by now, Lynn," he told her—proud that his voice held no hint of the torture in his heart.

"It isn't good-by, Jim. It can't be."

"Why do you say that?" he asked, forcing a smile.

"Didn't you know I'm to be a witness before the state hospital committee?"

"There's no need of that. And don't make it sound like a trial —it's only a routine hearing."

"I wouldn't be too sure," she said. "Dr. Frankel called me up yesterday—and I was glad to accept. My last final exam is on Friday. So it fits in perfectly."

"I'd rather you didn't come."

"But I'm your prize exhibit, Jim. Aren't you proud of me?"

"Too proud to share you with six politicians from the capital, and a gang of newspapermen."

"I've already been invited," said Lynn firmly. "And I won't be put off by a stubborn idealist—who should know better." She turned to the path as the bell's last note died out. "Good-by until Monday, then. Wish me luck with my exams?"

"You'll make your own luck, from now on."

"I intend to do my best," said Lynn—and lifted on her toes to kiss him lightly. "That's to wish *you* luck on Monday."

She left him quickly on that, running just a little to overtake a group of students converging on the portico of Fine Arts.

v

Twenty-four hours before the arrival of the investigating committee, Dr. Thaddeus Meeker summoned his staff for a briefing. Dr. Corwin's name was pointedly omitted from the invitation, as was Dr. Singh's.

Since both Jim and the Hindu were on ward duty at the time (and were thus unable to attend) it was possible to overlook the omission. Still, the hostility in the director's timing was unmistakable. Keegan, Jim reflected, was bombproof. So, because of his reputation, was Frankel. Young Welles (along with the three gray anonymities who completed the medical personnel) had stubbornly refused to take part in the drug program. Positive now that something lethal was brewing, with himself as the victim, Jim determined to spare Singh, if such a course was possible.

"Has Meeker asked for the final figures on our test?" he demanded, when their paths crossed at the day's end.

The Hindu shook his head. "Dr. Meeker hasn't spoken to me for weeks."

"Nor to me. He briefed the others this morning. Why hasn't he called us in, now we're off duty?"

"Perhaps it's a war of nerves."

"Meeker's too stupid to dream up that approach. Frankel was right: he plans to lie doggo at the hearing tomorrow—while Virgil Stobbs fires the book at us."

"But why, Jim?"

"Because he feels, quite rightly, I'm his mortal enemy. He'll kill me without a qualm—if only to cover the graft he has working here."

"Not just you, Jim. We ran these tests together."

"The original idea was mine."

The Hindu smiled gently. "Are you, by any chance, trying to hog the credit?"

"You know damned well I'm not."

"The blame, then?"

"It's mine—and I'm prepared to take it. There's no reason why you should be hurt too."

"There need be no blame, Jim. The program's a success."

"Not with Clark's death unexplained."

"It was coronary thrombosis."

"We can't prove it."

"True. If there had been time to complete the cardiogram——"

"Would it have shown anything?"

"It might. As I recall, I had completed two leads—perhaps three. The machine is an ancient one. It worked slowly."

"There's no ECG tracing on Clark's record," said Jim. "No one remembers it in the lab. It must have been tossed out as incomplete—and worthless."

"Surely a clinical diagnosis is worth something."

"Perhaps—if someone else had made it. It's too bad that Jack Hanley called us in that day—instead of Keegan or Welles. Either of us might be covering up for the other."

"You mean, implying that Clark did not die from the effects of reserpine?"

"Face it, Chandra. Whatever we say will be suspect."

"In my country we have a profound conviction that right will triumph—if we live long enough. Courage, my friend; I think that maxim still holds true in America."

At breakfast Jim learned that the committee's arrival had been a complete anticlimax. First, the seven-man group had stalked through the wards at top speed. (Jim could not suppress an inward chuckle as he pictured that whirlwind tour. It was obvious that Meeker had kept the visitors moving at a fast tempo, lest they recognize the difference between Brown and Lovell—and the rest of Leyden.) Shepherded by Meeker, they had next visited the occupational therapy workshop and the model farm. Finally, they had gathered in the lounge to compare notes. The staff had been ordered to appear there at ten, the hour at which the hearing would formally open.

Large as the staff lounge was, it seemed crowded when Jim entered. Frankel had insisted on informality, but the visitors were an impressive focal point as they sat bunched at a green-baize table between the two tall windows. At a small table to one side sat Meeker, with the state commissioner of mental health at his side. The staff doctors (trying hard to look at ease) lounged in a half circle of armchairs, with their notebooks beside them.

Behind the green table, Jim noted, was a clerk with a Stenotype machine. Two bored reporters occupied the window seats: in a tip-tilted chair an equally bored cameraman adjusted a flash-bulb holder before he resumed his doze. . . . Taking a place between Singh and Frankel, Jim felt that the same ennui had infected the whole gathering. He had expected oratory (if only for the benefit of the press), an instant passage at arms with Meeker. Instead, he gathered, the early hours of the hearing were to be devoted to a solemn parade of facts and figures, with the stress on Leyden's record for economy. At the moment, Meeker was reciting an apparently endless list, with frequent assists from his two private secretaries, who staggered from corridor to staff room with his ledgers.

Facts and figures (the two, it seemed, were synonymous) became part of the record as the stenographer transcribed them. Now and again one of the reporters scribbled a note before slumping into apathy: the photographer exploded a single grudging flash bulb to take in the scene as a whole. There was no other activity whatever. Save for Meeker's drone, and the muted chatter of the Stenotype, the room seemed lost in collective slumber.

"Why do we have to sit this out, Kurt?" Jim asked in a whisper.

"It has a purpose. Just wait."

If only to keep his own eyes open, Jim began to study faces in detail. Garvin Rogers, the chairman, was ramrod-stiff in his armchair. As Frankel had remarked, he was a gentleman of the old school, cut on old-fashioned lines: his resemblance to a plantation whisky ad was so startling it took the breath away. Above the shoestring tie and the broad linen collar, the man's face was claret-colored and completely in repose: Jim needed a second glance to convince himself that Rogers was sleeping soundly—with his eyes open wide.

Sam Wylie (Enoch Williams' brother-in-law) sat at the chairman's left, an old-young man in a rumpled linen coat: like Rogers, his thoughts seemed far away. On Rogers' right was Virgil Stobbs, the menace Frankel had described so ominously. At this distance he seemed the model, well-sandpapered lawyer with a jocular manner and a ready smile for his fellow members.

Dr. Stanton Potter, the medical member from the university, was brisk and obviously efficient. So far, it was impossible to guess where his sympathies lay. The two others at the green table were nondescript backwoodsmen, whose coats had long since been shucked. Their sweat-stained galluses seemed to form identical patterns as they leaned forward on their elbows and strained to follow the meaning of Meeker's drone.

At the side table the director was nearing the end of his formal accounting. Jim had not set eyes on Meeker for several weeks. He was shocked to note that the director's face was pinched and unwell.

Dr. Andrew Damphier, the state commissioner, sat unmoving at his side—a wizened man only a size larger than a jockey, the effigy of the old-style country doctor. Only the eyes were active; they roamed from face to face in the group, missing little in their restless appraisal. When the man caught Jim's stare, an eyelid fluttered in an unmistakable wink. Antagonists of long standing via the telephone, they had finally become friends of a sort, though this was their first formal meeting.

Garvin Rogers spoke as Meeker closed his last ledger. Considering his aristocratic bearing, the chairman's voice had a back-country flavor, with the hint of an evangelical whine.

"Any questions on the budget report, gentlemen?"

There was a collective sigh from the table. Sam Wylie opened his eyes and seemed about to speak, thought better of the effort, and contented himself with a shake of his head.

"Accepted as read, Dr. Meeker," droned Rogers. "Subject, of course, to the state auditors' approval. We've already found your hospital in excellent condition. So, it seems, are your books. Certainly your patient day-cost is well below average."

Meeker spoke with a glance at his notes—so ponderously that both reporters took out their folded copy papers to record the utterance. "We try to keep Leyden efficient, Mr. Rogers. Every servant of our great state has a sacred obligation to the people —and the people's trust."

"If you have finished, we will open the meeting to questions."

"I've assembled my staff for that purpose," said Meeker. "Ask them what you wish: we've nothing to conceal here."

"A commendable attitude, Doctor," said Rogers. "To save time, we'll make this an informal discussion." He turned to his fellow members. "Put any query you like, gentlemen. The chair will rule on points of order."

For a moment no one spoke—and Jim had a wild, irrational hope that the gathering was about to adjourn from sheer inertia. Then Stobbs raised his hand for attention. His voice was as brightly suave as his manner. For all its deceptive friendliness, it broke through the fog of boredom instantly.

"I seem to remember newspaper reports, Dr. Meeker—describing an interesting surgical technique to correct mental illness."

"Are you referring to our program of transorbital lobotomy?"

"That was the operation," said Stobbs. "How's it been progressing lately?"

"I'm afraid lobotomy has been virtually discontinued."

"*Discontinued*, Dr. Meeker? The first reports, as I recall, were excellent. You gave out two interviews, stating that it might open a new era in hospital procedure."

Jim glanced at Frankel, then held his tongue. Sensing the enemy's strategy, he had no way to counter it. To start defending himself before he was accused would only stress the implication of guilt.

"The first reports were indeed excellent," said Meeker. "I was able to add over eighty patients to my permanent work force. The fact accounts, in part at least, for the figures in my report."

"Yet the program was shelved?"

"For all practical purposes, yes. My staff so advised me—and I did not countermand the decision. As you gentlemen know, I am primarily an administrator. I put my trust in Dr. Frankel—and his judgment."

Jim found he was speaking at last, before Frankel could break the sudden hush. "Perhaps I am best qualified to explain what happened, Mr. Stobbs," he said.

Meeker flourished a plump hand by way of introduction. "Dr. Corwin, our neurosurgeon," he said. "He was in charge of the program."

"Then he's entitled to explain its failure," said Stobbs. The smiling mask was still in place. The voice behind it was a whiplash, hinting of real torture to come.

"Lobotomy is not a perfect operation," said Jim. "I know of no surgeon with a knowledge of psychiatry who endorses its final result unreservedly."

"But you *did* perform a hundred or more lobotomies when you first came to Leyden?"

"Yes, Mr. Stobbs."

"Even though you were dissatisfied with the results?"

"Are you entirely satisfied with the results of democracy?"

The whip lashed in earnest. "My beliefs are not in question here, Dr. Corwin. Nor is my competence. Proceed."

"Lobotomy has been fairly widely used on what were formerly called hopeless cases," said Jim. "But not because it was perfect. The operation was a short cut; it was never a cure. It did help many people, despite its drawbacks."

"I have read of no better treatment for mental disease," said Stobbs frostily. "Therefore, I see no excuse for discontinuing the surgical technique for which you were hired."

It was the most obvious of traps—yet Jim saw he must walk into it nonetheless.

"Allow me to update you, Mr. Stobbs," he said, spacing the words carefully. "There *is* a new treatment. We have been using it successfully here for some time. So successfully, in fact, that we've stopped doing lobotomies almost entirely. Even shock therapy has been discontinued in schizophrenia—the category that includes the greater proportion of our cases."

Stobbs glanced toward the stenotypist to make sure that Jim's words had been recorded. "Does this treatment you originated have a name?"

"Not yet—and we are not its originators. Basically, it's the use of two new drugs to quiet mental disturbances. They are called reserpine and chlorpromazine——"

"Reserpine? Isn't that a fancy name for Indian snakeroot?"

Dr. Potter spoke dryly, before Jim could answer. "Mr. Stobbs, reserpine is the pure principle derived from an Indian herb called *Rauwolfia serpentina.* It's a standard specific in the treatment of high blood pressure. Don't imply that Dr. Corwin has been using a patent medicine—or something that isn't pharmaceutically acceptable."

Stobbs's mask was still blandly unmoved. "Thank you, Dr. Potter. It's good to have an expert with us."

"I quite agree," said Potter. "I've watched you in action frequently. While I'm present, there'll be no Roman holiday in this room."

"Proceed, Dr. Corwin." The legislator's voice was in firm control, but Jim did not miss the red coals of anger that had exploded beneath each half-lowered eyelid.

"I began using reserpine on the wards after taking it myself," said Jim. "At the time, I was suffering from mild hypertension. I noticed how completely it brought about sedation without drowsiness—and felt it might prove valuable in extreme cases of derangement. After I'd tested my belief with a fifty-patient program, I learned that similar trials were afoot in other hospitals, with excellent results."

"You call this a 'trial program,' Doctor. Does that mean you experimented with patients under your care?"

"By no means. Dr. Potter just told you that both drugs are pure laboratory preparations, whose properties are well known. They have been used in treating other forms of illness. Here, I merely began a clinical test, to see how they might help our patients."

"Does that differ from an experiment, Doctor?"

"I think so. In an experiment, you're flying blind."

"It seems to me you're splitting hairs to justify a technique that might be dangerous to the inmates."

"Dr. Meeker approved it."

"In the interest of staff harmony?"

The director lifted a detaining palm. "Allow me to say this for the record, Mr. Stobbs. I asked Dr. Corwin why he'd stopped doing lobotomies. He told me that he wished to use this new medicine, instead, on a trial basis. Since he'd been taking reserpine himself, I assumed it was safe and gave him permission—so long as the state obtained it gratis from the manufacturer. I assure you that I did not know it was an experiment." Poor actor though he was, Meeker brought off this thundering lie with a flourish.

Sam Wylie leaned forward. His pale, back-country eyes opened wide with the motion, like a china doll's. "Do you call it an experiment *now,* Dr. Meeker?"

The director shrugged. "Naturally, I prefer to stand up for my doctors, even if they——"

"If they make mistakes?" asked Stobbs.

"You used the word—not I."

The legislator turned on Jim. The mask was gone now, the fanatic beneath it nakedly apparent. "*Did* you make mistakes with this new treatment, Dr. Corwin?"

"Yes, I did."

A flash bulb popped: this time, it was Jim alone who had been photographed. "At first I used too little reserpine," he said quietly. "I wanted to be entirely safe—and therefore proceeded slowly."

Stobbs, who had been awaiting a far different confession, controlled his disappointment with a shrug. "Does this mean you pushed the drug to dangerous levels later to get results?"

"We've always stayed within prescribed limits."

"What other errors did you commit?"

"It took us much too long to improve some of our older patients. Later results, I'm glad to say, have been——"

"Just a minute, Doctor! In the matter of the drug and its safety——"

Dr. Potter cut in on the attack. "Mr. Stobbs, is it fair to interrupt Dr. Corwin? When he's doing his best to explain his program to your limited understanding—and to justify it?"

The room was hushed as Stobbs looked from face to face at the green table. What he read there, it seemed, was to his liking: at least, his voice had lost its cutting edge when he spoke again.

"Proceed, Dr. Corwin."

Jim opened the file folder on his lap. "I am in the process of finishing a report for medical-journal publication and for the manufacturers who furnished us free drugs in the interest of progress. It covers three hundred patients over a twelve-month span—all acute cases of schizophrenia. Of those three hundred, about eighty per cent have been quieted to a remarkable degree. Many are now working in the hospital and on the model farm. With supervision they could be discharged to their homes tomorrow."

"What about chronic cases?" asked Potter, before Stobbs could speak.

"Even they are benefited. Since we began using reserpine, the decibel level in my wards—and in Dr. Singh's—has been halved."

"What of the people who have gone home?"

Jim shot a quick glance at Meeker. The director's hands were shaking as he sorted his papers. "Very few have left Leyden so far."

"Surely it would save the hospital money if they were permitted to leave."

"Possibly not, Dr. Potter. The beds would be filled at once from the waiting list. Processing new admissions might even bring costs up."

"Suppose that cost, and the cost of the drugs, was met. How many more patients could be handled here, on a yearly basis, if those now eligible for discharge were released?"

Jim breathed deep, knowing his next words would seal his fate at Leyden. "I'd say the number could be trebled."

"Then many of the patients here at present are on the rolls because they help with the work—and keep costs down?"

"You'll have to ask Dr. Meeker that."

"But you *did* recommend them for discharge?"

"A good many—at first."

"At first?"

"Until I was told that the policy of the hospital was not to release patients."

Potter turned to the director—and held up a warning palm as Stobbs attempted to speak. "Do you care to explain, Dr. Meeker?"

Meeker half rose from his seat: with both fists planted on the table and his nostrils distended he could have passed for a rampaging bull. "I refused most of Dr. Corwin's requests for discharge—because I did not consider the results of his treatment conclusive."

"Will you state your reasons?"

"In my opinion, few if any could function as normal individuals outside."

"How many did you actually release, Doctor?"

Meeker snatched a list from his secretary's hand. "Four, I believe. And I let those go most reluctantly."

"May I ask their names?"

"Susie Learoyd. Mrs. Rhoda Stanley. Miss Lynn Thorndyke. And Clint Prescott."

A murmur swept the room: Jim suppressed a grin as he recognized baseball fans on all sides. Clint Prescott had been one of the few lobotomy patients who had also been treated with reserpine. Only yesterday he had pitched a no-hitter in Cincinnati, lifting the Orioles to the first division and chalking up his tenth win of the season.

Potter sat down again, ignoring the murmur. This time it was Sam Wylie who rose to question the witness. The junior legislator gave Stobbs a leisurely glance before he spoke, as though daring an interruption.

"Were these four ex-patients schizophrenics, Dr. Meeker?"

"That was the diagnosis."

"You had reservations as to their cure?"

"I had—but I gave in to Dr. Corwin. I still say that the whole treatment was experimental. For all I know, I've sent four potential maniacs into the world."

Wylie turned to the chairman. "Mr. Rogers, will you permit me to introduce one of these alleged maniacs as a witness?"

"Of course, Mr. Wylie—if it serves a purpose."

"You may be the judge of that, sir. Will someone call Miss Lynn Thorndyke?"

vi

There was a slight delay while an orderly hurried into the corridor to summon Lynn. As the spectators settled into expectant quiet, Frankel scribbled a line on a scratch-pad and passed it to Jim.

They've thrown crooked punches. Now we're hitting *them.*

So the head physician's promise to use fire for fire had been no idle boast. He had obviously arranged with Wylie for this surprise effect—with the stormy petrel of the state house in the questioner's role. Jim did his best to look nonchalant when Lynn came through the door and took a seat at the head of the green table. Her color was high, but she betrayed no nervousness under the prod of these all-male stares.

"May I ask what you're doing now, Miss Thorndyke?" said the chairman.

"I'm waiting for my diploma at the university." The girl's voice was low but firm. "Last fall I returned to take up my studies. I'd dropped them—when my illness began." She spoke without embarrassment, her chin lifting.

Rogers nodded solemnly. Jim could sense the man's surprise at Lynn's self-possession. Like so many laymen, the chairman of the state hospital committee obviously felt that mental sickness left an indelible scar.

"Will you question the witness, Mr. Wylie?"

Sam Wylie pushed back his chair—and held the pose with casual competence while the photographer framed him in his lens. It was evident that fireworks and the junior legislator were synonymous.

"Miss Thorndyke, how long were you a patient at Leyden?"

"A little more than a year."

"What was the nature of your illness?"

"Catatonic schizophrenia—alternating with the disturbed phase."

There was a pause while Dr. Potter translated for the committee. Again Lynn betrayed no hint of embarrassment. While she waited she smiled at Jim as calmly as though they were alone in the overcrowded room.

"Is it true, Miss Thorndyke, that you were confined in a locked ward?"

"For over six months I was in constant restraint."

"This may be painful to you, but we believe it is important. Wasn't your case written off as hopeless?"

"Yes, Mr. Wylie."

"You were, in fact, what Dr. Meeker has just called a maniac?"

"One of the worst types."

"Yet you consider yourself cured today?"

"Completely."

"Do you concur in that judgment, Dr. Corwin?"

"Yes, Mr. Wylie." Jim spoke for the reporters and their briskly moving pencils—but the words were for Lynn.

"Do *you*, Dr. Frankel?"

"I do," said the head physician.

Wylie resumed his seat at the table. His voice, though it carried clearly, had dropped to conversational pitch. "To what do you attribute your cure, Miss Thorndyke?"

"To reserpine and phenidylate, two of the drugs Dr. Corwin is using. I was one of the first patients to receive them."

"Were they wholly responsible?"

"No, Mr. Wylie. The drugs made it possible for Dr. Corwin to give me psychotherapy. Until then, I would let no one come near me."

Stobbs cut in quickly. "Then it was psychotherapy that cured you, Miss Thorndyke—not the drugs."

Lynn accepted the interruption without a flicker. "Both, Mr. Stobbs. Psychotherapy finished what the drug began. Neither would have been effective without the other."

Wylie did not speak again for a moment. Instead, he fixed Stobbs with lazy-lidded eyes, a wordless challenge to speak again. When the older man refused the dare, he got to his feet and gave Lynn an awkward, backwoods bow.

"That will be all, Miss Thorndyke. Thank you for coming."

The girl moved away from the table but did not leave the lounge. Intent on her brief ordeal, Jim had not noticed that several nurses and orderlies were grouped at the back of the room. Among them were Enoch Williams and Jack Hanley. Janet Moore and Mrs. Foster sat on a bench together. Lynn took a seat between them.

The assembling of this impromptu audience had occurred without rebuke from the chairman—who nodded curtly as Stobbs asked permission to resume his questioning.

"You may have the floor, Mr. Stobbs—unless Mr. Wylie has something more to say."

"I've made my point, for the present," said Wylie.

Stobbs leveled a finger at Jim. "Dr. Corwin, would you call the medical experiment you've been conducting here a success?"

"I have so stated in the report I'm sending to *The Journal of Clinical Psychiatry*. Shall I read it into the record?"

"Thank you, no. We've had enough medical jargon for one morning. And more than enough calculated trickery from my distinguished colleague, Mr. Wylie." Stobbs leveled a scowl at Wylie, who already seemed to doze in his chair. "Miss Thorndyke, I'll grant, made an impressive witness—but Miss Thorndyke was but one of three hundred cases. Did you succeed with *all* of them?"

"Of course not," said Jim. "I've stated that our percentage of noticeable improvement was around eighty per cent."

"Isn't it true that many of your patients regressed? That one of the by-products of this treatment is intense depression?"

"Actually, depressive effects were much less frequent than we had expected. And they were usually controlled with phenidylate."

"Then you did not consider depression a serious complication?"

"No, Mr. Stobbs."

"The drug was in no way dangerous?"

"No more than other standard medications."

"Could it cause death, if used improperly?"

"Of course. Any drug can do that."

"Do you consider death a serious complication, Dr. Corwin?"

"Your question's idiotic, Mr. Stobbs. What can I say but yes?"

"Were there no deaths from this drug at Leyden?"

"I think not."

"You think not! Don't you *know*?"

"I presume you're referring to Lester Clark, who died of coronary thrombosis."

"I am. And he did not die of heart disease."

Dr. Potter's fist, smashing down on the table, brought silence to the room. "Since when did you turn diagnostician, Mr. Stobbs—or acquire a medical degree? And when did you examine the body?"

"I'm quoting an expert medical opinion," said Stobbs—and he was really shouting at last. "Dr. Keegan's—a staff member."

"When did Dr. Keegan examine Clark?"

Keegan spoke up with weary politeness. "Two days before his death, Dr. Potter."

"Did you find him suffering from reserpine poisoning at the time?"

"The patient complained of faintness when I examined him: I could see he was unfit to work, as the others were doing. I'm unfamiliar with reserpine, and I opposed its use at Leyden: I never permitted it on my own wards." Keegan's eyes were on the ceiling, his air of virtuous attachment absolute. "At the time I found no evidence of coronary thrombosis."

"Did you enter your opinions on the chart?"

The sad-faced doctor shrugged. "With five hundred patients, we don't have too much time for chart work."

"I can understand that, Dr. Keegan," said Potter tartly. "Just as I can understand that your examination was probably so cursory it would have missed all signs of reserpine poisoning, as well as an impending coronary. Isn't that true?"

"There wasn't time for a head-to-toe checkup."

"Yet you state categorically that Clark did not die of heart trouble?"

"That's my opinion."

"Forgive me, Doctor, but I'm not impressed."

Keegan flushed darkly and continued his bored inspection of

the ceiling. Stobbs was prowling behind the table now—dismissing the exchange with a windmill gesture as he closed in for the kill.

"Dr. Corwin, are you *sure* this patient did not die from the effects of reserpine?"

Jim rose to his feet and stood eye to eye with his inquisitor. This, he realized, was the climactic moment: he could not afford to hesitate.

"No, Mr. Stobbs, I am not."

The reporters' pencils were flying now. Jim felt his face muscles go rigid as another flash bulb popped. It was as though his honest doubt had been translated, in that flash of light, to a barefaced admission of guilt.

Stobbs pressed his advantage instantly. "Did you not discuss the case with Dr. Singh—and the probability that death was due to reserpine?"

Jim's glance moved from Meeker to Jack Hanley. The guard had been in the surgery at the time of Lester Clark's death. It was now obvious that he had returned to listen outside the door—after Clark's body had been taken to the morgue. Hearing Jim's admission (in his discussion with Singh) that reserpine might have played some part in the fatality, the attendant must have gone straight to Meeker with his report. An autopsy would have been mandatory at that time—if Meeker had accused Jim of responsibility for Clark's death. Instead, the director had waited until Hanley's spying would be of real value.

"We did discuss that possibility," Jim said. "But we concluded that death came from coronary thrombosis."

"Did you take an electrocardiograph?"

"We tried. The patient's heart had stopped before we could finish."

Potter cut in swiftly. "What was the report of the cardiograph, Dr. Corwin?"

"The tracing has disappeared. So far as I can learn, it was discarded by the laboratory."

"Couldn't there be another explanation, Doctor?" Stobbs's query was almost thundered.

"I'm not aware of one."

"What if the film showed no sign of coronary disease—and you destroyed it for that reason?"

"Are you accusing me of fraud?"

"I'm asking a straight question, Doctor. Answer it."

"It isn't a straight question, Mr. Stobbs. It's a cheap actor's trick, with reporters present." Letting his anger ride, Jim still kept his voice below Stobbs's near-hysteric shriek. "Your whole approach has been designed to make me seem responsible for the death of a patient: let's make that clear at once. There are still courts, and you've no legislative immunity here."

"I am only going by the evidence——"

"Give all of it, then. Jack Hanley's your informer. Ask him whether or not he heard me call Mrs. Clark on the phone and request permission to perform an autopsy on her husband. And warn him before he speaks that both Dr. Singh and Miss Moore were present."

"Dr. Corwin, you are not conducting this hearing——"

Dr. Potter's voice cut Stobbs short. "If it please the chairman, we're here to learn the truth! If Dr. Corwin *did* request an autopsy, it means he wanted the real cause of the patient's death established."

Rogers held up two soothing palms. "Let's have no more unseemly interchanges, gentlemen. Mr. Hanley is here. Will you ask him the question, Mr. Stobbs—or shall I?"

Stobbs held his ground, but his voice dropped as he faced the guard. "Mr. Hanley, did you hear Dr. Corwin ask permission to perform an autopsy on Lester Clark?"

Hanley's massive back was resting against the doorjamb. He began to squirm visibly, as though scratching an elusive itch. "He called somebody. I don't remember much about it——"

Janet Moore spoke from her corner. "Jack Hanley, it was you that told us Mrs. Clark lived at Ellenville. Don't be such a clumsy liar."

"Then Dr. Corwin did request an autopsy?" said Potter.

"Reckon he did, now you mention it."

"Nevertheless," said Stobbs, "Clark may have died from the drug. Dr. Corwin himself admits it."

Jim glanced at Meeker. He was strangely pale—and seemed to be biting his lips, as though to stifle a groan. Whatever the cause, it was evident that his courage was ebbing fast. Jim turned to the chairman, with his eyes still on the director. When he spoke, he addressed them both.

"May I answer what Mr. Stobbs has just implied with a prepared statement?"

"Certainly, Dr. Corwin."

Jim drew the closely written sheet from his file folder. He had composed it in longhand that morning while he waited to go before the committee. For a moment the words seemed to run together, as the last of his anger evaporated.

"You've heard Miss Thorndyke state that she is cured," he said by way of prelude. "A few years ago, she would have been judged hopelessly deranged. Today, a combination of drugs and psychotherapy has assured recovery in her case, and in others. You have also heard me testify that three times the number of patients could be treated at Leyden each year—if my methods were in full use, and people were discharged when they were ready to go home."

Still without glancing at his notes, he turned to Meeker. Though he did not address the director, the words were meant for his ear.

"This state, and many others, faces a difficult problem in mental illness. Our jails are filled with men and women in desperate need of the treatment Leyden offers. If we wished, we could set an example here, establish a record of which we could all be proud."

Again he glanced at both tables. Meeker seemed to be having trouble in breathing: his face, glistening with sweat, was even paler than before. Keegan, now that he had spoken his lines, continued to stare at the ceiling. Stobbs sprawled in his chair again, like a wary boxer resting between rounds. The others were listening intently. Jim began to read from his prepared paper—slowly at first, then with mounting fervor.

"'No responsible doctor using the so-called tranquilizing drugs today really believes they cure mental illness. Every trained scientist knows that the causes of the disease process are rooted deep in the personality—and in the early life of the victim. But we have proved beyond all doubting that these drugs do quiet the patient and separate him from his symptoms. We have proved that this separation helps the patient and the therapist to analyze those symptoms—and, eventually, to work out ways of adjustment. Out of three hundred such patients, all of them cases of schizophrenia, we have proved that two hundred and forty can return to something resembling normal existence.

"'Of these two hundred and forty, many are now ready to return to their families, where families are available. Perhaps they'll need psychiatric help from time to time. Just how long they'll go on needing the drugs we don't yet know. I suspect that in cases where we have been unable to carry out a complete program of psychotherapy—and discover the mental conflicts that originally caused the illness—the drugs will be continued indefinitely as a safety measure, precisely as insulin must be used in diabetes. In more fortunate cases, as Miss Thorndyke has just illustrated, the history can be closed, the cure complete.'"

He turned to Lynn as he read the words, and knew he would always remember her as she was at that moment—young and lovely and vibrantly alive as she sat listening to his reading. Did it matter that this was the last picture for his memory book—so long as he knew he had restored her?

"'Any new therapy, by its very nature, is potentially dangerous,'" he read. "'In his early treatment of rabies, Pasteur might have used an incompletely dried rabbit spinal cord—and given the patient the disease he sought to prevent. Does that mean the world should lose the benefits of the Pasteur treatment for all time? Practically all medicines are poisons, in sufficient dosage. Sometimes, in desperate cases, it is necessary to push that dosage near the danger level to get results.

"'When we began using reserpine here at Leyden, we realized there might be ill effects. We faced the fact that any drug may kill as well as cure. People die occasionally from injections of penicillin—because they have what doctors call an idiosyncrasy to the medication. We took every possible precaution with our three hundred cases—but we knew we must go on to the end. From the first we realized that we had stumbled on an amazing medical technique.

"'Later, of course, we found that others before us had made the original discovery. It strengthened our belief that we were correct in our major premise. Later still, after we had become familiar with the benefits of this drug, we realized we must follow a single guiding principle: the greatest good for the greatest number.

"'Let me repeat: *the greatest good for the greatest number*. Had we held back this new discovery from our patients, we would have been guilty of a crime transcending murder—the mass destruction of human minds.

"'When I came into this hearing, gentlemen, I knew I would probably be blamed for the death of Lester Clark. I cannot prove that Clark did *not* die from reserpine poisoning—only an autopsy could have done that. My considered medical opinion is that he died of a coronary heart attack. But I would continue this program regardless—even were I persuaded that I, personally, had killed him by ordering the medicine.

"'Let me sum up my findings: I am convinced that we have found, in these new drugs, a method that will revolutionize the treatment of disease—a way that offers hope to everyone—a way to bring psychiatric care to the entire world of the mentally ill.'"

Jim folded the prepared statement and placed it in his file. He had stated his credo. What he was about to add was far harder to utter than those written words.

"I will now offer you an item of testimony which Mr. Stobbs, for all the efficiency of his spy system, has somehow overlooked. Shortly before Lester Clark was stricken I ordered his dosage of reserpine to be increased."

He saw that Singh had half risen in his chair, and hurried on before the Indian doctor could interrupt. "If you examine the record, you will find that Dr. Singh signed the original order. But I was in charge of this entire program: he acted only on my instructions. The continuance and perfection of this technique is vitally important. Nothing must happen to endanger it. For that reason I will assume personal blame for Lester Clark's death—and certify that it may have been caused by the medication."

There was a stunned silence at the committee table when he finished. Stobbs pawed at the air with a cautious hand as he geared himself to resume the battle: clearly he could not believe his good fortune. Even Meeker, though his face had lost none of its odd, green-white pallor, looked relieved. The other committee members stared at one another blankly. The gesture of self-abnegation (in behalf of a cause greater than one's self) was simply beyond their ken.

When Potter spoke at last, his voice seemed to echo the general puzzlement. "What dosage had you ordered for Clark when he died?"

"Ten milligrams a day."

"That dose is not infrequently used for hypertension. It can hardly be called dangerous."

"I did not consider it dangerous, Dr. Potter. But the patient may have had an idiosyncrasy to reserpine."

"How long had he been receiving the drug?"

"Two weeks."

"Isn't that time enough for an idiosyncrasy to show up?"

"Usually, Doctor."

Stobbs found his voice and his bulldozing manner. "Dr. Potter, this Alphonse and Gaston exchange seems quite pointless. Dr. Corwin has confessed his guilt. That should be sufficient——"

"For *your* purpose, yes," drawled Sam Wylie. "Not for mine."

There was something in the young man's lazy voice that swiveled every head in his direction. Jim saw that he had opened a loose-leaf notebook and taken out a page—seemingly at random. It resembled a carbon from a ledger, with columns of well-checked figures crowding both margins.

Stobbs had already turned in fury. "What's your game now, Wylie? Are you going to waste more of our time—when we've already proved what we came here to prove?"

"So far," said the younger man wearily, "we've proved nothing. I intend to begin now, if you'll stop talking."

Stobbs made a spasmodic move in Wylie's direction, with both fists clenched. For a moment Jim was positive that the two would come to blows. Instead, Stobbs paused at the table's end, and gestured angrily toward the chairman.

"Must I endure these insults, Mr. Rogers? Corwin has condemned himself. He admits killing a patient. So far, we've seen only one he can *prove* he's cured——"

"That's where you're wrong," said Wylie. "We've another cure right in this room. Come up to the table, Enoch—where folks can see you."

Again the silence was complete as the little pharmacist detached himself from the crowd and sat down in a chair facing the committee. His manner was restrained, yet strangely gleeful. Jim had observed that cautious half smile a dozen times when he had stopped at the drug counter and watched Williams add the last ingredient to a prescription he had ordered.

Wylie presented his brother-in-law with another rustic show of manners. "I owe a great deal to Mr. Williams, gentlemen," he said. "Because of him I first became interested in affairs at Leyden. If memory serves, that was a full nine months ago—when he first applied for release from this hospital."

Jim risked a glance at Meeker. This time the director's pallor had been replaced by a rich, purple flush that was, if anything, even more alarming. Aware that every eye was on the committee table, he half rose to go to the man's aid, then subsided grimly. Such a gesture would have been ill-advised indeed.

At the table, Williams had begun to tell his story—diffidently at first, and then (warming in the evident show of interest) with real vehemence. He spoke of his years in the locked ward, of the partial success of the lobotomy—and, finally, of the course of reserpine which Jim had prescribed, and its wonder-working aftermath.

"When were you put in charge of the drug room?" asked Wylie.

"More than a year ago. Fourteen months, to be exact."

"When did you make your first application for a discharge from Leyden?"

"Around June of last year. Dr. Corwin signed it—but Dr. Meeker refused to accept the recommendation."

"Did you apply again?"

"I did—six months ago. I was refused a second time."

"Objection!"

Meeker had risen with the word, which had burst from his lips in a strangled cry. The chairman, absorbed in what Williams had been saying, turned in annoyance toward the interruption.

"Did you wish to make a statement, Dr. Meeker?"

"Mr. Wylie's insinuations are uncalled for. This is a mental hospital, not a prison."

"Do you deny you kept Enoch Williams here against his will?" asked Wylie. "When your own staff doctor recommended him for discharge?"

"How could I let a former lunatic go back to the drug business?" asked Meeker hoarsely. "Would you let him fill your prescriptions?"

"You allowed him to dispense medicine in the hospital. If he's sane enough to do that, he can run his own business. Shall I tell the committee the *real* reason you detained him?"

"Don't make insinuations you can't prove!"

"I haven't even started, Dr. Meeker—and I can prove every item. We're all aware that you and Mr. Stobbs conspired to make Dr. Corwin the scapegoat here. We all see how miserably you've failed. It's your turn now, and you can stop bleating."

Wylie held up a page of figures for the whole committee to see. "Here's the *real* Leyden ledger, gentlemen—not the fairy-tale figures you heard this morning. The three hundred dollars a month the state paid out for a pharmacist went into what the director calls his welfare fund—which means his own pocket. The thousand a month he saved on the laundry—by using female zombies there—went into other pockets: we'll identify them later. The produce from his model farm he's been harvesting with more slave labor, and selling to the state for twice its value——"

The room had been still as the recital went on. Now two sounds broke the quiet. The first was the pop of a flash bulb as the cameraman framed accuser and accused, with the small, neat figure of Enoch Williams between them—still seated in his chair, his lips quivering in a smile.

The second sound was the crash of Meeker's fall—a dull, thudding impact of his heavy body as he pitched face downward on the carpet and lay there, moaning feebly. Both hands were clutching at his left side, as though to ease a pain that had suddenly grown intolerable.

vii

"As coronary cases go, I've seen worse," said Dr. Potter cheerfully.

He stood with Jim in the doorway of the staff infirmary: a few moments ago the orderlies had brought Meeker there on a stretcher, after an injection of morphine had soothed his pain, and an oxygen mask (applied while he lay on the carpet of the lounge) had eased the burden of his laboring heart. From the moment of his fall—as in the case of Lester Clark—the symptoms of a collapsing circulation were self-evident. In the director's case, however, the chance of recovery was good—now that Potter had had time for a detailed examination.

"His blood pressure's holding up well," said the visiting doctor. "So's the heart action—considering the circumstances. Apparently there's nothing like a guilty conscience to bring on these attacks. May God forgive me—but I thought at first he was shamming—to get off the hook."

Jim shook his head: now that he was convinced Meeker stood in no real danger of death, the situation had an ironic inevitability which was almost comic. The director of Leyden, to put the matter bluntly, was a hog who had wallowed in the public trough long enough to grow careless. Sam Wylie, playing his attack by ear, had simply allowed Stobbs to overreach himself before striking back. True, the hearing had adjourned abruptly after Meeker's collapse. At the request of Stobbs, the chairman had asked that Wylie's last statement be stricken from the record pro tem, in view of the sick man's inability to defend himself. But there was no doubt that Meeker's political career was behind him. By the same token, Potter had already assured Jim that the committee (turning a deaf ear to Stobbs) would accept Wylie's motion tomorrow and vote in favor of his program at the coming session.

"I can't thank you enough, Dr. Potter," Jim said fervently. "Sorry there wasn't time to tell you sooner."

"Think nothing of it, Doctor. I'm a crusader too, in my own parochial way. Between the university and the state house, I've a hard row to hoe. Meeting a man with the same ideas is always refreshing."

At the hearing, the thin, alert internist had seemed an improbable saint, intent on slaying the same dragons that had menaced Jim at Leyden. Now he saw that Dr. Stanton Potter was only a tired man like himself—a bit older (and certainly much grayer), but no less grateful for small mercies.

"I'm damned glad you were here to handle Meeker," Jim said. "In the circumstances, neither Singh nor I would have wanted the responsibility."

Potter smiled. "That I can well appreciate. Shall we take another look at the patient before I wash up?"

The director of Leyden had been given the best room in the staff infirmary, and a special nurse. In the plastic frame of the oxygen tent, with his eyes closed in the tropic oblivion of morphia, he resembled an overfed baby without a care in the world. The pinkish glow of his cheeks (restored by the flow of the oxygen) and the deep relaxation of his slumber added to that grotesque image. Potter took the patient's pulse—and conferred for a moment with the nurse who would stay at the bedside until morning.

"All in all, Meeker's luckier than he knows," he said. "Now let's see if we can find a cup of coffee."

In the diet kitchen, Jim closed the swinging door. "Do you really think he has a chance to pull through?"

"An excellent chance. We won't bother him with a cardiogram until morning—but I fully expect it to sustain my judgment. He should be out of bed within a few weeks—and convalescent in a month or so. Naturally, there's no chance of his resuming full activity for a long time."

"That means Dr. Frankel will be acting head until further orders."

Potter nodded. "He's handled the job often enough before. Meeker's absentee record is notorious."

"What's your estimate of his future?"

Potter did not hesitate. "As of today, Dr. Corwin, Meeker's through at Leyden. Depending on circumstances, he'll either be prosecuted by the state attorney—or allowed to ease out in a way that'll save his face and Al Hanley's. Even if he gets a whitewash it's going to be bad weather for our politicos."

"May I tell Dr. Frankel what you think?"

"If I were you, I'd make haste slowly in that department. Frankel's had to walk a tightrope in this business: he was taking a real risk when he joined forces with Sam Wylie and arranged to have Miss Thorndyke testify. Until this business of the committee is settled, I'd keep to myself, do my job, and say nothing. There must be no hint of collusion."

Jim nodded soberly. "I see your point, of course. I'll do anything, if the committee will sustain my program here——"

"I'm voting for it, as you know. So will Wylie, since he has an eye to the future. So, I feel sure, will the chairman: Garvin Rogers lives in the past, but he keeps his ear to the ground just the same." Potter paused and chose his words with care. "You made an excellent showing today, Dr. Corwin. So excellent that Stobbs will play his cards close to the chest, for the time being. You might still draw a vote of censure. It depends on how the newspapers handle the story."

"Both those reporters seemed fair to me."

"They are. I know them well; they'll phone straight stories to their editors, with no attempt at slanting. But there's still that damnable business about Lester Clark. Your candor did you credit, of course—but Stobbs might use your own words against you later."

"In my place, would you have testified differently?"

"Of course not. Didn't I say we're two of a kind? The main thing is to make sure the committee votes for a continuance of the drug program. I think we can count on that."

"I could never have beaten Stobbs without your backing," Jim said gratefully. "I'm not fast enough on my feet."

The visitor shrugged off the compliment. "When it comes to trading punches with Stobbs," he said, "I'm a veteran infighter. But you'd have won on points—even if I hadn't been working in your corner." He paused, with one hand on the door. "Not that a vote of censure can hurt you personally. When this story hits the front pages you'll have every mental hospital in the country bidding for your services. To say nothing of every private sanitarium. You can name your job—and your salary."

"My job's here at Leyden," said Jim. "I'll never leave, unless they force me out."

Potter's tired eyes opened wide. "Such devotion must have a compelling motive."

"The girl Wylie brought in to testify was cured here. A lifetime's too short to pay back that stroke of luck."

The internist had already agreed to spend the night at Leyden, in case Meeker's condition worsened. When he had installed the visitor in the guest wing, Jim found he still had a half hour to spare before the ritual gathering of his colleagues in the lounge.

Unwilling to discuss the outcome of the hearing at this time, he decided to stroll about the hospital lawns until the dinner bell: it was a habit he had grown into since Lynn's departure. . . . Tonight, when he was passing the portico of Lovell, he was not too startled to hear his name called, from the shadows of the vine-covered stoop. He had guessed that she might linger here for a final word. It was, in fact, quite appropriate that she should wait on the porch of Lovell—on the threshold of the hell she had escaped.

"Can you spare a moment, Jim?"

"Of course, Lynn."

He sat on the bottom step, grateful for the deepening dusk that covered his slight awkwardness. Viewed from this angle, Lynn was only a white blur in the shadow of the vines.

"You must have known you'd find me here," said the girl. "After all, I was waiting to ambush you."

"Shouldn't you be getting back to Glenville?"

"Jay's gone into town to get his Jaguar serviced. We'll drive back later."

He had guessed that Jay Thompson was in the offing. The discovery did nothing to ease the painful thudding of his heart. "I wanted a word with you after the hearing," he said. "To thank you. Unfortunately, there wasn't time to find you after the room was cleared—I was too busy with Dr. Meeker."

"You knew I'd wait—didn't you, Jim?"

"I *hoped* you would." His hands were trembling a little while he fumbled for his pipe—but he felt he could carry off this meeting if she did not prolong it.

"I couldn't leave," said Lynn. "Not without saying how fine you were."

"If you mean the hearing——"

"I've been proud of you before. I'll probably be proud of you tomorrow. But I'll never be prouder than today."

"I felt like a fool, reading that statement. I should have made sure of my job and played safe."

"You'll never play safe, Jim. That's why I had to prove I was on your side. I felt I owed you that."

"Believe me, you owe me nothing."

"You've won, haven't you?" she asked softly.

"The program will go on at Leyden. I'm sure of that much. Stobbs may still have my head. Pray for me, when you open your newspaper tomorrow."

With an impulsive movement Lynn slid down to the bottom

step of the portico and took his hand in hers. "Jim Corwin—how can you be so *calm*?"

"I've said what needed saying," he told her quietly. "It's on the record that mental illness can be cured—or will be, in the fullness of time. My future doesn't matter too much—if that fact's established."

"But it does. Who else could finish what you've begun?"

"I'm not a pioneer, Lynn."

"Perhaps not. But you've the same kind of courage. And you *will* be at Leyden when they throw away the keys. Just wait and see."

"I'll wait," he said. "I'm good at waiting."

Her hand was still warm in his. She withdrew it with a smile when an auto horn bleated from the driveway.

"You'll get what you deserve, Dr. Jim. I'll take odds on that."

viii

Meeker was resting comfortably the next morning, though regular injections of morphine had been necessary during the night to ease his pain. A glance at the chart and a few words with the nurse convinced Jim that he was more than holding his own. Since Dr. Potter was still the attending physician, he kept clear of the director's bedside. Instead, he went straight to the staff dining room—knowing there was a morning paper on every table. So far, he had not quite dared to pick up his own.

Braced for hostile stares, he had seated himself beside Singh before he realized, from the Hindu's flashing smile, that the news was good.

"Read and rejoice," said Singh, pointing to the front-page headline. "Had I written this myself, I could hardly have bettered it."

The Atlanta paper had given the hearing a banner lead:

LEYDEN DOCTOR DESCRIBES
AMAZING TREATMENT
FOR MENTAL ILLS

The story was in the same laudatory vein, though the reporter's approach was factual rather than wide-eyed. Jim's statement to the hospital committee was printed in full: his photograph faced Lynn's, as she testified in behalf of his program. Much was made of his insistence that patient turnover could now be trebled. Wylie's threatened disclosures against Meeker were not spelled out—but it was clear that the director had collapsed in the midst of a rear-guard action.

There was only passing mention of the death of Lester Clark—and even this was presented as the exception that proved the rule. Virgil Stobbs and his bombast had been ignored entirely. The column-long story was news-pointed on the Leyden miracle with reserpine (the phrase seemed to drop naturally from the reporter's typewriter). From first to last, the name of Dr. James Corwin was stressed as its innovator.

Jim put down the paper with a great sigh of relief. It was evident that the reporter—a veteran of the hospital beat—had known Stobbs of old and had discounted his venom in advance. There was even a final paragraph predicting a vote of confidence for the program at the next session of the legislature. Sam Wylie, it seemed, had made the most of his position.

Dr. Potter entered the dining room as Jim was devoting himself to breakfast with a vastly increased appetite, and pulled out a chair at the table. He carried a sheaf of newspapers under one arm, and seemed almost boyishly exultant.

"Well, Corwin? How does it feel to wake up famous?"

Jim knew he was blushing at the praise, and hastened to change the subject. "Have you visited Dr. Meeker?"

"Ordered an ECG two hours ago. They're developing it now in the lab. Not that the clinical picture isn't diagnostic enough. Thad Meeker will recover—drat his hide. But he's manipulated his last hospital budget."

"You're sure you can force his retirement?"

"Damphier clinched that fact beyond a doubt: I've just had him on the phone. You know, of course, how he's hankered to retire. All that's kept him at his desk was the knowledge that Meeker would probably succeed him. In a few days Sam Wylie will threaten to put that page of figures on the record. Meeker knows it was lifted from his own files—and that at least three secretaries in his office will swear it's accurate. Sick or well, he'll go out to pasture. Damphier will bow out this fall—and the governor will appoint Kurt Frankel to the post."

"Frankel?"

"He's been slated for the succession—once we had the goods on Meeker."

"You couldn't find a better man."

"Amen to that," said Potter. "He'll put this state on the medical map. It's time the South stopped being tail end of the mental-hospital program in America. A born teacher like Frankel will really train our young doctors. With these new drugs we can handle every patient in need of treatment, without adding a single ward to existing structures."

Potter gave a sigh of content and poured a second coffee. "So far, that's been the curse of our state system: every appropriation has gone into building rather than medical brains. Give Frankel a free hand and he'll reverse the process. There'll be fewer mausoleums for our living dead—and better treatment to restore them to life." The visitor broke off with a chuckle and set down his cup. "Sorry, gentlemen: the urge to make a public pronouncement is always strongest when the enemy seems routed. How soon will you be qualified to practice psychiatry, Corwin?"

"In the fall—if all goes well."

"Yesterday you told me you were staying on at Leyden. Would you like to succeed Frankel as head physician here?"

"I've had no experience——" Jim knew he was gaping. His demurrer had been an automatic reflex.

"Maybe that's why Leyden needs you so badly—a man with ideas, who isn't afraid to test them. Are you game to try?"

Jim glanced at Singh, who was nodding a beaming endorsement. "I'd be honored, of course—if they'd have me. But I'm afraid you'll never swing it."

"Why not? Look at the facts. You've introduced a brand-new treatment of mental disease——"

"I was a fool for luck."

"It was more than luck, Corwin. Mainly, it was the fact that you *were* new to the snake-pit circuit. If you'd been crippled by tradition—or a timeserver like Keegan—reserpine would have scared you out of your wits. Instead, you moved ahead and proved its value."

"Your offer still floors me."

"Naturally, I can't make a commitment at this breakfast table," said Potter. "But I mentioned you to Damphier today—and he endorsed you instantly. When he brings up Frankel's name at the state house, he'll support yours as well."

"Retired or not, Meeker will try to block the appointment."

"If he does, we'll blow the lid off his playhouse."

"What about Stobbs? The papers didn't print his remarks on Lester Clark—but they're on the record. Even if the governor *did* appoint me, the legislature could vote it down."

Potter rose from the table. "Stop playing hard to get, man. We'll handle Stobbs when the time comes. Meanwhile, let's get over to your darkroom and take a look at Meeker's cardiogram."

In the hospital laboratory they found that the ECG film was still on the drying rack: photographed as it was, on a moving roll, it had been removed from the machine and immersed in a developer bath. Potter held the film under the light and studied it carefully.

"The picture's definite now," he said. "It confirms the sedimentation test I ordered yesterday. It's a coronary, pure and simple. You might even say it's an end mark on the pattern of evil that trapped Thad Meeker." Again he held the long strip of film under the light. "Unlike most end marks, however, this one seems to go on forever. I didn't realize the technician used so much film."

Jim, who had been studying the tracings over Potter's shoulder, beckoned to Singh. "Better have a look, Chandra—this is your bailiwick."

The Hindu took the film from the visitor's hands. "These are separate tracings. That would explain their length."

"And two case-history numbers," said Potter.

"That's impossible, sir. The correct number was copied from Dr. Meeker's chart."

"Just the same, there are two tracings here. See for yourself. The first part of the roll has a much lower voltage."

"Do they both show coronary heart disease?" asked Jim.

"Beyond question."

Singh had been studying the film with myopic care. Now, without a word, he moved to the wall phone and dialed the record room. Standing at his elbow, Jim could hear the voice of the clerk as the Indian doctor asked her to check both numbers against the files.

"What's going on, Chandra?"

Singh's face was a bland mask. "It is written in the Gita: *there will be much rejoicing, when that which was lost is found.*"

"This is no time for proverbs, man!"

"I speak of facts, Jim." Singh hung up the phone. "D'you realize whose history that first number represented? *Lester Clark's.*"

"How could it?"

"Clark died while I was taking the tracing," said Singh. "So I did not go on with it. Nor did I trouble to develop a film I thought was blank."

"Are you telling me this film stayed in the magazine—until we developed Dr. Meeker's tracing?"

"Yes, Jim. No one has touched this machine since Clark died."

Dr. Stanton Potter backed against the wall in an attitude of self-defense as the two doctors, arms linked, began a war dance around the developing sink. When he had grasped their reason he joined in heartily.

"I'll call the newspapers at once," he said. "It'll make a nice footnote to the first story—to say nothing of spiking Virgil Stobbs's guns. Your appointment is as good as confirmed, Dr. Corwin."

ix

An hour later, with the addition to Lester Clark's death certificate a part of the records, Jim entered Lovell One with a clear conscience. It was still a prideful thing to walk through a locked ward that was locked no longer. Today he could even pause at the door of the cell that had once prisoned Lynn Thorndyke—and tell himself, not too sadly, that his behavior had been perfect. As a psychiatrist, certainly—if not as a man.

Mrs. Foster was busy in the chartroom. There was a cat-and-canary quality to her smile this morning that cheered him mightily.

"Good news travels fast, it seems," he told her.

"So it does, Doctor. May I say how happy I am—for you both?"

"Thank you, Mrs. Foster. Dr. Singh was still turning handsprings when I left the record room."

"I wasn't referring to Dr. Singh. I mean the *real* news."

"Must you *always* be cryptic, Mrs. Foster?"

"Who's being cryptic? I'm only telling you that Lynn is back. She's working with her first class now."

"Lynn's at the university."

"She must be twins, then. Look out on the porch."

Last night he had never hoped to see Lynn again. Now, finding her moving serenely among the easels of her art class, her hair bound in the golden pennon he knew so well, it was hard to believe she had been away.

He did not go to her at once. It was only when Mrs. Foster joined him in the doorway (and eyed him with a reproving smile) that he forced himself to move out to the porch. Lynn—busily reshaping a charcoal line on one of the canvases—gave him a casually friendly wave as he moved into her line of vision.

"Don't look so blank, Jim," she said. "Didn't Dr. Frankel tell you I'd be starting work today?"

"I haven't seen Frankel since the hearing——"

"But you must have realized I'd come back. I said as much, the last time you were in Glenville."

"I'm afraid I misunderstood." He was near enough to touch her now—and let his fingers brush her shoulder. Only then did he really believe in her presence.

"Darling," said Lynn, "are you being dense on purpose?"

"Come to the chartroom," he said thickly. "We can't talk here."

The girl followed obediently as he strode from porch to corridor: at his nod, Mrs. Foster stayed rooted where she was. In the chartroom he waited tensely until Lynn had entered, then pulled the door shut behind her.

"Tell me why you're here," he said.

"Dr. Frankel offered me the job last evening. I'd just written out a fifty-thousand-dollar check to build a studio-workshop here—so he could hardly do less."

"Will you make sense, Lynn?"

"The moment I heard about the money, I wanted to give it to Leyden."

"You can't come back to Leyden. You're going to marry Jay Thompson."

"But I'm not. No patient can obey *all* her doctor's orders."

"He's in love with you."

"Jay was a useful beau, while I was still a college girl. But he was never in love with me. For a while, he was in love with love. *Then* I'm afraid it was the fifty thousand dollars." She was laughing a little as she moved closer. "Poor Jay—even that sport car was being bought on time. I'm afraid the finance company will take it back tomorrow."

"You said you were getting married. During graduation week."

"So I did, Jim. Did I mention my husband's name?"

She was in his arms with the words, and her kiss wiped out all the weariness of his doubting.

"Darling," said Lynn, "I'm buying my way back to Leyden, quite without shame. Don't make me propose, too. It's something I could never tell our children."

AUTHOR'S NOTE

The most sensational medical discovery of modern times seems to be the power of certain chemical compounds, now known as "tranquilizer drugs," to slow down the hyperactive minds of the mentally ill to a point where many of them can be rehabilitated to normal life again.

During the last few years, a mass of reports have appeared in medical journals. Most of these reports have been studied as background for this novel. It would be impossible to list them all. However, I do wish to acknowledge my indebtedness to the medical service division of Ciba Pharmaceutical Products, manufacturers of reserpine under the trade name of "Serpasil," and of the drug referred to in the text as phenidylate under the trade name of "Ritalin," as well as to Smith, Kline and French Laboratories, who manufacture chlorpromazine under the trade name of "Thorazine."

For the background story of the use of phenidylate in the treatment of the depression that sometimes accompanies the use of reserpine, I am indebted to the article, "Treatment of Reserpine-Induced Depression with a New Analeptic, Phenidylate," by Dr. John T. Ferguson (Annals of the New York Academy of Science, *Vol. 61, April 15, 1955*).

I am also grateful to Paul DeKruif and his book A Man Against Insanity (*Harcourt, Brace & Co.*), *which brought to my attention the pioneering work of Dr. Ferguson in the treatment of mental disease with drugs, as well as the experimental work of Dr. William F. Lorenz and Dr. Arthur S. Loevenhart in the temporary relief of catatonic stupor by the injection of sodium cyanide* (Archives of Internal Medicine, *1918, Vol. 21, pp. 109–29*).

The number of sedative drugs now used in the treatment of mental disease is legion. But in the early days of this movement—with which this novel is concerned—reserpine and chlorpromazine were the major items.

Frank G. Slaughter, M.D.